S

Rebecca had seen Aaron bare-chested before, but never this close. Her voice quavered, "W-what do you want?"

"To kiss you good-bye."

She had no time to protest before he dipped his head. Only his fingertips touched her, one hand bracing the side of her jaw, the other encircling her waist, but she felt a current surge through her at each point.

Then his mouth covered hers, and when his tongue flicked lightly over her lips, testing, urging . . . she could not keep herself from parting them, astonished yet emboldened by the silky warmth that invaded her mouth. A low sound escaped her throat, or perhaps it came from his—she could not be sure. Suddenly she was pressed hard against him, her fingers splayed against the firmness and heat of his chest. She tipped her head farther, seeking, discovering . . . welcoming. . . .

WHEN MORNING COMES

by

Robin LeAnne Wiete

AN ONYX BOOK

ONYX
Published by the Penguin Group
Penguin Books USA Inc., 375 Hudson Street,
New York, New York 10014, U.S.A.
Penguin Books Ltd, 27 Wrights Lane,
London W8 5TZ, England
Penguin Books Australia Ltd, Ringwood,
Victoria, Australia
Penguin Books Canada Ltd, 10 Alcorn Avenue,
Toronto, Ontario, Canada M4V 3B2
Penguin Books (N.Z.) Ltd, 182–190 Wairau Road,
Auckland 10, New Zealand

Penguin Books Ltd, Registered Offices:
Harmondsworth, Middlesex, England

First published by Onyx, an imprint of New American Library,
a division of Penguin Books USA Inc.

First Printing, January, 1993
10 9 8 7 6 5 4 3 2 1

 REGISTERED TRADEMARK——MARCA REGISTRADA

Printed in the United States of America

*To Mark, Eric, and Kyle,
the loves of my life.*

PROLOGUE

Near West Canada Creek
New York State
1782

They were trapped. The young man's stomach rolled sickeningly at the realization. He crouched behind a dense thicket of brambles, his eyes itching, straining to see into the dusk. A harvest moon slipped in and out of heavy clouds, occasionally illuminating the earth below. Blinking slowly, the young man swung his head to the left, glancing over his shoulder at the carnage behind him.

Here, where once a mighty oak had reigned before some jagged strike of lightning destroyed it long ago, lay a sheltered clearing amid the otherwise unbroken forest. In the dim light he could just make out the shapes of the others who shared this spot. An abrupt movement from one of the sprawled shapes on the ground drew his attention.

A feeble voice rose in a desperate plea. "Help me. Help me. . . ."

Quickly, Aaron Cambridge edged away from his post, scuttling toward his injured companion without raising his head above the level of the thicket. "Hold on, Mercer," he said, automatically feeling for the man's scrawny neck. Beneath his fingers a pulse beat erratically, growing weaker with every second.

"Cain't last much longer," came the raspy reply. "But mebbe it's best this way. Rather die now than get finished off by them heathen Mohawks."

Dipping his head, Aaron closed his own eyes, the better to concentrate on the sound of Mercer's uneven breathing. Even without an opportunity to examine the wound, he could sense it was mortal.

Isaac Mercer, then, would also die.

Overwhelming sadness filled Aaron, forcing his head upward. Though he had tried to avoid looking, his gaze was drawn to the edge of the clearing where another body, lifeless and broken, slumped against the bole of a sturdy maple. Two others lay nearby, but his burning eyes sought only the propped-up form.

Eli Winthrop. His teacher, his mentor . . . his friend. A lifetime of medical knowledge the wise old man had drilled into his sometimes resistant skull, and still Aaron had not managed to save him. Never mind that Eli's wound was a fatal one from the start. Never mind that from the moment the musket ball had pierced his chest Eli had known he was a goner. None of this kept guilt from pouring over the younger man like scalding water, or held the feelings of helplessness and shock at bay.

Those feelings threatened to drown him, to suck him down into a mire as deadly and paralyzing as any musket ball. But worse than the stunning horror and agonizing grief was a deep, bitter sense of shame. Shame because— even while surrounded by the dead and dying—the concern uppermost in Aaron's mind was whether or not he himself would survive this day.

He was only nineteen—too young to die, with so many plans for the future. He wanted to learn to *save* lives, damn it, not watch them drain away before his eyes. And what about 'Becca? More than anything else, he wanted to live to see her again. To love her again.

The sound of a snapping twig penetrated the stillness of the forest, bringing his head around with the force of a lashing whip. Through the dusk he watched the stealthy approach of yet another man, this one also stooped low to avoid detection.

"Leave Mercer be." The intruder's growling tone was scarce above a whisper. "He'll be dead soon if he ain't already. We got better things to think about."

Relief swept through the young man, along with resent-

ment that someone had put to words the very thoughts he
had struggled to deny. He squelched both emotions, hoping that his own voice would not crack from the strain. He
scarcely knew this corporal, who was from another unit,
but the soldier did not look nearly as frightened as Aaron
felt. "Is there a way out?"

A slight gesture from the corporal; a wag of his head,
a nearly imperceptible shrug. No wasted motion here, no
unnecessary sentiment. Just cold, precise efficiency. "Patrols all around us. Two British, one Hessian. A few injuns, to boot. And no trace of Willett's men."

Aaron bit down hard on the inside of his cheek. So it
was true what they had suspected earlier, when their units
had first been cut off from the bulk of the Colonial army.
They were surrounded by the enemy with little hope of
rescue from their own troops. Aaron thought of his brother,
only a year older but already a leader. Knowing Jacob, he
would probably insist that his own unit scour the woods in
search of survivors come morning. What would Jacob think
when he learned that Aaron had perished, close by yet
utterly beyond reach?

Just then the dying Mercer emitted a stifled groan, and
both remaining men reacted instantly. The corporal tensed,
his head cocked to listen for any sign of approaching danger, while Aaron resumed his place at Mercer's side. He
would offer comfort, if nothing else.

Before he could clear his throat to speak, however, his
words were cut off by a signal from the corporal—a raised
hand held palm outward. After a few tense moments, the
hand fell back to his musket barrel, where it caressed the
smooth steel thoughtfully. He leaned close.

"Someone's coming. I know you can stitch a fine seam,
Sawbones, but can you fire a pistol?" The challenge was
laced with barely concealed derision.

It was in the young man to reply with an indignant "Of
course I can!" but something in the corporal's expression
stopped him. Instead, he gulped at the thick clot of dread
in his throat. "You keep the gun," he whispered tautly.
"I'll carry Mercer."

Another groan, this one louder than before. The corporal glanced down at the wounded soldier, then turned

back to scan the dark forest, his hand moving from the stock of his musket to fumble around at his waist. Finally his cold gaze rested upon Aaron. "Is he gonna live?"

Aaron shook his head mutely, scarcely able to contain his own fear.

Again the corporal bent nearer. "Then let's make damned sure *we* do!" With a quick and certain movement, he slashed his hand out and over Mercer's throat. In the falling darkness it was not easy for Aaron to see exactly what the other man had intended; besides, the deed was done before his mind could register the glint of steel or the gurgling rush of air that rose like a horrified gasp before receding into dead silence.

"Y-you killed him!"

"Shut up. I had to kill him. Besides, he was already dead. Said so yourself."

"But—"

"Listen up, boy!" The corporal reached across the body, clasping Aaron by the throat. "This ain't no picnic! If we don't act fast—and I mean *now*—you and me'll end up just like the rest of these poor sods." He drew a pair of guns from the dead Mercer's belt. "Take these," he whispered with no hint of remorse and only a modicum of urgency, "and find yourself a hiding place. When they break the clearing, shoot first. Don't wait for no invitation."

Aaron scarcely heard; his hands felt like wood around the worn handles of the two pistols the corporal had tossed in his direction. His mouth opened and closed, but no protest emerged.

"Don't freeze up on me now, you son of a bitch!" With another merciless thrust, the corporal poked the bloody tip of his knife into Aaron's thigh. "I ain't about to die on your account."

Sharp pain lanced through his leg, and he stared in shock and disbelief into the corporal's emotionless eyes. They looked as hard and flat as metal—as gunmetal—but behind them was a kind of driving intensity that finally woke the younger man from his stupor. That, and the throbbing ache in his leg. The wound was not deep, but was just painful enough to keep him alert. "Are you . . . are you planning to kill me, too?"

The other man stared at him for a long moment, then replied, "Not unless I have to. Are you comin'?"

With an effort, Aaron nodded heavily.

"All right, then. Get ready."

As if on signal, the forest suddenly came alive with noise. A wind rustled the tops of the trees, sending a shower of leaves drifting downward. Those leaves which had fallen in days past now provided a crackling carpet beneath the feet of the approaching enemy, who were moving ever nearer.

Aaron's heart hammered so loudly in his chest he thought it would rise above the shuffling footsteps; even so, he moved to protect himself. Following the corporal's example, he quietly shinned up a nearby tree, not so high that he could not jump to the ground easily, but high enough to give him some advantage over his opponents. Settling on a thick branch, he winced when his movement sent another rash of leaves tumbling to the ground, though they fell almost soundlessly.

Irrelevantly, he wondered if the corporal was carrying extra shot and whether he would have time to reload. Or perhaps the experienced soldier had taken additional weapons with him. Not that one or two extra guns would make much difference now.

Despair clutched at his heart, but Aaron forced himself to think about the next few moments. Two shots. He had two shots, and then only his hands and his feet would remain between him and death or capture. How many were out there? He couldn't tell. One or two? Would more come running at the noise of a skirmish? What could he do but shoot and run? Shoot and run. Shoot and run.

This litany was still echoing through his head several minutes later when Aaron caught his first glimpse of reflected light on the barrel of a rifle. Startled, he squinted harder and glanced up, surprised to see that at sometime during his watchful sojourn the moon had made a grand appearance. With only a split second to pray that its light did not make him as visible as it did his enemy, Aaron lifted the pistol in his trembling right hand and tried to take aim.

"Fire!"

The shout jolted him at the same instant that the man below stepped into full view. Aaron reacted automatically, instinctively, squeezing the firing mechanism of his weapon. The resounding blast did not affect him nearly as much as the result of his pulling the trigger. His arm flung upward, striking a branch above him, but Aaron's eyes remained locked on the man. As if witnessing a pantomime or a poorly acted drama, he watched his enemy slump slowly to the ground.

Immediately, two more scrambling figures burst into the clearing, followed by accompanying blasts from the tree where the corporal perched. Without quite realizing that he had done so, Aaron shifted the second pistol and squeezed the trigger.

"Hold your fire! Hold your fire!"

At first he thought the command had come from below, but then he recognized the corporal's grating voice. Panic filled him at the thought that both weapons he held were now useless.

But the need for guns was over, at least for the moment. The three bodies lying on the ground were still. With jerking movements, Aaron lowered himself from the tree limb, wondering whether his oath compelled him to examine the men before he made a desperate bid for escape. They looked dead.

Shoot and run. Shoot and run.

"Hellfire and damnation!" The corporal swore as he landed beside Aaron with a rustling thump. "You're shakin' like a damn woman. Lucky for you I was here." He strode toward the nearest body. With the toe of his boot he nudged at the fallen soldier, then kicked the inert body all the way over. Where once had been a face, there was now little more than a gaping, bloody hole. "Damn!" he repeated. "This 'uns one of ours!"

"Wh—what?"

"It looks like we done ambushed our own reinforcements. These here's some of Willett's men. I recognize th—" He stopped abruptly, pausing over the third soldier.

Then he lifted his head to peer around at the young physician.

Something about his hesitant stance struck Aaron as odd. There was uncertainty in the corporal's expression, something Aaron had never seen before. But revulsion over their error left him no room to wonder.

"Holy Mary!" Aaron exclaimed in a choked whisper, stepping forward. "Do you mean to say we've killed some of our own—"

The words died in his throat, along with some part of himself that he knew he would never recover. Moonlight illuminated the upturned face of the mortally wounded soldier. Only the corporal's brutal grasp of his arm prevented Aaron's knees from buckling, but nothing could stop the horror from spilling like acid through his gut as he stared down at the man he had shot.

The hand on his arm tightened. "Come on, kid." The voice was almost sympathetic. "We gotta hightail it outta here. No tellin' whether the next bunch'll be redcoats or rebels. Can't do nothin' more here."

"N-no!" Aaron shook his head, shock making his eyes roll wildly. He fought to free himself of the corporal's fierce hold, but his limbs were astonishingly weak.

Almost effortlessly, the older man swung him against a tree. Aaron heard the impact of his head as it made contact with the hard trunk, but no feeling penetrated the cloud of desolation that already enveloped him.

"Now, lookee here! We were defendin' ourselves. That's all. There's nothin' wrong with that. Only mistake here was made by these men. They *knew* we was fightin' over here. If you don't snap out of this we'll both end up like them." The corporal jerked his thumb over his shoulder.

"W-we have to get help! J-Jacob!"

"Too late for that. What we gotta do is forget it. *Forget* it. You understand?" The command sounded as harsh and rasping as ever, but this time his tone was underscored with a menace too powerful, too threatening to ignore.

After a long moment, Aaron nodded weakly. *Shoot and run. Shoot and run.*

"Good." The corporal dropped his hands from Aaron's shoulders, turning to gather what weapons he could from the grisly scene. "Now that I think on it, it might be best if we was to split up. Remember not to say anythin' if you make it back to camp first. Y'hear?"

Again Aaron nodded, accepting a proffered rifle before stumbling out of the clearing. He thought he heard the corporal say "See ya later, Sawbones," but he could manage no response.

He moved as if in a trance. The trees enveloped him. The night closed in, suffocating and bleak. The sound of his own footsteps on the dried leaves seemed louder than rifle shots—so loud that he almost missed the telltale crunch just a few feet to his left.

His reaction dulled by shock and fear, Aaron pivoted slowly, opening his mouth to yell a warning to the corporal. But the sharp crack of a pistol muffled his cry. The last thing Aaron saw was the moon as it slipped behind another cloud high above the spidery branches.

Then all was darkness.

CHAPTER 1

Cincinnati, Ohio
1792

The man the Indians called Cain stood alone in the darkest
corner of the tavern. Daylight streamed through the open
door of split logs, and the single window contrived of
parchment soaked in bear grease glowed amber. But sufficient shadow still lurked beneath the low, soot-blackened
ceiling and against the rough-hewn walls to obscure a
man's features. Protected from both idle curiosity and genuine interest alike, Cain took equal turns staring into the
depths of an empty tankard and peering expectantly toward the sun-washed doorway.

With an elbow resting negligently atop a sturdy keg and
his weight balanced on one foot while the other toed the
dirt floor, Cain assumed an expression of boredom and
surliness combined: His expression was designed to discourage conversation from the other three customers in the
room, though in truth he would have preferred to join the
good fellows openly instead of snatching bits and pieces
of their conversation.

Seated about a crudely wrought table—this no more than
another keg with several rough boards nailed on top—the
citizens in question seemed not to notice their silent companion. Cain supposed they were rafters from the way they
referred to the river in terms both affectionate and profane.
And judging from the flaming red hair showing beneath
three hats in various stages of dilapidation, the men were

most likely brothers. He could only wish their talk would take a turn toward the army garrison up on the bluff outside town. Instead, the three seemed inclined toward outtippling each other. Indeed, they were so well into their respective cups that Cain might have stripped to his loincloth and stuck feathers in his hair without the jolly boatmen making comment.

So, then, what would be the harm in joining the lads?

Cain pondered his position carefully. In such an inebriated state, it was unlikely the young men would remember a few carefully worded inquiries about the situation at Fort Washington, nor would they recall afterward that he had not offered his name. But his face?

Now, there was the risk. A face so marked would not be easily forgotten, even by a trio of drunken river rats. The caution ingrained by so many years would not allow him to err. Cain was better served by waiting quietly, and listening, no matter how much the inactivity chafed at him like a rain-stiffened set of buckskins.

He only wished they would talk about something besides the damned river!

Impatiently, Cain signaled for the innkeeper's lanky son to draw him another tankard full of ale. He did not really want it, but it was only his third, and to stand without one would raise more question than should he fall besotted to the floor. Already the lad gawked at him with unabashed curiosity as he replaced the empty tankard with a full one, while Cain's more noisy neighbors earned no more than a glance with their ribald shouts and echoing belches.

"Here, now, boy," one of the brothers bellowed, waving a pewter mug over his head. "We'll not be idlin' sober while you crawl about your duties. Draw us another round."

To Cain's amusement, the youth remained unflustered by this cheerful abuse. With one hand, he deftly caught the empty tankard as it sailed toward him, placed it on the serving board in time to catch the next, then repeated the deed and stood ready to intercept the third and final vessel from his laughing patrons.

It landed with a loud crash, however, against a ceramic crock now lying shattered on a shelf behind the boy's head.

Cain frowned at the lad, whose hand remained upright and frozen, his eyes bulging wide and the knob in his skinny throat bobbing convulsively.

The rivermen's laughter died along with the last sounds of falling pottery as they turned in unison to face whatever had caused the youngster to fail at this familiar game. Cain dipped his head low and then slanted it toward the tavern's entrance.

A figure paused in the doorway, throwing even more shadows into the common room. Not tall or broad enough to block the light completely, the new arrival stood motionless, framed by shafts of bright yellow sunshine.

A woman, Cain determined immediately.

Instinctively.

Sunshine never limned a man to such utter perfection. Cain thought of a painting he had once seen, of an angel descending from heaven surrounded by luminous clouds and piercing rays of sun, an expression of great serenity and joy upon her face.

But this woman's face was still dimmed by shadows, though the rigid set of her shoulders and the defiant tilt of her chin bespoke not serenity, but nervousness . . . and perhaps fear.

It was not often that a woman ventured down to the riverfront taverns alone. To do so was to invite comment at the least, and most likely trouble of a more tangible nature. Though the newly named town of Cincinnati was largely populated by stalwart settlers and farsighted businessmen, it was still a frontier outpost sprung up around the walls of a military fort.

Women were scarce. Beautiful women were more rare than a gemstone mined from the black Ohio soil. He might have wondered if he were seeing things, might have doubted the reality of this vision, except for the gawking silence of the boatmen.

And then she took a hesitant step forward, and Cain *knew* she could not possibly be real. He had not thought to see her again outside his dreams.

His gaze dropped abruptly to the dark liquid quivering at the brim of his tankard. With an effort, he stilled the sudden trembling of his hands before he sent another wave of ale sloshing onto the dirt floor. Perhaps she had not noticed him. Perhaps it was someone else she had come to haunt.

Through the corner of his eye he watched her take a few more steps until she stood in the center of the tavern, her curious gaze sweeping the room. She was a small woman, slight of frame and delicate of features. The caraco gown she wore showed signs of age, but it was clean and made of a deep blue worsted instead of the more common homespun so often seen on the frontier. The gown's tight bodice emphasized luscious curves and a tiny waist.

A bonnet hung down her back, tied at her throat with a pair of blue ribands. Her hair was a riot of black curls, so fine and wispy around her face that it appeared to surround her head like a dark mist. She had tried to fasten it with pins, Cain could see, but with no luck.

He almost smiled, but then her voice rose softly, with a husky quality that he remembered well, softening a desperate edge that he did not. How in *hell* had she come to be here?

"I am looking for a man named Cain," she stated clearly.

He watched her turn to the three rivermen, who stared at her in stunned silence. Then she tilted a questioning glance at the innkeeper's son. The tongue-tied lad continued to gape, but his eyes flickered toward the man in the corner. She spun back.

"Are you he?"

Reluctantly, Cain continued to peer into his drink. What he wanted was to slam the tankard to the ground and escape from the room. His attempt to ignore her, however, came to naught. She did not address the other gawking men again, but remained steadfast, her lovely pointed chin aimed in his direction.

"Are you Cain?" she repeated.

After a long moment he felt a response leave his lips, though the voice was far deeper and more gruff than his own, the words carrying a harsh ring to them. He wondered what man it was who truly spoke.

"So you're lookin' for Cain," he growled threateningly. "Who wants to know?"

* * *

He could not be the one.

The woman hid her disappointment behind a tight smile while politely waiting for the stranger's response. She was foolish to have hoped so, even for an instant.

Her eyesight had not yet adjusted to the murky depths of the tavern after the morning's brightness, but she could see already that this slovenly drunkard was no physician—or at least not a respected one. Why, he could barely turn his head to look at her straight on. Even in the poor light she could see the grime coating his buckskins and the trace of dark beard shadowing his jaw. It was difficult to tell the color of his hair; the queued strands that showed beneath his brimmed hat were so streaked with dust and dampened by perspiration they might have been any hue.

But the worst was that he would not meet her eyes.

"It's . . . I really need to find . . ." *Be direct,* she commanded herself. *Firm.* She took a deep, sustaining breath to begin again. "My name is Rebecca Osborne. I am looking for a man known as Cain. I was told that I might find him here, or more accurately, that I might learn his whereabouts."

Through bleary eyes, the stranger slanted a glance toward her. "Whaddya want him for?"

The slight movement of his head sent a shaft of alarm through Rebecca. There was something menacing about the way he kept his chin tucked low, peering at her from beneath thick, frowning brows. She wished again that he would remove his filthy hat so that she could see his face. Swallowing her discomfort, she stood her ground.

"I don't see that my purpose is any of your concern."

"It is," the man drawled insolently, "if you expect to find 'im. A skirt and a pretty smile might get you something up at the fort, but I don't s'pose that's what you're lookin' for anyway. Or is it?"

Rebecca drew in a sharp breath. Hot waves of anger and embarrassment swept up to her cheeks, making her exceedingly grateful for the tavern's gloomy interior. She had been well aware that her actions might elicit this kind of treatment. It was a risk she had willingly accepted.

But that did not make the ordeal any easier.

"My inquiries at the fort were met with courtesy and kindness." Her voice rose indignantly, and she had to will her lower lip not to quiver. "Obviously you are not familiar with those particular traits."

She pressed her lips together, waiting, and then when he did not respond, she began to turn away.

"Not so fast," he said. A hand clamped down on her arm.

Rebecca's head snapped around. She tried to pull away but his grip was strong, though not vicious.

"Let go of me," she demanded in a voice far steadier than her pulse. She felt the blood race through her veins. Though not, as she would have anticipated, from fear, but from the sudden gentleness in his command, the unspoken apology she sensed just beneath his words. She grew still, poised between flight and a fierce resolve to see this through.

Slowly, he moved his hand from her arm.

"This man . . . Cain," he began, his tone once again gruff. "What makes you think he'll cotton to you trackin' 'im down?"

"Why would he not?"

"Mebbe he likes his privacy."

"But he is a doctor, is he not? Surely he'll be willing to help me."

Rebecca had not intended to raise her voice, but even she could hear the desperation threatening to burst through her crumbling control. Her plea, however, seemed to have no effect on the man. He once again dismissed her, ducking his head and lifting his tankard for a long draught.

Behind her, a chair thudded dully to the earthen floor as one of the other men stood up. Rebecca had paid them scant attention until now, assuming that the raftsmen were transients who would have little knowledge of the local population. But they could be no less helpful than the surly man before her. She turned hopefully.

"Beggin' your pardon, ma'am." The youngest of the trio took a half step forward, then paused to throw a sheepish glance toward the other two. A couple of nodding grins gave him courage. With his rawboned hands clenching and unclenching the battered brim of his hat, the young man appeared more nervous than an unbroken colt faced with a bit and saddle.

"M' name's—"

His voice cracked, bringing a soft smile to Rebecca's lips. She waited patiently.

"M' name's Seamus O'Day. These're Nevin an' Lonn. We ken tell ya all 'bout this Cain fella."

Through the corner of her eye, Rebecca saw the man at the whiskey barrel straighten his broad shoulders. It was the first time he had moved other than to raise his mug, and she was surprised by how that slight motion made him appear larger and more menacing than before. Still, he did not look up.

"I would appreciate whatever information you can give me," she said to Seamus, who continued to shift his weight awkwardly from one foot to the other. "So far, I have learned only that the gentleman stops upon occasion at this establishment. I fear it is quite urgent that I locate the physician today. If he truly comes here, as I was told," she added with a sigh, already suspecting that her efforts would come to naught.

Again, the tall man shifted his weight, but he did not interrupt the young Irishman, who answered, "Me 'n my brothers been here since y'st'day, we have. An' not a soul 've we seen but for that sort." He gestured without malice toward the silent stranger. "But we've been here times enough to hear the tales the injuns tell."

Rebecca, too, had heard stories. Wild tales peppered with incidences of great courage and great pain. At the fort, her friend Sergeant Skulley had regaled her with enough legends and lies about this Cain fellow to keep an entire village entertained throughout the long winter. The wizened old trooper told of a man so tormented by demons that he shunned civilized company and communed only with the creatures of the forest. He spoke with awe of a physician whose powerful medicine had gained the respect of the Shawnee, a tribe which openly disdained all aspects of the white man's world.

Skulley had warned her, too, of the dangers involved in seeking out such a man on her own. Rebecca had listened to Skulley's admonitions and dismissed at least half as pure embellishment of the truth. She was prepared to exercise the same caution when measuring Seamus O'Day's words against what she already knew.

"They say he walks with a half-tamed panther at his side," the Irishman said, genuine pleasure making his eyes gleam bright as his nervousness fled. "Half animal himself, he is, livin' in a cave from the time he was born in the year of the otter. That bein' only ten years ago, there's proof enough for me that he's not one from this world. Me ma always did say there was fairies and the like."

"Yeah, and you bein' the only one what believes in 'em!" Lonn shouted from the table. Seamus blushed profusely, but he did not back down.

"Well, then, what about the lass we saw last spring in Limestone Point? Didn't she tell us he cured her pox with the blink of an eye?"

"More like wavin' 'is wand," Nevin hooted. "Likely it was nothin' more'n a sniffle she had, anyways. People's apt to stretch the truth when it suits 'em, an' there ain't such a thing as an honest whore, boyo."

Though she was embarrassed by the crude remark, Rebecca's practical nature tended to agree. Still, desperation made her greedy. If Cain could boast of even half the accomplishments credited to him, she would be happy. Small hope was better than none.

"But do you know where I might find him?" She insisted quietly, "I must speak to him. If you cannot give me his direction, please do say so."

To her dismay, all three men looked abashed. Then the burliest of the brothers—Lonn, she recalled—cleared his throat noisily. "We'd be tellin' you if we knew, that we would. But there be only one man who knows, an' that's Cain himself. But they say he comes an' goes at all places, sometimes disguised like an' injun, an' sometimes just like a reg'lar man. You'd never know 'im. Why, it might 's well be him!"

Rebecca sucked in her breath. She spun on her heel, then planted her leather-clad feet on the earthen floor. She had almost forgotten about the scruffy stranger, but now she eyed him anew. Unfortunately, he had not remained slouched in the corner. A wave of dizziness threatened to sway her as she peered up at the man who now stood straight. His shoulders were no longer slumped nor his face averted, though his broad-brimmed hat still cast a shadow over his features.

All but his mouth. His lips were drawn thin and his jaw rigid, his fierce frown both menacing and compelling. Rebecca felt herself moving closer, though she was hardly aware that she had taken a step, and another.

"You *are* Cain!" Her voice faltered, then rose on the crest of disappointment and exasperation. "How can this be?"

For a long moment the man did not move. He merely stared at her as if divining her soul from the depths of her eyes. Then one large shoulder lifted a fraction of an inch.

"Hardly the stuff of legends, is that it?" His voice was heavy with sarcasm. Gone, too, was the backwoods accent he had used earlier. "Don't be so surprised. The lad was right." He jerked his head toward the stunned rafters. "Most people can barely distinguish a falsehood from the truth. The man you seek does not exist."

Rebecca's pulse fluttered in her throat like a captured bird. She swallowed convulsively, confused by the bevy of emotions his words aroused: anger, denial, pity . . . and the stirring of a memory so dim she could scarcely determine its shape. Easier, and much more important, to focus on the matter at hand.

"Then what man are you?" she demanded. "Surely the tales are not all flights of imagination. Are you or are you not a physician?"

Her words were commanding, but Cain heard the doubt underlying her authoritative tone. It irked him that she could dismiss his talent on the basis of his shoddy appearance, though anonymity was precisely the reason he had contrived the disguise. He studied the determined tilt of her jaw, then summoned an equal measure of resolve.

Lowering his voice so that the men at the makeshift table could not hear, he said, "It doesn't really matter. I can't help you."

"You say that without knowing my circumstance?"

Cain paused, his eyes flicking over her. The thorough

perusal might have carried insult, if not for his detached manner. "You seem healthy enough."

Rebecca drew herself taller. "It's not for myself. My son . . . it is my son who is injured."

"How?" Cain could not help it. He told himself it was only curiosity posing as concern.

"It was on the river." Encouraged by his unexpected question, Rebecca hastened to explain. "Samuel's leg was broken when our raft capsized. Because he suffered from a lung ailment immediately following, the bone was never set properly. Now he must use crutches in order to walk. I'm certain that the leg could be reset by someone competent, but it must be done soon, don't you think? Before the bones knit together wrong? Otherwise Samuel will be crippled for life! I cannot allow that to happen!"

Cain paused. "No sign of gangrene?"

"None."

"Then his health is not otherwise in danger?"

She bit her lower lip. "Not really. But even though Samuel rarely complains, I believe the pain is constant."

And not only for the boy, Cain thought with sudden insight. He spoke brusquely. "How long ago was the accident?"

"Six months."

"The boy's age?"

"Nine years. Ten this summer."

"And you have come alone, a woman without escort, to consult me?" The muscles across Cain's chest grew taut. "What of his father?"

His voice was deceptively low, yet it took only an instant for Rebecca's eyes to fly wide with shock. It was not his question that took her by surprise, however, so much as the veiled contempt behind it.

She knew the answer ought to have come easier. "My husband," she said evenly, "drowned in the same mishap that crippled my son." A long silence stretched between them, broken only by the hushed voices of the Irishmen.

She had changed little, Cain thought. And yet she was not the same. He wondered how she could speak of a husband dead for such a short time with so little emotion.

And then his conscience intervened, reminding him that

he was little better. Instead of regret at the news of Levi
Osborne's death, he felt only resignation . . . and a strange
sense of inevitability, of destiny propelling him toward an
uncertain future. One thing was certain. Neither of them
could call back the past.

"There are other physicians," he said, forcing his mind
to remain firmly fixed in the present. "Word came there
is now a doctor at the fort."

Rebecca signaled her disgust with a flip of her hand.
"A drunken quack," she spat, then lifted her gaze quickly
to determine if Cain had taken offense. It appeared not.
She continued. "Captain Tuthill gave Samuel's injury a
cursory look and suggested amputation. He visited only
once."

Cain's eyebrow shot up beneath his floppy hat. "Only
once?"

She paused, then a rueful smile twisted her full lips.
"He did call again, but after the first time I refused him.
Besides lacking the medical sense of a cur, amputation was
not the only ludicrous suggestion he made that day."

Despite himself, Cain's hands curled into fists at his
sides. Her expression of grim forbearance spoke volumes.
He didn't doubt she found herself receiving many such
"suggestions" from lonely frontier settlers and soldiers
starved for female companionship. The stubborn thrust of
her chin also told him how firmly she dealt with such interference. Even so, he wondered how long she would last
before some eager swain took her to wife. Widows did not
remain so for long in the territories. Or anywhere, for that
matter.

The thought left a bitter taste in his mouth, abetted by
the lingering taste of cheap ale. He had the uncontrollable
urge to clasp her slender shoulders tight and force her to
open her eyes to the truth. Instead he shrugged the notion
away, along with whatever sympathy her desperate plea
had begun to arouse in him.

"Will you examine my son?" she asked.

Her dark gaze continued to search his face, and he remembered that she still could not make out his features.
How would she behave if she could see him clearly? Would
her eyes dance with joy? Or shudder closed with revul-

sion? In truth, Cain was not certain which reaction he preferred.

Slowly, as if afraid to tempt fate yet unable to forestall it, he raised his hand to the stained brim and pushed his hat farther back on his head.

Even without the shadow cast by his hat, the tavern's dim light did not allow for an accurate study of Cain's face, nor did several days worth of whiskers or his unkempt mustache. Rising from his beard, high on one cheek, a scar marred his flesh, forever etching the path of some long-ago musket ball. The skin surrounding the scar was stretched taut and colorless; even so, Rebecca's glance skimmed over the superficial wound, seeking his eyes instead for the answer to her question.

It was difficult, given the lack of adequate light, to determine the exact hue, but she had never thought to see eyes so pale again in her life. Pale, though not without fire. After all, blue flames burned the hottest, she recalled distantly.

But these eyes offered her no warmth. Only a kind of watchfulness that she found more disconcerting than she cared to admit. Watchfulness . . . and unspoken regret.

Her heart plunged as she realized he had no intention of coming with her. Rebecca was torn between anger and despair, but she allowed only the first to surface. "You call yourself a physician?" she whispered furiously. "Yet you refuse even to *look* at my son?"

Cain tugged his hat back to its original position. "I never said I was a doctor," he replied, his voice gravelly and low. "Not a white man's doctor. The fact of the matter is, a lot of men around here would rather shoot me than let me lay a hand on one of their kinfolk. Most of the medicine I know came from the Shawnee. I'm surprised whoever told you about me didn't include that little piece of information."

"I don't care how you learned it, as long as you can help my son!" She choked down her tears. "I know what some of the soldiers say about you. If you're worried about interference from the fort, then I promise I won't say a word to anyone. You can examine Samuel at night."

Only once before in her life had Rebecca pleaded for

something so desperately. She remembered the same feeling of helpless frustration, with a marked difference. Then she had been little more than a girl, frightened and heartsick. Now she was a woman, strengthened by adversity. She could accept for herself that life's turns were often senseless and destructive.

She would not accept that for her son.

"If it's your fee that concerns you," she continued stubbornly, "my late husband left me with the means to establish a small dry goods store in the settlement just a mile or so west of here. With the flatboats coming through again this spring, we are well stocked. Gunpowder, grain . . . whiskey? Whatever you want. I could even order medical supplies from—"

"I'll think about it." Cain's voice was strangled as he pushed past her toward the door.

Rebecca turned her head to follow his retreat. With their positions reversed, she was amazed by the way the light framed his head and shoulders in stark silhouette. It made him seem even larger—almost unreal. For a moment she had the unsettling notion that she had been conversing with a ghost.

Panicked, she called out, "But . . . when can I expect—"

At the door he paused, though he did not turn around again, only tossed a parting comment over his shoulder in tones harsh and implacable.

"I'll think about it," he repeated.

The man the Indians called Cain vanished into the brilliant sunlight.

CHAPTER 2

John Percival Haskull—Skulley to his friends—squinted in the direction of the bustling frontier fort through his one good eye. The sound of a muffled command followed by the low drone of responding voices drifted over the palisaded ramparts. A series of loud cracks from the direction of the north ravelin signaled that at least one unit was getting in another round of target practice before the afternoon call to duty.

Yessir, he thought glumly. *Things is really hoppin'.*

Frowning, he rubbed the dun-colored sleeve of his fatigue jacket across his brow. Skulley knew part of being a professional soldier was learning to adapt to any situation, good or bad, but he couldn't help wondering why his back itched every time he noticed the increased activity at Fort Washington. He spat a stream of pungent tobacco juice to the muddy ground, then twisted his arm behind his back to give himself a thorough scratching.

From beside him came a moist sucking noise, then a much clearer stream of saliva landed in the exact spot as his own. Beneath his graying mustache, Skulley grinned. "Gettin' better, boy. Just don't you go practicin' on yer ma's plank floor, else we're both likely to git our hides tanned." He sent his young companion a conspiratorial wink.

"I know better than that," Samuel Osborne protested. He propped himself taller upon his crutches and followed the direction of Skulley's gaze, saying in a solemn voice, "It looks to me like the troops are ready. Do you think there'll be another Indian war this year?"

Skulley considered the question gravely. His mustache twitched. "I don't know, lad. But you can bet I been thinkin' on it some."

Indians were much on everyone's mind lately, especially since the resounding defeat General Arthur St. Clair had suffered at the hands of the Shawnee just six months earlier. Hundreds of troops had perished in that ill-fated campaign, and as a result, St. Clair had been summoned back to the new nation's capital in disgrace.

The only thing St. Clair had managed to accomplish during his "visit" to the river town was to change its name from Losantiville to Cincinnati. The name promised peace, but so far the small village had seen little of that elusive state.

Now the soldiers garrisoned at Fort Washington as well as the townsfolk all wondered what would come next. Skulley cursed silently. Damn, but his back itched something fierce!

He watched as Samuel swung forward, nearing the low stool where Skulley whittled away at a stick of hickory. Balancing on one foot, the boy let his crutches fall away, then dropped to the ground, sitting with his crooked leg thrust out in front of him. "Why do we have to fight the Indians anyway, Sergeant Skulley? Isn't there enough land for everyone?"

The old man drew a sighing breath as he peered into those quizzical blue eyes. "Oughtta be," he acknowledged. "But both sides cain't agree on it. The gov'mint wants ta make sure the settlers have all the land they want no matter who lived there first, and the Injuns don't see no reason ta leave their homes. Plenty o' folks here think fightin' is the best way to settle the dispute."

"Violence is never the answer," Samuel responded pragmatically.

Skulley ducked his head over his handiwork, hiding a grin. "Yer ma told you that, huh?"

"Yessir."

"Weeelll—" Skulley paused to spit again. "She's right, I s'pose. Might sound surprisin', hearin' that from an old soldier, but fightin' never seems to work as good as folks

think it will before they git goin'. It's afterwards folks start
thinkin' bout how gawdawful bad war can be.''

"Tell me about how you fought for independence,"
Samuel asked, curiosity lighting his eyes.

Skulley considered for a moment whether he ought to
discuss such topics with the boy, then relented. The lad
was as bright and eager as a young colt, and it was Skulley's opinion that Rebecca Osborne—good woman that she
may be—was coddling the youngster a tad too much. Not
that one could blame her, what with the lad's bum leg and
all, but he *was* a boy. And whether his ma wanted to admit
it or not, one day Samuel would be a man.

Some things a man needed to know.

"Those days I was infantry," Skulley began, his words
straining around a wad of tobacco in his cheek as well as
around the heaviness in his heart. "Joined up with Schuy-
ler in '77, just in time to git a taste o' the Battle o' Ben-
nington. Lost two o' my brothers there. Lost my eye at
Saratoga.''

He paused, glancing over at the boy's rapt expression.
"Already tol' ya that one, didn't I?''

"Yessir, but I don't mind hearing it again," Samuel
answered politely.

Skulley harrumphed and spat. "Some other time.''

Normally he enjoyed telling stories to anyone who cared
to listen, but today he couldn't manage to get up the urge.
Maybe it was the premonition of impending trouble that
nagged at him so; maybe he felt guilty because it was
partly his tall tales that had set 'Becca Osborne off on a
wild-goose chase. He wished she'd hurry back.

"I hope Ma doesn't come back too soon.''

Samuel's piping voice startled Skulley so, he nearly
dropped his knife. "Why'd ya say that?''

With frank admiration, the boy replied, "So I can stay
with you a little longer, Sergeant Skulley. You're my best
friend in the whole world.''

It took a moment for Skulley to summon back his voice.
"Well, now, Samuel, I 'spect you're jest 'bout *my* best
friend, that's a fact. An' I'm right glad ta have yer company anytime. But I'd feel a sight better if'n yer ma was
ta let me go 'long when she traipses down to the landing.''

The boy turned his head in the direction of the river, which was barely in view now that so many houses had sprung up along the banks. He pursed his lips thoughtfully. "Ma's scared of the water. Nothing will happen to her, will it?"

"Nawww. She'll be jest fine. All I meant was, I been dealin' with them flatboaters fer three years now, ever since this here fort's been built. An' she's such a purty little thing. . . ."

"But she can tangle with the best of 'em," Samuel added proudly. "You said so yourself."

Skulley stared at the boy for a moment, then grinned and reached forward to ruffle his light hair. "Yeah, I did at that."

A pang of fondness for this young pup clutched his heart. Soldiering could be a lonely profession, and he thanked the Lord nearly every day for tossing Rebecca Osborne and her son up on shore not fifty feet from where his foraging party was camped. In the six months since then, Skulley had watched over them protectively. He had used his position as the fort's quartermaster sergeant to help Rebecca establish her business, and had befriended the injured boy.

That the two of them brightened his old life considerably more than evened things up, he thought.

"My uncle died fighting in the war," Samuel noted quietly, "but I don't remember him. Lots of other people my Ma knew died, too. She won't talk about them much, just like she won't talk about my pa since he drowned. That's the worst thing about war, you know. People die, and then the people who are still alive have to be sad all the time. I don't want to be sad, and I don't want to *ever* die."

The abrupt change of subject did not surprise Skulley; he knew Samuel well enough. But he sensed there was more to this conversation than a childish fascination with death. He took his time answering.

"Folks don't *have* ta be sad all the time, they don't. An' sometimes dyin' ain't so bad, like when a fella's old an' ailin'."

"My pa wasn't old, but he was sick. Ma said he was probably happier in heaven because he got to follow his

dream than if he'd died in his bed all weak and tired. Is
that what you mean?''

Skulley laid his gnarled hand on Samuel's shoulder.
''That's 'xactly what I mean, boy. Lot o' soldiers feel that
way 'bout dyin' in battle. They'd rather take a bullet
through the heart than wind up old an' useless when the
war's done.''

''I know.'' Samuel nodded perplexedly. ''I heard Captain Jessup say it's a soldier's honor to die on the battle-
field.''

''Well, now, I wouldn't 'xactly say that,'' Skulley
cautioned. He silently cursed the recently arrived Jessup,
who was full of more swash than sense. ''I'd rather be
hon'rble *an'* alive. But the fact is, boy, I seen enough men
carrying scars, on their insides an' outsides, too, ta know
there's worse things war can do to a man than kill 'im.''

''What could be worse?'' Samuel asked incredulously.

Skulley hesitated, wondering again whether it was his
place to say such things to an innocent lad. There was no
point, though, in hiding the truth, any more than there
was in glorifying it.

''I seen wars turn cheerful men into lunatics, an' lunatics into soldiers. Once, in battle, I saw a man who'd not
flog a horse turn into the worst kind o' cold, murderin'
animal himself. An' I've seen them who can never git over
the killin', even long after it's done. Sometimes, boy,''
Skulley continued gently, ''a war can go on in a man's
heart for years after the last shot's fired.

''But let's say 'nough o' this morbid talk.'' Skulley suddenly slapped his thigh with his palm. ''The whole reason
you'n me is in this here territory is to start somethin' new,
ain't that right? So let's not be yakkin' 'bout the past.''

His blue eyes lighting up, Samuel, too, seemed more
than ready to drop the topic for now. ''All right, then,''
he said, his small head tilting precociously. ''Now will
you teach me how to fish?''

Nonplussed, Skulley gave a little snort. ''Fish, huh?''
he finally asked. ''Ain't we been through this before?''

''Awww, but Sarge—''

''Look boy!'' Skulley pointed his knife toward the road
leading down to the river. He allowed himself another grin

and a mental sigh of relief. "The fish'll just have to wait till next time. Here comes yer ma now."

It looked to Rebecca the same as always, this brambly woodland trail that widened and narrowed not by man's design but of its own accord. She had chosen to return home by this path over the more traveled river road for two reasons. First, because she had wished to be alone with her thoughts; second, because the woods usually had a calming effect on her. She narrowed her eyes, squinting against the bright sun.

The tops of the trees danced to the tune of a gentle breeze. Stately oaks spread protectively over the smaller hickory and maple, and beneath them all, determined dogwood gamely thrust their way toward the sun. This was her favorite time of the year in the forest. Bedecked with tiny green buds, each towering sentry bore the promise of new life, no matter how worn and scarred its trunk, no matter how thick and forbidding its branches. The trees reminded Rebecca that, like people, they were never too old to start over again, and never too staid and stalwart to deny the fresh beginning that came with each spring.

But discouragement soured her mood, so that even the lush, spring-sweet forest did not cheer her as it usually did. Such frivolous thoughts brought little comfort today. Not even when she turned her gaze to the solemn boy beside her.

"Look, Ma. There's some daisies. I'll pick a bunch if you want." Eagerly, Samuel hobbled toward the shaded patch of wildflowers, not waiting for his mother's response. "I'll be careful," he called over his shoulder, heading off the customary warning.

To Samuel, the worst part of having a crooked leg was the expression on his mother's face whenever she thought he wasn't looking. He wished he could walk better so she wouldn't worry anymore. For months it seemed like the anxious frown never stopped pulling at her mouth. Even when she smiled at him her eyes stayed sad.

And today she looked especially tired. Maybe she had walked too far to order those new shelves while he stayed with Skulley at the fort. Ripping one-handed at the thin-

stalked daisies, Samuel wished fervently that he could do
something to make his mother happier.

Rebecca watched his progress fretfully, resisting the urge
to tell him not to bother. She knew how hard Samuel tried
to pretend his injury made no difference. Countless times
she had cautioned him to slow down, but such solicitude
only made the boy shake his head more determinedly than
ever. And so she was gradually teaching herself to let her
son move as fast as he liked, which was never quite fast
enough to suit *him* but was always rapid enough to cause
her heart to thunder as she braced for the inevitable falls.

Luckily, those spills were becoming less frequent as
Samuel grew adept at swinging his slight weight upon the
pair of crudely fashioned crutches. She did not, however,
wish him to become too accustomed to his handicap. Not
yet.

"Ma, couldn't you find the man?"

"Wh-what?" Startled to find the boy already at her side
holding out a fistful of bright flowers, Rebecca bent her
head questioningly. "I'm sorry, Samuel. What did you
say?"

"Couldn't you find the man to build the shelves? That's
what you went to the landing for, isn't it?"

"Yes . . . yes, I found him," she fibbed. "But his price
was too dear. We'll wait until some other settler arrives
who can boast carpentry skills. One will come along
sooner or later, please God."

To cover her uneasiness, Rebecca recovered the bouquet
of wildflowers from Samuel's grip, twining one long stem
around the others and tying it off to secure the bunch.
"There. That will make a lovely centerpiece for the table,
don't you think? Thank you, darling."

"Uh-huh." With a bare nod of his head, Samuel set off
once again, leading the way along the trail.

Rebecca sighed quietly. She hated to lie to him, especially when his silence indicated that he sensed her hedg-
ing. But she did not want to raise his expectations
needlessly, only to have them dashed by someone who had
no care at all for Samuel.

Like that abominable backwoodsman!

Fury warred with mortification as Rebecca recalled the

recent interview. How could she have let herself hope for a miracle from a man so rude and uncouth? Cain! What kind of name was that, anyway?

Rebecca had lost no time trying to follow Cain from the waterfront saloon after his abrupt departure, but once her eyes adjusted to the blinding light she quickly realized that she would never find him among the dingy hovels that lined the public landing. Not if he did not wish her to find him. And Rebecca had no illusions but that he likened her to the plague.

So much for listening to fireside gossip, she had chastised herself as she stomped back toward the fort. Anger had fueled her as she climbed the bluff with the ease and agility of one of the white-tailed deer that populated the forest surrounding Cincinnati. Once reaching Fort Washington, however, Rebecca had purposely subdued her ire. She had not wanted Skulley or anyone else to ask questions in front of the boy.

There was nothing to do now but put both her anger and the incident from her mind, she decided resolutely. Unfortunately, Rebecca found she could do neither. Cain's dark and shadowed image continued to float before her, taunting her with a pair of intriguing eyes. She squeezed her own eyelids tight to cast the vision away, but succeeded only in stumbling over a root and nearly pitching herself headlong into Samuel.

"Be careful, Ma," he said in a teasing voice, obviously delighted at the chance to toss her own words back at her. "Not too fast, or you'll fall."

"Impudent child," she retorted, chuckling at her own folly.

Thankfully, the moment served to break her from her dark thoughts. Samuel seemed to sense the change as well, for he resumed the pace after giving one crutch a deft twirl and executing a small but joyful leap. His piping voice carried back to Rebecca.

"Next time we go to the fort, can I go fishin' with Skulley? He said I could if it was all right with you."

"I don't know, Samuel. The river may still be too high." Suppressing a frown, Rebecca tried to stave off the fear that squeezed her heart. "And besides, Skulley has duties to attend to. Sergeant or not, he can't just walk away from the fort whenever he pleases.''

"But he said he'd take me, Ma. Can I, please?''

"I said I don't know. Let's just wait and see, shall we?''

Silence was the boy's only response, and Rebecca could picture him chewing diligently on his lower lip. His small head bent forward as he concentrated on navigating the rutted path.

She despised herself for casting a pall over their day, but she could not put aside her fear of the treacherous Ohio River. It amazed her that Samuel could so easily forget the way those same swirling waters had robbed him of so much.

Until today and Cain's harsh reminder, Rebecca rarely thought about the incident in terms of her own loss. In many ways it was far easier to deal with Samuel's recovery than to examine her own feelings. The painful truth was, the changes wrought by Levi Osborne's death had been, in her opinion, for the better. At times she missed him, but mostly Rebecca felt only a vague sadness that his life had been cut short. Sadness, and a shameful sense of relief that the river had taken him swiftly, before the case of consumption he battled had done its worst.

Their marriage had taken on many forms over ten years, from mutual dependence and friendship to cold indifference. At the last, Rebecca had expended most of her energy nursing her husband while Levi wasted what little was left of his own with grandiose schemes designed to satisfy his perpetual wanderlust.

Rebecca sighed heavily. At least she and Samuel could now stay in one place for more than a year. Six months earlier, Levi had announced his plans to float a raft down the Ohio River all the way to the land known as the Miami Purchase. Much to Rebecca's surprise, he had saved up enough money from trapping and scouting over the years to purchase goods for a trading post and a couple of acres. It was as if he realized that his own traveling days were over, yet wished to wait out his death by living at the far reaches of civilization. One last time, Rebecca had packed up their meager belongings. She and Samuel had bid good-bye to their friends upriver in Pittsburgh, their most recent stopping place, and resigned themselves to obeying Levi's call.

Fortunately for her, Levi had shown uncharacteristic foresight this trip and had shipped his trade goods ahead to Cincinnati. And so, though she had lost her husband to the river, Rebecca had been left with the means to secure a future for her son.

She was quickly learning—to her amazement and secret pleasure—that widowhood had its advantages. Though she was scarcely six and twenty, people automatically granted her the respect of a woman much older. And she found that no more was necessary to discourage unwelcome suitors than a fluttering sigh and an oblique reference to her recent loss.

Sympathy worked to silence most of the men who now lived near the thriving village of Cincinnati. Whereas Cain had remained coldly unemotional when she mentioned Levi's death.

Damn him! Why *could* she not put the man from her thoughts?

Beyond her power to control it, her mind shifted once again to that single, heart-stopping moment when Cain had revealed himself to her. She recalled the dizzying anticipation, the inexplicable *certainty* that some momentous event would follow the action . . . then shattering disappointment when it had not.

But just what had she expected? Rebecca could not be sure. Something about the man's voice had caused her pulse to speed up a notch, tones as softly sculpted as a Carolina dune, a barely perceptible drawl that conjured images of sun-drenched earth and windblown palmettos. They were the sounds of her childhood; yet different, deepened by reality and sharp with sarcasm.

No, Rebecca thought sadly. Cain's voice had not been one she remembered. That was impossible. More likely she had allowed concern for Samuel to weaken her defenses against such bittersweet reminders of her past.

The invisible barriers she had erected over the years served her well most days; it was only during the lonely, haunting hours of the night that the memories invaded her soul. Oftentimes she dreamed of strong arms stealing around her, enveloping her with goodness and warmth. Occasionally she woke with her face soaked and stinging from anguished tears shed during the night.

But rarely in the past ten years had a flesh-and-blood man reminded her so strongly of Aaron.

That it had happened today was unsettling, to say the least.

That the man who could cause her nerves to grow as taut as a Shawnee bowstring was also a selfish, heartless miscreant only added fuel to the fires of her dissatisfaction! If it weren't for Samuel—

"Samuel!" Rebecca called out, hiding the moment's panic when she first realized the boy was gone. Her gaze swept the path ahead where the trees had thickened considerably. She had so lost herself in her thoughts that Samuel must have moved ahead without her noticing. Not that there was much danger when they were less than a mile from the settlement, but if he fell . . . ?

"Samuel, where are you?" Rebecca paused, ears tuned for any telltale sounds of movement. Surely he could not be too far away. Perhaps he was only teasing her. "If this is some kind of trick . . . Samuel, answer me!"

Vexed, yet nagged by concern, she started forward again, faster this time. Her worried gaze darted from one side of the narrow path to the other, attempting to pierce the gloom of the forest. Could he have stepped off the trail without her knowing? Had she already passed—

Rebecca stopped short. A slight bend in the trail had hidden Samuel from her view until she was nearly upon him. Now she could see him standing rigid, facing away from her with his attention focused straight ahead. Rebecca opened her mouth to speak, then froze, too, at the sight she beheld.

Indians!

A voiceless scream rose in her chest, choked back only by the knowledge that hysteria would not save them. Then in the next instant Rebecca saw what she had at first missed. Samuel's right hand held up at the shoulder height, fingers together and palm facing forward. It could have been a signal to silence her . . . but it was not. Samuel's gesture was clearly aimed at the youth glaring at him from less than ten yards away.

Rebecca's relief when she realized it was only a lad who confronted them was short-lived. No Shawnee tribe would send a boy this far south alone, she knew. There would be others.

At first the fear froze her limbs and throat so that she could not move, could scarcely draw breath. But an instinctive need to protect her son proved stronger, however, lending her voice a steadiness she did not feel, but made use of nevertheless.

"Don't make any sudden motions, Samuel. Do you hear me?"

"Y-yes, Ma." The boy's shoulders twitched above his crutches. "What should I do?"

"I'm thinking, Samuel. I'm thinking."

What *could* they do? She could see clearly the stone knife gripped in the Indian boy's raised fist. His dark eyes glittered, courageous yet full of caution. He, too, waited for her next move.

Never before had Rebecca despaired of Samuel's handicap as she did now. It was impossible for them to escape without pursuit; if this situation ended in a footrace, her son would surely lose.

Such a fate would not be Samuel's, Rebecca vowed silently.

"Perhaps if we move back slowly," she suggested, "he will let us return to the fort without interference." When no response came from her son, she called more firmly, "Samuel, did you hear what I said?"

At first she thought it was the sound of her voice that caused the Shawnee youth to stir. But within moments she saw that she was mistaken, and a new and entirely overwhelming terror turned her blood to ice.

She had been right to think the boy was not alone.

"Ma, l-look," Samuel stammered, his voice thin and quavering.

A few paces behind the boy stood a fierce warrior—at least Rebecca supposed he must be a warrior. His dark eyes stared unwaveringly; his bronzed face remained immobile and forbidding. Most of his head was bare, the hair

having been plucked or shaven. A single long lock fell
over one ear, with a twisted leather cord securing one mottled feather to the braid. He wore plain deerskin leggings
over a breechclout; another garment of leather similar to
a vest covered his chest, leaving his well-muscled arms
free of constraint.

Each and every one of Skulley's tales came back to Rebecca in a rush—tales of kidnapping and pillaging, torture
and hatred of the invading white men. She also recalled
that the Shawnee rarely murdered children. Instead they
preferred to adopt them into their tribes. Not so the adults
unfortunate enough to cross paths with a war party. Wordlessly, Rebecca prayed that Samuel would be spared the
horror of watching her die.

Should she stay to offer what scant protection she could
to her son? Or should she flee into the forest, hoping she
could race beyond Samuel's sight and hearing before the
savage brave caught up? Indecision paralyzed her.

"Naga e'tek, gusah."

The low command broke the silence like the stinging
rattle of a viper. Reluctantly, the Shawnee boy lowered his
weapon a few inches, though his fist seemed to tighten
more determinedly than ever around the crude knife.

Unconsciously, Rebecca straightened her shoulders, her
limbs tensing as she prepared to flee.

"Naga e'tek," the warrior repeated. Slowly, the lad relaxed his grip, finally thrusting the blade through a rawhide loop attached to his own leggings.

Just as slowly, Samuel leaned forward on his crutches,
his palm outstretched.

"No, Samuel! Don't—" Before she could do more than
raise both hands, Rebecca was stunned to see the Shawnee
warrior nod approvingly. After another terse command,
the Indian boy took a wary step forward.

Samuel shifted his crutches awkwardly, managing a
fumbling step of his own.

The tall Indian gave his son another nudge between the
shoulder blades.

Rebecca stifled a gasp. What on earth was he doing?
Was this some heathen ritual designed to lure victims into

a false sense of security? Or did he truly intend for the two boys to shake hands?

And then another movement gave her additional shock. Rebecca had been so intent upon Samuel that she did not notice when the trees behind the Shawnee warrior had parted, revealing three more figures creeping stealthily into the clearing.

What proved most surprising to her, however, was the nature of the new arrivals: another boy, this one a few years younger than the first, though remarkably similar in looks; a slender girl, taller than both her brothers but still lacking the curves of womanhood; and last, a stately Shawnee woman bearing a bundle of colorful cloth in the crook of her arm.

At last Rebecca realized her initial error. This was no raiding party they had chanced upon. This was a Shawnee family.

Not that the danger was any less, she cautioned herself. In fact, it was quite possible that she and Samuel were in worse trouble than before. A lone brave, or even two, might choose to ignore a white woman and a lame boy if they were in a hurry. But according to Skulley the Shawnee were known for their devotion to family, and especially children. If this man perceived the slightest threat to his flesh and blood, he would defend them to the death. Her death. Rebecca shuddered.

"Ma?" Samuel's voice bore the sound of suppressed excitement. She could envision his lopsided grin. "I think he wants to be friends, Ma. Look! They all do."

As Rebecca surveyed the waiting faces, she saw the truth in Samuel's words. The boy they first encountered returned her son's grin openly, and his father's countenance had softened slightly from a murderous scowl to a watchful frown. The other boy clutched his sister's hand; both wore shy smiles. Only the woman's expression remained apprehensive; Rebecca knew instinctively that the woman's concern mirrored her own.

Mothers, then, were the same everywhere.

That thought did more to ease her fear than any, and when the bundle in the Indian woman's arms began to wriggle and emit soft mewling sounds, Rebecca could not help herself. Her gaze fastened and held on the blanket, a sense of expectancy filling her.

With a hesitant step, the Shawnee woman drew next to her husband, then lifted a corner of the blanket and raised her elbow to display her bundle. From inside the deep folds peeped a red and wrinkled face, one tiny fist flailing about aimlessly.

"Ma, it's a baby," Samuel breathed, delight and awe mingling in his voice.

"Yes, I see." She tilted her head to get a better glimpse. Then she raised her eyes to meet the Shawnee woman's proud gaze. Slowly, Rebecca's lips curved upward.

"Can I look closer, d'ya think?"

"You'd best not," Rebecca said after a moment of solemn contemplation. Her own fear was rapidly dissipating, but she had no wish to test their luck.

The Shawnee mother glanced sideways at her husband, speaking in low, sibilant tones. He turned his head toward her, grunting once before answering with a brief flicker of amusement in his eyes. Then the woman drew the infant higher.

Now Rebecca guessed that the baby was only a few days old. She remembered that wizened look on Samuel's face in the days before his small limbs turned plump and rosy with good health. She smiled again, and this time the newborn child let out a sound that resembled a chortle of glee. The tiny mouth grew rounded, then twisted upward for an instant before opening in a wide yawn.

Quiet laughter filled the clearing, followed by an expectant hush when the oldest girl placed her hand on the baby's head, saying, *"Shemah, e'nau'bin nish-nas."*

"E'nau'bin nish-nas," the mother replied, nodding happily.

The warrior glanced down at his sleepy daughter, then raised his stern gaze to Rebecca. *"E'nau'bin nish-nas,"* he pronounced. Then he surprised her by repeating in English, "She smiles at strangers."

Rebecca was not certain how to respond. She did not understand what had transpired; she only knew that the danger had somehow passed. Moving closer to Samuel, she laid a gentle hand on his shoulders and smiled back.

"Your son." The warrior indicated Samuel, then held his palm above the dark head of his own boy. "My son." His hands spread outward in a gesture that could have meant almost anything. "Brave men," he said gravely, though Rebecca could have sworn the glint in his eye was hidden laughter.

With that he turned to place a protective arm around his wife. Immediately the children scurried into the under-brush, only to reappear with their own bundles of traveling gear slung across their backs—all but the oldest boy, who gripped the poles of a travois on either side of his waist.

"Fare-well," the Indian said to Rebecca as his family moved into the woods along a nearly hidden trail at right angles to the one she and Samuel walked.

She bowed her head briefly. "Safe journey," she called after him.

But the Shawnee had already disappeared into the trees.

CHAPTER 3

Cain crouched behind a thicket of hawthorn, his long legs folded uncomfortably beneath him.

Because it was nearly dusk, he could see little except for the foliage directly in front of his face. But all his other senses were attuned to the signs of the forest. He had been sitting here so long that the redbirds once again twittered in the branches above his head, now accustomed to his presence. From off to his left, the rumbling drum of a partridge sounded.

Automatically, his finger tightened on the trigger of his musket; then Cain forced his hand to relax. This was not a hunting expedition. Though someone in the village was always in need of meat, he could not risk a shot yet.

Again he concentrated on the telltale noises around him. More woodland creatures than the partridge were making their presence known. Above the rustling of the trees he could hear a dove's plaintive wail, and somewhere nearby a chipmonk chattered gaily. A gentle grunt from several yards down the nearly hidden path made Cain raise his head with a start, until he realized that it was no bear hidden in the brush, but was probably an amorous groundhog.

Underlying all was the steady rush of the Great Miami River wending southward toward the Ohio. Its flood-swollen waters covered the banks at this time of the year, but the song never changed. Cain remembered the old shaman telling him, "If one listens long and hard, one can hear the voice of the river speak great words of wisdom and guidance."

Cain grimaced. He could use a little wisdom and guidance just now. Indecision wore at him like the saw-edged tools the Shawnee women used to scrape hides for tanning. Bitterness and uncertainty left his emotions too raw for rational thought.

Best to wait until he could consult the shaman. Or better yet, maybe he should forget the entire incident. But Cain knew deep in his soul that he would never forget, that he did not truly want to. And why should he, when he had spent the better part of ten years trying to remember?

As if the ancient sage were standing over him, Cain heard the counsel of Snow Hair. "The heart will recall what the mind cannot. When your heart is strong enough, my son, then you will know what has gone before you."

Wise words indeed, Cain reasoned. Yet they did little to bring him ease. He struggled continuously between the memories that remained elusive as well as the ones that haunted him with all too vivid clarity.

And now this new question to consider.

Before his thoughts could take him further, the fluttering gobble of a tom turkey drifted toward him. Leaning forward, his thigh muscles straining inside his buckskin breeches, he responded with a throaty reply of his own.

Another rapid gobble sounded and Cain stood, using his musket barrel to lever himself up.

"Greetings, friend," he called out in hushed tones. Within moments the brush parted several yards from him, revealing a chest-high head of black hair adorned with the feather of a blue jay. "Little Otter," he said. "You move with the stealth of a tiger."

The Indian boy swaggered to a halt. "What is this tiger, Gentle Healer? Have you seen one? Is it wild and ferocious?" The young Little Otter launched into his usual spate of questions.

Cain chuckled, his eyes meeting those of Wind at His Feet, who now stopped directly behind his son. "A tiger, my curious friend, is like the panther who roams this land, only larger, with black and yellow stripes. I have never seen one myself, but I know of the tiger from the books of my people. And yes, he is a wild and ferocious warrior, as you will someday be."

Little Otter beamed proudly; then his head once again

tilted questioningly. "You have spoken of these books before. When will I see such a thing?"

"Enough." Wind at His Feet raised a palm for silence, though he bestowed an indulgent smile upon his son. "Later we will speak of books and imaginary panthers. Now we gather news of our friend."

"Yes," Cain agreed, motioning the Shawnee forward. From the shadows of the trees, Wind at His Feet's wife and other children appeared. Cain nodded respectfully. "White Star, I see that your childbirth went well with you. I am glad."

Wind's chest expanded visibly. "It is a daughter. It seems my mate was right in her vision. The child lives. I will call her Smiles at Strangers."

It was Shawnee tradition to name a child for some significant event surrounding its birth. Cain wondered how his friend had arrived at such an unusual name, but did not have a chance to question him before White Star moved forward. Shyly, she offered the tightly wrapped bundle to him.

Cain took the baby into his arms reverently, deeply touched by the trust implied in such an act, and awed by the responsibility. With great care he knelt, laying the infant on the ground so that he could unfold the blanket.

"Ahhh," he said a few moments later, relieved to find that Wind's pride was justified. He ran his thumbnail the length of one tiny foot, pleased by the instant reaction. Gently, he placed two fingertips upon the child's chest, then cupped her small, rounded skull with the palm of his hand. Cain smiled.

"Already she grows fat on the milk of her mother. You have done well, White Star."

Now it was the woman's turn to smile, and she did so openly as she knelt beside Cain to retrieve her child. Her smug expression told him she was well aware of her accomplishment.

He knew, however, that it had not always been thus. White Star had suffered three stillbirths in as many years. Cain had found no medical reason for the failed pregnancies, but since White Star was no longer a young woman,

Cain had regretfully advised Wind at His Feet that his beloved wife should risk her health no more.

But the stubborn White Star had not heeded this advice. She had convinced herself that the answer to her prayers lay in the location of her birthing hut. Her first three children were born overlooking the banks of the Ohio, before the Shawnee were forced north by the encroaching white settlers. There, too, must this last child of her loins be delivered.

After great pleading and many tears, White Star had talked her husband into making the perilous journey with her to the site of their old village. In the Shawnee way, the entire family went along. Cain knew the dangers they had risked. His friends had probably walked within shouting distance of at least one white settlement, and maybe more.

Standing, he addressed Wind at His Feet. "I have prayed for the safe return of you and your family. My happiness is great."

Wind acknowledged this blessing with a dignified nod. "And you, my brother . . . did you not find the signs telling you to return to your people?"

Cain shrugged enigmatically. "I don't know whether I'll return or not; first I must make myself known to them. But this, as I explained before, must be done carefully. There is much at stake."

"You have told me so." Wind paused, his expression expectant. "But I still see in you feelings trying to become thoughts, and thoughts waiting to become words, and words struggling to leave your lips. You will tell me the rest?"

"Not standing here in the forest." Cain frowned. "Are we moving or not?"

"My wife is tired," Wind said after a thoughtful pause. "And it is many miles since we last saw the smoke of the white man. We will make camp beside the river."

That said, the entire party sprang into action, preparing a nearby clearing for the night. So adept were the Shawnee children at handling their tasks that Cain's reprieve was short. Too soon, he found himself facing his companion over the glowing coals of a low fire. Around them, Wind's family slept.

"So, my friend. I wait to hear your words."

"I'll bet you do," Cain grumbled, then shook his head when Wind pursed his lips in consternation. He had forgotten that though his Indian brother's understanding of English was good, sarcasm clearly was lost on him.

There was no use delaying the inevitable. His friend would not allow him any peace until he told him what had transpired in the waterfront tavern. Besides, if anyone deserved to know, Wind at His Feet did.

"Something unexpected happened today." Quickly, Cain outlined his conversation with Rebecca Osborne, speaking in the Shawnee tongue for the sake of Wind at His Feet. When he completed the tale, his friend continued to stare at him pensively for several minutes.

After a long moment, Cain chuckled mirthlessly. "Well? Have I grown another head or something?"

"My brother," Wind finally said, "I can see you are greatly troubled by this dilemma. You have told me the danger of letting the white man know you live, yet you wish to heal this boy. This is a hard decision to make. You must give the matter great thought. But," he continued, "I sense by the look of foreboding in your eye that there is more you must tell me."

Cain was prepared to deny this charge, but he realized that it was no use. Wind at His Feet was his brother in spirit, if not in blood. He had seen Cain at his worst and at his best. To lie to him now would be to repudiate the honor of their friendship.

Quietly, he spoke. "I have known this woman before, in my life before the great darkness." He paused. "She is one whom I have loved."

"Ahhh." Wind nodded knowingly, as if this came as no surprise to him.

"It makes no difference now," Cain said wearily. "She did not recognize me after so many years. . . ." He touched the scar on his cheek. "And after so long there is no more love between us. So the only question is whether or not I can do anything to help the boy. It is possible that nothing can be done."

"You will not know until you examine him. How soon do you return to the white village, my brother?"

"I didn't say I was going!" Cain protested. But when

his friend did not answer, he lowered his gaze to the fire. His voice took on a wry twist. "Then again, you seem to know better than me what I'll do next. So tell me, Wind . . . what are the chances of my keeping my identity secret once Rebecca recognizes me?"

Wind at His Feet sighed bitterly. "Not good. This could mean the end of your freedom, I know. But what kind of freedom is it, if you cannot choose to ease the pain of a child?"

Cain remained silent, but Wind shifted his weight and cleared his throat.

"Ten winters ago, you were as close to death as any man can walk. I felt only relief when the demons that made you weep and scream and curse your life finally left your body, taking with them your memory. But now this place where the memory should be haunts you, like a hungering belly demanding to be filled."

"This is true," Cain admitted. "For too long I've pretended it didn't matter; now I want to know. But Rebecca has nothing to do with all that."

Wind grunted. "Then I will tell you this as well. The word you cried out in your dreams was 'beck-a, beck-a.' I did not understand it then. I do now."

Cain stared at him in stunned silence. Then he lowered his head resignedly. Fresh pain surged through him, the way a wound will bleed that has not healed well. As much as he would have liked to pretend his feelings for her had died along with that other part of himself, he could not. He closed his eyes to think.

All around, the night air was filled with the reassuring sounds of the forest: insects clicking softly, the gentle soughing of the wind through the treetops, even the occasional hoot of an owl. But none of these blocked the incessant rush of the river as it continued its ceaseless journey, never stopping for rest or showing hesitation or doubt. In a way, Cain thought, the river was a symbol of life itself. You could try to fight its mighty current, or even divert it, but sooner or later it would sweep you up again. The Shawnee believed the river was holy, a mighty goddess to be both revered and feared.

Just now, he was inclined to agree with his adopted people. He felt caught up in events he could neither avoid nor control. He had a choice. Live and forge bravely ahead, or hide himself once more and die inside.

Fed by a gust of wind, a single flame shot up from the fire, lighting the waiting face of his friend. Cain felt his lips turn upward in a parody of a smile.

"Wind at His Feet, my brother, will you make sure your children do not grow too fast until I can see them once more?"

The warrior lifted his palms. "I cannot stop them from growing, but I can make certain they do not forget my good friend, Gentle Healer. My children will sing of your greatness, and my children's children as well."

"I'd be content to have a warm place at your hearth once in a while, Wind." Cain cleared his throat against the thickness growing there. "But I am grateful for your praise."

"You will sleep before you go?"

He wagged his head. "Maybe. I think I'll sit for a while by the river." As if the pain in his heart had somehow settled into his limbs, he stood slowly.

The river was waiting, and there was no use trying to halt it. In his heart, Cain sensed that his time with the Shawnee had come to an end, and even though he couldn't remember all of the endings in his life, he knew that this good-bye would be one of the worst.

He only hoped it wasn't forever.

"Lordy, 'Becca! You might've been killed! Whatever possessed you to take Sammy out in them woods yesterday?"

Cringing at her sister-in-law's strident tone, which had abated little over the past twenty-four hours, Rebecca nevertheless nodded in agreement as she set aside the last of the pewter plates she had finished drying.

"You're absolutely right, Lenore. I suppose with all the talk lately of how the army's going to tame the Indians, I just forgot there are still dangers. Truthfully, the family we met never once threatened Samuel or me. In fact I'm surprised we saw them at all. There hasn't been an Indian this close to the fort in over a year."

"Least none that we know of," Lenore Braddock

scoffed. "What about that young girl from over near Columbia settlement just this past February? Nancy Gordon—wasn't that her name? Indians chased her brothers home when they were out collecting maple sap, but that poor gal hasn't been heard from since. How do you know there aren't heathens out in those woods we just haven't seen or heard yet?"

Lenore's angular face lengthened, and Rebecca was once again struck by her resemblance to Levi. As her brother had been, Lenore stood taller than average and was rather thin, though she was not by any means frail. She could hoist a sack of grain upon her gaunt frame as easily as she could carry one of her four offspring. Her work-hardened hands with their callused palms and knobby knuckles were as well suited to rough tasks as they were to soothing away childish tears.

Rebecca loved her dearly, though she often found herself viewing Lenore's dour outlook on life with exasperation. "Well, if they aren't bothering us, then we have nothing to fear, either, do we?" she reasoned. "Who knows how many friendly Shawnee there might be?"

Now that she and Samuel were safely home, Rebecca found her curiosity about the Indians far outweighing the memory of terror. Why had the family ventured so close to the white man's domain?

"Ain't no such thing as a friendly Shawnee," Lenore proclaimed. "Must've been Miami you saw. Or maybe Delaware. Don't matter much, though. I'm just glad you've still got all your hair in place. Bet them heathens'd put a high price on a scalp like yours. Now, mine, on t'other hand, is fair safe."

Rebecca laughed. The difference between their hair had long been a standing joke between the two women. Lenore often pretended jealousy over her younger sister-in-law's dark, curling mane, while Rebecca occasionally spoke her wish aloud for more manageable locks such as Lenore's pale, lank braids with their streaks of gray. That they could tease each other with comfort was a tribute to the close relationship between them. Ever since Rebecca had agreed to wed Levi Osborne ten years earlier, Lenore had been her staunchest supporter and dearest friend.

Having lost her own husband in the battle for Yorktown, Lenore had joined her household to that of her brother's. Many a young bride might have resented such an intrusion, but Rebecca had never known cause to wish Lenore and her boisterous family away. They had filled the long months—at times nearly years at a stretch—while Levi was gone trapping. And besides, it wasn't as if her marriage had been a love match. Lenore knew this as well.

Rebecca sighed out loud, catching herself too late to avoid earning a raised eyebrow.

"What's wrong?"

"I was just thinking . . ."

" 'Bout what?"

Rebecca paused, then answered quickly, "About how nice it was when we shared our meals, instead of just once in a while like tonight."

"Not likely," Lenore harrumphed. "I could tell you and Sammy were ready for some peace and quiet. B'sides, you needed this room for yourself, since your store takes up the whole front. And it's not like we're miles apart, bein' we're just the other side of the stockade. No, my passel is too rambunctious by far, and you can't say it isn't fine having more room, can you?"

Rebecca smiled. "I will admit to that much. But there are times when I miss all the commotion."

"Then what you need is a couple more young 'uns of your own, not mine underfoot!" Lenore snapped her wet dishtowel open, then spread it to dry over Rebecca's smooth-planked table. "Which is just one more reason why it's right, you having your own cabin. What man would come a-courtin' when he's likely to get hooted off the porch by my Ephraim. Why, that boy's plumb obnoxious!"

"High-spirited," Rebecca defended automatically, then shrugged her narrow shoulders. She had no intention of letting anyone "come a-courtin'," and especially not a man who would let himself be cowed by a boy.

What need did she have of a husband? Rebecca often reasoned. The idea of having a baby was not unappealing, but neither did she consider such an insubstantial yearning to be worth the trouble of another marriage.

It had been a different matter ten years ago. Then, she

was heartbroken and alone and had no other means to survive but to wed her childhood friend, Levi Osborne. Now she was an independent woman, with a boy to care for and a livelihood of her own.

A man would only force changes, and for once Rebecca was determined to keep her life and Samuel's on an even keel.

"That's right," Lenore continued as if Rebecca's response was not necessary. She bent to toss an additional log on the fire. "Before you know it, some tall stranger'll happen along to steal your heart, and then you won't have to worry about Indians or running a store or walking alone in the woods."

Arranging the pewter dinnerware on the open shelf above the hearth, Rebecca carefully kept her face turned away from her sister-in-law. She didn't want Lenore to see how the heat had filled her cheeks at the mention of a tall stranger. "Seeing as you're the one with the romantic notions," Rebecca said glibly, "I'm surprised you don't set yourself to finding a man."

"Who, me? I'm too old and ugly."

"Nonsense." Rebecca fiddled with a set of mugs, sliding them a fraction of an inch to the right. "You're a fine-looking woman in the prime of life."

Silence filled the small keeping room, broken only by the sounds of shouting laughter from outside, where the children played in the waning daylight. When Lenore finally spoke, it was in a tone that brooked no disagreement.

"And you're doing a poor job of trying to fool an old fool. What's really bothering you tonight, 'Becca? It's not missing me and the children, and it's not that run-in you had with the Indians. So the only thing left you haven't told me about is your trip to the fort yesterday. What did you find out?"

Rebecca tensed, then relaxed her shoulders with a resigned sigh. "I met a man who told me where to find Cain," she said quietly.

Pulling out a bench on one side of the trestle table, Lenore seated herself and motioned for Rebecca to take the other. She knew of her sister-in-law's search for the elusive physician these past weeks, and had never doubted that if anyone could get the man to leave his wilderness hideout for civilization, Rebecca could. "What happened?"

"I went to him. But it was no use. He's not what the legends say of him, Lenore. He was drunk and dirty and rude, and . . ." Her voice faltered as she slumped dejectedly to the bench.

"And he said no, is that it?"

Rebecca nodded.

"So what else is wrong?"

"Isn't that enough? My last hope for Samuel, and he could barely stand up straight. That's what's wrong!"

Lenore never removed her knowing gaze from Rebecca's troubled features, but her smile tightened. "Cain wasn't your last hope. He was just the one you wanted most. You can still take Sammy back upriver to Pittsburgh. There're good doctors there."

Rebecca squashed the shudder that threatened to rip through her. Instead she raised her chin bravely. "I am aware of that. And I will take him, if it's the last resort."

"I know, 'Becca." Lenore reached across the table and patted her hand. "I know."

A loud, raucous screech from just outside the door startled both women into sudden laughter. Lenore withdrew her hand, then pushed herself up from the table. "Time I got those youngsters into their own cabin, before one of them takes a notion to burn down the stockade."

"Thanks again for the pie and the preserves," Rebecca said, rising as well. "They were perfect with the stew."

"Pshaw." Lenore waved a scraggly hand. "Next time, you can bake and I'll dish up. Strawberries'll be out soon. If them Indians don't come back I'll send Ephraim to pick us some. In the meantime, will you promise not to go walking to the fort alone?"

Rebecca shook her head, but her lips curved up as she gazed at Lenore fondly. "You just don't give up, do you?"

"Not on you, honey. Will you promise?"

"You know that's impossible. The men here are too busy hunting game and clearing the new fields to escort me every time I have an order to pick up. But I will stay on the river road instead of taking the path through the woods."

"And a gun? You'll start carrying that old ball pistol of Levi's?"

"I don't think one shot will do much good if I'm attacked by a war party," Rebecca said lightly, then reached for Lenore's hand when she saw the worried frown her words caused. "But I'll take it, if it makes you feel better," she added.

"Hmmmph. That's better than nothing, I s'pose." Lenore placed a dry peck on Rebecca's cheek. "Better get on my way. I'll send Sammy in. You lock up tight, now."

"Yes, I will. And Lenore . . . thanks for worrying about me."

The older woman looked back, her rawboned frame nearly filling the doorway, her lips softening into a smile.

"Of course I worry about you," she said matter-of-factly. "That's what sisters are for."

It was some hours before Rebecca managed to get Samuel settled down. Lingering excitement over the previous day's adventure, coupled with the pleasure of relaying the tale to his cousins, kept Samuel energetic and talkative long after his usual bedtime.

Now, watching the gentle rise and fall of his chest, Rebecca sighed enviously. Sleep had eventually come for the boy; she feared she would not be so lucky.

Leaning over Samuel's pallet, she brushed a golden curl from his forehead. Even at this age, his hair remained the texture of spun silk, falling into unruly waves much like her own, only honey-colored instead of black. And by summer's end his hair would be as pale as corn silk.

Like his father's.

The thought startled her, not just because it was unexpected, but because it was the second such reminder in as many days. Why, after all this time, could she not forget?

Raising her hand reluctantly from Samuel's brow, Rebecca straightened and tugged her wrapper more tightly around her. Most likely it was the worry that caused her mind to betray her, she rationalized. Responsibility was a burdensome thing.

She would find no peace tonight, Rebecca decided tiredly, so she may as well not disturb Samuel's rest. Quietly, she tiptoed from the small bedroom she and Samuel shared and climbed down the narrow stairs.

The banked fire cast a paltry light over the keeping room, throwing teasing shadows into every familiar corner. But Rebecca was accustomed to the darkness. Settling herself in the rocking chair near the hearth, she laid her head back against the back rail and stared at the rough-hewn beams above her.

As a result of yesterday's disappointment, she now had a difficult decision to make—two, if she counted the question of whether or not to tell Samuel her plans. To do nothing at all was not even a consideration, so her choices were to wait here in the hope that the river would soon bring another physician to the territory, or to return to Pittsburgh with Samuel.

Both options had drawbacks. Common sense warned Rebecca that time was running out if Samuel's leg was to be reset correctly, and she had no way of knowing when—or if—a doctor might arrive.

For the same reason, if they were to return to Pittsburgh, she and Samuel would have to make the trip as soon as possible. Rebecca had money saved to pay for their transportation. She would have to sell off her entire stock of trade goods to raise enough funds to keep them in Pittsburgh for a few months, at best. How they would live after that, she did not know. She supposed she could manage by hiring out as a maid or laundress. Better yet, some shopkeeper might allow her to clerk for him.

The idea of working for another after owning her own store was disheartening. She would also miss Lenore and the children terribly, for she harbored no illusions that her sister-in-law would choose to make the trip again, knowing how Lenore was as glad to be permanently settled in a home as she. To ask her to leave once more would be unfair.

Rebecca, too, despaired of leaving the secure home she had made for Samuel and herself. And it was more than parting with their snug, two-storied cabin. Over the last months she had come to know her neighbors well and had relished the idea of staying in one place long enough to develop close friendships. Though the little settlement was less than three years old, there was a comforting sense of permanency in its sturdy blockhouses, fortified cabins, and tilled fields.

Rebecca despised the thought of leaving again. That emotion, however, did not come close to matching the unease she felt placing herself and Samuel at the mercy of the Ohio River.

Groaning silently, she bent forward, massaging her temples with the tips of her fingers. If the mere thought made her heart pound and her stomach clench up in knots, what would happen once she stepped foot on a rocking, shifting boat?

Rebecca remembered all too well the terrifying feeling of leaving solid ground behind. She could picture the muddy, roiling water with its demon currents, waiting to suck her and Samuel down into its murky depths.

How could she face the horror again? How could she not?

"Oh, dear God," she whispered prayerfully, "what kind of mother am I?" Rising from the chair, she tugged the robe's belt tighter around her waist, as if that determined movement would somehow bolster her resolve. She lifted the iron poker from the hearth and stirred the glowing embers in the fireplace until flames shot up, then she added a small log to the growing blaze.

For Samuel's sake, she could do anything! she told herself as she swung a kettle of water over the fire for tea. That begun, she moved to the upright cupboard beside the door, where she kept her sparse collection of books and writing tools.

She would start by making a list of prospective buyers for the stock. And a letter sent ahead to one of her old friends might help pave the way toward finding a job and suitable lodgings, as well as a reputable physician. All this planning would keep her very busy over the next few weeks—too busy to dwell on her fear. Why, if all went well, they might be on their way at the end of the month!

Seating herself at the same table where she and Lenore had chatted after supper, Rebecca lit a candle and spread out her writing instruments. Since vellum was precious on the frontier, she carefully smoothed out an old bill of lading from her last load of yard goods and turned it over to use the back for her list. After a moment's consideration, she scribbled two names. Before long she was completely caught up in making lists.

So engrossed was Rebecca in her plans that she paid scant attention when a dog barked somewhere nearby. She raised her head questioningly, however, when the noise grew. Several of the villagers owned dogs, and it was not unusual for one or more to roam around at night. But they generally kept quiet. Something must have set them off.

The thought of Indians would never have entered her mind if not for yesterday's incident, yet Rebecca gave little credit to the possibility of an attack. Only the northern-most settlements of the territory were still considered dangerous. Most likely the dogs had caught the scent of a rabbit or a fox.

She bent to resume tallying the estimated figures, already growing weary of the task. If she offered her store for sale before the spring traffic increased on the river, she would stand to make a larger profit. Sergeant Skulley could probably help her find a buyer from among the settlers arriving daily. But she took little pleasure in the knowledge. Once her storeroom of goods was sold, there would be no turning back.

Rebecca was just writing a letter to Gert Starkey, a former neighbor in Pittsburgh, when another noise drew her attention. By this time the dogs had grown quiet once again, so she clearly heard a grating sound from just outside the storefront door, where she and Samuel had spent days piling small stones to eliminate the number of muddy footprints tracked through the room. Silence followed the solitary crunch, and she had just decided that it was her imagination when another scraping noise sent her pulse skyward.

Quickly but quietly rising from her seat, Rebecca moved with stealth through the cloth-covered opening to the store, taking care not to walk in front of the candle so that no shadow would pass through the chinks in the heavy wood shutters covering the windows. Beneath a long counter where she measured out yard goods was the rifle, primed and loaded for emergencies. She did not yet feel threatened by the intruder outside, but six months on the frontier had taught her that it was safer to err on the side of caution.

By the time the soft knock sounded at the cabin door, Rebecca was ready, her rifle cocked and aimed at the center of the crossbar. "Who's there?" Her voice was calm and steady, belying the nervous jitter in her belly.

"Rebecca?"

The rumbling voice seemed to echo through the room, sending a thousand spiraling images swirling through her mind, tapping a well of aching sadness deep in her soul. For an instant she wondered if she had fallen asleep, for surely this was a dream—or a nightmare. It . . . it could not be!

She gripped the stock of the gun so hard she felt as if the metal would bend beneath her hand. Then slowly, Rebecca shook her head, biting down on her bottom lip to stave off unbidden tears. "Wh-who's there?" she demanded, but this time her chin trembled and her breath came in tiny catches.

At first there was no sound. Maybe he was gone. Or perhaps he had circled to the back of the cabin to try a window there. Frantically she tried to remember if she had barred them all, or if, as she sometimes did, she had left a shutter open to allow in the sweet spring air. Finally his words came again through the thick door. She froze, eyes wide and lungs burning from the expanded breath she had forgotten to release.

"Let me in, Rebecca. It's—"

He stopped abruptly, then after a long moment continued on in a slightly harsher tone than before.

"We met yesterday. Surely you haven't dismissed me so quickly. You asked for Cain, so now you've got him."

She stared at the heavy oak bar in disbelief. "W-what?"

"Just open the door, *Mrs.* Osborne. I've come to examine your son."

CHAPTER 4

Cain looked around the storefront, his bleak gaze raking the neatly stocked shelves. From the pyramid of cider kegs in the corner to a cheerful array of yard goods piled upon the long counter, the store appeared well maintained and welcoming. A small cast-iron stove stood alone in the center of the room. He had not seen one like it since he'd left Albany; it must have cost Levi a good bit to ship such a rare commodity so far, Cain thought dispassionately.

He sat with his elbows planted on his thighs, his nerveless hands dangling between his knees. With only a slight twisting of his neck he could see beyond the connecting doorway into the room beyond, where Rebecca had disappeared shortly after bidding him to sit on a three-legged stool placed in front of the cold stove. She had been wearing the same anxious expression he had seen on her face when she had finally opened the door to him. He knew that emotion well. It was the one that flayed him each time he stepped into the lodge of a dying man, crossing a threshold he did not wish to enter, yet knowing he must.

It ate at him to think that Rebecca's welcome—and it was a halfhearted welcome at best—came only on behalf of her son. On her own she would have turned him away. If not for the boy—Samuel, she had called him, and wasn't *that* a kick in the teeth!—she probably would have shown him the dangerous end of her rifle instead of lifting the heavy oak plank that barred the door.

But she had not, of course, and now he was sitting in her store, knowing she would soon reach a crossing of her own, one that might well determine whether or not he spent the next few years in a military prison. He wondered how she would take the truth when he told her; he sulked over the fact that he even had to.

Cain stood, too restless to remain still. His long legs made pacing impossible in the crowded store; two steps and he was face-to-face with a towering stack of feed sacks, three more to the right and he would bang his shins on a large spool of stout rope. When light footsteps tapped across the puncheon floor, signaling Rebecca's approach, he turned his head away quickly, pretending to study with great interest a tin candle lantern hanging from a nail above the counter.

"Are you planning to purchase a lamp, Mr. Cain?"

Rebecca's low voice breached the silence. It trembled a little, either with fear or expectation. More than likely, he would disappoint her on both counts, Cain thought wearily as he glanced over his shoulder.

"Just *Cain*," he said. "No mister."

"Very well, then. It's an unusual name, Cain. Do you spell it with a *C* or a *K*?"

He chuckled dryly. "No call for spelling among the Shawnee. They haven't got a written language. But I had to tell them something. Cain is easy to remember, and not too—" He had been about to say *not too different from my real name* but he caught himself in time.

"Not too *what*?" she asked quietly, quizzically.

"Not too difficult for the Shawnee tongue," he lied glibly. "They aren't used to pronouncing our words, and some syllables give them a hard time."

"I see." As she had in the tavern, Rebecca found herself wishing he would turn around and face her straight on when he talked. He was still wearing that blasted hat pulled over his forehead. It might have been more polite for him to remove it once indoors, unless he was carrying head lice, in which case she prayed he would keep it on. She sensed, however, that his reasons were far less prosaic. Was it the scar he tried so desperately to hide from view? Or did his eyes hold greater, more terrible secrets?

She crossed her arms to hug herself tightly, warding off a shiver of unease. Despite having quickly donned a wool gown, Rebecca was chilled. Yet she could not bring herself to invite Cain closer to the fire in the other room.

"You have lived with the Shawnee," she said.

It was a statement, not a question, though Cain could find no hint of accusation in her voice. She seemed as relieved as he to find some topic to latch on to, a safe haven from which they could listen and watch and judge one another. He understood her wariness; he would be wary, too, if he had something so precious as a son at stake.

"I spent some time with the Wyandot up near Fort Detroit a few years back," he acknowledged, "and some with the Delaware. But mostly I've stuck around here with the Shawnee."

"And you aren't afraid of the Indians?"

At last Cain turned all the way around to face her, though in the near-darkness she still could not read his expression. Beneath his scraggly beard a grin struggled to surface, and failed. "Afraid of what? Scalping? Death? There are worse fates than falling under a Shawnee tomahawk. Once a man understands there's more than one way to die, then he can put his fear into perspective. The Shawnee admire that."

"I've always felt," she responded slowly, "that a healthy fear of dying has kept many a man from taking foolish risks."

Now he did smile ruefully. "Funny. I figured you for a risk-taker yourself. Seems I guessed wrong."

Cain watched with grim amusement as Rebecca pulled herself up taller. The gown of cherry wool hung loosely from her narrow shoulders, though with her arms crossed beneath her breasts he could make out nearly every curve and hollow. She was still slender in some places, rounder in others. But her jutting chin was the same as he remembered.

"For someone who does not know me at all, you presume far too much, *Mr.* Cain. I hope you are not so hasty with your medical opinion when it comes to my son."

He met her inflexible gaze. She stared at him fixedly, and again resentment coiled deep in his belly. She was wrong. He had known her from the instant he saw her in the tavern yesterday, had known her forever, it seemed. But apparently he had meant little enough to her—now, or in the past.

And *she* accused *him* of haste!

"Ah, yes, your son," he said at last.

She appeared not to notice the sting in his voice. Or perhaps he was the only one who could taste the bitterness. It made him want to spit out the truth before it poisoned him, yet some shred of humanity made him swallow his anger and gentle his tongue. He would tell her, but he would ease into it the way he might approach an unfamiliar campfire, hoping to find a friend but prepared to meet with the enemy.

Rebecca studied him intently, struggling to understand this man who filled her with such a warring mixture of emotions. She was intrigued by him, and yes, frightened, for she sensed that beneath that stoic exterior lay passions dark and dangerous.

And she sensed something else, too. Something familiar, like the wafting scent of honeysuckle on a summer's day or the sound of children laughing at dusk. It made her happy and homesick all at once; her chest throbbed with a dull, empty ache.

"Y-your voice?" she asked. "Are you, by any chance, from the Carolinas?"

His head dipped lower. "What makes you say that?"

"You sound so familiar to me. It must be the accent, or—"

"We were discussing the boy's condition," he said abruptly.

Rebecca gave a start, then pressed her lips into a tight line. "Yes, of course. Would you like to see him now?"

"I want to ask you something first. The procedure you seem to think is required is sure to cause him some pain, and there is no guarantee he'll be any better off. The boy has already been through one ordeal, I gather. Are you sure you want to put him through another?

Rebecca stiffened, drawing a sharp breath. "If there is a reasonable chance of success, then yes. The alternative is to see him remain crippled for the rest of his life. As you undoubtedly know, this wilderness is harsh and unforgiving. A boy . . . a *man* has to have every advantage to survive. Without a father to guide him, Samuel will need those advantages more than most."

Cain nodded, his voice tight and controlled. "I can't say as I disagree with that. So we'd best get on with it."

He waited for her to lead the way, but Rebecca only stared at him, her gaze distant and unsettling. It was almost as if she had forgotten he was there, or was seeing someone else altogether. But then she snapped out of her trance, a rose blush suffusing her cheeks with color.

"W-what did you say?" she stammered.

His tone was almost gentle when he answered, "It's time I talked to the boy."

"I heard about you," Samuel Osborne said, his voice still thick with sleep. "Can you really turn into a panther?"

Propped against the two goosefeather pillows Rebecca had brought to his bed, he looked smaller than a ten-year-old should, his skinny shoulders nearly disappearing into the striped ticking.

Cain scratched his rough cheek and grinned. "Is that what they're saying about me now? Can't a fellow grow a beard without someone likening him to a wild beast?"

Despite the tired circles beneath his eyes, Samuel giggled. He liked this huge, shaggy man, even though he'd been scared when his mother first woke him up. Somehow, while his head was still full of dreams and his eyes not quite opened, he'd had the idea that this was his father come up from the bottom of the river. But that was silly. Besides, Cain didn't look *anything* like his father, even though Samuel already had a hard time picturing him.

Samuel shrugged. "I guess I didn't really believe those stories. At least the ones about you turning into an animal. But you are a doctor, right?"

Easing himself onto the edge of the bed, taking care to keep his back to Rebecca, Cain nodded. "Yes, I am, Samuel. Your mother asked me to take a look at your leg. Is that all right with you?"

The blue eyes peering back at Cain were solemn. "Sure, you can look. Captain Tuthill said my leg'll never get straight again, but you're a better doctor than him, ain't ya?"

"Aren't you," Rebecca corrected automatically. "And you must let Mr.—You must let *Cain* make up his own mind."

She stood at the foot of the small bed, holding the candle high so that the light spread through the tiny room with its slanted ceiling and single shuttered window. A niggling doubt had worked its way into Rebecca's mind, the same one that had kept her from telling Samuel earlier about

Cain. She did not want to fill the boy with false hope, only to see those hopes broken apart as mercilessly as the river had done to their flatboat six months before.

But Samuel's eyes remained fixed on the tall woodsman with a kind of awestruck wonder he usually reserved for men on horseback, or, more recently, for Skulley. Rebecca had expected her son to be intimidated by Cain's rough-shod appearance, but if anything, Samuel seemed more fascinated than frightened by the aura of untamed wildness surrounding the legendary man.

As she watched silently, Cain removed the bedcovers and began to run his palms over Samuel's leg. Even from where she stood Rebecca could see that his touch was firm but gentle, and she noticed for the first time that despite his otherwise unkempt demeanor, Cain's hands were surprisingly clean.

"Do you need more light? I can bring up the lant—"

"No, this will do." His abrupt answer startled her, until he explained, "I don't need to see so much as feel the position of the bone. Don't go to any bother."

She fell silent, watching as he examined Samuel's thigh. "Does it hurt when I do this?" he murmured in a low, soothing tone. "Or this? How about when you're walking?"

Samuel's responses came as no surprise to Rebecca, for she had often performed the same motions and asked the same questions. The difference was, while she had nothing but instinct to guide her, Cain examined her son with a smooth precision that was matter-of-fact, and therefore comforting.

Perhaps his training had been unorthodox, but Rebecca did not doubt that Cain's hands were those of a healer.

After a few more minutes of massaging the stringy muscles of Samuel's leg, Cain pulled Samuel into an upright position, then laid his head to the boy's chest.

"Why are you doing that?" Rebecca asked suspiciously.

"You said he'd suffered a lung ailment. Just wanted to make sure it's all cleared up."

Mollified, Rebecca relaxed again. She *had* told him yesterday about Samuel's illness last fall. And though she had forgotten, Cain obviously had not. His thoroughness heartened her.

As he continued to converse with Samuel in a low voice,

Rebecca let her thoughts wander. Samuel certainly had taken a liking to the man, and it was always said that when it came to instinctively judging character, you couldn't fool children or dogs. Cain certainly appeared to know what he was doing.

Perhaps she had been wrong to judge him so harshly yesterday, she thought. After all, she had taken him by surprise, and who was she to question the man's peculiar penchant for secrecy?

If he could help Samuel, she didn't care if he *did* turn into a panther once he left!

Several more minutes went by before Cain stood—or at least hunched—at the side of the bed. He shook Samuel's hand with mock gravity, then tucked the covers back up around the boy's chin. "You get some sleep now. A boy your age shouldn't be up so late."

Samuel's chin dropped, then he realized he was being teased and grinned tiredly. "Then I guess you'll tell Ma not to bother me if I sleep past chores, huh?"

Cain chuckled, patting a thin shoulder through the covers. "I suppose that's the least I can do. G'night, son."

Blue eyes widened momentarily, then drifted to half-mast. "G'night, Cain. Will I see you t'morrow?"

"That'll be up to your mother." With a sideways glance, Cain met Rebecca's gaze. She looked startled when their eyes made contact, as if he had caught her woolgathering over some forbidden delight.

Lowering the candle, Rebecca shielded it with her hand as she moved around the bed and bent to kiss her son on the top of his golden head. "We'll talk about it in the morning, Samuel. Sleep well."

Without another word, she led Cain down the narrow stairs to the keeping room below.

"I agree that resetting Samuel's leg could be a risk worth taking, provided you realize that the chance of a full recovery—at least the kind you're wanting—is slim, and that there are other things that could go wrong."

They had returned to the store's front room in order to keep their voices from carrying up to Samuel, and now Cain straddled the same stool he had earlier scorned. Rebecca had pulled a chair from beneath the counter, sitting with her hands folded primly in her lap as if she were making a Sunday call back in Beaufort County, Carolina. But he could see the pulse flutter at the base of her throat.

"What could go wrong?" Rebecca asked tremulously.

"A severed artery, gangrene . . . those are two possibilities."

"What else?"

Cain paused. "The broken ends have started to knit together already, though not quite in the right places. Sometimes bones'll grow a sort of shell around them—a protective layer, I suppose you could call it. If there's too much of that shell already built up, Samuel's leg may not heal as well as it already has. At least now he can make his way around on crutches. But if the new break won't mend, he could end up bedridden."

She paled, her eyes growing as large as two black pennies in her white face. "Have you . . . have you had much experience with this sort of injury?"

"With setting broken bones, yes. This is a bit different, though."

Cain could sense her uneasiness. His skills had been questioned before, but he had not expected it from her; after all, she had sought him out first. "Those are the risks, and I wouldn't feel right not telling you. I still think it's worth a try."

He waited for her reaction, anticipating her showing him the door. Doubt filled her eyes, followed by an expression he read as resignation. She nodded once, rose quickly, and said "Very well," before turning to leave the room.

Cain lunged from the stool, stopping her with a firm grasp above her elbow. "Wait! Do you mean you want me to do it?"

She twisted her head around. "Is there more I should know? Another adverse effect?"

"No, but there's something else we have to talk about first."

Rebecca swung back, flinching a little at the pressure of his fingertips, not because it hurt, but because of the exquisite pleasure that tingled up her arm. His movement had placed him farther inside the circle of light cast by the candle on the high counter. She could see the lines of weariness around his mouth, and the pale tint of exhaustion beneath his tan. Something akin to sympathy stirred

inside her, sending fans of warmth outward from her
breastbone to kindle her blood.

But the old caution returned quickly enough, and with
it a measure of anger at herself for becoming careless—or
perhaps for caring too much. She narrowed her eyes.
"Have you, or have you not come here to treat Samuel?"

"I have," he answered readily.

"Then I suggest we stop wasting time—"

"But not tonight," he continued, his hand dropping
abruptly from her arm as if he suddenly realized he was
holding on to a burning branch. "I didn't mean tonight. I
have to make preparations, find an assistant."

Rebecca now faced him fully, a puzzled frown pursed upon
her full lips. Cain had the urge to touch those lips, to see them
spring into a joyful grin or grow slack with passion.

Instead her frown deepened. "Then why did you not
wait until morning to wake me?"

He paused, shuffling his feet, unconsciously stepping
back into the shadows again. "That's part of what I have
to tell you about. I had to be careful about who saw me,
at least until I was sure this was worth doing."

Be careful who saw him? Why on earth—? "Are you . . .
Have you done something wrong, then?"

Cain watched as fear and defeat seemed to coalesce in
her dark eyes. Better for her to feel them now, he told himself grimly, while she still had the chance to change her
mind. "It was a long time ago. Ten years, to be exact."

He waited then. Waited for the dawning realization to
grow bright in her eyes, watched for a slow smile of rec-
ognition to spread like sunshine across her lips. None
came. Her expression remained bleak, guarded.

"What exactly did you do?"

Cain blew out a long breath. "Desertion will most likely
be the charge. Dereliction of duty. Cowardice in the face
of the enemy."

"You fought in the war?"

"Fought? That's not quite the way I'd describe what I did—
at least the parts I can recall. My memory of that last skirmish
is nothing but a hazy fog, but I do remember how I felt afterward. Nothing could have made me go back."

"Is that where you got the scar on your cheek?"

"Yes."

"But if you were injured you could hardly be expected to return to battle. And you must have been quite young then."

He looked at her intently, trying to fathom the depths of concern he heard in her voice. "Nineteen. But none of that will hold much weight with the military authorities at Fort Washington. When I tell them my real name they might decide that hanging is the most fitting punishment for desertion. I won't do Samuel much good then, now, will I?"

Rebecca pursed her lips again. "Do you have to tell them?"

Cain chuckled mirthlessly. "That's the catch, my sweet. In order to help Samuel I'm going to need certain medical equipment, and some help. The fort is the only place in this territory where I can get it. However, I can hardly walk in there as 'Cain.' "

He watched her duck her head and begin chewing on her lower lip in concentration. In silence he waited for her to ask the question, *If not Cain, then who?*

But she did not. She worried her lip some more, her smooth brow now deeply furrowed. "I could ask Skulley," she finally said, lifting her head hopefully.

"Who?"

"Sergeant John Haskull. He'll know what the penalty for desertion would be, and he might even put a good word in for you. After all, you *were* only a boy. The army might be more lenient than you think. And Skulley will help."

Cain felt his gut tighten inexplicably. "Why would another soldier put himself out on a limb for me?"

Rebecca shrugged unconcernedly. "He'd be doing it for me, of course. And Samuel."

"Is that a fact?"

His voice had taken on that sharp edge once again, and Rebecca looked up, surprised that he did not find her idea more inviting. And then shame washed over her. Now Cain was the one contemplating taking a risk, all for the sake of a boy he had only just met. And she was treating the matter as lightly as if they were discussing whether or not he might get his leather moccasins wet.

Cain saw the distress darken her eyes, though he read it to mean she was afraid he would change his mind. Not that he blamed her. She could not know that he had been flirting with the idea of turning himself in for months now. "You're probably right about the army's treatment of deserters. The Colonial army was plagued throughout the war with the problem. But I don't need your friend—what was his name? Skulley—to help argue my case. You may require a protector, but I'd just as soon take care of myself."

There was a moment in which Rebecca was certain she had misunderstood him, but the derisive tone he had used carried into his expression, and she saw the mockery drawing his mouth into a crooked smile. That smile, too, was oddly familiar; she immediately likened it to the knowing grins of the townsfolk in Beaufort so long ago. As it had then, her heart felt as if lead weights had been attached to it, though that did not prevent her from lifting her defiant chin.

"Sergeant Haskull is a friend," she defended. "*Only* a friend. But even if he were more, it would be none of your concern. How dare you question my actions? Of all the arrogant, presumptive—"

" 'Becca, I—"

"For your information, I've spent my entire life being 'protected' by men. First my father, then my fiancé, and finally my husband Levi, when I was too young or . . . or when I could not survive without them. There's no shame in taking help where it's offered. Not when it's a matter of life or death."

" 'Becca, listen to me."

But she was too far into her tirade to let him stop her now, too caught up in purging the frustrations of the past to notice his familiar use of her name, or to hear the painful ring in his voice.

"Would you let pride stand in the way of a life?" she cried, jabbing one furious finger in his direction. "Samuel's life?"

" 'Becca!"

He had not raised his voice, but this time his incisive tone cut through her tantrum and sent her anger shattering into a thousand disjointed pieces.

He took a step toward her, then another, and before she

knew it he was clasping her shoulders with a rough grip, as if preparing to shake her back to reality.

But he did not shake her. He only held her at arm's length, his eyes growing sad as he repeated, " 'Becca."

"My God!" Her gaze flicked up past his bearded chin and full, sensuous lips to his pale blue eyes, where shock and elation caught her in a mesmerizing spell. Those eyes were still hidden in shadows, but now she saw what she had not seen before. "My God!" she said again, unaware that though her lips formed the words, no sound emerged but a strangled gasp.

Her senses whirled; a maelstrom of emotions spun her so thoroughly that she thought she would surely faint. Denial, disbelief, joy . . . and then heartbreaking reality. She blinked hard, summoning the memory of his betrayal.

Slowly, he released her shoulders and took a cautious step backward, removing his hat to clutch it in both hands like a sheepish schoolboy. A fine sheen of perspiration glistened just below the sweep of gold-streaked hair that dipped across his brow. The scar on his cheek stood out from his tanned flesh like a smudge on a muslin sheet.

He looked different, she thought distantly. That's why she had not recognized him. But she realized deep in her heart that it was more than a hat or a scar that had disguised this man; it took time and tragedy and hatred to keep him from her all these years.

The Indians had called him Cain. To Rebecca, he was Aaron Cambridge, the only man she had ever loved.

CHAPTER 5

Rebecca went rigid with shock, then fumbled behind her
back for the counter, searching for the candle. Her nerveless fingers nearly spilled the flame until Aaron's hands
reached forward and captured the pewter holder.

"Let me, before you burn the place down," he said
harshly. Knowing what she had intended, he flung his hat
onto the planks and lifted the candle closer to himself, so
close he could feel the flickering heat against his scarred
cheek.

Even as she peered at him she was shaking her head
slowly, denial written on her lovely face. "How . . . how
can this be? A-Aaron?"

"Yes, it *is* me, 'Becca. I suppose you weren't expecting
an old friend after all these years, but I am surprised you
didn't know me a bit sooner than this."

"S-sooner?" A huge, welling sob burst from her, so
that her words were choked and broken. "I thought you
were d-dead!"

Now it was Aaron's turn to look shocked, though he
quickly recovered, his stern features drawing into a fierce
frown. "I don't see how. Even on the official reports I was
listed only as missing. Not deceased."

Rebecca could answer only with a weak moan as she
leaned against the counter for support. Her stomach muscles contracted, threatening to revolt, and she swallowed
hard to keep her supper from rising in her throat. So many
emotions erupted within her she could scarcely credit them
all, but the strongest of these, disbelief, still managed to
retain the greatest hold. "It can't be," she whispered

softly, her gaze raking him greedily. "After all this time, it can't be. Aaron."

He shrugged, moved by her reaction, too moved to trust his voice. There could be no feigning the turmoil in her dark eyes. Her surprise was genuine.

Surprise, however, meant only that he had come unanticipated. It did not necessarily mean he was welcome. "Maybe we better sit back down, 'Becca. It's—"

"Why didn't you show yourself to me yesterday?" she demanded quietly. Her words were clear and calm, in direct juxtaposition to the state of her nerves. "Why did you let me go on thinking you were someone else, this . . . this *Cain*?"

"I am Cain," he answered levelly. "Just as much as I was ever Aaron Cambridge. Maybe more."

With a slashing motion of her hand she silenced him, unwilling to listen to further excuses. Anger had now replaced disbelief, and she was filled with a blazing hot fury that ripped at her soul and singed her heart. "You tricked me! You knew who I was and yet you purposely hid yourself from me! Why? Did you think I would still hate you? That I wouldn't let you near Samuel?"

Aaron remained still in the face of her wrath, though his gut clenched angrily at her hard words. He had given her no reason to despise him so. Carefully he replaced the candle on the countertop, then stooped to pick up his hat, watching her out of the corner of his eye. She stood with her fingers laced together and pressed tight against her belly, as if holding herself together by sheer strength of will. He cleared his throat roughly.

"I wasn't aware that hatred was one of the lingering emotions you harbored toward me. Since it is, I could argue that it was one more reason for me to remain anonymous—until I was certain you would not pepper me with rifle shot, that is. But I told you the real reason I was silent. You'll just have to trust me that secrecy was the best way."

"Trust?" Rebecca tried to laugh, but the most she could do was to utter a high-pitched squawk. With her incredulous stare still pinned on Aaron, she groped for the stool she had vacated earlier, her knees having suddenly turned the consistency of gooseberry jelly.

She must get a grip on herself, Rebecca thought. Cackling like a lunatic would serve no purpose, nor would crying out her frustration and disbelief. If they could only discuss this calmly . . . rationally.

But she feared there *was* no rational explanation. At least none that she could comprehend. Utterly bewildered, and suddenly more heartsore than she had ever felt before, Rebecca fixed her gaze on Aaron's ravaged face. "Why, Aaron? Tell me why I should trust you. Make me understand."

Her plea drove straight to his heart, shearing his resistance in two. With her ebony hair billowing around her shoulders and her eyes as dark as midnight in her pale face, she looked once again like the young, guileless girl he had left behind him so many years ago. She had said something about believing he had been killed in the war. Perhaps there was some truth in that statement, after all.

"I'm not the same as I was back then, 'Becca. Let's get that said right up front. And I didn't expect to see you again any more than you did me, just so you know this doesn't come easy on this end, either."

"What . . . what happened?" she asked, despite an almost overwhelming dread of knowing.

Aaron hooked his stool with one foot, pulling it closer to her chair. He hunkered down on the hard seat, elbows resting on his thighs, his long fingers still worrying the tired brim of his hat. "What happened," he began slowly, "is that I found out the hard way that I was better at taking lives than I was at saving them. Do you remember me telling you about Eli Winthrop?"

Rebecca frowned, then nodded. "I think so. Wasn't he the physician you met in Albany? The one you apprenticed yourself to?"

"He was the finest field surgeon in Gates's army," Aaron said in low, respectful tones. "And a fine teacher, as well. Precise, yet patient . . . perhaps too patient. He could have driven me to learn faster—God knows the war gave us plenty of opportunities for practical experience. He should not have let me spend so much time with the medical books. What the hell good are books when a man is dying?''

Anguish etched his face, and Rebecca found herself longing to brush back the lock of hair that fell across his lowered brow. "What happened to Dr. Winthrop?" she asked softly.

Aaron lifted his bleak gaze to her. "He died, just like so many of them. I could do nothing for Eli in the end, except hold him as he strangled on his last breath. But he wasn't the worst. There were . . ." His face grew blank, then twisted into a frown.

"There was what?"

"I don't remember." Aaron stared at the floor helplessly. "Not from that last patrol. I can't remember anything about the night I was shot."

Now Rebecca's heart pounded with sympathy, and a wisp of doubt flitted through her thoughts. "I've heard of that—losing one's memory after an injury or a terrible shock."

"The medical term is amnesia," Aaron confirmed.

"Then you *couldn't* come home, because you didn't remember!"

The hopeful light in her eyes made his chest throb with remorse, and for a brief instant Aaron toyed with the idea of letting it stay there. But he could not. The road to finding his own peace was not wide enough for deceit. Not now. Not anymore.

He shook his head slowly. "I deserted, 'Becca. Plain and simple. The only memory I lost was that last bit, right before I got shot and up to the time I came out of the fever. A farmer found me wandering a few miles from where the skirmish took place. My fever was raging so bad by that time he feared moving me, so he kept me in his barn instead of taking me back to the regiment. Two weeks later I woke up."

"But . . . but you were still sick."

"Not so sick I didn't know I wasn't ever going back to my regiment. As soon as I was well enough, I walked south all the way into Jersey, staying clear of towns and army encampments. It was easy enough . . ." his voice took on a heavy irony, "since the British had surrendered.

That was a hell of a thing, to find out that last skirmish took place, by most accounts, after the war was really over.

"It was in Philadelphia I found out—and the fact that I was posted as missing. I decided after that to head west."

Rebecca's thoughts were all in a whirl, too tangled and frantic to make much sense. A thousand questions surged to her lips, a thousand possible responses lacerated her mind. None of them gave her much hope.

Though she lifted her chin bravely, her voice was no more than a hoarse whisper. "You did not . . . you did not think to let me know you were alive? Could you not have sent a message, a letter? Anything?"

Aaron's gaze focused on her trembling lower lip, and he had to force himself to remember that she was not the only one who had suffered a loss. "I did go back to say goodbye," he said tonelessly, "but you were already gone, you and Levi. Gone to Virginia, someone said. My old friend Levi Osborne and his pretty young bride. If I hurried I might catch up, they told me. You'd only had a week's head start and a man alone can make better time than a settler's wagon."

"Oh, Aaron," she murmured in a strangled voice, "why didn't you?"

He looked at her longingly, then rose, clapping his hat on his head. "Because it was too late, 'Becca. It was already too late."

It *had* been too late, Rebecca knew in the part of her mind that clung to rationality. But that did not erase the bitterness that spilled through her like a cold mountain stream, leaving her numb and aching all at the same time.

And even if Aaron had come to her before she accepted Levi's suit. What then? He said himself that he had come home only to leave once again. To say his good-byes. Could she honestly say that would have been better than thinking he was dead?

"Oh, dear God!" Rebecca moaned, resting her forehead in her hands as she perched on the edge of her bed. Dawn had already begun to tint the eastern sky, painting the clouds a pinkish gray. It was too late, then, for sleep, yet she was so emotionally drained she felt weak and shaky. The tears that had continually threatened during Aaron's terse recounting now refused to come. In their place was a solid lump lodged in the back of her throat; it tasted as sour and dry as an old turnip.

Damn him, she cried wordlessly. *Damn him, damn him!*

It was the same ineffective curse she had wept ten years ago, on the morning of her wedding. Lenore had found her then, curled up in a ball on a feather bed far distant from the one she now used, and pounding her soaked pillow weakly.

"No use weepin'," Lenore had said pragmatically, though her hand had been gentle as she smoothed Rebecca's hair from her damp cheeks. "If it was in us to always wail ever' time we're given a hard shake, why, we women'd be wrung dry to nothin'! Only way to face it ever' day, 'Becca, is to think on the good things."

"You're r-right, Lenore," Rebecca had hiccuped into the pillow. "I *do* thank God for you and Levi. But it's just s-so hard."

"Don't I know it, honey. Don't I know it."

Rebecca recalled how ashamed she had felt at that moment, remembering that Lenore had lost her husband only a short time before. Rebecca had pulled herself together, with her soon-to-be-sister-in-law's help, and had bound herself in holy wedlock to Levi Osborne with dry eyes and a clear head.

She would not look back, she had told herself fiercely. She would never look back.

And most of the time, Rebecca could freely admit, she had not. But there were days—and nights—when the memories came to her unbidden, like secret visitors that crept in without warning, bringing happiness while they stayed but leaving the house empty and grieving once gone. . . .

It was summer when he came home the last time, and the hot sun had turned the dunes into stiffened peaks, scorched white and rippling like frozen waves. Rebecca ran across the hard-packed surface, her lithe body rising and falling with each crest and valley, her skirts wantonly gathered to her knees.

"Aaron!" she cried, stopping long enough to wave at the tall figure standing thigh-deep in the surf. He looked up, and though she was still far up the beach, she could picture his slow smile spreading across his face. Laughing, she broke into an unladylike sprint.

But as she drew closer, propriety—or shyness, for she had not seen him for over a year—reared itself up, causing her to slow to a more regal walk. Self-consciously she lowered her skirts, adjusting the twin panniers and shaking out the sprigged muslin fabric until it brushed the tops of her slippers. Her *best* slippers, she remembered with a wry smile. They would be ruined now, but what did she care? Aaron was home.

He waited for her, impatient but not showing it, his arms bent and fists planted on his hips. Gentle waves lapped at the back of his legs, nudging him toward shore, so with a quick toss of his head he waded from the sea.

Rebecca stopped, stifling a joyful gasp. Had he grown taller in a year? Or was it just that his shoulders carried a new width? Her eyes skittered down the untied front of his white linen shirt to where his dark trousers clung to muscular legs, then back up to his strong, bare throat beneath his squared jaw. She could not quite bring herself to meet his eyes. Not yet.

"Hello, 'Becca," he said, the first to speak. "Come to help me draw in Levi's line?"

At the barely veiled amusement in his voice, she darted a glance to his eyes. *More blue than the sky,* she thought instantly. *Just like I remembered.*

"Of course not," she said, her pert nose tipped disdainfully upward. "A lady does not turn her hand to fishing."

"Only footracing, I suppose," he retorted lightly. "Remind me not to challenge you to a contest."

He *was* laughing at her, Rebecca saw at once. Her already flushed cheeks burned hotter, though she could not suppress the answering smile that danced across her lips. "Can't you tell I'm too old for such games, Aaron Cambridge? I'm grown up now."

"Yes," he answered slowly, no longer laughing. "I noticed."

By then he was beside her, within touching distance, if one of them but raised an outstretched hand. But neither did; instead they let their eyes reach for one another, hungrily, avidly, seeking and searching for the changes of a year as well as the comforting sameness, too.

Aaron had never felt so self-conscious around her, not even last summer when he had brushed his lips over her soft, upturned mouth before boarding the schooner for New York. She had been a child then, a girl of only fifteen. Now she wore the shape and features of a woman. She was right. She *had* grown.

Rebecca, too, was acutely aware of her newly blossomed body, for it seemed that she ached in all the places that had sprouted and transformed in the last months. And why was she so tongue-tied? After all, it was only Aaron who stood before her, not some strange young god risen from the sea.

"Walk with me back to Levi's?" Aaron offered, finally breaking the awkward silence.

"All right."

They fell into step together, she skirting the dancing surf, trying to salvage what was left of her dignity, he trodding barefooted through the churling foam.

With an effort, Aaron turned his thoughts to the details of home he had so missed during his absence. It occurred to him that Rebecca *was* one of those details, but he settled for a topic less inflaming. "How does your father fare?"

"Papa? He seems fine, though he was bad again this winter past. He continues to claim it is nothing but an ague." She glanced sideways demurely. "Will you call on him?"

Aaron's exposed neck grew red, though she could tell he was pleased by her request. Suddenly she felt as if the air around her had grown less confining, somehow brighter.

"I'm not certified yet, 'Becca. Dr. Winthrop said it'll be another year, at least. We're marching out with General Gates's army next month, though, so I expect I'll get more experience then." He glanced at her face, saw the slight frown there, and added quickly, "But if you want me to, I'll talk to your father first."

Rebecca nodded, her happiness already dissipating. So soon! She bit her lower lip miserably, but refused to let her disappointment show. After all, the war was making demands on everyone; she would not snivel and whine like a baby. "He will be pleased to see you again, too, Aaron. So many of the young men who used to come around to hear him talk have gone away. All but Levi, and you know he never enjoyed Papa's philosophizing the way you did."

Aaron chuckled, the rumbling sounding deeper than Rebecca remembered. Another change. "Poor Levi," he commiserated. "Always itching to be away. He's taking it hard, being stuck here now. I keep trying to tell him that the war is no adventure, that we'll have our chance to strike out for new territory when the fighting's done. But he's chafing, I can tell."

"Can you? Levi never said one way or another to me." Rebecca wasn't sure which bothered her more, the idea that Levi had not shared his feelings with her, or the thought of her two friends traipsing off into the woods without her. It was bad enough that Aaron had been gone off and on for most of the past three years. And now he was filling Levi's head with the wanderlust. "What's wrong with staying here in Beaufort anyway?" she countered. "What's wrong with staying home?"

With me! she added silently.

They had reached the top of the rise, where sand gave way to thin grass. With casual ease, Aaron stepped over the ridge, reaching back for Rebecca's hand to help her over. And then it seemed the most natural thing in the world to let her slender fingers slip between his.

He tightened his grasp. "There's nothing wrong with this, 'Becca," he said, waving his free hand to indicate the sun-drenched beach and scruffy brush around them. "But don't you want to see something different? Trees so thick and green you can scarcely see the sky? Wide rivers and earth as black as midnight? I saw all those things when I went to Fort Pitt last year, and they're ours for the taking."

Aaron paused, glancing over to gauge her reflection. He had surprised himself, talking like he was planning to take her along. But now that the seed was planted, he sort of liked the idea. Rebecca had tagged after him and Levi so often while the three of them were children it just wouldn't seem right to go without her.

Rebecca was nearly dizzy from all the feelings cascading through her. Her hand had gone tingly with awareness, clasped inside of Aaron's. She thought she would never catch her breath again, at least not while he was walking so near that his shoulder brushed hers. And she was afraid to look at him. Afraid that if she caught his eye she would see the glint of laughter in those wide blue depths, and he would say, *I was only teasing, 'Becca. You're just a girl— you're too young to come with us.*

But he did not. And so she continued to walk in silence, the stitch in her side growing worse from not taking deep breaths, uncertain tears hovering just behind her eyelids.

When they came to the road that marked the beginning of town, Rebecca thought he would drop her hand, but instead Aaron stopped and turned toward her.

She peeked up at him hesitantly, her heart clamoring in her throat as his azure gaze met hers. She had never noticed before how dark and thick his lashes were, how his sun-streaked hair dipped so low on one side it nearly covered the bold slash of his eyebrow. She noticed those things now, along with the new strength in his jaw and the sureness of his firm lips.

'' 'Becca,'' he said softly.

His voice was a husky rasp. Rebecca's heart swelled. He was as shy as she! She leaned closer, barely more than an inch, but enough to show him that she wasn't afraid anymore. "Do you have to go back to Levi's yet?" she whispered. A timid smile tugged at the corner of her mouth. "I mean . . . you could come to see Papa now. He might invite you to stay for supper."

Aaron paused, then answered with a smile of his own. "I sure would like that, 'Becca."

That afternoon had set the tone for the remainder of Aaron's time in Beaufort. With his own parents dead and his brother, Jacob, already fighting with the Colonial army, Aaron was free to do as he pleased. He boarded with Levi, crowded into the clapboard house with his friend's mother, widowed sister, and four young nephews.

Each night Aaron sat before the fire, listening to Levi bemoan his fate, shackled to the fishing business that had been his father's and unable to join the army because his family could not survive without him. In the mornings Aaron either helped his friend or studied the medical tomes borrowed from Eli Winthrop.

During those times Rebecca rushed through her duties keeping house for her father, her heart beating a happy tempo as her thoughts dwelled on Aaron. He usually arrived some time after lunch, while Papa was upstairs resting, and the two of them would sneak off to the beach or to the piney forest outside of town.

Despite the war, despite the knowledge that Aaron would leave soon, they were the happiest days of her life. . . .

When the distant howl of a wolf awakened her, Rebecca jerked upright, clutching her shawl tighter around her throat. The sky outside was still gray. She had only dozed off for a few minutes, though it had seemed longer as she relived nearly every moment of that magical summer.

Slightly disoriented, she gazed through blurry eyes around the cramped room. The bare walls were stark and rough and somehow mocking. Her thin mattress crackled as she moved, and when she lowered her hand to the pillow she was astonished to find it wet with tears.

This, then, was reality. Not the girlish fantasies of her dream, nor the romantic notions of a child. Only a hard life, and a heart so bruised it still wept in the night.

What a fool she had been, both then and now, Rebecca railed against herself. She had let him see how very vulnerable she was to him, and that was a kind of power she needed to protect herself against.

Rising quickly, she changed into her only other dress. If and when Aaron returned, she would let him know in no uncertain terms that whatever personal feelings were between them in the past, they had absolutely no bearing on today. She *could* not allow him to wreak havoc on her world.

Once, long ago, she had allowed him into her life, trusting him with her heart. She would not make the same mistake again. For Samuel's sake—and for hers.

CHAPTER 6

He camped on a wooded knoll some two miles from Rebecca's store. He did not sleep. Instead, he sat with his back as rigid as one of the aged oak trees surrounding him, his legs crossed and knees spread wide, his palms upturned. The position was one the Shawnee used for silent meditation, but there was nothing peaceful or relaxed about Aaron's posture.

Accusations hurled around inside his head, none more stinging than those he had cast upon himself. Rebecca's anger was well justified. He *had* wanted to maintain an advantage over her before revealing his identity. With Samuel's fate hanging in the balance, he had known she would be less likely to dismiss him out of hand if she didn't recognize him.

And as for the rest? Even without the parts he could not remember, Aaron figured he had enough sins against him to head him straight to hell. He had no regrets about choosing not to drag Rebecca down with him. She didn't realize just how lucky she was to have chosen Levi over him.

Nevertheless, her pride was hurt and it wouldn't sit right with him until he made it up to her. *If* she'd even let him now.

Impatient to begin, Aaron scanned the slope before him, watching for signs that the village was awakening. All was still—all except the Ohio River snaking through the valley like a silent gray serpent shrouded in early morning mist.

The fortified settlement rested on a plain well above flood level, clearly visible now that dawn had lightened

the eastern sky. The original fort was made up of a group
of ten or twelve cabins arranged in a rough rectangular
shape and joined by a connecting barricade of spiked logs.
The backs of the cabins themselves formed a part of the
defense, with a two-story blockhouse on each of the corners.

But most of the residents had abandoned the stockade
after Fort Washington's establishment nearby had effectively reduced the threat of Indian raids. Now many small
buildings clustered beyond the shadow of the log walls,
and arable fields stretched in an erratic circle nearly a mile
wide, dotted with cabins and zigzagged with split-rail
fences.

Another mark of civilization, Aaron thought with grim
resignation. Ownership designated by a few sticks of
wood. Shawnee fields were rarely fenced, because The
People did not believe in owning the land. The earth and
all its fruits were gifts from the Great Mother, and squab-
bling over a gift was a sign of disrespect toward the giver.

Besides, what did these settlers think they were protecting themselves from? Aaron questioned more pragmatically. A mere fence could not stop the floods or the
ravaging funnel clouds that often swept through the valley
each spring. Drought and disease knew no boundaries,
either. These were the elements that should most concern
the brave frontiersmen. Not scarring the land with parti-
tions and pettiness.

No amount of talk, however, would convince the white
men that this rich, fertile valley did not belong to them
alone. They argued that the recently drafted Northwest Ordinance gave them the right to turn the lush forests into
fields. And with determination and courage they would
survive the natural disasters and conquer the unnatural
ones, including those who had prior claim by right of thousands of years.

Aaron closed his eyes, sadness and weariness washing
over him. Possession of the Ohio Valley was a question
that had long plagued his soul, but he could admit he was
pondering it now only to avoid confronting his own problems. And had he not told his friend Wind at His Feet that
he was prepared to face his past?

Yes, he was! Aaron told himself firmly, rising to stretch his stiffened legs and shaking out the tension in his shoulders and back. Facing the morning sun just peeping above the rolling hills to the east, he narrowed his eyes intently, his gaze focusing on his inner soul as much as the verdant landscape.

For ten years he had lived with the knowledge of his own cowardice. In all that time he had never tried to understand his driving need to learn the healing arts of the Indians. Not until Snow Hair, the wisest of the Shawnee shamans, had counseled him had Aaron witnessed his first glimpse of the truth buried deep inside. Something had happened that night of the skirmish that had marked him, not just physically, but emotionally as well. Snow Hair had presented the possibility that it was not his injury which had caused the loss of his memory so much as the traumatic events leading up to it. Only by remembering that night would Aaron find peace with himself.

He had to confront his past in order to get on with his future. Only then could he return to the life he had made for himself with the Shawnee. Presenting himself at Fort Washington to face the charges against him would be the first step toward accomplishing this goal. Making amends to Rebecca would be the second.

Rebecca. For so long his memories of her had been tainted by the venomous sting of betrayal. After a time, however, the razor edge of his emotions had dulled, and he had trained himself to think of her only in terms of the lesson she had taught him. Her love for a gallant young physician's apprentice had been a bright and wondrous thing, but when that man had ceased to exist, her love had disappeared as well.

Or so Aaron had told himself. But now he wondered. Rebecca seemed to be telling the truth when she said she had believed him dead. Remorse weighed heavily upon him when he thought she might have grieved for him needlessly. He could, however, by helping her son, atone for the sadness he had caused. If not, then his life's work had been for naught.

Spurred by renewed ambition, Aaron turned from his view of the valley. From his pack on the ground he with-

drew a muslin shirt and a dark coat made of broadcloth.
Tan-colored breeches and a pair of stiff leather boots completed the outfit, which Aaron had purchased more than
three years earlier and had worn only twice, once on a
surreptitious trip to Marietta for medical supplies, and once
to attend the funeral of a trapper friend who had insisted
on being buried downriver in the civilized town of Louis-
ville. The garments would serve him as well for the brief
time he would need them now, he hoped.

The clothes were in need of a good airing, but Aaron
figured he could hang them from bushes beside the stream
where he planned to take a much-needed bath. Bundling
them under his arm, he pushed through the thick underbrush until he reached the nearby pool.

Spring or not, the water was as icy as a midwinter sleet
storm, so he made haste with the handful of soap root and
a shell comb with half its teeth missing, emerging at last
feeling invigorated and cleaner than he had since leaving
the Shawnee village nearly a week before. The Indians
themselves were meticulous about personal hygiene; it was
only when Aaron reentered the world of the whites that he
donned filth as an acceptable disguise.

When he was finally dressed in the unfashionable yet
sturdy clothing, his beard shaved off and his hair combed
back and tied in a short queue with a ribbon instead of
rawhide, Aaron repacked the soft leather satchel and slung
it over his shoulder as he stood to look out over the valley
once more.

Now wisps of smoke, as limp and wrinkled as the dark
ribbon in his hair, curled up from the chimneys of the
distant cabins. The settlement was waking. Rebecca would
be, too, if she had slept at all after his hasty departure.

He wondered if she thought he had gone far away, for-
saking his promise to help Samuel. He wondered as well
what her reaction would be when he appeared at her door
again, not as Cain this time, but as Aaron Cambridge fully
returned from the dead. The thought made his mouth twist
into an uneasy smile. Not many men were offered a chance
to be born again.

He only hoped to God he didn't foul *this* life up as badly
as he had his first.

* * *

Rebecca glanced up, not quite surprised when a soft knock sounded at her door, yet not quite prepared, either. She gave the corn mush one final stir before sliding the lid back onto the iron kettle, then stood away from the fire, automatically smoothing her skirt and patting her hair into place as if she had not checked her appearance just moments before in the tiny sliver of mirror she owned.

From the thumping overhead, she knew Samuel had heard the light rap as well. Rebecca smiled distractedly. His ears were as keen as a hound's. *And there would be no privacy,* was her next unbidden thought.

Now, what on earth do I want privacy for? she scolded herself, moving quickly through to the store. When she confronted Cain—*Aaron,* she corrected mentally—she would remain as frostily proper as any other well-bred woman would behave toward such a heathenish character. He was *not* the same Aaron she once knew. She would do well to remember that.

But when she opened the door, fully prepared to order her reluctant guest to leave his pest-ridden hat hanging from a nail on the outside post, Rebecca was stunned to find herself standing face-to-face with a total stranger.

At least for a moment he was a stranger—until a slow, cautious smile transformed his face.

"A-Aaron," she stammered, then clutched her apron into her fists and spun around. She forced a cynical note into her voice as she walked away. "Come in. I'm surprised you had the nerve to come back."

Since this was exactly the reception he had expected, Aaron was not at all perturbed. "Are you? I told you I would try to help Samuel. What passed between us last night . . . or before . . . does not relieve me of that obligation."

Rebecca had moved back to the boiling kettle and snatched up a stick to swing the crane out from the fire. From behind she could hear Aaron's footsteps follow her through the store and into the keeping room. Tendrils of heat bathed her face, making the springy curls around her temples cling to her cheeks and brow. She gritted her teeth. "You have no obligation to me." With greater force than was necessary, she slammed a bowl to the table. It made a loud, clattering ring that unnerved her more than the following silence.

Aaron did not answer at once, and Rebecca could almost feel his penetrating stare dance up and down her spine. Her heart drummed a crazy rhythm beneath her breasts, sending added heat to her face. She glared up at him, daring him to deny her statement.

"I have an obligation to anyone who needs medical attention, Rebecca. Surely you know that," he finally said.

His tone was curt, telling her more clearly than words that Samuel's condition had brought him back, and *only* that.

"So you took it, then?" she asked, still fumbling with two wooden porringers. "That oath you talked about?" Curiosity helped to mask the hurt.

"The Hippocratic oath," Aaron supplied. "In a sense, yes."

"And the medical school in Philadelphia, what about that?"

He hesitated again. "No, that would have been too much of a risk. Besides, I've learned much from the Shawnee."

Rebecca looked up in time to see him shrug. The gesture was so reminiscent of the Aaron she used to know that she drew in a sudden breath to combat the stab of pain in her chest. Here, with the morning sun spilling through the open window, she could see him more clearly than ever.

His hair was the color of aged ale when firelight dances over it. Clean and shining and slightly damp, the thick waves were drawn back into a neat braid at the nape of his strong, corded neck. His jacket fit snugly across broad shoulders and a trim waist, and the muscles of his thighs bulged beneath trousers of cloth, not buckskin.

Rebecca's avid gaze returned to his face, and she was startled by the hungry look in his blue eyes. His dark brows were drawn into a frown, and for the first time she took a really close look at the scar that slashed the right side of his face from his cheekbone nearly to his ear. The scar was a symbol of the years still standing between them. It also reminded her how truly close to death he had come.

She swallowed the sudden overwhelming rage that drove tears to her eyes, not even certain who or what had done this to him, knowing only that she hated it.

Swiftly she turned back to the fire.

For a while the only sound in the room was the whispered hiss of steam from the kettle still suspended over the flames. Rebecca kept herself from sniffling out loud, but could not prevent one huge, swollen tear from rolling down her cheek and plunging from her chin to the hearth below.

Then Samuel clambered down the ladder, his crutches swinging below him. " 'S breakfast ready?'' he asked no one in particular.

Rebecca pretended to wipe the perspiration from her forehead with the back of one hand, catching another tear before it fell. "Almost. I thought you'd sleep in today." Her voice was raw, but Samuel did not seem to notice. She could hear him drag out a chair from the table, depositing himself with a light *whoosh*.

"Did you sleep here last night?"

This time Samuel's question brought her head around, one glance over her shoulder confirming that he wasn't speaking to her. Aaron must have moved silently while her back was turned. He paused in the connecting doorway to the store.

"No," he answered stiffly. "I only came by this morning to give your mother a message."

"Then aren't you stayin' for breakfast?"

"I can't, Samuel. I have many people to see today."

"But Ma says it's important to eat breakfast, *especially* when you've got a lot of things to do!"

"She's right. But I've already eaten, thank you."

"But—"

"Samuel." Rebecca turned now, having chased the last of her tears away. "You're pestering. Mr. Cambridge has said he cannot stay."

She carefully avoided Aaron's eye, so she did not know that he was avoiding hers as well. Samuel looked from one to the other glumly. Then his small face screwed up into a frown.

"Mr. Cambridge? You told me he was Cain. Was I dreamin' last night? Aren't you the doctor?"

Rebecca bit down on a sigh. She could hear in the high-pitched query his confusion and disappointment, and found herself breathing a silent prayer that Aaron would spare him of both. Her prayer was answered, at least for the moment.

"I am Cain to my friends, the Shawnee. But I am also Aaron Cambridge." After a slight pause he added quietly, "Have you ever heard my name before?"

"No. Was I s'posed to?"

Rebecca's heart dropped all the way to her toes as she waited for Aaron's response. What was he trying to do? With one question he could bring her world crashing down around her once more, and she suddenly knew just how much more was at risk than she had first thought.

But Aaron only stiffened, his blank stare shooting right past her to the window beyond. Whether it was relief she felt or sorrow, she was not sure.

"Never mind, Samuel." His voice was emotionless. "It's not important."

"Out with it, 'Becca. Just who in blazes was that?" Lenore had scarcely mounted the two oak puncheons that acted as porch steps before her strident voice pierced the morning.

Still ladling grits into Samuel's bowl, Rebecca glanced up. She grimaced as she watched her sister-in-law push through the store, her tattered wool shawl flapping behind her like crow's wings. "Good morning, Lenore. Have you had breakfast yet?"

" 'Course I did. Been up since before dawn, what with Zeb running back and forth to the privy from eating those green apples yesterday. And I was up early enough to see you had company already, so don't be changing the subject on me. Who is he?"

With a meaningful look toward Samuel, who was concentrating just a little too hard on his porridge, Rebecca asked calmly, "Is Zebulon all right? I could make him some peppermint tea if you'd like."

Lenore hung her shawl on the back of a chair and struck

a perplexed pose, balled fists planted upon narrow hips and shoulders hunched nearly to her ears. "The boy's fine, 'Becca. Now, will you—"

"I certainly hope so. Poor Zeb. Someone should have told him it's too early for apples around here." Rebecca shot Lenore a scathing glance over Samuel's head, which had the effect of drawing Lenore up taller. But the gangly woman appeared to have understood, for her mouth snapped shut on whatever she was about to say and she gave a quick nod.

Samuel, however, was not about to go long without having a say in the conversation. After gulping down a glass of buttermilk, he wiped his upper lip with the napkin Rebecca had placed in front of him and grinned up at his aunt. "If Zeb's sick," he said cheerfully, "then maybe the doctor can fix him up, too."

"Doctor?" Lenore switched her sharp gaze to Rebecca. "What doctor?"

"He has two names, Aunt Nora. Isn't that funny? One of 'em's Cain, and the other one's Aaron something-or-other."

There was a long pause before Lenore managed to choke out a whisper. "Cambridge. Aaron Cambridge. I thought he looked familiar."

"Yeah. D'you know him?"

Rebecca watched her sister-in-law's shocked expression with a cross between pity and amusement. She wondered if her eyes had looked ready to pop out when Aaron first revealed himself to her, or if her jaw had gone quite so slack. Wiping her hands on her apron, she moved around beside the stunned woman and gently pushed her into a chair.

"If you're finished, Samuel," Rebecca ordered quietly, "I want you to go outside for a while."

"What's wrong with her, Ma?"

"Nothing. You can leave your chores for later. I'll call for you when it's time to come home."

Fortunately, the prospect of a morning free of chores was enough to make Samuel lose all interest in whatever the adults were talking about. "Can I see if Zeb feels good enough to play?" At twelve, Zebulon was the cousin closest to Samuel in age, and the two boys were constant companions.

Rebecca nodded. "That's fine. Go on, now." She stopped to kiss Samuel, but he evaded her good-naturedly, shrugging away her hug as well. She settled for tousling his wheat-colored hair. "Be careful."

"I *will,* Ma," he groaned on his way out. "Don't *worry*!"

Shaking her head after him, Rebecca then turned back to Lenore. The brief exchange had obviously given the woman time to get over her initial shock, for her gray eyes now snapped with curiosity.

"Aaron's alive?" Her voice held a mixture of disbelief and chagrin.

Rebecca sighed and nodded. "Very much so. It seems Levi was given the wrong information when he wrote to that officer in Aaron's unit, the one who told us he remembered seeing Aaron fall. Aaron was only wounded, not killed."

"Then why didn't he come home?" Lenore's puzzled frown reflected the very same question Rebecca had wrestled with from the moment she learned Aaron's identity. Now that it had been voiced again, she realized Aaron had never truly answered her.

She stiffened, her hands clenched tight within the folds of her skirt. "He said he had, but not until after . . . after we were already on our way to Virginia."

"I see." Lenore's shoulders jerked higher.

"It doesn't really matter"—Rebecca shrugged—"because Aaron wasn't coming back for me anyway. He said he was only planning to say good-bye before he headed west himself." Her voice grew small as she continued. "He didn't seem at all surprised to learn that I was married to Levi."

"Did you tell him why?"

Rebecca looked up sharply, then sighed. "No, and I don't intend to. What good would it do now?"

Lenore considered the question for a long moment; then she frowned thoughtfully. "Seems to me he has a right to the truth. It's not as if you played him false. You only took

Levi because you needed a husband bad and you thought Aaron was dead."

"That sounds . . . that sounds so terribly callous now."

"But it's the way it was. No use prettyin' it up."

"I suppose not." Rebecca sighed. Her sister-in-law was absolutely right. But that didn't give Aaron the right to simply step back into her life!

"Are you gonna tell him?" Lenore pressed.

Summoning back some of her earlier resolve, Rebecca shook her head fiercely. "Why should I? This whole misunderstanding is Aaron's fault. He could have contacted me sooner, but he didn't want to."

Lenore looked doubtful. "How do you know that?"

"Because he told me, that's how!"

Just as it had the night before, Rebecca's heart ached with the knowledge that Aaron had not loved her enough to come back to her. But instead of overwhelming anguish, today the pain spurred her to anger. "There was no excuse for him not to get word to me that he was alive. No excuse at all, except that he doesn't . . . *didn't* love me."

"Honey, I know that can't be—"

"It's just as you said, Lenore. There's no use prettying it up, so let's not try. Aaron Cambridge turned his back on me just the same as he did on the Continental army."

Her words seemed to reverberate through the small room, echoing over and over as if to emphasize her anguish. Rebecca squeezed her eyes closed to block out the pain.

It seemed a long time before her composure returned, but when she opened her eyes again Lenore still waited patiently, her expression sympathetic, if a little perplexed. From outside came the sounds of the awakening land; sleepy voices rose to greet the new day, the plaintive lowing of a milk cow demanded attention, and somewhere a door slammed open and a child's carefree giggle capered through the air.

Normal sounds, Rebecca thought. Comforting sounds. Funny, but she found it hard to believe she would ever feel normal again. Aaron had seen to that, damn him!

"So," Lenore continued, her voice gentler than before but just as determined. "Aaron Cambridge is also Cain

. . . or is it the other way around? And whether or not you decide to forgive him for runnin' out on you ten years ago, he's still your best chance at gettin' help for Sammy, ain't that right?''

With a burst of bitter laughter, Rebecca shook her head once more. ''Who knows? After all he's done, how can I be sure I can trust him with Samuel? I don't even *know* all that he's done!''

When Lenore cocked her head quizzically, Rebecca explained about the desertion charge Aaron faced. Surprisingly, the older woman clucked her tongue and gave her head a sorrowful wag. ''Poor Aaron. He's been through a lot, I'll say that. And to think now he might be thrown into prison.''

''Poor—?'' Biting off an angry retort, Rebecca fumed silently. What about all that she had been through? And surely Samuel was the most innocent victim in all this. What about her fatherless son?

Turning to face the window where the morning light now streamed into the room, Rebecca looked out toward the east, in the direction of Fort Washington. ''As far as I'm concerned,'' she said scornfully, ''prison is too good for him.''

CHAPTER 7

At the sound of footsteps outside the door, Aaron drew himself to attention, his backbone growing as rigid as one of the gateposts guarding the entrance to Fort Washington. Every muscle in his body remained taut and wary; instinct warned him that he was not out of danger yet.

Four hours. He had been escorted to this room more than four hours ago, and though he had witnessed a succession of officers and answered every question he had anticipated—as well as some he had not—no one had bothered to offer him food or relief from the stifling confines of the cell-like room.

He might just as well get used to it, Aaron told himself archly, and be glad they had not yet resorted to baser means of extracting information. His fists clenched involuntarily. The longer the afternoon wore on, the more convinced he was that he would not be leaving this place anytime soon.

Now the footsteps stopped just on the other side of the heavy oak door. He held his breath, wondering which of the officers had thought of something else to ask him. Whatever the question, he would answer with the truth and damn the men who refused to believe him. He would stand up to them with dignity, by God!

However, when the door opened and a grizzled head poked inside, Aaron was almost embarrassed by the extent of his relief. He stifled a sigh, but allowed a wry grin. "Sergeant Haskull, come in."

"Don't mind if I do." Kicking the door wider with his booted toe, the old soldier entered bearing a tin tray covered with a stained and frayed napkin. "An' you can call me Skulley. Any friend of Miz Osborne's is a friend o' mine.''

Motioning the tray toward a rickety table in the corner, Aaron grimaced. He had tried all morning to push thoughts of Rebecca to the farthest recesses of his mind, with little success. Every moment brought him the memory of her stricken expression last night and the cold distrust in her eyes come dawn.

Aaron paced. ''I warned you before, Rebecca may no longer consider me a friend. In fact, I wouldn't be surprised if she denies knowing me at all.''

''Doubt that.'' Skulley grunted, skidding the tray across the table and giving his mustache a tug. ''She spent too much good time lookin' for you.''

''But that was before she knew who I was.''

''Don't matter. If you do what you can for the boy, my bet is she'll fergive you just about anythin'.''

Aaron still had his doubts, but he silently conceded by pulling up a chair to the table. Without hesitation Skulley appropriated the only other chair and eased his stiffened joints into a sitting position.

The first thing Aaron had done upon arriving at Fort Washington that morning was ask for the Sergeant Haskull that Rebecca had mentioned. He could admit to himself now—albeit sheepishly—that he had done so out of pure jealousy. He had wanted a good look at the man whom Rebecca called friend.

But a single glimpse of the one-eyed codger had reassured Aaron, and after talking with the man he found himself feeling absurdly grateful that Rebecca had lucked into friendship with the kind and capable old soldier. There was nothing dishonest about Skulley, from the haphazard irreverence of his shabby uniform to the way he talked as straight and true as he could spit a stream of tobacco juice.

Apparently, straight talk was on Skulley's mind now.

''You're in a mess o' trouble, boy,'' he said cheerfully as he watched Aaron devour his ration of venison stew and hard bread. ''But it could be worse. It'd sure help some if'n you could remember ever'thin'.''

Considering that Skulley had not been present during the interrogations and that Aaron had not had time to tell the sergeant the whole story before his request to see the fort's commandant was granted, it was amazing he knew as much as he did. But Aaron did not question the soldier's sources; it was enough to have someone like Skulley on his side.

"I would gladly tell the army all they want," Aaron said around a mouthful of stew. "If I only knew. Believe me, I wish I could remember that night as much as anyone. That's part of why I'm here."

Skulley nodded sagely. "That's what I figgered. You don't strike me as one who'd lie just to protect his own hide."

Lowering his fork, Aaron pushed back from the table and eyed the other man thoughtfully. "In a sense that's exactly what I've done for the past ten years. Just because I don't remember what I was running from doesn't justify the fact that I deserted during a time of war."

"No, I reckon it don't." Skulley fiddled with the gray patch over his blind eye, then hooked his thumbs in the waistband of his regulation britches. "But you got some things goin' in your favor. One, the war ended purty near the same time you up an' run, so it weren't like you missed out on much. Two, there were lots of deserters ever' year, an' if the army tried to hold 'em all we'd be bustin' at the seams with boys who had to go home to help plant the crop or daddies who just couldn't wait one more day to see their young'uns. Three, comin' in here on your own two feet makes you 'pear to be an honorable man, and there ain't nothin' Major Carswell likes more'n a man of honor."

Aaron resumed eating, feeling somewhat reassured by Skulley's opinion. Each of the other officers who had interviewed him had spoken of Henry Carswell, the current commandant of Fort Washington, with respect and deference. Aaron was almost looking forward to this final and most important meeting.

It turned out he did not have long to wait. Just as Aaron was using the remains of a half-eaten biscuit to sop up the last of his stew, a young corporal strutted into the room like a bantam rooster, banging the door against the wall.

"Stand at attention!" he barked, stepping aside and

throwing his own hand upward to shade his brow in formal salute. The corporal held himself erect—all five and a half feet of him—but his eyes flickered disdainfully in Aaron's direction. "On your feet, soldier," he hissed.

Slowly, Aaron pushed himself away from the table and rose. Skulley moved a little more deliberately, his one eye gleaming with amusement. "You puff up any more, Lutz, an' you're gonna explode. An' that ain't the way to make an impression, nosirree."

The younger noncom turned a furious shade of purple. His mouth opened and closed ineffectually, his diminutive frame quaking with suppressed rage. He did not break form, however, until a sonorous voice ordered, "At ease, Corporal."

The officer who entered the room behind Corporal Lutz commanded immediate attention, not because of the service stripes on his arm or the double row of gleaming buttons on his uniform, but because he exuded a strength and dignity that was illustrated in his erect bearing and direct gaze. That gaze fell on Aaron with all the intensity of a noonday sun.

Unconsciously, Aaron straightened. "Commander-Major Henry Carswell, I presume."

"At your service, Mr. Cambridge. But 'Major' will do just as well." He turned his authoritative gaze to Skulley. "Sergeant Haskull, thank you for attending to our guest's needs. I might have known I could rely on you even when the rest of my staff seems to have overlooked the midday meal." Addressing Aaron once more, the commander offered an apologetic nod. "Had I been present upon your arrival, Mr. Cambridge, you would not have suffered such shoddy treatment. You're not a prisoner here."

Not yet. "No harm done, sir." Aaron's words were precise and wary.

"Very well, then . . . let us proceed to the purpose of your request."

Without another word, Skulley gathered the dirty bowl and utensils. He managed a wink in Aaron's direction before turning back to the commander, the heavy tray held out before him. " 'S there anythin' else you'll be needin', sir?"

"No, that will be all, Sergeant."

After jerking one shoulder high in a gesture that might have passed for a salute, Skulley exited. Aaron noticed that on his way out the grizzled old soldier also winked at Corporal Lutz, who had barely moved from his original position.

There was a long pause in which none of the remaining men spoke; then Major Carswell cleared his throat and said, "Please close the door as you leave, Corporal Lutz."

This brought a flustered expression to the noncom's face, but after another perfectly executed salute he followed Skulley's example, pulling the heavy door shut behind him.

"As you were, Mr. Cambridge." Carswell moved toward the chair where Skulley had been seated and indicated that Aaron resume his own place. Once sitting, he crossed his long legs and folded his arms over his chest.

Now, Aaron thought to himself, *this is it.*

At that moment he would have given his right hand to be traversing the Little Miami River with Wind and his family. Anxiety twisted his gut into an unrelenting knot, while frustration flooded through him at having to face the humiliation of confessing his sins—such as he could remember them—once more.

"Suppose you tell me what this is about," Major Carswell began.

Aaron braced his legs firmly, but forced his hands out of the tight fists they had formed. "You already know who I am and why I'm here, so can we dispense with the formalities?" He had not intended to sound belligerent, and feared he had offended when Major Carswell pinned him with a thoughtful stare.

After a few moments, the officer answered, "It is true that each member of my staff has made a report, but it is also my policy to judge a situation myself. Trust me, Cambridge, when I say you should be glad that I indulge in that particular idiosyncracy. With the exception of Sergeant Haskull, the rest of my officers wish to see you jailed indeterminately."

Aaron's jaw twitched in rebellion, but he nodded acquiescence. "Very well, then," he began. "In 1782 I was attached to the seventh unit of Colonel Willett's battalion in the Colonial Army of New York. The war in that part of the country had effectively ended after Burgoyne's surrender at Saratoga, but the frontier still held pockets of Tory regiments and Iroquois loyal to the British. It was our job to subdue these elements and defend the gains already made.''

Carswell massaged his short beard pensively. ''As I understand it, that campaign was considered a success. The British never did regain a foothold in the region. Weren't there only one or two battles of note?''

''That's correct,'' Aaron continued slowly. His gaze grew distant as he peered at the rough-planked wall; again the memories clamored to be free, but were blocked by some resistant part of his mind. Automatically, his hand reached for the scar and he rubbed his cheekbone absently. ''I was apprenticed to Dr. Eli Winthrop at the time, so I remained in the field hospital during the worst of the fighting. Fortunately, we took few injuries. In fact, we generally patched up more British prisoners than our own men.

''Weeks would go by without a shot fired, but the last time was up by West Canada Creek. There was a British regiment—hardly more than few scattered patrols, actually—that had set out to cross the German Flats. We went after them at dawn on the twenty-fifth of October.''

''I take it you were a part of this excursion.''

Aaron grimaced painfully. ''Not intentionally. We set up the field hospital too close to the lines, and the last thing I remember clearly was the sight of redcoats swarming over the hill behind us. We must have been cut off. . . .''

He felt as if a band of iron had tightened around his head, the mounting pressure causing his vision to blur and his ears to ring. As it always did when he pushed too hard to remember, his chest grew heavy with dread and—inexplicably—with self-loathing. Finally, when both the physical and mental strain became too great, he pressed the heel of his palm against his brow and bowed his head.

Major Carswell waited with solemn patience for Aaron to resume the tale. When no further information was forthcoming, he rose from the chair and stood with his hands clasped behind his back. "And so this is where your memory fails you. Is there anything else you can recall?"

"Nothing," Aaron said, his voice rasping with effort. "Not about that day, or the weeks following."

"Were you unconscious for so long?"

"Technically, no." He shrugged, feeling the tension pull at his shoulders like heavy ropes. "There was a farmer who found me three days after the battle suffering from exposure and loss of blood. He says I talked like a crazy man. I can only assume that I took the wound in the battle, and that it was the fever that caused me to lose my head.

"As for the lapse in my memory . . . I had an opportunity to study a medical journal during a brief stop in Marietta a few years back. This book reported a similar case of memory loss brought on by a severe blow to the head. In that instance the boy regained his memory after several months passed. The theory was that his brain needed only sufficient time to recover from the trauma. There's even a name for the condition now—amnesia."

Carswell frowned. "So your scar *is* from the war. And your injury was the cause of this amnesia?"

"Perhaps." Aaron wished he could leave it at that. But he had spent too many years struggling with doubt to draw such a simple conclusion. "The book mentioned several other possible causes, including severe fatigue, illness . . . or an incident so shocking that one's mind refuses to recall it."

At this Carswell looked up sharply, his dark brow furrowed in concentration. "I *have* heard of this!" he exclaimed. "When I was a boy in Massachusetts, there resided in our town a woman who lost her husband and three children to scarlet fever. Everyone thought she would go mad with grief, but she finally recovered. At least to the point where she behaved in a normal manner. The odd thing was, afterward she could never remember having been married or bearing children. It was as if her mind could only function by completely eliminating her memory of those she had loved and then tragically lost."

"That sounds like what I'm talking about," Aaron agreed. He paced to the other side of the room, then turned to face the commandant. "I imagine that anyone could

experience a similar reaction under circumstances too horrifying to bear.''

With sudden comprehension, Carswell's eyes narrowed.
''Do you believe this is what happened to you? Granted,
war can be a terrible thing, but men have gone for years
witnessing all manner of brutality and still survived. What
makes you different?''

Aaron's voice was a choked whisper. ''I wish I knew.
I'm not even certain anything unusual happened at all, it's
just that I've had this feeling . . . I know it sounds contrived, and purposely vague, but I remember coming out
of this . . . this fog that surrounded my mind with the
unarguable sense that I had done something wrong. But
what it was, I can't seem to remember. And I *have* tried,
Major Carswell. Believe me, I want to know exactly what
happened on that day.''

After a moment of silent contemplation, Carswell sighed
heavily, then returned to his chair, again indicating that
Aaron should do the same. ''You might have learned the
answers had you gone back to your unit at once.''

''I realize that.'' Aaron's smile was without humor. He
lowered himself into his chair defeatedly. ''But at the time
returning seemed the worst possible solution. I'm not sure
why I felt that way, other than the fact that I was only
nineteen and had never seen a dead man until that same
year. But my gut tells me there is a far more complex
reason than youth and inexperience.''

A faint smile, the first since he had entered the room,
softened the harsh lines of Major Carswell's weathered
face. ''Mine, as well. And I do believe you seek the truth.
Though I'm still not certain why, after all this time, you've
decided to come forward. You might well have lived out
your life in complete anonymity without ever having to
face charges. This country has better things to do with her
fledgling treasury than chase down deserters, particularly
since there are so damn many of them. When the army
does run across known deserters on occasion they are generally pardoned.''

''But your case,'' he qualified, ''appears to be more
serious than a mere bout of homesickness.'' He paused,

then cleared his throat noisily. "I'll need time to investigate further."

A lump of dread formed in Aaron's chest, not only at the thought of what such an investigation might divulge, but at the prospect of spending whatever weeks or months such a search might entail confined to a cell, when for ten years he had enjoyed unrestricted mobility. And how could he help Rebecca if he was in prison?

"Will there be a trial?" he asked, not expecting an encouraging answer, but wishful nonetheless.

"Perhaps," Carswell answered. His gaze remained fixed upon Aaron, studying him. "And perhaps not. I can't promise you anything. I'll begin here at Fort Washington. Many of the officers served in the Continental army. Perhaps one or more of them were present at West Canada Creek. Failing that, I'll send to the capital for complete records. But rest assured that your case shall be handled promptly and with justice."

Aaron's jaw twitched. "I suppose that's all a man can ask."

"Follow me." Without warning, Henry Carswell stood, reaching the door in two long strides. With only a moment's hesitation Aaron obeyed.

They exited down a narrow hallway, then out onto the fort's interior palisade. Below, an artillery unit drilled with a pair of three-pounders, while a group of soldiers trotted in unison across the muddy commons with another small cannon—called a grasshopper for the way it looked—on their shoulders. One officer lounging against a hitching post looked up with an open smirk. Aaron stared at him blankly. He was not concerned with anyone's opinion, except the one that counted.

Focusing ahead, Aaron now studied Carswell's ramrod back. The major had promised him a prompt investigation. But would he move fast enough? While the thought of a prison cell was not appealing to Aaron, far worse was the knowledge that for every day he was held captive, Samuel's chances for recovery diminished.

He would need to send a message to Rebecca, he thought distractedly. Skulley would do it. And he could write to the medical school in Philadelphia on her behalf. If she had to take Samuel back east, he would have the best.

The major stopped abruptly, turning left through another door on the upper level of the fort. Aaron followed more slowly, blinking as his eyes readjusted to the darker room after the bright sunlight outside. He found himself face-to-face—or rather chest-to-face—with the inflated Corporal Lutz.

"Shall I call for the guard, sir?" Lutz fairly chortled with undisguised glee.

"That won't be necessary, Corporal. See that we're not disturbed."

With that the major ushered Aaron through yet another door. This room was not much larger than the outer office. It boasted only a single desk and two narrow-backed chairs, as well as a cluttered map table, but a pair of windows gave it a more spacious feeling. Aaron's anxiety lessened slightly.

"Please be seated," Carswell said, moving behind his own desk. "I'd like to discuss something with you. Are you willing?"

Aaron lowered himself to a spindly chair. He could almost smile at the irony behind the commandant's courteous request. For someone who held the reins, Major Henry Carswell was suspiciously cordial. "I'm at your disposal, sir."

"It has occurred to me that you might strengthen your own position within the military by taking positive action—just as you have already done by presenting yourself here. Would you consider such a direction?"

"What do you mean?" Wary but curious, Aaron leaned forward in his seat. A lock of light hair fell across his forehead and he swept it back impatiently with a sure hand.

"What I propose is that you sign on here at Fort Washington, purportedly to finish out your original conscription. You said you had only three months service remaining at the time of your injury. If, in a few months, your story can be verified, then I feel confident you will be discharged without further questions."

"And if there are no answers? What then?"

"Then I will be forced to pass judgment based on your

word . . . as well as your current service record. I ought to say that as company physician you will have many opportunities to prove your worth.''

Aaron snapped his head upward, wondering if in his fatigue he had misheard the officer. ''Ten years ago I held the rank of private, and served only half my apprenticeship with Dr. Winthrop.''

''Yet you are known as a healer in these parts. Have you not come by your reputation honestly?''

Carswell's black eyes gleamed, and Aaron had the sudden inkling that the commandant had planned to spring this on him all along, and that there was more—much more.

''I have not been certified.''

''By whom? You know as well as I that there is no standard for certification in this land. Any man may call himself doctor who practices medicine, and certification is only a piece of paper from another physician who may or may not be competent himself.''

This much Aaron knew was true. Nevertheless, he was surprised that a man of Carswell's rank and station looked so lightly upon a tradition that was commonly accepted, if not utterly reliable. Not everyone would agree. Aaron had encountered enough prejudice in the last few years to be certain of that.

And so, even though the prospect intrigued him, Aaron continued to doubt. ''What about the physician already here at the fort—Tuthill?''

''Ah, you have heard of him,'' Carswell exclaimed softly. Again his mouth curved upward beneath his luxurious mustache. ''Captain Tuthill will be leaving us soon, discharged at his own request. You will take over his duties effective immediately with the simulated rank of captain. By agreeing to this you will be doing both of us a great favor.'' He glanced at the closed door. ''Corporal Lutz is an efficient aide, but he does take himself and military protocol rather seriously. Unfortunately, he's not the only one around here who does. You may find yourself up against some resistance from the other officers. If it helps, you have my backing.''

The offer was almost too generous for him to credit it.

Aaron narrowed his eyes, meeting Carswell's direct gaze with his own skeptical one. "There's something else, isn't there?"

A long moment passed; then the commandant let forth a burst of laughter, hunkering forward in his own seat. "You are more astute than most, Cambridge." His pose was relaxed, his gloved hands resting upon his desk. "As a matter of fact, there is another matter I would like to discuss. It has to do with the Indian situation."

Uneasily Aaron waited for the officer to continue. The tensions between the red man and the white had long been a source of personal pain for him. Torn between two worlds, Aaron had realized that he might someday be forced to choose. But just because he was here now did not mean he would turn his back on his adopted brothers and sisters. "If you expect me to take part in your butchery, you can forget it," he said with quiet intensity. "I'd rather rot in prison."

Carswell raised one dark eyebrow smoothly. "You may do just that if you refuse to obey orders while in command." Then his smile returned. "However, I have no intention of ordering you into action against your friends. My plans are of a different sort altogether. Are you familiar with the recent campaigns of Generals Harmar and St. Clair?"

Aaron nodded cautiously. "I am, though not in the way you might think. Many young men from the Shawnee village where I once lived helped repel the attacks, both from Harmar in '90 and St. Clair this past fall in '91. Despite the great victory, several of my friends did not survive."

"The battles were victories in the eyes of the Indians, yes," Carswell conceded. "But for the settlers of the Miami Purchase, those two failed campaigns ushered in an era of fear and unrest. To the frontiersmen who want only to farm and hunt in peace, the current situation is intolerable."

"As it is to the Shawnee," Aaron added dryly, "who want also to farm and hunt in peace . . . on the land they claimed long before the first white men set foot on these shores."

To his surprise Carswell did not argue the point. The

commandant merely continued in a dispassionate voice. "It is a dilemma not easily solved, I fear. But we can take steps to alleviate the tensions if we but try, do you not agree?"

"How?"

"By letting reason and common sense guide us, instead of prejudice and fear. Let me be perfectly honest with you, Cambridge. My posting here is a temporary one since St. Clair was called back to the capital, and my orders are to hold the tribes at bay until we have time to regroup. But I am *not* a great military strategist; my strengths lie in other areas. Rumors abound that by summer a new general will command the western army, one who will direct the troops to a resounding victory."

"In other words," Aaron said bitterly, "the government will continue to drive the Shawnee and Miami and all the others off their land. And if you don't do it, someone else will."

"If I don't do *something*, then yes, some other general will certainly take the helm. Most likely 'Mad' Anthony Wayne."

Carswell paused. His attitude at the mention of the great war hero was one of respect, but it was obvious that he had more on his mind. Aaron slanted him a look. "What can you do?"

"The better question is, what can you and I accomplish together? I humbly believe that I was given this position to allay the fears of the people of Cincinnati and her outlying settlements because of my reputation as an honest and dependable officer. I am conceited enough to believe I can make a difference here—not with victory in battle, but perhaps with a more subtle triumph. But I'll need your help.

"You are familiar with the tribes and their customs, and most importantly, they trust you. My goal is to devise a peaceful coexistence between the settlers and the Indians."

Aaron sat upright, his chair scraping back on the floor. Not so much stunned as he was skeptical, he allowed himself a moment to ponder Carswell's suggestion. Such idealism was rare, and unfortunately difficult to put into

practice, particularly when few other men held similar be-
liefs. But if the commandant could bring around the feelings of the settlers and Aaron could talk to Wind at His
Feet . . .

"My contact with the Shawnee is limited," he admitted
doubtfully. "I was adopted into one small family tribe,
but there are many other factions within the larger tribe,
and many tribes which comprise the entire Shawnee nation. As for the Miami and Delaware, who knows what
they will do?"

Carswell was not to be put off easily. "You do yourself
a disservice, Cambridge, if you think you have no influence among the Indians. And your word will bear weight
with the settlers as well. I have heard the tales and legends
of Cain, the great healer. So have many others."

"Believing the stories is one thing," Aaron scoffed.
"Learning to accept the differences between two remote
cultures is another."

"But you will help me."

It was a command, yet it was one which Aaron knew
could not be enforced. Carswell realized it, too, for though
his look was determined, his smile was wry.

Aaron studied his own hands clasped tightly together.
They were ordinary hands, ten fingers held together by a
broad palm, flesh and sinew and bone working together in
perfect order.

But they were also not ordinary hands. He had held
within them the lives of many people: babies entering the
world, slippery and vulnerable and yet strong with poten-
tial; old men ready to relinquish their souls to the spirits,
weary of life but afraid of dying; and most incongruous of
all, young men praying for recovery so they could face
death in battle once more. His hands had done much that
was good, Aaron realized with silent wonder.

And God willing, they would do more.

"I will help you," he said, raising his eyes until they
met Carswell's avid gaze, "on one condition. I want no
restrictions as to whom I treat. Soldier, civilian, Shawnee
. . . only I will decide who needs medical attention and
who does not. I want free use of whatever facilities are

available here in the fort for all my patients. And one other thing.''

"Yes?'' Major Caswell's voice was leery.

"When do you expect Tuthill to leave?''

"With the first party traveling west, if we're lucky. The man is totally incompetent. You'll want no advice from him.''

"But he *is* accustomed to an operating theater. He can assist me on a case I wish to take on immediately.''

Major Carswell appeared to brood on this for a moment, but the eager light in his eyes proved he would accept any qualification, provided Aaron would agree to his proposal. He rose then, stretching his gaunt frame as he reached out his hand. Aaron stood also, at least willing to meet the officer halfway.

Carswell smiled triumphantly. "I am quite pleased that you have arrived at a decision, then. Shall we proceed to your new quarters and introduce you to some of the other officers?''

This surprising twist was better than he expected. Aaron followed the officer gladly now, his heart far lighter than before. He still would not pretend to himself, as Carswell had, that the decision to return to the military was one he made without reservations.

But after ten long and torturous years, it felt good to be taking a step toward redemption.

CHAPTER 8

As Wind at His Feet and his son crouched beside the morning fire, Little Otter announced, "Today I will kill *two* rabbits, and perhaps a fox as well!"

"Shhh," his mother cautioned. "You will wake your sister with your boasting. And then instead of frightening rabbits you will spend the day with a crying baby. How is that?"

Wind hid a smile at the astonished indignation in his son's expression. But the boy had been taught well, and did not retort. He only nodded once and resumed eating his corn cake.

"Your skill with a bow has improved," Wind consoled in a low voice. "Soon you will grow tall enough to handle the long bows. By next summer, perhaps."

Little Otter's dark eyes danced. "I could do it now; I know I could. Then we would have venison for dinner instead of rabbit, and I would have a new pouch from the hide—"

"Not so fast, my son." Wind placed a gentle hand on Little Otter's shoulder to prevent the boy from shooting from the *wigewa* like a misfired arrow. "You may think you are grown enough, but it takes great strength to draw a long bow, and there are reasons for young men to practice first on the smaller game. The gods guide your arrows straight to the heart of the rabbit and fox, but if you were to shoot at a deer, your arrow would wobble and fall, or worse, only wound the deer. Also, in the spring it is unwise to kill the female, for her young need her to survive.

It takes a skilled hunter to track the young buck after he has shed his antlers in the spring. Do you understand?"

"Yes, Father." Little Otter squirmed impatiently. "May I go now?"

"Yes, you may go."

Both Wind and his wife smiled indulgently as the boy scampered from the *wigewa*. Wind's own fingers itched to curl around a smooth ash bow, and his eyes narrowed as they would if he were sighting game at the end of his arrow. But Wind was expected today at the council lodge, and so he must trust his son's developing skills to the older youths assigned to guide their younger brothers.

"You wish to hunt also?" White Star teased as she scooped up the last of the corn cakes to be reground into tonight's bread. "I will hide the feathers from your head and remove the chest piece that marks you as a tribal leader; then you can run with the boys."

Wind at His Feet chuckled, patting her rounded bottom as she bent over to bank the fire. "I would stay here with my wife, now that our children are occupied and the babe sleeps. Or is it too soon?"

"It is too soon." White Star smiled over her shoulder. She knew her husband was well aware that she could not share love with him for several more weeks, but she relished his attention nevertheless. His black eyes gleamed appreciatively in the darkened *wigewa*, and White Star's breasts ached for his touch even more than they did for her baby's eager mouth.

"Ahhh," Wind sighed. His voice was husky as he rose. "It is good, then, that I must attend to the council. Rest easy today, wife. I will bring the water for your washing so you need not go to the stream."

"Huh. Am I an invalid, then?" White Star replied lightly.

"No, you are a woman who has borne four beautiful children, the last only seven days ago. Besides, I would have you regain your strength quickly."

With another playful swat, Wind exited the bark *wigewa*, stretching his muscular limbs as he stepped into the misty morning. The cool air played along his bronze skin and tugged at the scalplock lying over his shoulder. The three feathers he wore, signifying three great battles in which he had fought with honor, ruffled lightly in the same breeze that caused the white maple trees to sway around him. He could hear the low murmur of voices as other men rose for the day, and the soft giggles of the young women who readied themselves.

Wind stretched again, glorying at the feeling of his strong heart pumping blood to his waking limbs. His soul stretched as well, filled with the happiness of a man who is blessed with all that he needs, and who wants no more.

It would be a good day, he thought contentedly. Only one thing could make it better, and that would be the return of his friend Cain. But that was a selfish desire, Wind chided himself silently. Better to wish that his friend find peace in his own heart. Then, if that peace brought Cain back to his blood brother, Wind could rejoice without reservation.

With an inner smile to warm him, Wind at His Feet strode confidently toward the council lodge, eager to begin the day's discussions. But as he approached the large, bark-covered shelter, the sound of distant shouting halted him. Pivoting on one bare heel, he turned to face the eastern path into the village, where a noisy group of youngsters, including his own son, now gathered.

"Ho!" Wind at His Feet raised a hand as he neared the agitated crowd. Out of respect, most of the others fell silent at the arrival of a warrior chief, but a few excited young men continued to rant and gesture wildly. Wind caught a glimpse of one angry, tear-streaked face and felt his heart grow heavy. "What has happened?" he asked.

"It is Red Water and Bear Follower. The white men have killed them."

This was spoken with great bitterness by one of the young men Wind had first spotted. The youth stood stiff and proud despite the blood that streaked from his shoulder to his hip. Wind knew he was one of a scouting party sent to watch the movement of the white men along the beautiful river, the O-hi-oh. But the party had been instructed to observe only, otherwise it would not have included untried youths such as this one, and Red Water and Bear Follower.

"Where are the others?" Wind asked. The crowd had grown to include women and girls from the village, and a few other warriors. Emboldened by the attention, the young man threw out his chest.

"I was chosen to return with the news," he boasted. "The others have gone to a place where they can hide and wait for the white murderers to come closer. They will have blood."

Clenching his jaw, Wind hid the dismay these words brought to him. How could they expect to build a lasting peace with the white intruders when revenge was the instant response to any and all incidents? He wanted to shout his anger at the foolish young brave, but realized that the present mood of the village was one of retaliation, not caution.

"They attacked us at night, without warning," the lad continued, inciting his audience to a low-pitched muttering. "There were over fifty of them, but we fought them off with courage and cunning. I myself killed at least ten."

At this even Little Otter looked dubious, for he glanced sideways up at his father. Wind at His Feet shook his head imperceptibly. To boast without proof was not proper behavior for a warrior; this lad had much to learn. And Wind did not like the way the crowd was beginning to mill about fretfully.

"Come," he commanded, stretching out his hand to motion the young man forward. "Your wound must be cleansed. But first you must tell the entire story to the council. Only then can we decide what to do."

"We should destroy them all," a voice shouted. "They have stolen from us long enough."

"Not all white men are the same," Wind replied calmly. Inside, his chest felt as if it had been filled with stones.

"That is what you say, because you are the friend of Gentle Healer," called out another. "But it was not your son who was murdered in the night. What will you tell Dancing Bird? That she should honor the butchering white men who killed her firstborn?"

Sadly, Wind turned without answering, leading the battered youth toward the council lodge. His people had a right to be angry, he knew. But they also needed to realize the futility of trading atrocity for atrocity with the eastern settlers. The Shawnee villages outnumbered the whites for now, but Wind had seen the great town of Marietta from the safety of the river, and he had seen the hundreds of sturdy wooden houses there, each containing many people. If the settlers continued to arrive on the banks of the O-hi-oh in the same numbers they had, soon Cincinnati would also be a great town, and there would be more white men with guns than Shawnee warriors.

And then where would The People be?

Vance Jessup was proud of his rank as captain in the army of the United States of America, and never more so than at a moment like this, when the flush of victory sent the blood roaring through his veins like a demon unleashed. With a bloodcurdling cry, he straddled the limp body below him, then sent the stock of his rifle crashing down against the already lifeless skull.

"That'll teach 'em, the murderin' redskins," he shouted triumphantly.

His men laughed in reply, staggering about the scene of the ambush in varying degrees of drunkenness. It was Jessup's rule that a cask of whiskey be opened for every Indian killed; tonight the revelry would be profound.

"We goin' back to the fort now that we scared 'em off, Cap'n?" From his precarious seat on a fallen log, Silas Carter grinned up hopefully at his superior officer. They had been two weeks on the trail, scouting for Shawnee war parties and Delaware villages, as well as carrying on a little business of their own. Silas ached in every joint and crevice of his aging body from too much riding, though he managed to hold the discomfort at bay with frequent nips from the flask hidden beneath his regulation coat.

Vexed at the interruption, Vance Jessup tossed aside the bloodied rifle and stepped over the dead Indian, reaching down to drag the body by the feet to the spot where the other one lay. He frowned. Though his men had handled themselves well during the surprise attack, he couldn't help wondering why he always ended up doing most of the work himself.

"You're the laziest bunch of asses I ever did see," he

allowed, grunting at the weight of the dead Indian. Not one of his men moved to help, but Jessup hadn't really expected them to. He had handpicked this party himself, choosing men by their lack of scruples instead of their individual initiative. So if he had to personally see to most of the details, he could only blame himself. At least he wouldn't be hearing a lot of gripe about how they shouldn't have shot these two Indians in the back.

"Oughtn't we ta go after the rest of 'em, Cap'n?"

The query came from young Joe Kinkle, who was one of the few of this hastily formed unit who appeared discontent with stopping at two kills. Unfortunately, Joe was also drunker than most of the others. The reedy young man swayed unsteadily, his thin lips drawing back into a sheepish grin. Jessup eyed him balefully.

"Private, if you want to stay with this unit, you'll have to learn to hold your liquor. And you'd best learn who gives the orders around here, too."

"Thass right," Silas quipped. "Weren't it the Cap'n's idea ta wait 'til them two injuns moved away from the rest of 'em? Them damned redskins never knew what hit 'em!"

"But shouldn't we have followed them for one more day? They mighta led us back to their village."

"And they might have led us into a trap, too." Vance Jessup swung around angrily to face yet another of his men. Jessup had had his doubts about Avery Fellows from the first minute he signed him on for his unit, but he had needed a replacement for old Burris, and he had needed one fast. Now it looked like this Fellows was going to give him a hard time. "How long you been in the army, boy?" Jessup challenged.

"Th-three years, sir."

"Three whole years, eh? And how much of that three years you been on the frontier?"

"Sir, this is my first assignment west of Fort Pitt." Fellows's voice was incredulous. The captain was well aware of his service record; they had discussed his background at length before Jessup had agreed to take him on.

"Then what the hell makes you think you know more about soldierin' than me? Private, I was stickin' bayonets in them Hessian devils while you were still wettin' your bed. And just 'cause the war ended didn't mean I stopped bein' a soldier.''

That was the problem he always had, Vance Jessup thought. The army was the only life he knew, and the only thing he'd ever been good at. He loved the feeling of power that came whenever he was part of a group; he loved it even more now that he had worked himself up to being an officer. After the war ended he'd been afraid there would be nothing left for him to do, but thanks to the reorganized First Regiment, he'd found another place for himself. Still, there were folks who didn't appreciate his special skills.

''When you've had a few years on you, mebbe you'll learn that sometimes even the righteous have to draw the first blood. It's kill or be killed.'' His tone had taken on a mocking edge. He grinned murderously, then reached into his boot and withdrew a long knife before placing one foot square in the middle of the dead Indian's back.

As the onlookers watched in stunned silence, Vance Jessup grabbed up a handful of black hair in one fist, then carved his blade in a circular motion around the Indian's head. With a vicious twist he lifted the bloody scalp, holding it high in the air for all to witness.

''See what happens to any filthy redskin that crosses with Jessup's Rangers,'' he shouted triumphantly. ''Is there any man here who doesn't want to help drive every lousy Injun out of these parts?''

When only silence followed, Captain Vance Jessup lowered his prize, his smug gaze scanning the circle of slack faces. ''Good. Then let's open that second cask.''

CHAPTER 9

"Ma, he's back!"

Samuel's shrill voice carried clearly from the front of the cabin to the rear yard, where Rebecca bent over the space of earth that would soon be her vegetable garden, Lord willing. Her head snapped up at the sound of her son's cry; at the same time her heart gave a queer little jump.

Aaron!

Three days had passed since he left for Fort Washington—three days in which Rebecca had done little but relive the shock of finding him alive and fight the sweet memories of the past that continued to slip unbidden into her mind. All her attempts to keep busy with the store proved fruitless; too often she caught herself daydreaming at odd moments, poised over a ledger or standing indecisively before a crate of sundries that needed to be shelved.

It had not helped that most of Samuel's conversations also revolved around the mysterious Cain, for that was how the boy continued to refer to Aaron. Rebecca did not doubt that "Cain, the Great Healer" presented a far more romantic image to Samuel than plain old Aaron Camridge, physician. She, too, could not help wondering how much of the legend was true and how much was the product of pure fancy.

But she would find out soon enough.

Dropping her spade to the ground, Rebecca straightened, brushing her hair from her face with the back of one dirt-stained hand. Damp tendrils clung to her cheek and brow, and she could feel the bun she had fashioned earlier drooping at the nape of her neck. She must look a sight, she thought. Then Samuel's voice again interrupted before she could mentally scold herself for such vanity.

"Come quick, Ma!"

This time she sensed an urgency to his tone that she hadn't heard before. Frowning, Rebecca took a step toward the cabin, then stopped short as three men rounded the corner.

"Oh! It's you," she said in soft dismay, her hands clenching automatically at the sight of the burly officer and his two disreputable-looking men.

"Mornin', ma'am," Vance Jessup responded. Whipping his hat from his head, he bent forward in a half bow. Rebecca shivered and crossed her arms as his eyes dropped to her breasts, then flicked upward to leer at her openly.

She had encountered Captain Jessup only twice before, which was two times too many as far as she was concerned. The first occasion had been a month ago, shortly after his arrival at the fort. She had stopped to give Skulley a basket of fresh-baked bread in exchange for a packet of steel needles when Jessup sauntered into the quartermaster's storeroom. He had not shown blatant disrespect—most likely because of Skulley's presence—but Rebecca remembered the feeling of being watched like a defenseless rabbit targeted by a bird of prey.

She had felt the same way two weeks later when Jessup and his men rode up to her store, supposedly to purchase supplies on their way to scout the western hills for renegade Shawnee. Without Skulley's protective eye to deter him, Jessup had made no attempt to hide his interest in her. Only Lenore's timely intervention had saved her from having to show him out of the store with the business end of her rifle.

Her sister-in-law could not come to her rescue today, Rebecca thought frantically; she was visiting friends in the town. And Rebecca's gun was propped behind the counter inside the cabin, out of reach and utterly useless now.

She drew a deep breath, then took a bold step forward. Samuel still waited, hugging the corner of the cabin. She looked him straight in the eye. "Samuel, go tell your cousin Ephraim I'm ready for him now.'' The boy nodded, then swung about on his crutches.

She wasn't sure how much help a pair of boys could be, but Ephraim was large for fifteen years, and he was better than nothing. She turned her unwilling attention to the waiting soldiers. "Good morning, Captain Jessup. I fear my supply of tobacco has not been replenished since your last visit, but if you would care to wait at the front of the store, I shall be with you in a few moments.'' With a reserved smile that was hardly welcoming, Rebecca waited for Jessup to go back the way he had come. Unfortunately, the squat officer stood his ground.

In the few moments she had to study him, Rebecca noticed that his uniform of blue worsted was torn and stained. He had removed his tall beaver hat; it now dangled from between his stubby fingers, the once proud plume dragging the dirt. The look in his eyes sent a draft of bone-chilling fear through Rebecca. Though he still wore a derisive smirk, his eyes showed no sign of amusement—only a scaring intensity that made her stomach churn.

"Now, what's your hurry, Miz Osborne? After me and my men've risked our lives protectin' you from the heathen savages, seems the least you can do is to be sociable before you take our coin. Besides, maybe it's not tobacco we've come for." Jessup again let his gaze drop insolently, then rake slowly upward until it rested on her burning cheeks. His lips widened into a grin.

Rebecca willed her voice not to tremble. "Whatever it is you want," she claimed firmly, "you'll not find it back here." She attempted to move swiftly past Jessup, but before she took two steps his hand shot out, clasping her elbow roughly. She tried to jerk her arm free but could not break his hold.

"I *said* I'm here to protect you. And believe me, it's a real pleasure," he said, his voice lowered to a soft croon.

Rebecca glared back fiercely. "Let go of me, you oaf! The only protection I need is from the likes of you. You've no right to accost me this way!" Despite her forceful tone, she wasn't surprised when he did not obey.

"Now, now. Listen to them fancy words. Just where do you think you are, missy? That kind of talk might get you somewhere in a big city like Philadelphia, but out here it pays for a woman to appreciate what a man goes through to keep her safe. That's all I want—a little appreciation and respect for us soldiers.'' With that he released her arm.

Rebecca stepped back quickly, rubbing the spot where his fingers had dug into her flesh. His expression was so odd that she wondered if she was actually in danger from this man. It was true that an uneasy tension existed between the townspeople of Cincinnati and the soldiers garrisoned at Fort Washington. No one was completely certain which had jurisdiction, the local government or the military. The army was present to rout the Indians and maintain the peace, but how much authority should it have over civilians?

This controversy had scarcely touched Rebecca before. Now she saw firsthand how unsettling the dilemma could be. If she refused to sell her wares to Captain Jessup he could just as well confiscate everything she owned in the name of the U.S. Army. But neither would she allow him to take advantage of his rank to abuse her.

Rebecca lifted her chin. ''As I said, Captain Jessup, you may come around front to purchase supplies from my store. But that is *all* you will get from me!''

''Is that a fact?'' With surprising agility for his stocky frame, Jessup sidestepped abruptly to block her as she tried again to move past.

Rebecca just barely avoided bumping against his barrel chest, but when she changed directions Jessup suddenly fell back, his thick arms pinwheeling crazily. He seemed to hang suspended in midair for a long moment before dropping to the ground with a resounding thump, landing hard in the middle of the moist earth Rebecca had freshly turned.

Rebecca stared at the officer in surprise, then glanced down toward the discarded spade that had caused him to trip, before returning her gaze to his face, now mottled with rage. The two men Jessup had brought with him burst into guffaws of laughter, which only made his face turn a deeper shade of red. With a feeling of impending doom, Rebecca silently wished they would shut up. If Jessup had been in an uncooperative mood before, she shuddered to think what his frame of mind would be now.

But try as she might, she could not quite hide the amusement that tugged at her own lips.

"Damn you, Carter!" Jessup's curse hissed through the morning air like a striking serpent. "Kinkle, don't just stand there like a grinnin' idiot. Go grab us a rasher of bacon and another keg of powder." He struggled to his feet, wiping clumps of earth from his backside and glaring murderously at his men.

Still snickering, the younger of the two soldiers ambled toward the front of the cabin. Rebecca moved to follow.

"I've plenty of powder to sell you," she stated, "but you'll have to stop at Henderson's for fresh meat. I'm sure he'll—"

"We ain't buyin'," Jessup interrupted in a low voice. "We're takin'."

Dismayed, she turned to face him. "You can't be serious?"

"But I am, Mrs. Osborne. Considerin' how you ain't exactly been friendly—" his eyes once again slid downward, "I'd say you're gettin' off easy."

Rebecca's mind raced. A whole keg of powder was an expensive way to appease this man's wounded pride. On the other hand, she was not certain what he might do to her—or to Samuel—if she refused. "Can you not requisition powder for your men from Sergeant Haskull? What little I have left is for the settlers to defend themselves here."

"I got it, Cap'n!" Behind her, the young man Jessup had called Kinkle hefted a small keg from one shoulder to the other. "An' there's a fine-lookin' blanket in there. Can I have that'un, too?"

Vance Jessup's broad face cracked into a taunting smile, his evil gaze never wavering from hers. "Sure thing, boy. Whatever you want."

Rebecca felt herself grow hot beneath his stare, but she would not allow herself to back down. She suspected that Captain Jessup was the kind of man who enjoyed seeing others cower before him even more than he relished a fight.

"That blanket is worth two dollars. Your men must pay just as any other customer would."

Her steady voice and uplifted chin seemed to have an amazing effect on Jessup, for he suddenly straightened. Then she realized that it was not her he stared at; his gaze was drawn to a point above her shoulder.

Rebecca looked around with a combination of expectancy and dread. But the emotion that swept over her when she saw who stood behind her was one of vast relief.

"Two dollars sounds like a fair price to me," Aaron drawled. His back was to her and Jessup, his attention focused on Kinkle, who stood so motionless his spindly legs looked like saplings that had taken root.

After several long seconds passed, the flustered private let the wool blanket slip to the ground. 'I-I don't really need a new blanket."

"Good. Then you'll put that one back where you found it. And the powder as well, unless you intend to pay for it in coin."

Jessup's hand twitched involuntarily when Kinkle jumped to obey—and much more quickly than he had ever done for *him*. He switched his glare to the man who had just arrived and summoned his most authoritative voice. "Sir, you are interferin' with official army business. This is none of your affair, so I suggest you get on outta here."

Aaron pivoted slowly. Rebecca was as surprised by his appearance as she was by her reaction, for he no longer wore the leather buckskins of a frontiersman or the plain wool garb in which she had last seen him. Now he was clad in a dark blue coat with buff-colored facings and spotless blue trousers. From the polished shine of brass buttons to the dusty sheen on his blackened boots, Aaron Cambridge was every inch the soldier.

Rebecca had to remind herself to breathe.

Then Jessup's harsh, indrawn gasp startled her out of her reverie, reminding her that she and Aaron were not alone.

"You!" he seemed to say, though his voice was so choked she could not be sure. She glanced at him curiously, but within a split second the disheveled captain had resumed his air of complete control. Now it was Aaron who seemed momentarily stunned.

Though his expression had changed little from the forceful frown he had turned on the hapless Kinkle, Rebecca detected a slight paling of the flesh around his old wound. With his hair now tied back in a neat queue, the scar was more prominent than ever. But to her, overshadowing the slight imperfection were his expressive eyes.

Just now those eyes registered something that might have been contempt.

Aaron's mouth drew thin. "I don't know who you are, *Captain,* but no officer of the United States Army has the privilege to take unfair advantage of a civilian."

Jessup seemed to shrink. "I wasn't takin' advantage," he whined. "We been out on the trail for nigh onta two weeks, and my men deserve a little refreshment. We don't have time to go all the way back to Fort Washington for supplies. Or money," he added with a hasty smirk.

"Then your men will have to do without." Now looking her way, Aaron said quietly, "Go inside, Rebecca. I'll handle this."

"I'm all right now, thank you," she retorted softly, incensed by his presumptive tone. "I can finish this myself."

"Do as I say."

"I most certainly will not!"

"Rebecca . . ." he warned.

"Looks to me," Jessup interjected rudely, "that you're the one the lady wants to get rid of. And since you're the same rank as me, I ain't about to take orders from you, neither."

But despite his boastful words, Jessup was already moving toward the horse which the soldier named Carter had led around from the front of the cabin. When he was safely in his saddle, he leaned over the pommel and grinned maliciously.

"Whoever you say you are, mister, that spanking-clean uniform ain't gonna do you any good out here. While you're polishin' those boots I'll be out savin' your ass from the savages." Reaching behind him, he fumbled with a strip of rawhide tied to the saddle and swung a strange-looking bundle forward across his lap. Something dark and shiny, like ebony silk, fluttered in the breeze, but Rebecca could not make out precisely what he held.

"And just to set your mind at ease, Mrs. Osborne," he sneered, "I wasn't about to leave you with nothin'. These here're worth more than anything you got in that store, 'cause you never know which one of these devils is the one that could've got *you*."

With that he flung the bundle forward so that it landed on the ground in front of Rebecca. She forced herself not to jump back, though when she finally looked down at the unwelcome gift Jessup had offered, her stomach pitched violently and her head began to spin.

Lying on the fertile soil at her feet were two bloody scalps.

Inside the cabin, Aaron drifted toward the window as he waited for Rebecca to change out of her mud-streaked dress. Sunlight and fresh air streamed through the opening, along with the muted laughter of Samuel and his young cousins as they played beneath the stockade's log walls some distance away. Farther off, two men trudged toward their cabin from the field beyond, one hauling a pair of oxen by a lead rope, the other cradling a long-barreled rifle in the crook of his arm.

Such a peaceful scene did little to ease Aaron's troubled mind. He wondered how Rebecca was faring. She had appeared to remain calm enough while he disposed of the scalps after Jessup's departure, but he could not forget the expression of horrified revulsion that transfixed her at the moment she realized what Jessup had done.

Vance Jessup. Even the name conjured uneasy emotions—disturbing because he could not understand them. Grasping hold of the windowsill, Aaron clenched his hands tightly, feeling the wood dig into his palms and his knuckles ache from the steady pressure. Why had the sight of Jessup nearly paralyzed him with unaccountable fear? Who was he?

Mesmerized by Aaron's stark image silhouetted against the bright sunlight, Rebecca paused silently at the doorway. He seemed to be engrossed in some activity outside the window, for he had not heard her approaching steps.

"Have they come back?" she asked anxiously.

After a long moment, Aaron turned. "No. Did he hurt you?"

Rebecca shook her head adamantly. "Certainly not. The man is a bully, but he must know he could not get away with any serious offense against me, or against anyone else, for that matter."

"Except the Shawnee." Aaron's voice was carefully guarded. "Don't fool yourself, Rebecca. Vance Jessup is a dangerous man."

"You know him, then?" she exclaimed with quiet curiosity.

"I don't know. I have a dim recollection of him from before my injury. And one of the officers at the fort told me he was pretty sure Jessup was at West Canada Creek. Beyond that . . . I just don't know."

Now Rebecca became aware of Aaron's uniform once again, and she remembered his original purpose in going to Fort Washington. "It looks as if your past doesn't matter anyway," she said blithely. "It's obvious you are not under arrest for your past transgressions."

"I'm not under arrest, though I'm not exactly a free man, either." Briefly, Aaron filled her in on his conversation with Major Carswell, particularly the part having to do with his status as medical officer of the regiment. To his amazement, Rebecca did not appear pleased to hear the conditions he had set. She had been removing a row of dishes from a shelf along one wall; he had suspected all along she was making work to keep her hands occupied. Now she stopped in mid-motion, a smooth brown bowl clenched between both hands.

"Must you take Samuel to the fort?" she protested. "I thought you would repair his leg here."

"I would if I thought the procedure could be done easily. But I may need some assistance, and at least Captain Tuthill knows his way around an operating theater. And since he'll be leaving eventually, I'd like to take you and Samuel to the fort tomorrow morning."

"Tomorrow! So soon?"

Aaron studied her anxious eyes, dark and tumultuous as
storm clouds. Her slim figure was as taut as a bowstring,
and her lustrous black hair now billowed around her shoulders in unruly waves.

"Surely you can make arrangements to be away for a
few days," he said, puzzled by her indecision. "I thought
you wanted to have this done quickly."

"I do," she said hesitantly. "It's just that . . ."

And then it hit him with the unleashed force of a winter
gale. Aaron's heart thudded slowly, inexorably, each beat
pounding the message into his brain. She did not trust
him, after all. He was not even certain why it should bother
him, since many others had refused his care before. Perhaps it was because he was so certain he could help Samuel.

Or perhaps because he merely needed to do this one
thing for Rebecca in order to atone for past sins.

In one long stride he reached her. His hands gripped her
shoulders, causing her to drop the wooden bowl, which
fell to the floor with a hollow thump and spun around
crazily until it fell still at last. "Don't do this, 'Becca,"
he implored, his voice low and intense. "Don't punish
Samuel because of what I've done. A few days ago you
pleaded with Cain to help your son because you knew he
had the ability. I am still that man. Maybe everything else
has changed, but not that."

Helplessly, Rebecca shook her head. "You don't understand, Aaron. This has nothing to do with us."

"Then what?"

"I just need time to think, that's all." Breaking free of
his hold, she bent to recover the bowl, willing her hands
to cease their trembling. "When you left here I was so
. . . so sure you would never come back. Now you walk
right in and want me to go with you on a moment's notice.
I need some time. I haven't even had a chance to explain
to Sam—"

"What are you afraid of, 'Becca? Me?"

His gentle, persuading voice stopped her. Rebecca
raised her gaze to meet his, surprised by the disarming
tenderness there. "No, though perhaps I should be more

afraid of you. You hurt me once. I'm not at all certain you no longer have that power.''

Aaron's mouth quirked once. "You're honest, at least. And I suppose it was arrogant of me to assume I could stand between you and Samuel's well-being. But something does. Won't you tell me?''

With a wilting sigh, Rebecca replaced the bowl on the shelf, allowing her hand to linger over the smooth wood. Reluctantly, she tried to give voice to the nameless fear that held her in its sway.

"I *do* want what is best for Samuel,'' she said solemnly. "But how do I know when I'm doing the right thing? It was all so simple a few weeks ago when finding a doctor seemed the only obstacle. Now you're here, and willing. And suddenly I'm frightened.''

This last was spoken on a shuddering breath so fragile Aaron thought it would shatter in the stillness that followed. He ached to comfort her, but the rigid set of her spine warned him she would not welcome his touch. Instead he moved back to the window, groping for the words to allay her doubts, but knowing that words could not soothe a mother's anxiety—only results would.

"Do you think I'm not frightened, too? Every time I examine a patient I have to face the knowledge that I may be doing more harm than good. But we weigh the risks against the benefits, and hope that God, or nature, doesn't make fools of us. Medicine is an inexact science—much like being a parent.''

"That's what scares me so,'' Rebecca admitted. She still had not turned to face him again, but her shoulders relaxed slightly, either in acceptance or defeat. "I should know by now that life doesn't promise anything except change. Samuel has experienced enough unwelcome changes these past months; I just want to make sure this one is for the better.''

"If I could swear to you that it will be, I would,'' Aaron murmured hoarsely. "But I won't lie about what's ahead. There is a very good chance of success, but even in the best of circumstances there will be some pain at first, and perhaps for a while afterward. The muscles in his leg have become accustomed to stretching one way when they should be working in another. He might have to learn how to walk all over again.''

''And if he can't it'll be my fault.'' She clenched her fists so tight against her thighs it hurt. ''Just as it will if I allow him to remain crippled for the rest of his life.''

Silence filled the room; then Rebecca sighed wearily, pressing her fingertips to her temples. The throbbing she felt there matched the pulsing beat of her heart, more rapid than usual in Aaron's presence. Even with concern for Samuel wracking her nerves, her senses were alive with awareness; though he stood across the room from her, she imagined his every breath moving the air next to her face, could feel the heat of his virile body warming her back.

He had moved silently, though out of habit, not stealth. When he laid a gentle hand upon her arm she jumped like a startled rabbit trapped by a predator, whipping around with eyes wide and uncertain.

''It's not your fault, 'Becca,'' he said in a low and husky voice. ''Any more than it was your fault he was hurt, or that there was no doctor here to set the bone properly in the first place. You can't take responsibility for events you can't control—only for yourself.''

''But I . . . I have a responsibility to Samuel, too.'' His nearness was unsettling, more so than she cared to admit.

''Yes, you do. And that's why you'll do what you know is right even though it scares the hell out of you.''

He still held her arm loosely, though his fingertips seemed to burn through the sleeve of her thin cotton dress and his gaze was piercing and intense. With sudden insight she realized that Aaron was speaking as much of his own ordeal as he was Samuel's, and she remembered that he had recently faced a kind of hell of his own. Despite her resolve to remain hardened toward him, Rebecca felt her defenses crumbling.

But he was not the same as before, she reminded herself harshly. This was not the Aaron she remembered; the angry scar slashing across his face was only a small reminder that greater wounds lay beneath the surface. Without moving at all she withdrew from him once more.

Aaron fought to keep himself from pulling her against him to kiss her luscious, generous lips. But instead he remained still, taking care that his expression betrayed none of the emotions coursing through him. He had nearly forgotten how beautiful she was, but when he looked in her dark eyes for the gentle yet spirited girl he had loved, he saw only wariness and mistrust. Regretfully, he released her arm and took a step back.

"So what is your answer?" he asked, his tone more brusque than he intended.

Rebecca glanced down at her hands, laced together so tightly the knuckles stood white upon her fingers. "I'll need to make arrangements with Lenore and gather some things together. And of course I'll have to talk to Samuel . . . but we'll be ready to go in the morning."

She looked up again to meet his penetrating gaze. The uncertainty she felt no longer had as much to do with Samuel as it did her own unmanageable emotions, but there was nothing she could do now except keep them to herself.

And pray that Aaron did the same.

CHAPTER 10

The day sped by as Rebecca concentrated on readying the store for her temporary absence. She had no qualms about leaving its care to Lenore and her willing but unruly son Ephraim, but she much preferred to stay busy tallying receipts and grading pelts than to let herself dwell on thoughts of Aaron.

He had managed to throw her into a fine state. His low-pitched voice was always within her hearing, even when he went along with Samuel to fetch water from the stream, and his habit of sneaking up behind her without a sound had her looking constantly over her shoulder.

Rebecca had scarcely tasted their hasty dinner of re-heated venison and stewed apples; fortunately, Samuel's incessant chatter had covered her obvious silence.

Now, with the table cleared of dishes at last, she added two blankets to the pile of provisions she had gathered for their journey to the nearby town. The sight of those blankets and thoughts of what accommodations they might find at the fort made her wonder if Aaron would need a place to sleep that night.

"He can sleep under a tree," she muttered while rolling her best dress and a clean chemise into one of the blankets. She thought it likely that Aaron would prefer the open space of outdoors anyway, since he was accustomed to living with the Indians. She didn't know a lot about the Shawnee, it was true, but she did know that entire tribes could pick up and move at a moment's notice, and that young warriors could live in the wilds for weeks on end. She could easily picture Aaron like that, clad in his buckskins and carrying only a small bundle of plunder, traveling free of all encumbrances—encumbrances like a wife and child.

Sudden guilt snapped her from that train of thought, causing Rebecca to sigh and shake her head. She should be thankful Aaron was willing to help them now, and shouldn't be dwelling on old hurts. Instead of thinking about Aaron she ought to concentrate on preparing Samuel for the ordeal before him.

With yet another heartfelt sigh, she closed the basket she had filled with dried meat and fruit for the journey. When she turned to reach for Samuel's warm jacket she was startled to see Aaron lounging against the doorframe. "I wish you would stop that," she said petulantly.

"Stop what?"

"Creeping about like an Indian. It's unnerving."

Pushing off against the oak jamb, Aaron straightened. "I suppose like everyone else you consider all Indians savages," he said tonelessly, not questioning her so much as stating an unpalatable fact.

Bewildered by his assumption, Rebecca faced him with her head tilted to one side, her hands planted on her hips. "Whatever gave you that idea?"

"Why wouldn't you feel that way? Between the government's irresponsible treaty policy and the number of myths and exaggerations about them, it's no wonder most settlers come out here expecting the worst. They can't help—"

Aaron stopped. The situation Carswell had outlined, abetted by Jessup's inhumane display that morning, had raised his deep-seated anger to the surface, an anger he could scarcely understand or quell. But it wasn't Rebecca's fault that he got his back up at the slightest reference to his friends' ways. And if he was to spend the next few months in Fort Washington he would have to guard his tongue there as well.

"Sorry." His voice was contrite, at least, if not completely gentled. "I came in here to ask if you wanted me to talk to Samuel for you. It might come easier from me, and if he has any questions I can answer them."

Her first impulse was to offer a curt denial, but instead Rebecca drew in a slow breath, holding it there until her lungs ached and then burned. Exhaling shakily, she pressed her fists just below her breasts, unconsciously scrunching up the soft wool of Samuel's coat.

She angled her chin upward. "Thank you, Aaron, but I'll tell him myself."

"Are you sure? I thought perhaps you were waiting for me. It's obvious you haven't told him yet. The boy just offered to take me fishing tomorrow. Maybe both of us should—"

"I'm his mother. I'll choose the best time to tell him."

The silence lengthened as he regarded her with a speculative look. Eventually he said, "You're right, of course. I won't interfere."

Sighing, Rebecca allowed her arms to drop. "Now *I'm* sorry. It's not that I don't appreciate your help, but I'm used to handling Samuel on my own. I don't know why I got so defensive." *Liar!* a voice inside her claimed. *You know exactly why.*

"I'll leave now if you wish," Aaron offered quietly. "We're both a little tense today, after that scene with Captain Jessup." *Not to mention the way his heart contracted every time she looked at him with those dark, shining eyes.* "Besides, you're busy getting ready."

"Getting ready for what?" Samuel chose that moment to appear in the doorway. He limped inside with only one crutch, having discarded the other in exchange for two stout poles that just cleared the lintel as he passed beneath. "I found 'em just where Zeb an' me left 'em, 'round behind Aunt Nora's cabin next to the woodpile. Ephraim said he was surprised he hadn't chopped 'em up for firewood, but he was just teasin'. . . ."

Samuel's words trailed to a halt as he stopped before the table piled with bedrolls and food, his bright blue eyes widening at this new discovery. "Where're we goin', Ma? With Cain?"

Rebecca moved closer to Samuel, placing herself between him and Aaron as she cupped one hand around her son's cheek.

"That's what we need to talk about, Samuel. Mr. Cambridge would like to try to straighten your leg. He says it's best to go to Fort Washington with him."

"Tonight?" Samuel's eagerness was barely contained.

"Morning will be soon enough. I still have packing to do."

"Will we walk?"

"No," Aaron answered after Rebecca shot him a questioning glance. "I'll bring two horses back with me tomorrow. They're still down at the fort."

"Two horses? Are they both yours?"

Rebecca could see Samuel's excitement rising, along with his already significant estimation of his newfound friend. She should have been glad, but instead her heart seemed to slow to a sluggish pace. She wanted Aaron to help Samuel, *not* become a part of their lives. But how could she fight this, after all? More to the point, should she?

Aaron watched her expression change from anxious to stoic in the space of a second; his chest tightened with sympathy. She was thinking about Samuel's leg again, he figured. He knew what it was to inflict pain on a loved one in order to prevent a greater anguish. She might never know how well he understood.

Dredging up a smile, he responded to Samuel's question. "One of the horses belongs to me and the other I borrowed from a man your friend Skulley knows in Cincinnati. That's one reason why we have to leave tomorrow—I don't relish the thought of being hanged as a horse thief."

Samuel laughed, then his small brow puckered. "If we ride, then do I have to take my crutches?"

"You won't be riding once you get inside the fort," Rebecca reminded him softly. She knew what her son was really asking.

So, apparently, did Aaron, for he hunkered down beside the boy, laying one large palm on Samuel's shoulder. "You'll need to hang on to those crutches for a little while yet, son. In order to fix your leg I'll need to break it again first. Even if it heals right you'll have to keep your weight off it for several weeks."

"Will it hurt?"

"Yes, it will." No wonder Rebecca hadn't wanted to do this, Aaron thought. Samuel's normally cheerful smile looked forced, and his blue eyes had lost their inquisitive gleam. Aaron experienced a queer sensation in his gut when the boy's sharp chin tilted bravely in just the same way as his mother's. "But I'll make you a drink beforehand that will help you sleep," he promised, "and when you wake up the worst of the pain will be gone."

Curious, Samuel pursed his lips. "A magic potion?"

"You just may be right about that." Aaron's chuckle died in his throat when he saw the anxious frown begin to pull at the boy's mouth. He continued gently. "There's nothing wrong with being scared, Samuel. That's what your mother and I were talking about before you came in. I know it's hard going through the hurt all over again, and I can't promise your leg will be perfect when I'm done. I will promise to do the best I can, son. Do you understand?"

Samuel nodded gravely. "I am scared . . . a little. But Skulley said soldiers get scared, too—even the brave ones. Courage is when you do what you have to anyway, right?"

"That's exactly right, Samuel."

Now Samuel's eyes lit upon Aaron's uniform. Rebecca could see him working up to a whole new series of questions. But before she could intercede he was already asking, "Were you ever scared?"

Crouched down as he was, she could not see Aaron's face, though his spine stiffened and the taut muscles in his thighs grew more rigid. His wool jacket stretched to near bursting across his well-muscled shoulders; even in this position he seemed too large and indomitable to know fear, though Rebecca realized that strength and size had nothing to do with the measure of a man's courage. Still, she was surprised when he replied in a gravelly voice, "Yes, Samuel, I've been afraid many times."

"Then you have courage, too," the boy declared happily. His impish grin returned as he jerked his head toward Rebecca. "Sometimes women are brave, you know. My ma is, I guess, because she's afraid I'll get hurt all the time, but she lets me play with the other kids anyway."

Now Aaron rose, and she saw that he wore an almost identical grin, though his eyes remained troubled.

"Now, that's what I call real courage. In fact, your

mother may be one of the bravest people I know. Did she tell you how she had to face a whole saloon full of drunken rivermen just to find me?''

Rebecca gave an indelicate snort. "Three, more like. And they were no drunker than you, and far less intimidating. Now, young man," she addressed Samuel in a stern tone that was softened with a smile, "if we are to travel in the morning you'll need a bath." She stroked her son's silky hair, pleased that he had taken the whole thing better than she had expected, thanks to Aaron's sensitivity.

"Aw, Ma, it ain't even Saturday!"

"It *isn't* Saturday, but you will have a bath anyway."

Watching them face off, Aaron experienced a pang of longing so keen he had to close his eyes for a second. But he opened them again, determined to keep wishful thinking at bay. It was one thing to enjoy their company for a short while; it was quite another to forget that Rebecca had chosen another, and that Samuel was not the son he had always wanted.

"The Shawnee usually bathe before a special event," Aaron offered sagely. Two pairs of eyes turned to him, one full of curiosity and the other, relief. "They believe bathing makes them stronger and more worthy to embrace battle."

"Do you think we'll run into a battle tomorrow?"

Taking the two fishing poles from Samuel's hand, Aaron leaned them in a corner and gestured toward the door. "Not the kind you're talking about. But you could think of the next few days as a test. Shawnee boys go through a similar sort of test when they're your age. That's when they earn their *pa-waw-ka.*"

"Their what?" His protest forgotten, Samuel hopped along with his single crutch, following Aaron to the woodpile just outside the door. He managed a few sticks with one hand while Aaron loaded his own arms high.

For the brief time they were outside, Rebecca could distinguish only the sound of their voices, Samuel's high and clearly excited, Aaron's deep and resonant. She smiled and filled a kettle with water from the barrel before swinging it over the flames to heat, then tugged a large tin tub out from under the counter in the store and dragged it to the fire. About the time she had it in place, Aaron and Samuel returned with the firewood.

"If a *pa-waw-ka* is a sign from God, then is the Bible a *pa-waw-ka*?" Samuel was asking.

"For some people." Aaron appeared to give the matter great consideration as he spied out the water barrel, then thoughtfully lifted it to dump the remaining water into the waiting tub. "The Shawnee consider the *pa-waw-ka* a symbolic source of an individual's own strength and courage. To find such a symbol is one step toward manhood."

His voice had dropped to a hypnotic pitch, and Rebecca could almost picture him crouched beside a fire, speaking to a circle of avid listeners, their bronzed faces shining in the flickering light. It was no wonder Samuel hung on every word he said; she had forgotten how mesmerizing Aaron could be. She remembered listening to him for hours on end when he spoke with enthusiasm about medicine, or the rebel cause, or even about traveling to the western territories. Now, apparently, his heart was bound to the Shawnee.

Determined not to miss a word, Samuel leaned his crutch alongside the abandoned fishing poles, then hopped over beside the table, where he began to unselfconsciously strip. "But how do you find a *pa-waw-ka*? I think I could use one."

"It's not always easy," Aaron explained with a slow grin. "Nothing worth having is. One boy might dive into an icy river in the middle of winter to scoop a special stone from the bottom. Another might set out alone, traveling far away from his family until he discovers the proper signs to lead him to his *pa-waw-ka*. In the Shawnee towns, boys are taught from the time they are little to anticipate the trial of finding one."

"Then I can't get a *pa-waw-ka* of my own, can I?" Samuel stuck out his lower lip. "I'm not Shawnee." His skinny frame looked even thinner without clothing and with his arms laced around his sides. Despite his lameness he bobbed up and down to ward off the evening chill.

Aaron stooped to gather Samuel's discarded clothing into a bundle, depositing it on a nearby chair. "Neither am I.

At least not in the strictest sense. But I have a *pa-waw-ka.*"

"Where is it?"

"Right here." After tapping his chest, Aaron used one finger to hook the cord that hung around his neck, tugging until he pulled from the collar of his uniform what appeared to be a jagged stone. It glowed amber in the fire's rippling light.

Rebecca worked her mouth, unable to resist asking. "Is that a tooth?"

"A claw." For the first time since Samuel had come in, Aaron looked at her fully, his expression unfathomable. Then he turned back to the boy. "A panther claw."

"Gosh!" Samuel's eyes widened appreciatively. "That's what I want, too."

"You have to take the *pa-waw-ka* the gods choose to give you, son. But don't worry," he added, tousling the boy's blond hair before striding back to the fire, "I'll help you."

As Rebecca watched, Aaron tested the water in the kettle with the tip of one finger. She had already returned to the task of sorting Samuel's clothing, and she was surprised by how pleasant it felt to have Aaron's matter-of-fact assistance. Almost as if they were a family, she thought wistfully. The way things might have—

"H-how did you come to find a panther claw?" she asked abruptly, squelching her traitorous thoughts.

Almost reluctantly, Aaron answered, "It was a few years back. I happened to come across a Shawnee brave who'd been cornered by this cat. Together we drove the panther off, then later the brave hunted it down and presented me with the four paws as a gift in exchange for his life."

"Your *pa-waw-ka,*" Samuel cried gleefully. "But why do people say you can turn into a panther?"

Aaron shrugged and grinned. "For a while I carried those paws from a belt. Maybe they thought I put them on at night, like changing boots."

"D'ya still have 'em?"

"Only this." He fingered the smooth crescent. "But I found something better than a *pa-waw-ka* that day, Samuel. I found a new friend. His name is Wind at His Feet, and his family became my family; his home, my home. Sometimes a search for one thing in life brings us something entirely unexpected.''

At that moment Aaron looked up and his eyes claimed hers. A surge of awareness unlike any she had felt before shot through her, sending tendrils of heat licking up from the pit of her stomach.

Blushing, Rebecca lowered her head quickly, but not before she saw the look of astonished lust that crossed his face. It had turned his eyes into narrow, glittering beacons and deepened the flesh around his scar to a russet hue.

So. He was surprised, too, by the return of old feelings, she thought. But would he be content to deny them, as she hoped?

He bent to remove the hissing kettle from the fire, using a faggot of wood to swing the crane outward. By no accident the movement turned his face away from her, and away from Samuel's bright gaze as well. Aaron had seen the desire in her eyes as they captured his; he had seen, too, the regret settle over her expression as her glance dropped to the slashing blemish adorning his cheek. He wouldn't blame her if she was repulsed by his scar.

Perhaps it was even better if she was, since the old wound was the visible symbol of that which would keep them apart forever.

Mentally shaking himself, he poured the steaming water into the tub, then grasped Samuel's arm gently to help him into the warmed water. Halfway there, the boy cocked his head and stared up at him skeptically.

''Are you *sure* you can't turn into a panther?'' he asked.

''Yes, son. I'm very sure.'' Aaron chuckled wryly, but his heart held more regret than amusement. Without looking at Rebecca again he straightened, then lifted his hat from a nail near the door.

His tone was unusually brusque as he said, ''I'll be back for you in the morning.''

CHAPTER 11

I'll be back for you in the morning.

Rebecca rolled onto her side and thumped the feather pillow forcefully. How many times had she heard that very phrase, spoken with hushed anticipation and eager hope? During that long-ago summer Rebecca and Aaron had made a pact to never say good-bye; instead they parted each night with promises for another day.

Even now, with age and experience to remind her that some promises are destined to remain unfulfilled, Rebecca could not help feeling the same sense of expectant longing those words had evoked years ago.

Lying awake in her tiny room and surrounded by the black stillness of night, she crushed her palms hard against her breasts to relieve the throbbing ache that began there. Her nipples hardened as the rough linen of her nightgown scraped the sensitive tips, but instead of providing relief, the pressure of her own hands only left her craving another's touch.

And remembering how it had all begun—just before the end came. . . .

Aaron had been home for more than a month—longer than Rebecca had dared hope he would stay, though not nearly long enough. Ever since that first day on the shore, a new and stimulating awareness had blossomed between them like one of the wild hibiscus that grew amid the marsh grasses, and each hour they spent in one another's company only heightened her senses and honed to a keen edge the unfamiliar yearnings that now possessed her.

Then one evening Rebecca had gone out behind the kitchen garden to dump the dishwater and was surprised to find Aaron waiting for her beyond the gate.

" 'Becca," he had called to her softly, smiling crookedly when she let the tin dishpan slip from one hand to bang against her hip.

"Aaron, you scared me! I thought you were a redcoat."

He leaned against a fence post and hopped over the low gate, landing just inches away from her. "There are no redcoats in Beaufort." His smile fell away as he gazed at her earnestly. "But there are still plenty to be fought. I got a letter from Eli Winthrop today. He's marching out with the northern army next month, and he wants me to join him in Albany. My brother's in Albany. I'll be with Jacob again."

"N-next month?" Rebecca's voice choked on a stifled moan.

"Uh-huh. But I'll have to leave on Saturday's packet to Jersey and sail the rest of the way up the Hudson to meet them. I'll never catch up if I travel overland."

Rebecca sensed his excitement, both in his voice and in the avid gleam in his eyes. Disappointment welled in her. Already she was losing him, and she hadn't yet had the chance to tell him how much she loved him. Tears trembled on her eyelids, but in the half dark she was certain he would not see them. "Saturday is the day after tomorrow," she said bleakly.

"C'mere, 'Becca."

With a slight tug he urged her nearer, until she stood with her nose only inches from his chest. The strings on his shirt hung untied, the neck gaping in a deep V that revealed his muscular torso. She had seen him bare-chested before, but never this close, and never when the urge to bury herself in his arms was so strong. All of a sudden her knees felt watery and her jaw quivered. "W-what do you want?"

"To kiss you good-bye."

The dishpan slid to the ground with a metallic clang. "Oh!"

She had no time to protest—not that she truly wished to—before he dipped his head, raising his free hand to hold her chin still. Only his fingertips touched her, one hand tracing the side of her jaw and the other encircling her wrist, but she felt a current surge through her at each point, and she dimly wondered if she would be able to bear it if he embraced her fully. Surely the wondrousness of it all would cause her heart to explode.

Then his mouth covered hers, tentatively at first, barely brushing the corner, as though she were the most delicate of flowers or as fragile as spun glass. Aaron had kissed her often in the past weeks, but never quite like this. Now his mouth lingered, and she did not dare to breathe. When his tongue flicked lightly over the center of her lips . . . testing, urging . . . she could not keep herself from parting them, astonished yet somehow emboldened by the silky warmth that invaded her mouth.

A low sound escaped her throat, or perhaps it came from his—she could not be sure. Either way, it shattered the stillness of the creeping dusk and disintegrated the timidness they each had felt until now. Suddenly she was pressed hard against him, her arms squeezed between them and her fingers splayed against the firmness and heat of his chest. She tipped her head further, loving the fullness of his mouth slanted over hers, seeking, discovering . . . welcoming.

When finally Aaron broke away, his breath was a convulsive shudder that fanned her cheeks and mingled with her own shaky exhalations. Rebecca clung to him weakly, pressing her forehead against the unsteady pulse at the base of his throat. His hands stroked her back, following every curve and indentation through thin cotton that did nothing to block out the scorching heat of his exploration.

" 'Becca."

Her name was a rasping whisper, as sweet and seductive as any kiss. She arched instinctively, letting her eyes drift closed as she lifted her face to him once again.

"Listen . . . I should go now."

It took a second for comprehension to dawn; then Rebecca's eyes flew open. Her face, already suffused with blood, grew still as misery swamped her. "Oh, Aaron! You can't leave yet. You said Saturday!"

"I mean for tonight." Even in the shadowy garden she

saw his mouth curve upward, though she detected the rueful twist that she had seen often lately. "Can we . . . will you spend tomorrow with me?" he asked. "The whole day? I'll have to be at the dock early the next morning, but I've already packed my gear and Levi said he won't be needing me to haul lines. We could go on a picnic. Or something."

It was the "or something" that frightened and intrigued her, but not the space of a heartbeat passed before Rebecca nodded eagerly. "All right, Aaron. I'll be ready."

"Good. Then I'll be back for you in the morning."

There followed an excruciating night wherein Rebecca lay awake, reliving the magic of that kiss and wondering how she could live if he never kissed her again. And while her mind replayed the moment, her body remembered in other ways. First she felt an odd sensation in her chest, a fleeting warmth that raced from her heart to the pit of her stomach and back again, then was gone, leaving her feeling hollow and empty inside.

But gradually the heat returned, only this time it centered low in her belly, and instead of receding it continued to pulse and grow. Rebecca had never felt this way before, and she was not sure whether she ought to be ashamed or scared. These new sensations were not altogether unpleasant, but they left her panting and uncertain and alternately wishing them away and hoping they would stay.

Tentatively she lowered her fingertips to the place where the pressure seemed the strongest, and was surprised by the moist heat radiating even through her nightdress. When she pressed harder the throbbing eased somewhat, and though her cheeks burned at the idea of touching herself so boldly, she did not stop.

And then Rebecca had another thought—one so utterly shocking that she lay quivering on the bed at the mere suggestion: How would it feel if Aaron were to touch her there?

But such thoughts were reserved for marriage, and though she could not imagine herself married to anyone but Aaron, Rebecca knew that what she felt now was wrong—terribly, sinfully wrong. Quickly she snatched her hand away and clutched the edge of her blanket, hugging it under her chin as she closed her eyes and squeezed her legs tight together.

Don't think about it, she commanded herself. *Don't think at all. Just go to sleep.*

But sleep was a long time coming. And when it did come, it was filled with uneasy notions and strange longings that weighed on Rebecca throughout the night and well into the following morning.

As she and Aaron walked hand in hand toward the waterfront, her heart somersaulted inside her chest and her knees wobbled treacherously. "W-where are we going?" she managed to ask, pleased that at least she was able to speak. They were moving through the village streets at a breathless pace.

"To the island. I borrowed a sailing skiff from Jonathan Barnes. We can be alone out there."

He did not look around as he spoke, but Rebecca detected a trace of doubt underlying his words. Did he think she would disagree? she pondered while struggling to match his eager stride. She grabbed his hand, skipping forward to catch up.

"That sounds wonderful, Aaron. I haven't been to Carrot Island in ages."

He did glance down then, but his pale blue eyes were unreadable, and before she had time to offer more than a quick smile, his gaze had returned to the unfolding scene before them.

They had reached the end of the village, and Aaron stopped there so they could both scan the horizon. The sun was a golden orb hovering just above the most distant island, its white head already making the palmettos look like shimmering waves of green and brown. The water between the coast and the islands was as flat and still as gray pewter on this day when not a breath of wind stirred; the only movement came from above, where careening gulls danced a pirouette around invisible partners, their raucous cries lending counterpoint to the rhythmic lapping of the sea against a single rickety pier.

Rebecca glanced toward Carrot Island just across the waterway. It was a popular spot for picnickers and children, who regularly swam the placid waters to play on the island and chase the wild, shaggy horses that roamed there. Normally one could detect some movement—either horses galloping over the strands or birds taking flight from the trees. But not today.

She looked back at Aaron. "I don't *see* anyone else."

His eyes seemed to burn with unusual intensity as he raised them to meet hers, and she could not help but notice the deep russet tinge beneath his tan. "I thought we'd try somewhere new today," he said at last. "There's another island farther out with wild horses on it, but not many people bother to go there, with Carrot Island so close."

For a moment Rebecca forgot to breathe; then her heart's urgent beat forced her lungs to expand and contract. Her voice was almost natural as she replied, "Wherever you want to go is fine with me, Aaron."

The next half hour passed with little conversation as they boarded a skiff and Aaron concentrated on rowing the boat at a determined pace and Rebecca battled to keep her thoughts from straying to the deserted island and whatever else lay just ahead of them. The silence was broken once as they passed a fishing boat just heading to shore with the morning catch. Aaron shouted a greeting in response to the fisherman's cheerful hail. Rebecca, too, lifted a tentative hand, but she felt her cheeks grow hot all over as she wondered if the friendly passer-by would guess what they were up to.

But there was nothing wrong with going on a picnic, was there? Rebecca cast another surreptitious glance toward Aaron. He was rowing with all his might, his head turned away from her and his chin tucked into his shoulder as he steered them past a channel marker. His face was set in an intense frown.

Before long they arrived at one of the small outer islands. When the craft scraped bottom Aaron hopped out and dragged the skiff a few yards closer to shore. Rebecca eyed the several inches of water in which he stood, then leaned forward to unfasten the lacings of her own shoes.

"Don't do that," Aaron said huskily. "Grab the basket and hang on." Taking her hand, he helped her to stand in the listing boat, then bent, scooping her into his arms.

Rebecca felt weightless as he lifted her high against his

muscular chest, and she attributed the slight sense of dizziness to the speed with which he turned and strode toward the band of ivory sand skirting the island. Her left arm circled his neck while the right clutched the basket of food against her belly. She was too surprised to say anything, until he reached dry land and slowly set her back on her feet.

"Th-thank you, Aaron. I could have waded, though."

"I know." He grinned sheepishly. "I wanted to carry you."

She met his eyes with a steady, solemn gaze that told him without words that she had not minded his holding her at all. He seemed about to say something else, for his Adam's apple moved higher up his throat, but then he merely took her free hand again and led the way toward a natural path cut through the foliage after dragging the skiff higher onto shore.

"We're more likely to see the horses on this side." His voice grew more tender. "And it's shaded over here, so you won't get sunburned."

They tramped through brush and sand for nearly a mile before reaching a small copse of pines on the ocean side of the island. By unspoken agreement, they chose a patch of ground that sloped from the trees toward the beach several yards below. Waves lapped at the shore, and far down the beach a few of the island's wild horses flirted with the roaring surf.

And at last he faced her, taking up both her hands as she and Aaron dropped in accord to their knees upon the cushion of pine needles and loamy earth.

" 'Becca," he started, clearing his throat of the hoarseness there. "I want to ask you something. I thought it would be a couple of years before I could, because of the war making the future . . . *our* future . . . so uncertain. With me leaving tomorrow things are worse than ever. But I don't want to wait anymore, 'Becca. I have to ask you now."

"Ask me what, Aaron?"

He squeezed her hands tighter. A muscle jumped in his jaw. "Do y'love me?"

After skipping a beat, her heart tripped forward as if

she were running downhill and could not stop. His earnest face blurred as tears filled her eyes. "Of course I love you."

"Then will you marry me when I come home?" His hands gripped hers so hard now she nearly winced, until he realized what he was doing and relaxed his fingers. But he did not let go. "You don't have to answer right away if you want some time to think about it. But I just thought . . . well, it would make being away easier if I knew I had you to come home to."

"Oh, Aaron!" Rebecca raised their hands, pressing his knuckles against her trembling chin. "I don't need time to think—I've thought about little else for the past few weeks. You're the only one I ever wanted to marry. But—" she paused, nibbling her lower lip shyly, "do we have to wait?"

His Adam's apple lurched again. "There's no time now, 'Becca, with me leaving in the morning. Even if we found a willing preacher today. . . . But I would if we could!" he exclaimed at the sight of her stricken expression.

Untangling their hands, he wrapped his arms around her, pulling her close. They clung together, hips to hips, belly to belly. Rebecca's breasts pressed hard against his solid chest, and they throbbed at the mixed pleasure and pain. His harsh breath bathed the side of her neck and her cheek with warmth.

"Oh, Aaron, I've loved you for so long, but I wasn't sure you loved me," she cried.

He chuckled softly. "How could I not love you, 'Becca? All last year in Jersey, whenever I got discouraged or tired, all I had to do was think about you and I felt better. Sometimes I would remember how you laughed when Levi and I got tangled up in the lines beneath his pa's shack. Or the sound of your voice when you'd call after us when we were running off to play. But mostly, 'Becca, I would picture your smile. Do you know when I saw you on the beach that first day home I nearly told you right then I was in love with you?"

"Why didn't you?" she choked out, drawing back to search his eyes. "I wanted you to love me, too, but sometimes these past few weeks you acted like you didn't want me near you."

"It wasn't that." Aaron shook his head, then pressed a kiss on her temple.

"Then what?"

"I wanted . . . I *want* you too much."

His confession sent a thrill of excitement and relief spiraling through her, along with an increased awareness of where they were, and the utter solitude of the island. Her cheeks flamed as she squeezed her eyes shut and whispered against his bare throat. "I . . . I feel the same way, Aaron. Only I'm s-scared."

"Don't be." Aaron stroked her hair, while struggling for mastery over the raw emotions that had nearly erupted from him at her shy admission. "I promise I won't do anything to you. That's not why I brought you out here, I swear."

She shook her head, lifting her lips just high enough to graze his ear. "I didn't mean I'm afraid of you. Never that. It's just that before it was bad enough, knowing you would leave tomorrow. Now I can't . . . I can't bear the thought of letting you go." Her voice breaking along with her heart, Rebecca clung to him, allowing the scalding tears to flow unchecked.

"It's only for a while, my love. I promise I'll be back soon. The war *can't* go on much longer. I'll be back, 'Becca. I promise."

His words did not soothe so much as incite, for as he murmured these vows, his hands and lips became more urgent. They carried a silent, solemn plea that Rebecca could neither ignore nor refuse, for with each touch, each kiss, she felt Aaron's love for her embrace the deepest reaches of her soul.

When he drew her closer, taking all of her weight into his muscular arms so that he completely supported her, she did not protest. And when he lowered her to the ground slowly, bending over her as he deepened his kisses, Rebecca held him even tighter to her and opened her mouth in absolute welcome.

She had never experienced anything like this before—this shameless abandon, this growing, aching need to have him close . . . closer. And the joy of it all was that he needed her as much, and that by answering his need she could answer her own.

Rebecca was amazed by the hot slickness of his tongue probing and teasing, enticing her to join him. Tentatively, she returned his movement with a hesitant foray of her own, and was shocked by the incredible pleasure that streaked through her when he suckled her tongue gently, then with greater force. A racking tremor shook them, but she could not be sure whether it began with him, or if it came from deep within her own breast, or from them both.

With one hand he smoothed the damp curls from her face, his fingers weaving through her hair as if to find a safehold. His other hand inched slowly from her waist, seeking the soft swell of her breast. Arching against his palm, Rebecca pressed upward until hesitation turned to certainty and he cupped her wholly, his thumb tracing the outline of her budding nipple through layers of muslin. Just when she thought she could not bear the exquisite torture for another moment, Aaron broke away from kissing her, his mouth traveling down the length of her throat until it came to rest on the sensitive tip of her breast.

"Oh!" Rebecca moaned softly, gasping for breath as she clung to his broad shoulders. A white heat seared her, enveloped her, so that when he loosened the ribbons at her neck she felt no fear, only gladness.

Then cool air rushed over her—coolness where before there had been only warmth. Rebecca's eyes widened to see Aaron holding himself rigid above her, his lips quirked and his blue eyes bearing an expression of great tenderness, and even greater restraint.

"We have to stop. I can't . . . I can't take much more."

Somehow his gaze was apologetic and beseeching all at once, which served to embolden her. With a shaking hand, Rebecca laid her palm against his sweat-dampened cheek. "But I don't want you to stop. You said we'd be married soon. Please, Aaron?"

He responded with a low groan. " 'Becca, are you sure? Do you know what you're doing?"

She blinked slowly, her teeth catching her bottom lip to keep it from trembling. "Don't you?"

He looked stunned for a moment; then a smile creased his face. "Oh, Lord, 'Becca. That's not what I meant." Aaron's hoarse voice shook with mirthless laughter.

Even though he tenderly cradled her head between his palms, she was embarrassed by her ignorance. Red heat crept up her neck to flush her cheeks, and she squirmed beneath his crushing embrace. "Then what did you mean?"

" 'Becca, darlin' . . ." The endearment was spoken softly, though with just enough imperative to bring her wiggling to a halt. "I love you more than I ever loved anybody or anything. Do y'believe me?"

Silently, with tears clogging her throat, she nodded.

"I wouldn't do anything to hurt you, 'Becca. Never. That's why I want you to be sure you love me, too. Because if you're not . . . if you're not, then we should wait."

A long moment passed before she moved again, and this time it was to expel the breath she had unwittingly held throughout his declaration. Now she met his anxious eyes with confidence and overwhelming love. "You could never hurt me, Aaron. I know that better than I know my own self. I *want* us to be together. Today. Not next month or next year. Now."

His groan was muffled against her lips as she raised her head to kiss him once more. Rebecca savored the taste of his mouth as well as the roughness of his cheek and the welcome weight of his body flattening her into the bed of pine needles. And as he shifted over her she was aware, too, of the hard ridge that pressed insistently against her lower belly.

A moment of panic besieged her; then she remembered who it was and why she was here. It was Aaron, who loved her, and for him she would conquer her fear. *With* him she had no need to fear. She relaxed beneath him, allowing his knee to nudge her legs farther apart.

"My love," he whispered, his voice a pleasurable rasping sound against her ear. Wordlessly she moved against him, her shy boldness encouraging his caresses to greater lengths. She did not flinch when his hand found the edge of her petticoat and slid it up and over her flexed knee, nor did she stop him when the remains of her blouse fell from her shoulders. Rebecca closed her eyes and arched back, savoring the sensations he aroused in her with his hands and mouth and body, even while she wondered how it was possible that something considered sinful could feel so good.

Those thoughts, however, fled easily from her mind as Aaron's kisses grew more demanding and his tender foray more insistent. Her loving surrender was complete, and yet Rebecca was not prepared when his palm cupped her intimately. Seemingly of their own will her limbs quaked and shivered, and when he slid one finger along the crevice of her womanhood she cried out softly at the exquisite torture and clamped her legs tight, trapping his hand.

"God, 'Becca, don't be afraid now!" came Aaron's rasping plea.

"I-I'm not." With an effort, she forced her body to relax against his hand. "It's . . . it's just that I didn't know . . ."

Her voice trailed off as he continued the gentle stroking he had begun, sending mounting waves of pleasure rolling through her. With hooded eyes he watched her, his own weight eased from her body as he brought her ever closer to the peak. She was dimly aware of the rigid control with which he contained himself—his jaw was as rock hard as the muscles in his arms and back—but before she could dwell on his state of mind Rebecca found herself swept away on a greater tide of rapture than she had ever thought possible.

She clutched Aaron's shoulder, her parted lips pressed against his throat in a silent shout of ecstasy. Flames seemed to lick at the backs of her calves and wrapped tendrils of heat around the soft flesh of her thighs, creeping higher until at last it reached the core of her and exploded into one brilliant burst of fire and ice.

And then, before her shudders could subside, he was above her, raising her so that he could fit against her shivering warmth. Eagerly she lifted herself to him, cradling his hips as she instinctively sought the fulfillment that was just a heartbeat away.

"I love you, 'Becca," he murmured in the same moment that she felt the mingled pain and pleasure of his entrance.

"I love you, too, Aaron," she whispered back as her body, still throbbing with tiny convulsive waves, welcomed and held him. "Please don't leave me. I'm afraid something will happen to you."

He grew still, his eyes searching hers. "You know I have to go, my love. But nothing will happen to change the way I feel now. Do you hear me, 'Becca? *Nothing!* And I promise, no matter what, I'll come back to you."

Then she heard no more, for the roaring in her ears began again, and whether he whispered or ranted or remained completely silent mattered not a bit, for his love was spoken to her clearly. When at last he tensed above her in the final throes of his own desire, Rebecca wept at the sweetness of it, only to have him later kiss away her tears with smiles and promises. . . .

Broken promises, she thought now. Ten years and a thousand miles away, and still the remembered passion caused her body to ache and shiver.

And sadness for promises lost still enveloped her within its chill gray cloak.

Unmindful of the hour, or of her weariness, or even of the unnatural dampness of the pillow beneath her cheek, Rebecca lay staring into the black night. Sleep, too, she decided, was but a casualty of war.

CHAPTER 12

It was still dark when they set out, with a damp wind at their backs to remind them that spring was not yet ready to relinquish her hold over the land to summer. A night squall had left the ground spongy and hazardous, while lingering storm clouds forestalled the sun's appearance to the east.

"Can't we go at a gallop?" Samuel urged. "We coulda walked this fast."

Aaron answered with a dour laugh. "It only seems that way. Actually, we're making good time."

Rebecca glanced across the rutted path at the two riding beside her. What Aaron said was true. The winding river road was less direct than the steep forest path she usually took, but horses traveled faster than humans, even walking, and besides, without the horses they never could have carried the extra provisions Lenore had forced them to bring. Rebecca was glad now for the surefooted little mare she rode.

At her side, Aaron straddled a tall, one-eyed roan, which he had explained to Samuel had cost him only half its true worth because some men couldn't look past the empty eye socket to see the gelding's rare spirit. Samuel rode behind the saddle, his thin arms locked around Aaron's waist and his fair head swiveling so as not to miss so much as a rabbit on the trail.

By dawn they spotted the first cabins lining the plateau above the river, and once the trees thinned they could make out the buildings closer to the river as well, barely visible through the protective mist that rose from the water.

When they passed the tavern where Rebecca had sought out Cain, Aaron grinned over his shoulder. "Intimidating, huh?"

She fought a smile. "Only because it was dark and you smelled so bad. Thank God you got rid of those filthy hides."

"My buckskins and other gear are still at the fort. I'll only be in this uniform for a few months, remember?"

Rebecca guided the mare silently, following as Aaron led them through the bustling village, heading up the incline toward the stockade on the hill. How could she forget, indeed? Aaron would not stay in these parts long, he had just as good as reminded her. She should forget about a future that held no promises; making it through the next few hours was quite enough to think about. Frowning, she gazed ahead.

Though Cincinnati was still little more than a garrison town, vestiges of civilization had begun to take hold, as evidenced by the wide roads and evenly spaced plots laid out by Israel Ludlow, one of the town's principal landowners. Not every lot boasted a cabin as yet, but most were clear of trees and underbrush, affording an unobstructed view all the way down to the riverfront area, where most of the town's businesses were located.

Farther from the river were rows of larger houses, not rude log structures, but frame homes occupied by prosperous merchants and high-ranking army officers. Several boasted two stories, and one was even flanked on two sides by a pair of massive stone chimneys. Rebecca admired the elegant structure without envy—her snug cabin suited her just fine—though she marveled at how quickly the town was growing. Why, before long Cincinnati would be a regular city!

Just ahead, Fort Washington loomed protectively on a slight rise in the land. Rebecca observed activity outside its gates, and from inside a piping reveille reminded her that the day was about to begin, whether she was ready for it or not.

At the fort's entrance a sentry stopped them. Despite the silk epaulet of a captain on Aaron's right shoulder and his ranking uniform, the guard waved them on only after

Aaron produced a folded square of parchment from his jacket. Rebecca noticed the straining muscles of his jaw as he answered the guard in terse phrases; she noticed, too, the soldier's eyes lingering suspiciously upon Aaron's scarred cheek as they passed.

It reminded her, for the moment, that Aaron's elevated status was only a temporary reprieve. He was still under investigation, the charges of desertion merely waived until further notice. And from the way that soldier had treated him, she decided, Aaron would need more than a pardon to earn the respect of the men.

Finally they stopped in front of a structure built against the western wall of the fort. Beside her, Aaron dismounted quickly. When he reached for her reins she gave them up without question. "This is it."

His palms slid around her waist, pulling her toward him before she could protest. Automatically her hands found his shoulders, and though it took only an instant for him to swing her to the ground, her flesh tingled and her blood raced as her body brushed against his intimately.

And then, just as quickly, he stepped back. "Wait, Samuel," he said in a hushed voice. "I'm going to carry you in."

Samuel demurred, citing his grand age of ten years as reason enough to decline. But Rebecca well understood how Aaron wished to keep her son's leg relaxed and limber, and how even a short walk might strain the overworked muscles in the boy's thigh. Aaron chuckled and cajoled, finally convincing Samuel that carrying him would be a privilege and an honor.

Despite her uneasiness, Rebecca smiled ruefully at Aaron's back as he carried her son through the cabin's wide door. He could probably coax an angel out of heaven if he but tried.

She followed them inside, leaving the door open so that the early morning sun could light their way. Rebecca glanced around. To her left was a crooked table stacked high with books and parchment that looked ready to topple to the floor at any moment. On the wall directly across from the door was a shelf bearing glass jars of all shapes and sizes, though most were so coated with dust it was impossible to tell whether they were empty or full. Beneath this shelf was a disheveled bunk which was sadly in need of a few extra slats, the mattress nearly sagging to the floor. Another doorway to the right was covered by a filthy piece of cloth tacked to the lintel with two rusty nails.

"Damn!" Aaron murmured under his breath. He stepped forward, allowing her to move farther into the room. After lowering the boy to a chair, he moved to light a fire in the round stove in one corner. "I asked the major two days ago to see that these rooms were cleaned out before we came back. I should've checked last night after reporting to him, but he said he'd passed the order on to Captain Tuthill."

"Isn't this where you sleep?" Samuel asked curiously, scanning the narrow room as Aaron lit a lamp hanging on one wall.

"My things are at the officer's barracks," he answered. "This bed is for use whenever there's a patient in the infirmary who might need attention during the night."

Samuel studied the bed with bewilderment, then shrugged and said brightly, "Captain Tuthill was sleeping there when we came to see him last fall. There was no one else around then, but I think maybe he was too tired to walk to his quarters. He could hardly stand up."

"Yes . . . well." Aaron frowned, glancing sideways at Rebecca. "Let's hope Captain Tuthill won't be too tired today. He shouldn't be, at least not if Major Carswell has explained what I need of him."

Rebecca read concern in Aaron's eyes, which only added to her own. Her mistrust of Tuthill and his methods ran deep, and she could not help but wonder what possible use the man could be during the procedure Aaron described. Did Aaron honestly prefer Tuthill's assistance to her own?

No sooner had this thought appeared than a scuffling sound outside the door indicated someone's arrival. "That's probably him now," Aaron said in a low voice.

Captain Reginald Tuthill was everything Rebecca had remembered, and worse. Leading with his paunchy, food-stained stomach, the regimental physician reminded her of a child's toy she had once seen, a pear-shaped wooden doll which wobbled and spun on its rounded bottom. His fat, rheumy eyes stared ahead with a burning intensity, though it seemed his vision was turned inward, since his response to others was often slow and sometimes vague. A ripe odor surrounded him, a combination of stale whiskey, urine, and fetid breath that caused Rebecca's nose to twitch uncomfortably.

"Mrs. Osborne," he said in a slurred voice, which was also inexplicably loud, "I'm surprised to see you back here. But not as surprised as I am to see the boy. Thought he'd be in the ground by now." With the wave of a hand he dismissed them both, then turned to face Aaron. "So you're the fellow Carswell told me about. Injun-lover, I hear. But it looks like you've got the muscle for a surgeon, though. This here regiment's full of tough old birds. You'll have to do some 'rastling first before you go cutting off any limbs."

A smirk twisted his fleshly face as he glanced over at Samuel, who remained silent upon his chair. The boy's injured leg was propped on a low stool.

"That one shoulda come off," Tuthill said glumly. "You'll get nowhere trying to fix it now."

Shocked that he would make so blunt a statement in front of Samuel, Rebecca opened her mouth to protest. Aaron's voice, quiet but forceful, stopped her. "So you say. But I did not ask for your opinion." Lifting Samuel, he murmured to the boy, "Why don't you wait in here for a minute?" He carried him past the curtain into the other room, then returned. To Rebecca, he said, "I'll need boiling water. Will you see to it?"

"Of course." Glad to have something to do, she moved to the stove without acknowledging Tuthill. The man's very presence offended her, but if Aaron said he needed his help . . .

"What do you want with water?" the surgeon demanded.

"I'll ask you to keep your voice down," Aaron replied ominously. "There's no need to frighten the boy. To begin with, we're going to clean this place up. Then I plan to prepare a poultice, as well as a mixture of roots and herbs to produce an anesthesia. Remove that rag from the doorframe, if you please, Captain Tuthill. And then wipe off the table in the surgery.''

Having poured water from the pitcher Aaron had indicated into a tin pot on the stove, Rebecca looked around to see what else she could do to prepare the room. But her gaze was drawn by Captain Tuthill's complexion, which had darkened from its usual florid pink to a deep shade of vermilion. Though he sputtered ineffectually for a moment, the words soon flew from his mouth like bitter seeds. ''Wipe off the— I most certainly will not! I am the regimental surgeon, man. Not your damned squaw!''

With cool aplomb, Aaron slipped out of his own uniform coat, revealing the clean linen shirt and white waistcoat beneath. ''You *were* the regimental surgeon, sir. Now I am. And if I'm not mistaken, you are under orders to assist me until such time as you have obtained passage back to Pittsburgh.''

''Assist, yes! I thought you wanted me to help hold the lad down while you twisted—''

''You were mistaken,'' Aaron growled, his hands curling into fists as he towered over the portly captain. Then, sensing that a show of temper now would not further his aims, he relented, taking a step backward. ''It won't be necessary to 'hold' anyone. And as for making the surgery ready, I'm not asking you to do anything I would not have done myself had I opportunity. This entire infirmary could use a thorough scrubbing, but for now we have time only to prepare a small portion.''

Tuthill grew flustered once more at the intended barb, though suddenly his watery eyes narrowed and he said suspiciously, ''What do you mean, I won't have to hold him? You're not going to use any of that crazy Indian medicine, are you?''

Rebecca found the silence which followed more ominous even than Tuthill's words. She looked to Aaron for reassurance, but the defiant expression in his eyes only increased her trepidation.

''Crazy only because you don't understand it,'' Aaron finally replied, his voice deceptively calm.

''Who would want to?'' Tuthill crowed. ''That's not medicine—it's black magic! Let me warn you, Cambridge, you may be an Injun-lover at heart, but if you want to keep your neck out of the noose around here you best forget all this mumbo jumbo before you kill the boy.''

"He won't be hurt. Just put to sleep through the most painful part of the procedure.''

"I never heard of such nonsense!''

After staring long and hard at the elder surgeon, Aaron at last replied, "But *I* know what I'm doing.''

And you do not was the unspoken implication, though Tuthill seemed to have no trouble grasping Aaron's meaning. His food-stained coat rose as his chest puffed higher than Rebecca could have imagined. She hardly realized she was clutching the stove's iron poker so tight her knuckles stood out pale against her hands.

"I'll have none of it, I tell you!" Tuthill raged softly. "And furthermore, I'll do everything in my power to have you thrown into the holding cell where you belong. Wielding witchcraft on innocent people—my word! I was warned about you, Cambridge. I didn't want to think a fellow man of medicine could be so misguided. But it's true''—he leaned forward to make a show of sniffing the air—"you've lived so long with the Indians you're starting to smell like one.''

Glaring at him, Rebecca rammed her fists against her hips. "I'm surprised you can tell, with the scent of strong spirits filling your own nose!" Indignation for Aaron's sake made her quiver like a sapling braced against an autumn wind. "And as for refusing to help, why, six months ago I disdained to let you touch my son. Now I remember why!''

At first Tuthill seemed to waver under this fresh and unexpected attack, but then the sneer resumed its place on his thick lips and he lurched to a taller stance. "I suppose he promised you a miracle, eh? Or is it something more than your boy's leg that lacks for attention, *Widow* Osborne?''

Rebecca blanched, then felt her cheeks grow hot with fury. But before she could offer a scathing retort Aaron stepped in front of her and faced Tuthill.

"If you know what's good for you," he gritted through clenched teeth, "you'll get out of my sight now.''

"And if you know what's good for you," Tuthill replied defiantly, his voice gradually rising so that his last word was nearly a shout, "you'll go back to the heathens where you belong. This town has no use for quackery!"

With an unsteady withdrawal, the officer pivoted, aimed himself for the door, and was through it before Aaron could help him out, as he so richly longed to do.

For a long moment the only sound Rebecca could hear was the clamoring beat of her own heart. She was afraid to look at Aaron, afraid of what she might see. After all, the other officer had made some very serious accusations.

But when she lifted her eyes, meeting Aaron's steady blue gaze, she was surprised and relieved to see a glimmer of something that might have been humor, as well as the shadow of a wry smile. Suddenly Tuthill's parting statement seemed less threatening and merely ridiculous; she felt the tension slip away from her.

Samuel's piping voice broke the silence as he hobbled through the doorway. Rebecca looked down at him, concerned that he was upset by Tuthill's earlier words. But the expression he wore was quizzical.

She held her breath as he glanced from Aaron to her and back again. Then, with all the resilience and cheerful enthusiasm of a ten-year-old, he asked, "What's quackery?"

For the next hour Rebecca was grateful to engage herself in the purely physical tasks of scrubbing and sweeping the small surgery. The work kept her hands occupied as she listened with half an ear to her son asking questions of Aaron, who had set a handful of herbs and roots to boiling on the stove. The odor emanating from the kettle was somehow sweet and noxious all at once; she could not imagine what he intended to do with the concoction.

Her question was answered soon enough when Aaron ducked through the low doorway with Samuel in his arms, placing the boy on a bench against the surgery wall. The small room was built adjacent to the infirmary—almost as an afterthought, it seemed—holding nothing more than a high table placed along one wall.

It was while she was scouring this table that Rebecca had noticed the signs of its previous use. Edging the two longest sides were beveled furrows that led to a wider, scooped trough at the foot of the table. Dark stains discolored the wood inside these grooves as well as the center of the table, where deep scars cut into the smooth surface. No amount of scrubbing could remove those stains, Rebecca determined with a shudder of disgust.

So it was that she felt immensely relieved when Aaron pulled the table away from the wall to the middle of the room and draped a length of clean muslin over it. Next he moved to the window, unfastening the shutters and throwing them wide.

"Just as I thought, the fog's completely lifted."

Bright sunshine streamed through the open portal, eliminating the pervasive gloom that had first characterized the room. Rebecca breathed deeply of the mixed scents of soap, wet wood, and fresh morning air, and her own spirits climbed.

"So this is why you brought us out so early. I wondered."

Aaron turned and nodded. "Why some people continue to cloak the medical profession in secrecy and stealth is beyond me. I'd much rather see what I'm doing. And so far as I know, good clean air never hurt a soul, either." He lifted Samuel from the bench with ease, depositing the boy on the table. "Well, son, are you ready for a nap?"

Samuel grinned and shook his head doubtfully. "I'm not a bit tired. 'Sides, it's too light in here."

"You're right. That's why I made you a special drink to make you sleepy." Aaron laid a gentle hand on the boy's shoulder. "Remember I told you about it?"

"Uh-huh. Is that what you were making? How does it taste?"

"Not too bad. A little bitter, but I added some rosemary to sweeten it up." Aaron's voice drifted as he walked back to the first room, returning with a shiny tin mug in his hand. "Let me know how you like it. It's been a long time since I tasted any of this myself, and then it was made by an ancient Shawnee woman. I always suspected she added a little something extra to test the mettle of the braves she healed."

"Is it—" Rebecca stopped, biting her lip. She imme-

diately regretted her words. They sounded too much as if
she were challenging him again, and that was not her intention.

Glancing sideways, Aaron said expressionlessly, "It's
safe in the right dose. But most physicians don't know
much about the medicinal qualities of plants, as Tuthill
pointed out."

"Captain Tuthill can scarcely point his own nose out of
his bed in the morning, so do not fear that I value his
opinion over yours." Giving Samuel the bravest smile she
could muster, Rebecca moved to his other side. "Go
ahead, darling. I'll be right here the whole time."

Over Samuel's head Rebecca's gaze met Aaron's, and
the look of compassion and approval in his eyes caused
her pulse to thump erratically. Then her gaze dropped to
the large hand gently enveloping the boy's thin shoulder,
and the warmth spread outward, blossoming like a flower
beneath the summer's sun. They looked so right together.
She opened her mouth to speak again, then closed it on a
sigh. Some things were better left unsaid.

Aaron's hand remained in place while Samuel took the
cup and quaffed its contents as if it were a mug full of
sweet, creamy milk, then wiped his mouth with the back
of one hand. "All at once—that's how Skulley says a man
should take his licks. I guess I'll have to tell him the same
thing goes for medicine, too, 'cause it wasn't so bad."
Samuel's wrinkled nose belied his statement; then he
handed the mug back to Aaron with alacrity, as if afraid
to look inside in case there was more. "I'm gettin' sleepy
already!"

"Oh, you are, are you?" Aaron's throaty chuckle
seemed to curl around Rebecca's heart. "Then use this,
before you keel over and knock your head." Taking the
coat he had earlier doffed, he folded it into a compact pile
and placed it at one end of the table. "Lie down."

Pillowed against the dark blue wool, Samuel's tousled
blond head looked small and vulnerable. Rebecca reached
out to stroke his brow, and was gratified when he did not
pull away as he sometimes did of late, whenever he took
a mind to assert his independence.

"While you're lying here," she murmured, "why don't

you tell Aaron about the *new* fishing pole Skulley's making for you?''

Her suggestion was met with a grin, and immediately Samuel launched into a lengthy description of the project, from the selection of the perfect sapling to the finer intricacies of bending wire into hooks. Aaron appeared to listen with avid attention, making all the appropriately envious remarks, but Rebecca noticed that he had taken one of Samuel's hands and was surreptitiously counting the boy's pulse.

Shortly after, Samuel's words began to slur. His response slowed, and within a few minutes more his eyelids drooped and he emitted a gaping yawn. '' 'M tired now,'' he muttered, '' 'S good?''

''It is good, son,'' Aaron agreed softly. ''You're doing just fine. Just fine.''

Rebecca continued to stroke Samuel's hair a little longer, until Aaron stayed her hand, clasping her wrist in a gentle grip. ''I'm going to need some help, 'Becca. That's one of the reasons I wanted Tuthill here this morning. Wait here while I see if I can find someone else.''

''Can't I help? I'm strong, and Samuel's so little. What would you want me to do?''

''It's nothing to do with strength, or size.''

''Then let me stay.''

''You don't understand.'' They were still speaking in whispers, but Aaron felt the new intensity in her voice. ''This won't be pleasant, and even though Samuel is unconscious now, his body may still react. Do you really want to be here to see this? It won't do me or Samuel any good if you faint dead away just when I need you most.''

Rebecca's back grew rigid as she drew herself up to face him. ''*You* don't understand. I told him I'll be here the whole time, and I meant it. So you can fetch another man if you wish, but I am not leaving! And I will *not* faint.''

And then, as if to prove that she was inadequate to the task, tears welled in her eyes. She blinked them away rapidly, thankful to see that Aaron had turned his attention back to Samuel.

''I can't let you stay, 'Becca.''

''You can't make me go.''

Now Aaron studied her uplifted face, seeing anxiety mirrored in her dark eyes, and her determination as well. It reminded him once more that this was not the Rebecca who had once turned squeamish at the sight of a dead mouse or squealed over a gasping fish. Life had made her both sensitive and sensible, it seemed, along with adding a fair measure of steel to her spine.

"Very well, then. Come over here."

Rebecca could only hope that he would not see how her hands trembled as she placed them according to his direction beneath Samuel's shoulders. While Aaron manipulated the injured leg, her task would be to hold Samuel still, and to prevent him from lurching to the side should the potion prove weaker than it ought. The very idea that her son might be hurt made Rebecca's stomach harden to a tight ball, but she remembered, too, that he had suffered some degree of pain ever since the accident. At least he would be spared the worst of it.

Though the day had barely begun, the early sun fell directly upon them. Rebecca's dress clung to her uncomfortably, and she could see beads of sweat on Aaron's brow as he unfastened Samuel's knee britches and removed them.

With an expression of intense concentration, he began his examination. His hands, as gentle as always, moved up and down the area of the leg where the bone had first been broken, until at last they stopped at a place a few inches above Samuel's knee. "Here it is," he said, frowning. "I can feel the ends of the bone because they aren't quite aligned."

"Can you correct it?"

He did not answer, but again his brow gathered and the grooves on either side of his mouth deepened. After placing a block of wood beneath Samuel's thigh and positioning it carefully, Aaron looked over at her once more. "'Becca—" he started.

But she forestalled his question with a grave nod. "I'm ready."

He was struck all at once by her quiet strength, by the serenity which masked her own fears. Her dark eyes were wide and unblinking as they watched him, and he suddenly felt as if he had sunk into a deep abyss. For an instant he could not move, his fingers inexpert and numb, his limbs grown heavy and his chest hollow. The import of what he was about to do had not truly hit him until that moment. And with it came an awful certainty that chilled his blood.

If he failed her again she would be lost to him forever.

It had not even occurred to him that he wanted it otherwise, but now he realized it was the truth, and had been since the moment she stepped through the tavern door in search of a myth.

"A-Aaron?"

Her husky voice, tremulous now despite the firm resolve in her eyes, cleared his mind and unlocked the paralysis that had held him temporarily in its grip. *Reality now,* he thought with a self-deprecating grimace. He skimmed his fingers once again over the crooked thigh.

Rebecca focused her eyes on his hands, watching them move almost reverently over the soft, vulnerable flesh. She could see why the Indians believed him to possess great healing powers. With hands such as his, anything was possible.

Even conjuring a miracle.

And then they stilled. She could see the tendons on the back of his wrists grow taut, could see the pressure he exerted on Samuel's leg. Even in his deep sleep her son twitched uneasily, and Rebecca bent closer to hold him steady, praying all the while for the strength to withstand this ordeal. Her own hands felt cold and her legs oddly quivering, as if the blood had left her fingers to pool at her feet.

Remotely, Aaron was aware of her state, but he could not ease away from what he was doing in order to help her. "Sit down if you need to," he growled, unwilling to abide any distractions.

She shook her head savagely, as much to clear away the encroaching blackness as to gainsay him. When that brought no response she glared at him.

Aaron hesitated for only a moment, then leaned his weight farther over the table. Beneath his hands he felt the tendons giving way to the pressure; a raw, grinding sound filled the tiny room, underscored by Rebecca's terrified silence.

Then, with a loud report, the bone separated cleanly.

Swallowing hard, Rebecca squeezed her eyes shut against the waves of dizziness assailing her. She bit down hard on the inside of her cheek, relenting only when the coppery taste of blood and Aaron's voice drew her back from the edge of darkness.

"Don't give in now, 'Becca. We're almost done."

"I'm fine," she said tautly.

"Then you can let go of Samuel. There's a bowl of comfrey leaves near the stove. Pour in enough boiling water to soak them, then bring it to me along with what's left of the muslin. Hurry, now."

Only slightly off balance, Rebecca pushed away from the table to do as he bid. Aaron still held Samuel's thigh firmly between his hands, but the tension had gone from his shoulders and arms. Now he appeared to massage the leg with his thumbs, until another—lesser—grating sound indicated the bone ends sliding into place. Rebecca stifled a shudder, then exited to fetch the items he had requested.

When she returned, Aaron was no longer touching Samuel, but was arranging two wooden stakes on either side of his leg. "Hold these," he directed softly, "while I tie them together."

"That's not much of a splint," Rebecca said doubtfully, already anticipating the time when Samuel would want to hobble about. Neither stake looked strong enough to withstand much weight.

"This is only temporary, to keep him from disturbing the area of the break while he's waking. I want to watch for signs of swelling or redness for a few hours. Later I'll peel a circlet of bark from a tree the same size around as his leg. That will help keep him immobile until he heals."

"Then he'll be all right?" she asked hopefully.

Aaron swirled the steeping comfrey around the bowl, glancing at her sideways. "Time will tell, 'Becca. I've done what I can . . . no less than if Samuel were my own son."

"I know," she whispered bleakly, turning away.

He glanced down at the boy then, and so did not see

the quick tears that filled her eyes. For all his secrets, he was still a man capable of great strength and even greater gentleness, and she knew unequivocably that he spoke the truth.

So why was she so reluctant to do the same? *Because,* she told herself, *already he has captured your heart.*

And with even one more slender thread to hold her, Rebecca thought wretchedly, how could she ever hope to be free of him?

CHAPTER 13

Despite Aaron's efforts to encourage her to rest, Rebecca remained standing beside the makeshift bed for the remainder of the morning. Once it was clear by the lack of swelling that Samuel was in no immediate danger, Aaron left in search of further supplies, returning a short while later with a bundle which he placed in the corner before coming over to check her son again.

She could tell by his calmly attentive expression that he was pleased with the looks of Samuel's leg. Still, she would not budge from her place until a sharp rap interrupted the waiting silence. She looked up as Aaron left the room to answer the outer door.

It was full noon by now. With the sun directly overhead, the surgery was not as well lit as before, though brilliant light still bathed the floorboards nearest the high window and dust motes danced a tuneless reel to the accompaniment of a gust of fresh air. It was a day for fishing, Rebecca thought, stroking her son's hair. And a day for frolicking. Soon Samuel would be doing both.

From the outer room, she heard the entry of a scraping pair of boots. "How's the lad, then?" came a gruff query. Rebecca smiled at the familiar voice.

She pushed a lock of flaxen hair from Samuel's brow, straightening to greet their visitor. "Hello, Sergeant Haskull," she said as Skulley inched into the room with unaccustomed hesitation. "Please come in."

Skulley had attempted to make himself presentable. His lanky gray hair was clubbed crookedly and his cheeks were unusually slack, minus the customary wad of tobacco. His efforts touched Rebecca deeply; if she'd had any doubts as to his affection for Samuel, they would certainly now be assuaged.

"Sure it's all right?" He glanced over his shoulder at Aaron, who continued to urge him forward. "Just wanted to check, y'know, not be a bother."

Rebecca's smile widened encouragingly. "It's no bother at all, Sergeant. I'm sure you'll be the first person Samuel wishes to see when he awakes."

Skulley's weathered face grew a shade darker, the lines that bracketed his mouth deepening as he held back a pleased grin. He looked first to Rebecca, then back to Aaron. "Well, mebbe the third," he admitted happily. He moved closer to the boy.

Rebecca stepped back to allow Skulley more room, and her heart caught in her throat when the crusty old soldier gently fingered the lock of hair on Samuel's brow with a gesture as tender as her own.

"He's a brave 'un, ain't he?" Skulley crooned to no one in particular.

"He is," Aaron acknowledged from just behind Rebecca.

His voice was so close she imagined she could feel his breath stir the hair at the nape of her neck, though the sensation could have easily been the same bristling awareness that beset her each time he came near. With as much dignity as she could manage, she glided to the other side of the room and lowered herself to the chair Aaron had abandoned earlier.

"Samuel's leg will soon be healed," she informed Skulley. "Isn't that right, Captain Cambridge?"

Aaron looked startled by the unexpected form of address, though he recovered quickly enough. His tanned face twisted into grimace. "I said I *hope* it will heal quickly. God willing," he amended.

"Then the lad's in good 'nough hands, I reckon," Skulley added cheerfully. He bent to peer at the temporary splint Aaron had fashioned, then pinched the soaked muslin between two fingers and peeked beneath it. "Set a bone or two in my day—not many old coots my age ain't—but nothin' as tricky as this. Didn't doubt but that you'd serve the lad well, Cambridge.''

"Thank you, Sergeant. Unfortunately, not everyone will agree.''

Skulley straightened, nodding in agreement. "You got that right. That fatass Tuthill—beg your pardon, ma'am—he's already crowin' 'bout black magic. Any idea what he's talkin' 'bout?''

Quickly Aaron described the concoction he had brewed to ease Samuel's pain, adding that the prescribed roots had been used by herbalists for centuries, and not just by the Shawnee. "But I'm not surprised Tuthill doesn't know that," he added acerbically. "His idea of alchemy consists of transferring whiskey straight from the bottle into his gullet.''

"And from what I've heard, he's mighty handy with a rusted saw, too," Skulley agreed. He turned his narrowed eye toward Aaron, squinting thoughtfully. "But that doesn't change what he's sayin' 'bout you, boy. An' he's got his supporters, too.''

"Who?'' Rebecca cried out indignantly, before she remembered that rushing to Aaron's defense hardly proved her indifference to him.

Skulley glanced once in her direction with a benign expression, then turned back to the taller man. "You had any run-ins lately with a fella name o' Jessup?'' Aaron's grim silence appeared to be answer enough. "Hmmph. Thought so. Otherwise there'd be no reason for 'im to jump in so quick once Tuthill started blabberin'. Jessup an' the boys he calls his 'rangers' just rode in this mornin', an' already he's stirrin' up trouble.''

There was a stretch of silence that lasted but a few moments, though to Rebecca it seemed much longer. She fidgeted in her chair until finally she could stand the suspense no more. If Aaron would not ask, she would!

"What are they saying?'' she blurted curiously.

"It doesn't matter, 'Becca,'' Aaron replied with a small shake of his head. "I expected this. One of the reasons I wanted Tuthill here this morning—remember I said there was another reason?—was to curry some favor with him before he left in order to gain the men's acceptance.''

"I should think," she said dryly, "that just the opposite would be true. Any physician would be preferable to him—even you."

She said it with such a matter-of-fact tone, he could not help grinning at her double-edged compliment. "Thank you, m'dear. But the army is a strange organism. Closing ranks is not unusual. The men will go to great lengths to protect a fellow soldier, even one who does not deserve such loyalty."

"But you *are* a fellow soldier," she argued. "That doesn't make sense."

"It does to the troops," Skulley cut in. "Some o' these here represent the last o' the First American Regiment, an' just because they got whupped this past winter, they're still a proud bunch. The old-timers that fought with Harmar and St. Clair don't cotton to these new recruits from Fort Pitt. It'll take another battle or two 'fore they decide they's really just one army. This one here"—he gestured toward Aaron—"ain't one o' them yet."

"On top of which," Aaron added dryly, "I'm a known 'Injun-lover' among men whose sworn duty is to kill as many of the 'red-devils' as possible."

Rebecca had no response to that, though he still hadn't answered her first question, what was Jessup saying about Aaron? "But Jessup—?"

"The gal's right, Cambridge," Skulley interjected. "This is worse than the usual 'testin' out' period you're thinkin' of. Tuthill's madder'n I've ever seen 'im. An' this Jessup's sayin' he heerd of ye durin' the big war. Once he got wind that the doc was spreadin' fire, seemed he couldn't wait to add a spark or two of his own."

Rebecca opened her mouth to speak again, but she snapped it shut at the sight of Aaron's face. His tanned complexion had gone suddenly pale, and by the rigid set of his jaw she knew that he was feeling something worse than chagrin over the slurs to his reputation.

Finally he spoke in a dim, gray voice. "Jessup. I remember him, but not . . . not anything specific. Perhaps I should be grateful to him for shedding some light on my past."

"Wouldn't thank him too soon, 'f I were you."

Rebecca had the impression that if Skulley could spit at that moment, he would have.

"He's tellin' the men you was a deserter and a suspected traitor. Reckon most o' the fellas coulda looked past the first 'un. But turnin' against your own is a mighty serious charge."

A palpable silence invaded the tiny room. Though by the very act of sharing this information Skulley had shown where his loyalty lay, his statement had nevertheless carried the subtle inflection of a question. Rebecca's eyes flew from Skulley's openly inquisitive expression to Aaron's frozen features.

Aaron's hands were balled into fists, his knuckles white and prominent, though when he spoke his voice was outwardly calm. "Does he say more?"

He almost sounded casual, Rebecca thought in bewilderment, as if he were merely curious. But she remembered how he had described his mysterious loss of memory, and she knew with rare certainty that Aaron was desperate to learn whatever secrets Jessup held.

"Nothin' that'll help you, lad," Skulley said, "but that don't mean he's tellin' all he knows."

Aaron's stare remained fixed on the older man. Then, with a resigned shrug, he relaxed his stance. "You might be right. Then again, Jessup may know nothing at all about my past." With a quick, apologetic glance toward Rebecca, he continued, "This could be his way of getting even for the other day."

An unwelcome shudder raced through her at the reminder of Jessup's suggestive behavior. But she was forced to agree. In a twisted way, it made sense that Vance Jessup would feel compelled to undermine his fellow officer's authority.

With nothing more to add, now that both his support and his warning were conveyed, Skulley bid them goodbye and left with Rebecca's promise that she would tell Samuel of his visit when the boy awoke. In the wake of the old sergeant's departure, she turned her attention fully to Aaron. He looked as if he was waiting for her questions. He also looked as if he'd just lived through the worst kind of torture, but wished he hadn't.

Sucking in a deep breath, Rebecca said softly, "You really don't remember, do you?"

"Did you doubt it?" There was no censure in his tone, but perhaps a shade of disappointment.

"Yes," she admitted with a frank nod. She felt suddenly ashamed that she had so hastily dismissed as an exaggeration what was now painfully clear. "I doubted you. Not completely, but I didn't believe your . . . injury was as bad as you implied. It's difficult to understand how a person can forget important events in his life. And I suppose I was hurt and angry to think you had forgotten me as well."

He brushed a hand over his forehead, then studied it distractedly, moving his fingers through the filtered rays of light. A wry smile turned the corner of his mouth upward.

"I didn't forget you, 'Becca, and I'm sorry I led you to think that. I was hurt and angry, too, you know. How was I to know you had feelings for Levi other than friendship?"

Was that what her feelings for Levi had been? Rebecca wasn't certain anymore. Too much had passed between them to call it merely friendship, but how could she admit that she had never loved her husband as much as he wanted her to, as much as he deserved?

Aaron read the distress in her dark eyes as sorrow. Moving closer, he knelt before her, wrapping his fingers around her ice-cold hand. "I'm sorry, 'Becca. I didn't mean to open old wounds. Not yours, anyway. It's me that has to do the remembering."

Sighing, she leaned toward him. Without a thought to what dangers she invited, she reached for his face, gently tracing the scar with the soft pads of her fingers. "I'll help you, Aaron, as much as I can." She smiled crookedly. "It's the least I can do, after all you've risked for Samuel."

Bowing his head, Aaron said thickly, "Thank you, m'dear. I don't know that it'll do any good, but at this point I'll try just about anything."

She was touched by his openness, by his vulnerability. He was no longer the stranger to her that he was a week ago, or even yesterday. Not only had their mutual concern for Samuel drawn them together, but she had noticed that his manner toward her was less reserved—not quite intimate, but certainly less reluctant than before. He had, she remembered with a surge of warmth, begun to call her by the more familiar 'Becca.

Her fingers ached to touch the sun-streaked head bent over her hands, to cradle his head to her breast, to—

No! She would not allow such thoughts to interfere with her life, she told herself firmly. He was asking for assistance, nothing else. She owed him no more. She *wanted* no more.

Carefully withdrawing her hands, she folded them primly on her lap. Thankfully, Aaron responded to her silent message by retreating to the chair on the opposite side of Samuel. They could watch for signs of his waking while talking quietly, and it would be easier to converse, she decided, with her son between them.

"What do you want to know?" she finally asked. For some reason her stomach was fluttering uncomfortably, and her palms had begun to sweat. She tried to dry them surreptitiously on her skirt, but only succeeded in drawing attention to her nervousness.

Aaron chuckled humorlessly. "This isn't an interrogation, 'Becca. Rest assured, I won't ask for intimate details. Let's start off with what you heard about my death. Did you receive a message?"

He said it with such cool indifference, Rebecca was momentarily stunned. Then she managed a rueful smile. "Levi did, and as I recall, that first letter wasn't even about you. It was from the commander—Willett, was it?— and since it was addressed to you the post rider brought it to Levi."

"A letter to me? What did it say?"

"That Jacob was killed in battle." Rebecca had not thought to cushion her words, assuming that Aaron had known of his brother's death. But from the way he paled, the muscles in his neck standing out like thick cords, she was suddenly frightened. "You knew that, didn't you?" she asked. "Weren't you part of the same regiment?"

As she watched, Aaron forcibly relaxed, but when his

eyes once again focused on her they remained bleak and empty. "Yes, I suppose I did know. But until you said it just now . . . it's as if it were a piece of information there in my mind that I hadn't really examined yet. Go on."

"Shortly after that letter, Levi received another, this time telling us you were missing." Rebecca hesitated, then swallowed hard before continuing. Whether he thought so or not, these memories were as difficult for her to confront as for him, though not for the reasons he might believe. "For a while we all hoped, then one by one the others came to accept . . ."

"And you held on?"

She shook her head disconsolately. "As long as I could. But then my father passed away, too, and I had no choice but to give up. You had to be dead, I believed, or else you would have come back to me."

The resolute pain in her eyes nearly drove Aaron to rush once more to her side, but he restrained himself by remembering that she had not welcomed his comforting touch before, and would not again. Still, he could not let her suffer her doubts.

"I would have sent word to you, 'Becca, if I could have. But it was a month before I even knew I was alive, and another before I could travel." He sighed heavily. "And to be honest, any message I sent would have had the same result. The Aaron you knew *was* dead. What was left . . . what was left of me, you wouldn't have wanted to know. You were better off with Levi."

"Was I?" Rebecca didn't know which angered her more, his assumption that *he* knew better than she what she wanted, or the fact that he hadn't believed her love would stand up to a test. Shame crowded her throat. She had married in haste with unfortunate results, and she could not help but blame herself. First Aaron had not loved her enough to return, then even good-natured Levi had turned cold and bitter toward her.

She lifted her chin. "Levi missed you nearly as much as I. At times I thought the reason he wouldn't stay in one place was because he was looking for you. But that's not really why he was so restless. I tried to be a good wife, but gratitude isn't enough to make a marriage, any more than duty."

"I still say you were better off," Aaron insisted. His mouth twisted. "Though I'm surprised you didn't mourn for me just a little longer."

Rebecca shot to her feet. "I'll tell you something about mourning!" Her hands were clenched in the folds of her skirt, her voice quavered with suppressed rage. "If your idea of mourning is merely a prescribed period of time, something to be waited out until one is satisfied that propriety has been served, then no, Aaron, I did not mourn you. What I felt toward you was not an obligation, it was my very life! But how can I expect you to understand?"

Frustrated, she paced from one end of the tiny room to the other, halting in front of him, her small shoulders heaving with the force of her breath. "How can you berate me for not mourning you? I wanted to die with you. I would have, too, if Lenore and Levi had not convinced me that dying was too selfish to consider. And as for time . . . well"—she flipped her hand dismissively—"time was something I did not have to spare."

Aaron rose and took a step forward, clasping her upper arms in a gentle but firm grasp. He tightened his hold when she tried to wrench away. "Why?" he asked achingly. "If you loved me so much, why didn't you wait? Only a few more weeks and I would have been home."

"But I didn't know that!" she insisted, shaking her head frantically. "And I could not wait any longer! I was alone, Aaron. Frightened and alone. I needed help. I needed a husband, not time!"

His eyes bored into hers, seeking the truth with an intensity that caused her to shiver and burn all at once. His strong hands scorched her arms with a searing heat that weakened her resistance.

And then his fingers loosened, his grasp suddenly gentle, though his expression was one of dawning horror. She wished at that moment she could recall her words, for the shock and anguish on Aaron's face was unbearable to see. Rebecca raised her fingers to his cheek, letting them hover just above the surface, wanting to offer comfort, yet afraid to touch him . . . wanting to acknowledge what he was surely only guessing at, yet afraid of what would come of the truth.

She hadn't planned on telling him—not yet—but now that the knowledge was inevitable she wished she had broken the news to him kindly, not blurted it in anger.

" 'Becca," he rasped uncertainly, "is this about Samuel?" His eyes never left her, though she tried to elude them. "Answer me, 'Becca. Is Samuel mine?"

No other words could have given her the power to resist. But his sudden claiming of the one thing that had given her strength over the years caused her to bristle with resentment. Jerking out of his arms, she took a step backward, stopping when her spine met with the table in the center of the surgery.

She drew herself tall, answering in a voice as firm and sure as she could muster. "You may have fathered my son, Aaron, but whatever else you think, Samuel is mine."

CHAPTER 14

Aaron stared at her, nameless emotions crowding the voice from his throat. Ignoring the fact that her chin was thrust forward defiantly and her eyes sparkled with both tears and an unmistakable challenge, he stepped closer to Samuel, reaching out a shaking hand to tentatively touch the boy's head. He almost expected her to slap his hand away, but instead he heard only a sharp, indrawn breath as he ran his fingers lightly over the tousled blond hair.

His son. Samuel was his son.

His chest ached with mounting pressure, and to his chagrin, Aaron realized he was perilously close to tears himself.

"Why didn't you tell me before?"

In the interval before Rebecca answered he heard the hollow thump of drums calling the troops to inspection, their echo sounding far away and disconnected from this place. This was how he felt himself, Aaron thought. His life had changed so radically in the past week, he felt suspended in midair, ungrounded and uncertain. From freedom to duty, from Shawnee to soldier, all because he wanted a few weeks of his life back from the deep, black well of his mind.

And now this. First Rebecca, and then his son. More than he had wanted—more than he deserved.

"I—I wasn't sure I wanted to tell you," Rebecca replied haltingly, but with a frigid quality that warned him not to ask for what she would not give. "But my conscience, and Lenore, convinced me that you had the right to know, because it's the truth. That's all."

All? Aaron peered down at Samuel, seeing now what he had not thought to examine before. The boy's fine-boned features and pointed chin were the same as Rebecca's. Aaron had assumed that Samuel's thinness was the result of Levi's heritage, for his friend had been lanky all his life. But now he recalled that he had also been small and wiry as a child, with the same agility and quickness that Samuel, despite his injury, had apparently enjoyed. The downy wisps of fair hair Aaron now caressed had matched his own before the years had touched him. He thought, too, of the sister who had not lived past childhood, and how Samuel's lively blue eyes echoed his memories of Sara. And most obvious of all, the name Samuel honored not Levi Osborne's family, but Aaron's own father—and himself, Aaron Samuel Cambridge.

His heart twisted inside his chest. "Will you tell him?"

Rebecca made no move, but he thought he could feel the rush of air as she sucked in a deep breath.

"I hadn't thought of it."

"He has a right to know, too."

"Why?"

"Because it's the truth." He looked up in time to see the irritation flicker through her eyes as she realized her own words had turned against her.

She recovered quickly, though, and said in a dignified voice, "Truth or not, I don't see what good it will do Samuel. He would have questions . . . doubts. He's always believed Levi was his father. There's no good reason to tell him otherwise."

With an effort, Aaron suppressed the first retort to spring to mind, knowing instinctively that anger would drive Rebecca from him. Taking a step away from the table, he crossed his arms stubbornly. "That rationale may have been valid before, but not now."

Apparently unperturbed, Rebecca pinned him with a steady gaze. "Why not? Nothing has changed."

"You're wrong, 'Becca!" he exploded. "Everything has changed."

"What has? The fact that you are alive? I'm willing to concede as much, but no more. It doesn't alter the past. You abandoned us, Aaron." There was accusation in her voice; otherwise, she seemed as composed and emotion-less as if she were reciting the alphabet. It made him fu-rious.

"If I had known you were carrying our child—"

"You would have done what? Let me know you weren't dead? Returned to me out of a sense of obligation? Forgive me, Aaron, but I hardly find that a comfort."

His head began to throb in time with the dull ache in his chest. But worst of all was the knowledge that she was right. Samuel's existence didn't change the fact that he would have been a poor excuse for a husband. He had been trapped in a nightmare then, a living hell that had scarcely abated over the past ten years.

He had spared her one kind of pain in exchange for another.

Shoulders sagging dispairingly, he dropped to the hard wooden chair. With rough fingers he raked one hand through his hair, heedless of pulling loose his formerly neat queue.

"You're right, 'Becca. It wouldn't have made any dif-ference then. I was in no shape to do you or Samuel any good. I still say it was better that I didn't burden you with my problems."

He waited for some kind of response from her, but she kept her dark eyes fixed on some point beyond his left shoulder, and except for the minute trembling of her lower lip, she did not confirm or deny his statement. With a sigh, he continued.

"Levi took care of you in my stead and for years got nothing from me except bitter resentment, though he never knew it, thank God. Now, at least, I can repay him in kind. I don't know what the future holds, but whatever it brings, I'll do my duty by you, 'Becca. I owe you that much."

Her heart sank. Duty? That was exactly why Levi had married her, and look how miserably that had turned out. "You don't owe me a thing."

Her eyes flashed with indignation and something else he could not fathom, but which she obviously did not want him to see. She moved briskly away, gathering up the bowl and dried cloths discarded that morning. Her voice was tight.

"As you said, Levi cared for us well enough, and I'm no longer a frightened young girl. I've a prosperous store and money set aside. So you see, there is nothing I need from you."

She made to escape to the outer office, but Aaron leaped up, sidestepping quickly to cut her off just this side of the door. Through her sleeve he could feel the tremor that shook her arm; she refused to look up at him but stared stonily ahead.

"What of Samuel?" he asked quietly. "A boy his age needs a man to show him his way."

Rebecca's fingers tightened around the bowl. "He has his older cousins to look up to, and Skulley. Samuel won't be the first child to grow up fatherless, and I daresay he won't be the last."

"He is not fatherless," Aaron insisted. "And I cannot give back the knowledge that I have a son. Let me try to make up for lost time, 'Becca."

She gnawed on her lower lip, then shook her head sadly, resolutely. "I shouldn't have told you, because it's too late for that."

Releasing her arm, Aaron watched her slim, straight back as she slipped through the doorway. "We'll see," he remarked softly, more to himself than to her. "We'll see."

Rebecca refused to allow herself the luxury of tears. Not while she bustled about in the outer room, pretending to busy herself with straightening the disorder, nor when she returned to the surgery and saw Aaron bent over her son, studying Samuel with a look of anguish and heartbreaking wonder on his face.

She ought to be rejoicing that Samuel's recovery was proceeding well, but instead she felt miserable and bone-weary. Leaning tiredly against the doorframe, she was overwhelmed with an aching desire to be home.

Home with Samuel, healthy and whole. Home where each moment of the day was carefully arranged and well within her control.

Home—and far away from Aaron.

As if reading her thoughts, he lifted his head to gaze at her with solemn eyes. If she hadn't known better she might have mistaken his look as one of tenderness.

"You're exhausted," he said, coming around the table to grasp her elbow gently. "Come here."

"I'm fine."

"No, you aren't. You're about ready to drop."

At first she thought he intended to lead her to a chair, but with a firm tug, he pulled her toward him. He gathered her into his arms with a compelling force that allowed her no room for protest, and for the moment, at least, she offered only a token resistance, though she remained stiff and unyielding.

"Relax, 'Becca, you've had a rough day. Let me hold you. Stop being stubborn for just a minute."

"I can't," she protested, her voice muffled against his shirt. She tried to muster some genuine indignation, but her words came out sounding plaintive and ineffectual. "I have to be strong for Samuel."

But his warm hands felt so good pressed lightly against her back that for a moment she almost wished she could let go, that she could let all her worries slip away while she simply rested her head on Aaron's broad shoulder. She opened her mouth to protest again, and all that came out was a shuddering sigh as he began to move his hands up and down in a comforting caress. Before she knew it, she was melded against him like tallow fitted to a candle mold, and her own arms had crept around him, her hands splayed over his muscular back.

She could feel his heart beating a steady, reassuring cadence beneath her ear. His chest rumbled as he spoke; his breath fanned her brow.

"This isn't so bad, is it?"

"Mmmh," she murmured in return, afraid that if she spoke, she would choke on the tears of weariness that lumped in her throat. She let him speak instead, allowing his words to flow over her like a healing balm.

"You've been so brave, m'dear, for such a long time. I'm proud of you. You've become a beautiful and courageous woman, 'Becca. More beautiful than a field full of wildflowers, more courageous than a Shawnee warrior.

Samuel is lucky to have you for a mother. I'm glad you came to me for help. It's right that we're together now—''

"No, Aaron!" Pushing away from him, Rebecca roused herself from the seductive web he had tried to spin around her. "I told you before, nothing's changed. I've worked hard to make a life for Samuel and me, and I won't let you step in and ruin it. I won't have him hurt again."

He appeared stunned by her sudden reversal; then his eyes narrowed perceptively. "Is it Samuel you're worried about, or yourself? You're the one harboring old resentments, while from what I've seen of the boy, he'd welcome me as a father."

"Don't flatter yourself," she said derisively. "I got over you years ago, and as for Samuel . . . why, he'd take to *any* man that paid him some attention. I've *seen* the disappointment in his eyes when his fa—when Levi ignored him. On top of that, Levi was scarcely home more than a few months a year, not nearly enough for Samuel to get to know him. Do you think I want to see him go through that again?"

"You can't blame me if Levi had the wanderlust," Aaron retaliated.

"And why not? It was you he was trying to emulate, you who put the stories of far-off places into his head. And you're every bit as bad as Levi, wandering around the forest, living with the Indians."

She stopped, realizing that now her arguments had begun to sound less valid. First Aaron had slipped past her defenses with kindness; now he seemed to be diverting her anger away from the main subject. Rebecca sighed dejectedly.

"Trading accusations will get us nowhere," she pointed out. "What happened in the past is over and done with; we both made choices and now we have to live with them."

He looked as if he was about to disagree, but she quickly continued, forestalling any protest. "What happens to Samuel and me from now on is *my* decision. I want a normal life for him—and yes, for me too. He doesn't show it much, but I know Levi's death has affected Samuel. This isn't the right time to tell him . . . to tell him about you."

Aaron's frustration grew with every passing minute, but he forced himself to speak rationally. "I'll concede that it might be better to tell Samuel later, after he has a chance to get to know me. But that doesn't mean I'll stay away from him while I'm waiting. I want to spend time with him while I can, 'Becca. And with you."

With her? For an instant her heart cascaded to a stop. Then she remembered that he had already admitted to feeling an obligation to her, a debt. It was Samuel he wanted. She was merely an afterthought.

Rebecca wrapped her arms around herself as if she were cold. "So you want to spend time with him?" she asked caustically. "Let him get to know you better, maybe even begin caring for you, is that right?"

"Yes, damn it!" Aaron cursed in a low voice. "What's wrong with that?"

"Nothing." She shook her head sadly. "Until you have to go. How will he deal with the loss of *two* fathers? What happens to Samuel then?" *What happens to me?*

Aaron paused a moment before saying, "You have an even lower opinion of me than I thought."

The hurt and disappointment in his voice was undisguised, but Rebecca could not allow herself to be moved by them. It was Samuel she must think of. Samuel she was trying to protect.

"What else am I to think, Aaron?" she asked, her tone gentle now, tinged with regret. "You claimed you loved me once, yet it wasn't enough to hold you. You've spent years living in the wilds, free of all that is civilized and decent. You've thrown away your life, Aaron, and you can't even remember why."

"The Shawnee would take exception to your opinion," he replied in a tightly controlled voice. "They consider themselves both civilized and decent. And as for throwing my life away, I'm a valued member of the Shawnee tribe. But that's not the point. Samuel is my son, and I'm here now!"

"But for how long? You were right, Aaron, when you said you're a different man now. You live a life I don't understand, and even though you're trying to reconcile with whatever happened during the war, what if you can't?

What if you do remember, and whatever horrors sent you off the first time take you away again? Can you promise that you'll come through this without worse scars than before? My God, you can't even promise that you won't hang!''

For an endless moment he stared at her. Tears pooled in Rebecca's eyes as she watched indecision ravage his face. Then his shoulders slumped in defeat.

"You know I can't make those promises," he finally said. He lifted his head. "But neither could any other man, 'Becca. What you're asking is impossible. *Every* life is full of risk. Granted, right now my situation is more uncertain than most, but you can't expect guarantees."

"I don't," Rebecca retorted, squaring her shoulders and tilting her chin high. "But I won't ask for heartbreak, either. Not for myself, and especially not for Samuel. You chose a life that didn't include us. Until you're ready to give it up, don't even consider interfering with mine."

Before he could answer, a sound from the nearby table made her swing her head around. Samuel was stirring.

"He's waking," she said unnecessarily, rushing to her son's side.

Aaron's jaw tightened as he struggled to hold back his anger at having her dismiss him so easily; then he, too, moved closer to his son. Though still held by sleep, Samuel tossed his head slightly, his pale eyelids twitching as if the eyes beneath them were dancing merrily. A light film of perspiration dampened his brow; Aaron checked for signs of fever and was gratified to find none.

"He is gaining consciousness," he confirmed. "It may be a while before he's fully awake, so let's get the splint on now."

He was glad he'd gone out earlier in search of just the right tree to use as Samuel's splint. The length of curled bark lay where he had placed it in the corner after returning to the surgery. It needed only to be cut to the proper size before he could set the boy's leg properly.

He worked quickly and efficiently, measuring the elm bark against Samuel's thigh before peeling a couple of inches from one end. Rebecca watched, silent and suspicious.

Aaron could not put from his mind her belief that he
would hurt one of his own. "Hold him quiet, now," he
said more curtly than he intended. Removing the dried
poultice, he carefully wrapped Samuel's leg with a length
of soft muslin. Next he pried open the curved bark, set it
around Samuel's thigh, then allowed it to resume its natural shape. With strips of cloth he tied the bark closed,
binding it firmly so that the result was a perfectly fitted
splint, one which would not bend, no matter how much
the boy thrashed or flailed.

He stepped back to survey his handiwork. *As easy as
always*, Aaron thought. But to his surprise, his hand shook
as he scraped his fingers through his own damp hair.

"Th-that's very clever," Rebecca commented, prodding
the rigid bark with one finger. "And much stronger than
a regular splint."

"It's a method the Shawnee have been using for gener-
ations," he said acerbically before pulling a light blanket
over Samuel's lower body. "One of their more 'civilized'
accomplishments." He turned away, striding toward the
other room.

She had deserved that, Rebecca admitted inwardly. In
making her point she had inadvertently insulted him and
his friends. But she held fast to her resolve.

Lowering her gaze to her son, she was surprised to see
that Samuel was awake now. His skin was pale, but his
lips twitched in a valiant attempt to smile.

"Good afternoon, sleepyhead," she whispered, her
voice nearly breaking. Rebecca wondered if she should
call out for Aaron, then reconsidered. Just for a few more
minutes, she would keep Samuel all to herself. "How do
you feel?"

"Funny," he croaked weakly. "My head's spinnin', an'
I'm thirsty."

"That's probably from the medicine, darling. I'll ask
Aaron in just a second if you can have some water."

He nodded, and she touched his brow, pushing a lock
of golden hair back from his eyes. He felt clammy beneath
her hand, but not feverish. "Does your leg hurt?"

"A little. Not as bad as last time. I guess Cain fixed it
good, huh?"

Her pulse fluttered a bit, and she smiled reassuringly. "Yes, he did. You'll be right as rain in no time."

Samuel nodded again, this time with more vigor than before, yet Rebecca was quick to note that his eyes had filled with tears. "What is it, Samuel? What's wrong?"

Though he struggled manfully to contain them, one large teardrop spilled down the side of his face. "Nothin', Ma," he replied stoically. "I just want to go home."

Her heart nearly breaking in two, she leaned forward to brush his forehead with a kiss. She ached with love for him, and her mind raged with helplessness at the knowledge that she could not protect him from pain forever. But she would try, by God! She would try.

"Soon, darling," Rebecca whispered prayerfully. "We're going home soon."

CHAPTER 15

Out in the drill yard, Infantry Captain Vance Jessup swaggered across the hard-packed earth made firm by the weight of thousands of boots. His own leather footwear gleamed, reflecting the sun's brightness just as the buckle on his sword belt and the double row of pewter buttons lining his coat did.

He was, self-admittedly, the image of a perfect soldier. He hoped the time he had spent sprucing himself up would not prove to be wasted. Carswell had an eye for such things, Jessup had discovered. Jessup would need every edge to get past the wily old coot. A man who noticed one little detail might just as easy hone in on another.

When he reached the outer doors of the major's quarters he gave the door a single hard rap. Within moments it was opened by a red-faced Corporal Lutz.

"Captain Jessup," he squeaked, "how good to see you again, sir." Once the door was closed firmly behind him, however, Abner Lutz dropped his facade of military protocol and wrung his hands together gleefully. "I'd heard you rode in today, sir. I was hoping you'd report soon."

"I wanted to wash off some of the travel stain . . . if you know what I mean." Jessup had wandered over to look at the clutter of papers on the corporal's desk. Now he looked up sideways, his mouth stretched into a grinning leer.

"Oh . . . oh, yes!" Lutz paled, but he stiffened his spine and tried to affect a look of great worldliness. "It's amazing how some people despise the sight of a little blood. Especially when it's only Injun blood."

"Exactly. You're all right, Lutz. Maybe there *is* more to you than a puling clerk."

Abner Lutz gulped noisily, choosing to ignore the insult in favor of the captain's goodwill. After twenty years of bearing his brothers' cruel teasing, Lutz was inured to most unkind remarks. At least here in the army he could rise above—figuratively, anyway—the other common enlisted men. All it took, he had learned, was sticking with the right people. Major Carswell wasn't bad to work for, but he wouldn't be around long enough to help Lutz. Jessup, on the other hand, fit in with this untamed territory like he was born to fight redskins. Lutz admired his swaggering confidence more than anything.

"I *know* I can be a good soldier, if only someone'd give me the chance. And I can help you, too, sir. I would be willing to give you information. If you were to want it, I mean."

Jessup's eyes narrowed suspiciously. Ever since coming to Fort Washington, this Lutz fellow had been hanging to his coattails, yessir-ing and bobbing up and down like a damned puppet. Jessup didn't really think this whining pup could help further his career, but obviously the pudgy corporal thought the reverse was so. And truth to tell, Jessup didn't mind the adulation one bit. "What kind of information?"

"In*side* information." Lutz puffed up like a toad. "Like who's been spending hours on end with the major, poring over old maps. And who rushed in here last night to whine about how his Injun friends are getting scalped."

"Cambridge!" Jessup hissed. He felt his neck grow hot beneath the tight stand-up collar. "What else did they talk about?" Suspicion gnawed a raw spot in his confidence.

"I don't know for sure, Cap'n. But I can find out. Major Carswell didn't bring his own aide with him, being as this is a temporary assignment. *I* handle all his paperwork: officer's records, troop assignments . . . even personal correspondence. Some of it," he added slyly, "is *very* sensitive."

Vance Jessup did not have the opportunity to ask how sensitive before the door to the outer office opened to admit the major. He and Lutz both snapped to attention as Carswell halted just inside the door, his piercing eyes shifting from one to the other.

"C-Captain Jessup to see you, sir," Lutz said hastily. "He *just* arrived."

Major Carswell gave a noncommittal grunt. "In my office, then," he said curtly. "Follow me.

"Well?" said Carswell the moment the door closed with a resounding thud. "What have you to say for yourself?"

Jessup stood with his feet braced apart, his hands clasped behind his waist with his hat dangling from clenched fingers. Though his mouth twitched nervously, he managed to dredge up a wheedling smile. "The expedition went well, sir. We got sightings on two villages up the Miami and another west of that, near the Whitewater River."

"I did not *ask* you to site villages, Captain Jessup. Your orders were to spot hostile activity only." Carswell's tone was clipped and cool, his eyes revealing nothing as they pinned Jessup with a penetrating stare.

Jessup forced himself not to fidget, but he could not control the beads of perspiration that sprang out on his scrubbed forehead. "But sir, ain't they all hostile? The villages are where they go to make plans and such, and hold their war dances."

"Is that what those two boys were doing when you killed them, Captain? Making plans?"

Jessup swallowed hard, bile forming a bitter taste in his mouth. "What cowardly skunk of an Injun-lover came complaining back here?"

Silence permeated the room for a long moment, until Major Carswell finally stirred from his frozen stance long enough to kick the chair beside his desk into the center of the room. "Sit!" he commanded in a voice that was quiet, but lethal. When Jessup obeyed, he came around the desk to pace back and forth in front of his subordinate. "First off, no one came to me directly with complaints of your atrocities. I heard several of the men discussing it yesterday, a full day before you deigned to report in."

"Uh, we tried to get back, sir, but when we stopped for ordinance at one of the settlements to the west they was all out. So we circled round to McHenry's for supplies."

"Liquid supplies, I presume." Major Carswell paused to peer over his shoulder at Jessup. "I know all about your attempts to harass settlers into providing you with whiskey, and I've heard the gruesome details of your little expedition. In fact, it was probably the soldiers stationed at McHenry's who carried your tale back here so speedily, since you were . . . delayed." He turned his head, shaking it as if too disgusted to go on.

Inside, Jessup felt his blood begin to boil with anger and humiliation. Just who did Carswell think he was, talking to him like he was a schoolboy too stupid to mind his lessons? This situation with the Indians was war, damn it! And war called for drastic measures.

But despite his rage, Jessup realized also that Carswell could ruin more than just his career for him. "Sir, my men were tired and saddle sore and thirsty. After two weeks on the trail, I thought they deserved to have a little celebra—"

"Celebration?" Carswell's dark brow shot up. "Is that what you do after killing youngsters in cold blood?"

"Sir, they was *injuns*!" Jessup leaned back in his seat, stunned by the pigheaded obstinacy of his superior officer. "They were mere boys."

"Boys with loaded British rifles and knives in their belts!" Jessup retorted. "Sir, I'll admit that at the time I didn't stop to ask 'em how old they were. I don't know what you heard, but the two we killed were with a raiding party that nearly jumped us first. We couldn't wait around to make sure they saw us before we fired. I had to consider the safety of my men. It's kill or be killed—if you'd been out there you'd know."

Studying him icily, Major Carswell did not answer right away. Vance Jessup raised his head, meeting the major's gaze unflinchingly despite the trickle of sweat stinging the corner of his eye.

"Very well," Carswell finally said, returning to his chair behind the desk. He seated himself stiffly. "I have no choice but to trust your judgment on the subject of the attack, though you can rest assured I will question your men on the matter. But as for your methods, I'm afraid I must make my position perfectly clear. You are not—I repeat, *not*—to lift another scalp while under my command.''

Jessup cleared his throat. ''If I may argue to that, sir . . . there's a couple good reasons for taking scalps. One is that it confuses the injuns. They never know for sure if it was another tribe that hit 'em, since they're all bloodthirsty savages. The other reason is it puts the fear in 'em bad, sir. An injun believes he can't get to heaven without that scalplock of his. Any one of 'em'll think twice about messing with us, if he knows we're like to kill him *and* lift his hair.''

Carswell remained silent through all this, though a muscle in his jaw worked up and down. He steepled his hands beneath his chin. Jessup kept his attention peeled on those smooth, pansy hands, his own spirits beginning to rise as he saw that his explanation was working with the major.

''What of the rumors that your men *boasted* about these killings?''

'' 'Course they were happy, sir. Happy to be alive themselves—glad to be back among friends. And I suppose one or two of 'em might've stretched the truth. Is there some new regulation against bragging a little?''

After another lengthy silence, Carswell was the one to release a breath. ''No, there is not, Captain Jessup. I simply want it understood that I cannot condone brutality, nor will I put up with attacks which do not comply with army procedure.''

''I hear you, sir,'' Jessup nodded. His relief that Carswell could not pin him with insubordination was mixed with scorn for the commander's obvious weakness. ''Believe me, I'm just trying to do my duty, sir.''

''Part of your duty is seeing to the behavior of your men, Captain. And to your own. If you must end a mission with drunken revelry, then let the men do so here, in their own quarters. I want no more reports of harassing the settlers. We *are* ordered to protect them, remember.''

''It seems I'm not the one forgetting that,'' Jessup replied as he stood. But he regretted his incautious statement as soon as the words left his mouth, for Carswell's own lips tightened to a thin, hard line.

''There's one more thing before you go,'' the major said

with dry contempt. "I've been checking over your records, and I see that you fought under Colonel Marinus Willett's command during the war. Were you, by any chance, present at a battle near West Canada Creek in 1782?"

Jessup froze just an arm's length from the door. He turned slowly. "Yessir, I was. What's wrong with that?"

"I don't recall saying there was anything wrong. But I'm interested in hearing about your experience sometime." Carswell's tone was smooth, his expression calculating. "Not today, however. I'm sure you'd like some time to freshen up—after your *ordeal.*"

A droplet of sweat rolled from Jessup's forehead down the bridge of his nose and poised there, a fraction of an inch away from falling to the floor. His fingers itched to wipe it away, but he didn't want to call attention to the fact that Carswell's questions made him uncomfortable. Very uncomfortable.

On the other hand, it was shameful to have to stand here like this, with sweat pouring off his face. He wasn't even sure whether the major noticed or not; the bastard just sat there and watched him like a fat cat waiting to pounce on a mouse!

His tension mounted as he waited, wondering miserably which would occur first, Carswell's dismissal or his own disgrace. And the longer he waited, the more Vance Jessup seethed with hatred. Hatred toward the major, for making him squirm. Hatred toward the man who had put him in this position.

Even hatred for the army, which had trapped and held him for so many years.

And when the bead of sweat finally plunged from the end of his nose, dropping to the wood floor with a silent splat, he vowed that his hatred would also be his strength. He would show them. He would show them all.

"You are dismissed, Captain," came Carswell's sanctimonious command.

Without another word, and forgoing the customary salute, Vance Jessup turned and left the room.

CHAPTER 16

"I'm hungry, Ma. Can I have something to eat?"

Rebecca woke from a half doze, blinking hard. Her neck ached from falling asleep in the rocking chair with her chin tucked against her shoulder. It made a slight cracking sound when she turned fast to stare at Samuel. "W-what?" she croaked.

"I'm hungry. And thirsty, too. Did I miss supper?" Propped against the headboard of Rebecca's bed, Samuel gazed around the chamber in search of the absent meal. Though his face remained pale, the half circles beneath his eyes had disappeared and his voice was nearly cheerful.

"Oh, Samuel!" Rebecca hurried to his side, lowering herself to the feather mattress carefully, so as not to jostle his leg. She gently cupped his cheeks. "How do you feel, darling? I'm so glad to see you awake again."

"Me, too." His grin was genuine, if a little weak. "I was afraid you'd sleep all night, and then I'd miss breakfast, too!"

Tears of happiness and relief stinging her eyes, Rebecca laughed and hugged his thin shoulders close. "Well, we can't have that. I'll just go see what I can find downstairs, shall I?" She paused, almost afraid to add, "Does your leg hurt much, Samuel?"

Shrugging, he gingerly poked the bark splint, then thumped it a little harder with his knuckles. Rebecca could see his toes wiggle beneath the thin blanket. "Just a little. It's kinda sore inside, but I didn't even think about it till you asked 'cause my stomach was growling."

"That's a very good sign," a voice from the doorway stated gravely.

Rebecca whipped her head sideways, her arm tightening protectively about her son's shoulders. But Samuel wriggled free, leaning forward to peer around her.

"Hiya, Cain . . . I mean *Captain*. Guess what? You were right. My leg doesn't hurt anymore—much," he said proudly. "And I *was* brave."

"Yes, Samuel, you were very brave."

His presence filled the room, Rebecca thought, even before Aaron ducked through the doorway and came to sit on the other side of the bed. She had not seen him since yesterday, but it seemed almost a lifetime since then.

The previous afternoon was already a memory, and Rebecca was quite willing to have it remain so. She never wanted to go through a day of emotional ups and downs like that again, and had wasted no time in making arrangements to bring Samuel home after her promise to him.

It had not been so very difficult. Aaron had returned to the room when he heard voices, and after inspecting Samuel's leg, had given him another dose of the potent sleeping medicine and announced that he was progressing well. Rebecca needed only to wait until later in the evening, when Skulley arrived to sit with her while Aaron left for his nightly meeting with the fort's commandant, Major Carswell.

Even convincing Skulley that Samuel was best off at home had proved easier than she expected. True, he was reluctant at first, but in the end the old soldier's loyalty to the boy proved stronger than his untested friendship with Aaron, and he had rounded up a stout wagon in which to carry them back to the settlement at the top of the incline.

Most amazing to Rebecca was that Aaron had made no attempt to stop them. Surely he had discovered their escape last night, and on a fast horse could have easily overtaken the plodding wagon. Looking at him now as he peered at her from across the bed with an unfathomable expression, it was easy to believe he would go to any lengths to lay claim on her son. On her.

She would not let him, of course. Removing Samuel from Aaron's domain was her first line of defense. Keeping herself and Samuel both out of his sight would be her second. And from the way her heart tripped every time Aaron leaned his head close to Samuel's, she knew it would be the most difficult battle she had ever waged.

She stroked Samuel's cheek with the tip of one trembling finger. "What would you like to eat, dear?"

He tilted his head, giving the matter great thought. "Bread and honey, please, or jam. And some bacon, too, or maybe a big piece of cake, or pie and—"

"Whoa, there," Aaron interrupted, holding up his palm. "Not so much at once. A little broth, if your mother can manage it." After glancing down at Samuel's disappointed face he added, "And a slice of bread and honey."

"But I missed supper today!"

"And yesterday," Rebecca interjected softly. "It was *yesterday* morning that Aaron fixed your leg, and *yesterday* afternoon when he put the splint on. You've been quite a sleepyhead."

"I have?" Samuel looked doubtful, before he proclaimed triumphantly, "But then I should eat twice as much!"

"And you'll have twice the bellyache," Aaron warned. "Broth and bread for now, but you can have more later if you'd like. Fair enough?"

"Fair enough." Samuel stuck out his hand, which was quickly engulfed in Aaron's much larger one. He grinned up happily at his mother. "Make it a thick slice, all right?"

"All right," Rebecca said, laughing and shaking her head.

Aaron watched her as she left the room, his gaze following each graceful movement as she slid from the edge of the bed and shook out her skirts. The expression of maternal love she bestowed on her son before turning away made his chest ache.

His mouth flattened. His son, too. She could not change that, no matter how regal her manner. No matter how cold her heart.

An impatient rustling sound from beside him forced his attention back to Samuel. "Well, now," he said with strained heartiness, "how about letting me have another look at that leg?"

Downstairs, Rebecca fumed as she set about preparing Samuel some supper and returning to him as quickly as possible. Aaron's presence made her uncomfortable, but she was more distraught now, knowing he was alone with the boy. Would he ignore her wishes and tell Samuel the truth of his parentage?

But her attempt to hurry was forestalled by Lenore's quick footsteps on the low porch. The older woman took one look at Rebecca's stricken face and cried out concernedly, "What's wrong, 'Becca? Is Samuel feelin' poorly?"

Rebecca shook her head, realizing that her dour expression was misleading. She dredged up a smile. "Not at all. Samuel is much better, in fact. Captain Cambridge has said he can have something to eat."

"He's here?" Lenore's graying head swiveled toward the staircase, her dancing eyes narrowed speculatively. "I thought you said—"

"Never mind what I said," Rebecca hushed her. She did not want their voices carrying upstairs. "He came to check on Samuel, that's all. He'll be leaving soon."

"Why don't I take that?" Lenore offered, whisking the tray from Rebecca's hand. "You look half dead yourself."

"That bad?" She arched a brow.

"Sit down here a spell, an' I'll see that Samuel doesn't starve. I'm surprised Aaron hasn't told you himself to rest up. 'Course if you were to take sick, then Aaron'd get to doctor you."

"He wouldn't want to," Rebecca blurted. "He's only concerned about Samuel."

Lenore grinned gamely. "I'll believe that when the hens start layin' gold eggs." She paused at the bottom of the stairs, looking back over her shoulder. "You told him, didn't you?"

"Yes, and I'm sorry I did," Rebecca whispered vehemently. "I don't want him coming back here again."

"Hmmph." Lenore cast her one last doubtful look, then trotted up the stairs.

Rebecca sighed, slumping onto one of the benches pulled up to the trestle table. The hard edge of the table cut into her shoulder blades as she leaned back wearily.

Lenore was right. She was dead tired, and just now the idea of a hot bath and a good night's sleep nearly reduced her to tears. She squeezed her eyes closed, swallowing away the lump in her throat.

Lord, what a weeping fool she had become! And it was all Aaron's fault. It was bad enough she had to suffer along with Samuel through his ordeal. Adding the confusion of emotions that Aaron aroused in her was all she needed!

Footsteps sounded on the staircase just then, and Rebecca braced herself for another round of probing questions from Lenore. But when she opened her eyes, it was not her sister-in-law who gazed down at her, but a pair of ice-blue eyes.

From her position on the bench, Aaron looked taller than before, and the well-fitting coat with its silk epaulets made his shoulders appear broader than ever. Hatless, his gold-streaked hair gleamed in the afternoon sunlight spilling through the open windows.

"Lenore said you wanted to talk to me."

Sitting upright, Rebecca just managed to keep herself from sputtering a denial. Instead she squinted up at him with a frown. "Yes. Yes, I do want to have a word with you."

"Good, because I have some things to say to you."

Abruptly, he grabbed a nearby chair and swung it around, its legs scraping noisily across the planked floor. He straddled the seat, his arms resting atop the top rung of the ladder-back. The chair was pushed so close to her knees that Rebecca could not have escaped without shoving him away, which she sincerely doubted she had the strength to do.

"You had no business sneaking away last night. I wanted to keep a close eye on Samuel."

"And I wanted him home."

"What if it hadn't been safe for him to travel yet?"

"It was safe. You told me yourself the bark splint would hold his leg no matter what."

"Then if you wanted to leave, why didn't you ask me?"

Why, indeed? Rebecca met his compelling gaze with a challenging lift of her chin. "I'm unaccustomed to asking permission to come and go."

Aaron's jaw gave a frustrated twitch. "That's not what I meant, and you know it. I would have brought you home myself. I won't let you shut me out, 'Becca. You both mean too much to me."

"That's a switch." The acid comment was out of her mouth before she could recall it, and its effect was immediate. Aaron gripped the chair so hard his knuckles turned white, and she waited dispassionately for the rungs to snap.

His mouth twisted. "I won't bother to explain the circumstances again. Either you believe that I regret what happened ten years ago or you don't. But regardless, Samuel is my son and I want to be a part of your lives."

He had not said what portion of the past he regretted; his failure to return to her after the war, or the fact that he had placed her in dire straits to begin with. Willfully, Rebecca glared back at him. "There's only one problem with that happy scenario. I *don't* want you to be part of our lives. I don't even know you anymore."

With as much dignity as she could muster, Rebecca stood, trying to skirt around his legs without touching him. But he snatched her arm before she could move away, rising and tossing back the chair in one easy motion.

"You're lying, 'Becca," he growled, catching her in his indomitable embrace. "And I'll prove it to you."

She pushed at his chest, but he held her so tightly she could gain no leverage. One arm was wrapped around her shoulders like a steel band, the other gripped the back of her head, his fingers lacing through her hair. She could not move, could not escape him, but determination still outweighed for the moment the growing lethargy in her limbs.

"Let me go, you savage!" she cried hoarsely. She did not even notice that her voice was no stronger than a whisper.

"Not until you stop fighting me. I'm going to kiss you, 'Becca, and if you can still tell me you don't want to see me again, I'll leave."

She parted her lips on an exclamation of surprise, but he did not wait for her to speak. He touched his mouth to

hers, his kiss a gentle counterpoint to the forcefulness of
his embrace.

There was no haste in his kiss. It was slow and deliberate, recalling for Rebecca all the precious memories that
lay hidden deep in her heart. Though she fought to keep
from yielding to him, her mouth opened under the spell
of his firm lips, molding itself to the shape of his.

Dear God! she moaned wordlessly. She had remembered this in her dreams: the soft union of tongues, the
hard shuddering length of his body throbbing against hers.
Years slipped away and then stood still, locked in a time
of wild sweetness and desperate need.

Her hands sought his face, and though her eyes were
closed she could see the beloved features she remembered,
superimposed over those that were less familiar, yet no
less dear. Searching, she gently traced his damp brow, her
fingers fluttering over his closed eyes and the fringe of
lashes that brushed his high cheekbones. The coarse drag
of his whiskers was more pronounced than before. No
wonder she had not recognized him with a beard.

She continued her exploration, but when the tip of her
fingers touched the uneven ridge of flesh, Aaron pulled
away with a sharp, indrawn breath.

"Did I hurt you?" she asked fearfully, her eyes opening
wide.

But the expression he wore was not one of pain, but of
unconcealed triumph. Startled, and suddenly ashamed, she
jerked backward, banging the backs of her legs against the
bench.

"There!" she whispered furiously, gulping air into her
constricted lungs. "Are you satisfied?"

"Hardly." Aaron's eyes danced like blue flames. A
muscle jumped in the side of his jaw, the only indication
that he was not completely at ease. "This is only the beginning, 'Becca, darling. Or rather, the continuation."

"Don't count on it." Swinging away, she averted her
face so he would not see her scalding cheeks or the feverish light in her eyes. She could not believe she had succumbed to his seductive ways. It was such an obvious ploy.
"You said you would leave after one kiss. I'll thank you
to keep *that* promise."

For a moment Rebecca thought he would grab her again—in fact her entire body quivered with anticipation that he would. But when no hand reached for her, no touch jolted her sensitive flesh, she realized he would not. The silence behind her remained unbroken except for the harsh rhythm of his breathing.

After a lengthy pause, he spoke emotionlessly. "I'll have Skulley come by tomorrow with a mixture of herbs to make a special tea for Samuel. You can let him get up whenever he's ready, since he's already accustomed to using crutches. The bark should hold up well enough. If you have any problems, just send word."

She did not turn around as he moved across the room; she could mark his progress by the shuddering of the planks beneath his heavy tread. She knew when he reached the door because a shaft of sunlight fell across her feet when he opened it, just as she could tell it was closed when the light disappeared.

And she knew when he was gone by the wretched ache in her heart.

"We'll send an expedition here, north of Fort Hamilton, and another eastward along the bend in the Little Miami." Henry Carswell pointed to the inky line squiggling across the map spread out on a table. "That, along with the villages you've already placed, should give us a rough idea of what we're up against. Are you listening, Cambridge?"

From his place at the head of the table, Aaron lifted his head guiltily. Carswell smiled at him benignly from beneath his luxurious mustache, but his dark eyes snapped with impatience.

"Sorry, Henry," Aaron apologized. "It's been a long day."

Indeed it had. Rebecca's parting jibe still stung, and he'd had a hard time putting it out of his mind. Worse, though, were the lingering emotions their encounter had aroused. He had meant that kiss to teach her a lesson; instead he kept going over and over it like a schoolboy committing a poem to memory.

But those were excuses which would carry little weight with Henry Carswell, who was continuing forward with his plans for a peaceful settlement with the Indians, thanks to the progress he and Aaron were making at their nightly meetings.

Progress that could have been seriously undermined by a handful of fools.

Aaron peered at the upside down map and frowned. "Any more campaigns like the last one and we may as well forget the whole plan. The idea is to win the Indians' trust, not send them into a rage."

The major straightened, rubbing his ink-smudged hand over his beard. He gazed thoughtfully at the map for a few moments longer, than nodded. "You're right, of course. I'll be the first to admit that I erred in allowing that platoon to leave without specific instructions. My only excuse is that I thought Captain Jessup would exercise good judgment, as he has experience with scouting parties. And quite frankly, I can't be certain that he did not. Who's to say that the circumstances were not exactly as he described them?"

Aaron quelled the uneasy feeling that rose in him each time Jessup's name was mentioned. Part of that, he knew, was due to the captain's rude behavior toward Rebecca; recalling that suggestive leer was enough to raise the bile in anyone.

But it was the notion that Jessup was somehow involved in his past that most disturbed Aaron. Carswell had already confirmed that Vance Jessup was present at the Battle of West Canada Creek. This news had not surprised Aaron, but only increased his desire to get to the truth. The more he learned about the officer, the more disturbed he became.

"Tell me something, Henry," he asked abruptly. "Do you trust Vance Jessup?"

Carswell's leonine head swung around, and he raised one bushy eyebrow. There was a trace of amusement in his eyes, but he was careful not to let it show in the craggy lines of his face, or on his firm mouth. "I won't remind you that you're in an awkward position to question another's honor," he said evenly. "I'll just assume that your doubts about Captain Jessup's character stem from the unfortunate incident involving your . . . friend, Mrs. Osborne.

"As to my official opinion—yes, I believe Captain Jessup is a competent military man, worthy of mine and any other commander's trust. His service record is commendable, and though he lacks some of the, er, refinement of some of the other officers, I have no apprehensions about his willingness to perform his duties."

"Fair enough," Aaron stated, with only a slight tightening of his mouth. "It was inappropriate for me to pose such a question. My apologies."

"Apology accepted. Now, unofficially . . ." Henry Carswell seated himself in his chair, leaning back in a more relaxed manner than Aaron had yet seen him. "Unofficially, I don't *like* the man. But I learned long ago that it's not necessary to make friends to run a successful regiment. Captain Jessup does his duty, and for the most part he does it well. My only reservation about him is that he seems to *enjoy* that duty just a little more than a man ought. What is your opinion, now that you've had an opportunity to meet him?"

"Not much of an opportunity, if you ask me," Aaron said, shrugging. Other than the words they exchanged in Rebecca's garden, he had not actually conversed with the man. He told this to Henry Carswell, ending with a sketchy explanation of the vague, familiar feelings Jessup stirred in him.

"You know there's only one way to find out," the older man advised. "Eventually you'll have to talk to him. More to the point, my investigation into the charges against you demand such a meeting. Perhaps an enlightening dialogue will show me exactly where I stand . . . with both of you."

Aaron looked up sharply at this, and his gaze met Carswell's unblinking eyes. He swallowed the quick retort that sprang to his lips. The major was right. *He* was the one Henry should not yet trust. It was *his* past that was in question.

Automatically, his hand rose to touch the smooth ridge of scar tissue on his cheek. For an instant a vision flashed into his mind—a vision of terror: darkness and cold, the smells of gunpowder and blood. And screams.

His own? Aaron could not know for sure, but just as
quickly as it came, the vision passed away, leaving him
slightly nauseous and more than a little frightened.

"Cambridge? Are you all right?"

Carswell's concern pierced the fog that surrounded him,
and Aaron lowered his hand to the table to hide its shaking.

"I'm fine," he muttered, blinking hard to clear his eyes.
"And you're absolutely right. I should talk to Vance Jessup about that time."

"Very well," the major assented. "I'll make the arrangements." He leaned forward once more, effectively
ending that part of their discussion. "Now, to get back to
our original purpose, we still need to send out another
scouting party in these areas. I'll instruct Lieutenant Fos-
ter personally, so there is no mistake this time about how
he is to proceed."

Almost relieved at the change of subject, Aaron resumed studying the crude map drawn up by Henry Carswell's own hand. His friend had explained that while he
could have used the services of a cartographer, he had
wished to keep this particular project a secret, at least until
he and Aaron had made definite progress.

For all that, the map was fairly accurate, Aaron observed. He had located several of the Shawnee towns himself, and could assume that the others were reasonably
placed.

"Another expedition may confirm what we already
know," he commented, "but it'll take more than just
knowing which areas to avoid. Unless the tribes understand that we don't intend to invade their territory more
than we already have, they'll see any movement as threatening—any movement at all."

"Precisely." Henry Carswell rubbed his bearded chin
once again, a sign that he was deep in thought. "That's
why I brought you in on this, Cambridge . . . or should I
say, Cain? You're the only one that can win the trust of
the Shawnee. And if the Shawnee fall in line, so will the
other tribes."

Aaron's mouth twisted into a rueful smile. "That's a big
assumption, Major. It's like presuming that whatever the

Spanish do, so will the French, just because they are both white and live on the same continent.

"But it *may* work," Aaron added thoughtfully. "The tribes in this area usually maintain peaceful relations. And if there's one thing sure to unite them, it's a common enemy."

Carswell frowned, his gaze becoming distant as he stared at the wall opposite him. "But can the same be said for a common ally?" he asked. "Will they work together in the cause of peace? That's what you have to find out."

"When would you have me go?" Aaron asked, surprised at his own lack of eagerness. Rebecca's image flashed into his mind, and her words echoed through his head. *You say you want to be a part of our lives, but for how long*? The truth was, now that he had her and Samuel near him, he was in no hurry to leave for an indefinite period of time. To Aaron's relief, Carswell responded as if he had read his thoughts.

"Seeing as you have one patient already to care for, there's no need to hurry off. Frankly, that will allow some time for the men to grow accustomed to your place here. It's too bad Captain Tuthill caused such a stir. It would fuel their mistrust if you were to disappear too soon."

Carswell tugged at his beard thoughtfully. "I suggest that you wait a few weeks before approaching the Shawnee. We'll continue to gather information on the towns and villages, and when you feel the time is right you can lead a party out to make contact."

Aaron remained silent, though he longed to inform Carswell that it was not Tuthill, but Vance Jessup who was causing his reputation the most harm. He would not, however, hide behind the major's rank. He would do what Henry asked because he believed that biding his time was the only solution, both for him and for the Shawnee. The problems with the men were his own.

And as for Jessup—he'd deal with him when the time came, as well.

CHAPTER 17

In the following days Aaron threw himself into the task of sorting the odd collection of notes and receipts that Tuthill had amassed in his year or so as regimental surgeon.

The handwriting on the scraps of paper was so spidery and smudged, Aaron could scarcely tell which were methods of treatment and which were lists of medical supplies. Tuthill's records were as shoddy as his methods, it seemed. After an hour of scanning the mess, Aaron shoved it all from him with a disheartened grunt.

He was too distracted to think properly anyway, he decided. Rebecca's accusations still reverberated inside his head like a cannon shot echoing through the valley.

Had she truly remembered nothing of their love but the pain it brought? Cradling his aching head in his palms, Aaron grimaced. The pain had not been one-sided. But Rebecca had not wanted to hear that. She could not see beyond the heartache and hurt she still felt. Worse, she was using Samuel as an excuse to avoid confronting the problems between them.

Not that he blamed her, Aaron thought with self-contempt. He was a fine one to talk about confronting the past. Even though he knew Jessup was back at the fort, he had made no attempt to talk to the man.

A sound outside the open door gained his attention. Aaron looked up to see Skulley poking his head inside, his one eye squinted. "Come in, Sergeant Haskull. I didn't expect to see you back so soon."

Skulley hitched his left leg forward and limped into the room. He hobbled over to a chair, lowering himself with a grateful sigh. "Didn't see no reason to linger, seein' as the boy couldn't do nothin' but lie 'bout. An' it 'ppeared 'Becca was itchin' to get things back to normal. Not that she weren't hospitable, mind ya, but ah'm not the man what oughta be sharin' her table."

Choosing to ignore the broad hint, Aaron leaned back in his own chair, presenting a picture of professional detachment. "Then Samuel's doing well? No complaints?"

"None that I heard." Skulley crossed his left ankle over his right knee and tugged at his worn leather boot. "He spent most of the day talkin' 'bout what he's gonna do next month when his splint comes off. That there's one fine lad. A *fine* lad. What I wouldn't give to have one like 'im of my own, I couldn't say."

"I'm sure you couldn't," Aaron said dryly. "Now, what seems to be the problem with your foot?"

The sergeant had succeeded in removing his boot, and was now working his way out of a stringy stocking that looked to be made more of holes than wool. Even from across the room Aaron could see the flaky patches of skin and spots where the flesh was rubbed nearly raw.

"Woulda been fine, 'cept the mare came up lame on my way back, 'bout a mile outta Cincinnati. Had to lead 'er the rest of the way in, an' now I'm worse off than the bloody horse!"

"I can see that." Aaron circled the desk, stooping in front of Skulley's propped-up foot. He took care not to inhale through his nose as he examined the inflamed blisters. "I'll fix a solution to soak it," he offered. "That'll ease the pain some, and draw off any poison that might be thinking about setting in. But what you really need is a better pair of boots. How's the other one?"

"Nearly as bad." Skulley looked as if he were about to spit on the freshly scrubbed floor, then thought better of it. "An' as for boots, this here's one o' the best pair in the camp, 'cept them the officers are wearin'. Noncoms like me, an' enlisted men, we take what we can get. An' it ain't much."

Aaron sat back on his heels, grim-faced. "Are boots the only necessities in short supply?"

"Nope. There's always plenty more we can use . . . of *some* things," he qualified.

"You're the sergeant quartermaster. Why is there a shortage?"

"Because up till now, Tuthill's been in charge of approving the ration list. We'd put through a request for goods, then he'd go changin' it to suit himself."

"Don't those lists go across Major Carswell's desk as well?"

Skulley gave a pained grunt when Aaron lightly pressed on one of his blisters. "They would if that aide o' his, Corporal Lutz, ever put 'em there. But he was in cahoots with Tuthill, and now with that Cap'n Jessup. Carswell's a good man, mind you, but he's too busy lookin' at the whole valley to pay much attention to my feet."

Aaron stood, pacing the length of his office while Skulley wrestled with his other boot. "Are there funds enough to pay for the supplies you need?" he asked, his expression thoughtful.

"Just 'bout. Word was that the gov'ment voted us more money this past winter, after St. Clair got 'imself whupped. That's why we're swarmin' with new recruits."

"But Tuthill diverted those funds. Why?"

Skulley hesitated while he shifted the wad of tobacco in his mouth to the other cheek. "Lotta whiskey been comin' through this here fort. More'n even Tuthill could drink. But I ain't seein' the men gettin' it, either."

"So where is it going?"

"You tell me, Cambridge." Skulley squinted up at him. "Couple months back we had us an Indian attack up at Dunlap's Station. Two of the witnesses swore them Indians was drunk as lords, a whoopin' and fallin' all over themselves. It's not like Injuns ta go 'bout so poorly. But then, a man'll do crazy things when he's got the whiskey thirst in 'im."

Aaron stood frozen as his thoughts raced back over something he had heard from Wind at His Feet not long ago. The chieftain had shown concern for those of his people who regularly traded with the settlers. It seemed that the vigorous Shawnee were uncommonly vulnerable to the potent drink. Even in Wind's relatively isolated village, there were already a few men who allowed their lives to be dictated by the need for whiskey.

White traders had used this knowledge to their advantage for years. This was nothing new. But if someone here at the fort were doing so . . . Aaron's mouth tightened into a resolute line. "Was Tuthill in this alone, do you think?"

"Don't 'xpect so," Skulley replied, "seein' as he was scared to leave the fort without an armed escort. He musta had someone doin' his legwork—someone with plenty o' chances to run inta thirsty Injuns."

"Someone like Jessup," Aaron said with quiet intensity.

Skulley grunted. "That's a strong accusation. I don't like the cap'n any more'n you, but without proof . . ."

"It makes sense. You said yourself that Corporal Lutz has switched his allegiance to Jessup now that Tuthill is gone. There must be some connection in that. And Jessup has perfect opportunity to make contact with the Shawnee and other tribes whenever he's supposedly out on patrol."

"Hmmph. He strikes me as the sort what'd druther shoot injuns than deal with 'em."

Aaron made no comment, though he was not convinced by Skulley's argument. His distrust of Vance Jessup went far beyond what was rational; the man struck a chord within him, one that filled him with a deep sense of dread and impending disaster. At the very least, the officer was a hindrance to his and Carswell's attempts for a peaceful resolution to the Indian wars. That in itself was enough reason to be wary of the man.

But wariness would not gain him answers, Aaron decided as he stirred a handful of dried herbs into a tin tub of boiling water. And the solution would not be as simple as tending to Skulley's feet. As he listened with half an ear to the sergeant's continuous anecdotes about some of the other officers and their foibles, he came to a conclusion that left him both eager and apprehensive.

There was no sense in waiting for Major Carswell to instigate a meeting. At the first opportunity, Aaron would confront Jessup on his own.

* * *

His chance came sooner than expected, for not long after Skulley hopped barefoot from Aaron's office clutching his battered boots in one hand, another patient appeared at the door. Silas Carter, whom Aaron recognized from that morning in Rebecca's garden, paused with his fist raised to knock just as Aaron looked up from where he was reshelving the jars of herbs he had used to treat Skulley.

"How can I help you, Carter?" Aaron said cautiously.

"Umm . . . er . . . don't know that you can," the grizzled and filthy private replied. "Got me a problem with my feet."

"You've got blisters, too?" Aaron's brow shot up.

"Unh-uh." The man wagged his head. "Gout."

Aaron perched on the corner of his desk, crossing his arms. "What are your symptoms?"

"Don't know nothin' 'bout simpins, but my ankles is swollen, an' my toes are so puffed up I cain't hardly walk on 'em."

Though Carter at first appeared embarrassed to admit to his troubles, once Aaron began to examine the offending appendages, it was clear that the man was anxious to reveal every nuance of the disease for Aaron's consideration.

"Thought it was just the rheumatism when it first come on," he explained, "but then my stomach started actin' up, too—you know, passin' plenty o' gas and not much else. Joe Kinkle said his old uncle died of it."

"That may be, but your case doesn't appear to be too far advanced for treatment." Aaron massaged the swollen, hairy ankle propped up before him, hoping that this day was not an indication of his future as a regimental surgeon. He never wanted to get within ten yards of a soldier's foot again.

"Eating a lot of meat, are you?" he asked, then added casually, "And drinking plenty of whiskey?"

Carter nodded. "Both. But if I'd known they was the cure, I wouldn't o' come in here."

"They're not the cure," Aaron said, rising. "They're the problem." Quickly, he described a diet of grain and vegetables, along with regular doses of dandelion wine for the ailing private. Carter paled and gulped loudly. "I cain't eat no weeds."

"You must if you want this swelling to subside. And stick to vegetables and bread if you can. No game."

Carter looked doubtful. "That won't be easy on the trail."

Aaron caught himself just short of telling the private that his platoon would not be marching anytime soon, then thought better of it. Such an order should come from Major Carswell; interference from him would only add fuel to the fire.

"As for the alcohol, you ought to give that up as well. If you must eat greasy food out in the woods, at least you can wash it down with fresh water. No whiskey." Almost as an afterthought, Aaron continued conversationally, "Do the other men drink when out on patrol?" He handed Carter back his boots.

"Sure, but none of 'em's hurtin' bad as me," the private fretted.

"I'm surprised your officer allows you to carry whiskey rations. He must be quite a jolly fellow."

"He is at that. The cap'n always brings along plenty o' kegs for special occasions."

Aaron turned his back so Carter would not see his frown. So Jessup was toting whiskey out of the fort. But enough for just his men, or enough to possibly undercut the Shawnee resistance? He pivoted slowly. "I think I'll have to talk with your captain about the dangers of mixing alcohol with duty."

"Now, don't go doin' that!" Panic showed on Carter's splotchy face. "I won't drink no more, but don't go sayin' nothin' to the cap'n!" The soldier scrambled to his feet, tugging at his bootstraps as he stumbled to the door.

"Why not, Carter? Surely your captain won't blame you for seeking a cure for your illness."

"He tol' us to stay clear o' you," the flushed man admitted. "Said you was a quack an' a murderin' traitor, an' that you'd likely dole out poison as cures."

This came as no surprise to Aaron, but he was amazed at how the insult burned nevertheless. Taking a deep, calming breath, he said to Carter, "I won't mention your name if you don't wish to suffer the repercussions. But trust me, I will attend to this matter. In the meantime, you

come back later today and I'll dose you. Wait until dark,
if you want."

Carter hesitated, his hand on the door latch. The mangy
fur robe across his shoulders seemed to grow heavy as it
drooped lower. "An' you won't tell the cap'n I saw you?"

"Not without your say-so."

"All right, then. I'll be back."

Aaron watched the private peek out the door warily before slipping through. Then, after a moment's thought, he
donned his uniform coat and fastened the double row of
buttons up to his throat, snatched up his hat, and followed
the hapless Carter out.

The officers' quarters were located along the same side
of the fort as the surgery, and so only a few long strides
later he was pounding on Jessup's door.

"Whaddya want?" Vance Jessup bellowed. "I'm not on
duty till first sentry."

"Captain, a word with you, please?" Aaron insisted. It
was all he could do to keep himself from kicking his way
in. Anger seethed through his every pore and determination overshadowed any reluctance he might have felt toward confronting the truth.

There was a lengthy pause, then the grumbling voice
again. "Come back later."

"Now, Jessup. Unless you have something to hide."

Again several moments passed, then the door swung inward and Jessup, his hair stringy and his huffing breaths
reeking of whiskey, stood glaring at Aaron.

"Now, ain't you the one to talk about hiding something," he crooned menacingly.

His voice was low. Aaron had to peer around him into
the darkened room to see why. Three other officers, all
off-duty, by the looks of their disheveled appearances,
huddled over a low table sporting a half-dealt deck of playing cards and a few small stacks of coin. Two empty bot-
tles rolled around on the floor, and another stood ready in
the center of the table.

"As you can see," Jessup sneered, "I'm busy. Besides,
I've got nothing to say to you."

Aaron pushed his way in, unwilling to let this opportunity pass. "Well, I've plenty to say, Captain. And I don't

mind talking in the presence of witnesses. Unlike you, I'd much rather call you a blackguard to your face.'' He was gratified by the astounded expressions of the other men.

Jessup's skin grew mottled, but he managed to choke out a snarling laugh. ''So you don't like me, huh? What's your point, Cambridge? I got no time for this.''

Aaron almost had to admire his bravado; Jessup hardly showed concern over his accusation. Either that, or the man was truly innocent of any wrongdoing.

Aaron discarded that possibility quickly enough. ''By what right do you order your men not to seek medical attention? It's an officer's duty to put the welfare of his men first.''

''Which one of the bastards told you that?'' Jessup scowled.

''Then you don't deny it?''

''Why should I? Of course I told the men to stay away from you. They don't need any of your heathen doctorin'.'' Jessup looked to the other officers in the room for support, and received a couple of snickers in reply. ''Tuthill might've been a tad quick to chop off a leg here and there, but at least he wasn't an Injun-lover.''

Aaron took a step closer, his fists clenched at his sides. ''Tuthill was an incompetent fool. He was also a thief. But I wouldn't doubt you're completely aware of how much whiskey he ordered each month, since you and your men never seem to lack for a drink.''

''There ain't no law against drinking whiskey,'' Jessup spat, but his stance appeared to waver a bit.

''There is one that says regimental property shall not be sold or traded by anyone other than the quartermaster or his designated agents. Did you know that, Captain, or did that one conveniently slip your mind?''

''Are you threatening me, Cambridge? I wouldn't do that, if I were you.'' Jessup's voice had dropped to low timbre, gravelly and thick. ''Not considering what I know about you.''

Here, then, was the moment Aaron had waited for. He glared at the grinning captain, the tension hanging between them like a cloud of acrid smoke. A familiar rush of terror swept upward from the pit of his stomach; he remembered this feeling distantly, like a boy recalls the dizzying panic of falling from a tree or the repulsive odor of an animal carcass. He could scarcely dredge up the strength to ask, "What do you know?"

The other men in the room waited in silence while Jessup stared at Aaron through hooded eyes. After a moment he seemed to arrive at some decision, for he nodded his head slowly and said, "I remember you from West Canada Creek," he said. "Pompous young ass, you were, strutting around on the doctor's coattails like you were better than the rest of us. Never seeing battle yourself—no, no! You were too much of a coward for that—you were only good for patching up the real soldiers afterward."

The description numbed Aaron, made him want to cringe and turn from the room in sorrow and shame. For all he knew, it was the absolute truth, no matter how his mind rebelled at such a portrait of callow youth.

He was no youngster now, however, and Jessup could not get by with slandering his name. Not without good reason.

Aaron pulled himself straighter. "So what did I ever do to earn such contempt from you?" he challenged, grateful that his voice sounded much more confident than he felt.

Jessup started to open his mouth, then closed it again. He cocked his head perplexedly and sneered. "Nothing in particular. I didn't have much to do with you then, and I'd just as soon keep it that way. You see, I don't care to have truck with a murdering traitor."

CHAPTER 18

Rebecca stood at the window, nervously wringing a dish-rag that had long since given up its last drop of water. Outside in the fading light of early dusk, Samuel hobbled on his crutches, making his way across the grassy commons in pursuit of his cousins, who were absorbed in a vigorous game of tag.

"I'm gonna catch you, Zeb," his voice rang out in the still evening air. "Just you wait and see. In a week I'm gonna catch you."

"Maybe even sooner," Lenore commented, her blunt voice startling Rebecca. She had not heard her sister-in-law move closer behind her.

Rebecca turned with a sigh. "He is doing well," she admitted. "And I suppose I'm a goose for worrying so. It's just that—"

"You can't help it," Lenore finished with a brusque nod. "You're a mother, that's all. Worryin's part of the job."

Laughing sheepishly, Rebecca returned to the table, where a freshly baked apple cake waited to be sliced. She had invited Lenore and the boys over to sample the treat, partly to celebrate Samuel's rapid progress and partly to assuage the intense loneliness she had felt these past two weeks.

It's only from being cooped up in the cabin, she told herself firmly. *I should have gone to town today myself and let Lenore look after Samuel instead of the other way around.*

The problem, Rebecca thought as she reached on the

shelf for her carving knife, was that she was a coward.
She did not want to chance running into Aaron at the fort,
not because she was afraid of what he would do, but because she was afraid of what *she* would do. Why, even
thinking about him made her cheeks flush and her skin
grow damp with perspiration.

She glanced up quickly to see if Lenore had noticed,
but the other woman had taken her place at the window
and was following the boys at play with a pleased eye.

"Samuel's doin' just fine," Lenore pronounced. "It's
lucky for him Aaron knows so much about physicking, no
matter what everyone else says."

What everyone else says? Rebecca bit her lip to keep
from asking it out loud, but her ears perked up despite
herself.

Lenore did not disappoint.

"Folks in town are full of all kind of talk," she continued blithely, though Rebecca doubted she was unaware of
the reaction her words caused. "And the soldiers at the
fort are even worse. Seems most of the officers are refusing to acknowledge Aaron, though I suspect their poor
opinion has more to do with his past than his medical
skill."

"Do you mean the fact that he lived with the Shawnee?"

"That's part of it." Lenore turned, her craggy face
drawn into a frown. "That toad, Tuthill, started the talk
about black magic. Now this Captain Jessup is puttin'
around worse. He's sayin' Aaron isn't to be trusted because he's a traitor."

"A traitor! That's ridiculous."

"That's what I said to anyone who'd listen long enough
to hear it," Lenore said with a resolute nod. "But not
many was in the mood, I can tell you. I don't know how
to break it to you, honey. There're some who want Aaron
to hang."

"Hang!" Rebecca squeaked, the result of trying to
speak with her heart in her throat. She felt the dishrag slip
from her fingers as all sensation completely fled her ex-
tremities. With a movement deft and agile for a woman of
her size, Lenore caught the falling cloth and then eased

the knife from Rebecca's numb hand before that, too, plunged to the floor.

"I'm sure if that Major Carswell was planning to have Aaron executed he'd have done it by now," Lenore offered by way of consolation. "I wouldn't worry."

With a slight shove between her shoulder blades, Lenore propelled Rebecca to the table, where she slid bonelessly into the nearest chair.

"Is there anything else I should know?" Her voice was bleak.

"Well, there was some talk, too, about Aaron and you. I'll be blunt, 'Becca. Folks are wonderin' whether there's more between you than just Samuel's leg."

"I hope you told them that was ridiculous as well," Rebecca declared with a gulp. She frowned when Lenore did not answer. "You did, didn't you?"

"Oh, I told a few to mind their own business," the older woman finally admitted with a mirthless laugh. "But I don't think it's such a bad thing for folks to get used to the idea of you an' Aaron together. That way it'll seem natural-like if you take up with one another again."

"I have no intention of taking up with anyone," Rebecca replied weakly.

She didn't know which had taken the gumption out of her more, Aaron's dangerous position or the thought of weathering another scandal. She never should have let Aaron kiss her. What would her sister-in-law have to say about that?

But Lenore did not press further; she seemed content to grin at Rebecca like a cat playing with a cornered mouse. No need to pounce yet. "I talked with Aaron today, you know," she said slyly.

Rebecca's head snapped up. "You did?"

"Uh-huh." Lenore bided her time.

"How did he look? I mean, is he taking this hard? All the rumors and suspicion?"

"Uh-huh. Can't help but, now, can he?"

Nibbling on her lower lip, Rebecca toyed with the edge of the cake plate, rubbing her fingertips along the rim. "Do you think he'll be all right?"

Lenore waited until Rebecca looked up impatiently before answering, "Why don't you ask him yourself? He'll be along anytime now."

"What?" Thrusting herself away from the table, Rebecca jumped up, then hurried to the window where she could see clear across the commons to the top of the trail leading down the incline. Sure enough, a tall silhouette stood limned against the dusky sky, moving only to bend over close to the smaller figure limping toward him.

Her heart spun crazily for an instant before settling back into a rapid beat. She turned, pressing her hands to her flaming cheeks. "My God, Lenore! What have you done?"

"I invited him for cake, to celebrate," the grinning woman replied. "I told him how Samuel's up an' about, an' that it was high time he came a'callin'."

With a groan of pure frustration, Rebecca stalked over to the hearth, where she swung the kettle over the fire with a noisy clang. "I don't *want* him here, Lenore. Please go out there and tell him to go back to the fort."

"Too late," Lenore whispered back. The clump of boots on the wooden porch punctuated her words, followed by Samuel's high-pitched voice.

"That was fun, Cain. Swing me up again!"

"Next time, Samuel," came a throaty reply. "Though if you get any heavier you'll have to start carrying me."

His deep chuckle contrasted with her son's delighted laughter, reverberating through the cabin, and sending curling tendrils of heat around Rebecca's heart. She stood frozen for an instant, lost in a reverie of unspoken hopes and wistful longings.

Then Aaron ducked through the door, led by Samuel on his crutches, and the spell was broken.

"Evening, 'Becca," he said quietly. "Lenore."

"Glad you could make it, Aaron," Lenore greeted him. "Wasn't sure you'd want to come up so late in the day."

He glanced at Rebecca, who remained before the fire with her back to him. "It gave me a chance to finish some paperwork first," he said evenly. "And I don't mind walking in the dark as much as some people."

" 'Cause you're not scared of Indians?" Samuel piped.

"That's part of it, son. There's also something peaceful

about the woods at night. I enjoy listening to the trees talk to one another while I'm sneaking by.''

She had often felt that way, too, Rebecca mused as she watched the kettle of water begin to bubble. Funny, but she never imagined Aaron having such a fanciful thought. Behind her Rebecca heard Lenore push out a chair for him, and from the scraping sound knew when he had pulled it up to the table. But she waited until Lenore's noisy passel of sons entered the cabin before turning around.

''Hello, 'Becca,'' Aaron said again. Even amid the scuffling din, his voice rang deep and clear.

''Hello,'' she replied in cool tones.

''Ephraim! You move over now and let your brothers share that bench,'' Lenore erupted. ''Latham, stop pickin' your teeth. Lester and Zeb, if you two don't settle down we're gonna go straight home and no cake!''

''No, don't leave!'' Rebecca exclaimed, then cringed at the note of panic. She lowered her voice. ''Don't even think of leaving, Lenore. The boys are just excited. They'll behave for a piece of cake, now, won't you?''

''Uh-huh!'' answered five eager lads. Samuel and his four cousins immediately ceased making a racket as they eyed the cake hungrily.

Aaron nearly chuckled at the sight, though it was not the youngsters that amused him as much as Rebecca's obvious efforts to ignore him. It didn't bother him a bit. Sooner or later Lenore and her brood would have to go home. He would talk to Rebecca then, since he wasn't planning on leaving until he had his say.

Rebecca, too, knew she could not forestall him forever. Outwardly she appeared calm, serving up cake and milk to the boys and coffee to the rest. But inwardly she seethed, irritated at Lenore for interfering, and angry at Aaron for breaking his word.

Too soon, her duties as hostess came to an end, and despite Rebecca's efforts to make the party last, Lenore shooed her boys out the door one by one.

''Now, don't make your ma have to chase you to bed, Samuel,'' she said gleefully, ''else you won't be able to come pick strawberries with me tomorrow. Good to see you again, Aaron. Don't be a stranger. G'night, 'Becca.''

"Good night," Rebecca said in a strangled voice.

To her utter surprise and chagrin, Samuel hopped toward the staircase almost as soon as the door closed behind his kin. "I best get to bed," he stated. "I don't want Aunt Nora to leave without me in the mornin'."

"Shall I tuck you in?" Rebecca moved to follow him.

"Naw, I can do it myself. I'm almost ten, Ma!"

Stopped short, she watched him as he scrambled nimbly up the stairs using his hands and one foot, scarcely impeded by his broken leg. Happiness over his rapid improvement warred with a bittersweet sense of loss that he no longer needed her.

But neither was stronger than the dread which filled her at the thought of the inevitable confrontation to come. She clenched her hands in her skirts.

"I don't need to look to see that Samuel's leg is improved," Aaron said softly, from his seat at the table. "He wouldn't be moving around so well if it pained him much."

The truth of his statement disarmed some of her anger. "He *is* much better," Rebecca admitted. "And I do appreciate all you've done. However," she turned, lifting her chin in subtle challenge, "I thought we had agreed you would not come back here."

Aaron rose, returning the bench to its place beneath the window and moving two chairs closer to the fire as if he were completely at home. He approached Rebecca, raising one tightfisted hand from her side as he pulled her toward the waiting chair. "Wherever did you get that idea?" he asked pleasantly.

Blushing furiously, she pulled back. "When you forced me to kiss you."

"I said I would leave. I did not say I wouldn't be back."

She snatched her arm away from him. "Then you lied."

"No, 'Becca." His voice deepened, sounding almost menacing in the too-quiet room. "The one thing I have never done is lie to you. Now will you please sit down so we can talk?"

Against his overwhelming reasonableness, Rebecca could do little but comply. With reluctant grace, she slipped past him and lowered herself into one of the chairs.

After a long moment in which Rebecca sensed him studying her, Aaron finally settled his large frame onto the other
chair.

"I came back because I wanted to talk," he began
calmly.

"I thought it was because Lenore invited you."

He smiled. "That provided me with a handy excuse,
I'll admit. But I would have come soon anyway. You've
had two weeks now, to consider our situation and to think
about how you'll tell Samuel."

"*If* I tell Samuel," she retorted. "I'm not sure I will."

Leaning back in his chair, Aaron clasped his hands
against his flat belly and crossed his booted ankles. His
blue eyes glittered dangerously as he stared at her. "It's
not a question of if, 'Becca, but a question of when. I'll
tell him myself if I have to."

His implacable tone, his quiet intensity, were more convincing to Rebecca than if he had ranted and screamed.
Though he seemed as relaxed as a sleeping panther, she
knew he could spring to action, or to alert attention, at a
moment's notice. And suddenly she had no desire to test
his patience.

"Is that why you came back?" she asked softly. "To
threaten me?"

"No, 'Becca. I came to make a deal."

He closed his eyes, his chin resting on his chest in
thoughtful repose, but she could tell by the throbbing pulse
at his temple that he was as tightly wound as she.

"Do you believe in fate?" he asked suddenly, his eyes
flashing open to peer at her.

Startled, Rebecca could only stare back. "I-I don't
know. I believe in God."

"That's not what I mean." He paused again, his mouth
pulling down into a frown. "I use to think every man
guided his own destiny. It's easy when you're young and
ambitious to believe that everything will turn out the way
you want as long as you work hard and honestly. I lost
that . . . that *faith* in myself and in life after the war. I
suppose I wanted to remember what happened, but it was
easier to believe that my efforts made no difference, that

no matter how hard I tried, the whole thing was out of my hands.''

"But God wouldn't have wanted you to suffer the way you did," Rebecca said with gentle conviction. "Not without a reason."

He smiled wryly. "That's what the Shawnee finally taught me, along with their belief that a man must both shape his own destiny *and* accept what fate gives him. Perhaps it's a contradiction, but in a muddled sort of way it's perfectly logical. You see, 'Becca . . .'' he leaned forward, his gaze almost beseeching as he tried to make her understand, "I chose to stay with the Shawnee because I was running away from my own tortured mind. But for whatever reason, I found peace with them, so the choice was the correct one. A few weeks ago I had to make another choice—whether to continue ignoring the past or to go after the truth. And I realize now that I did the right thing, because in doing so I found you and Samuel.''

He sat back, running a hand through his hair. "Does that make any sense?"

"I-I suppose." To be honest, Rebecca believed it went far beyond making sense; deep in her heart she knew what he said was true for her as well. It was not coincidence that had brought them together here, but the long ago plans Aaron and Levi had made to come to this place.

And yet, she understood now that a more compelling force bound them together. If men had souls, then hers and Aaron's were one.

"What I'm trying to say," Aaron said gently, reaching for her hands, "is that I've given a lot of thought to what you said last week, about us not knowing each other anymore. In a sense it's true, but at the same time I feel as if I know you better than I know myself. One thing I'm sure of: It's too important to ignore any longer."

Her fingers were cold and stiff, but the warmth that flowed through them at his touch seemed to revive her. Bolstering her defenses, Rebecca blinked the mist from her eyes and straightened her spine. "Last week you said it was Samuel you wanted, not me."

Shaking his head, Aaron gave her a rueful smile, his hands tightening around hers. "I don't blame you for thinking that, 'Becca. Especially after the way I abandoned you ten years ago. Now you're afraid that might happen again, aren't you?''

His directness caught her off guard. She pulled her hands from his, but could not escape his perceptive gaze. Her chin quivered shamefully.

''It wasn't you I rejected, m'dear.'' His voice was soothing despite its rasping undertone. ''It was myself, and what I would do to you. I'm sorry that you ever believed otherwise.''

She very nearly fell under his spell, but with an effort she armored herself with the same shell of anger that had protected her for so long. He was sorry! Well, sorry did not begin to make up for what he had done.

''For years I thought it was my fault you didn't come back,'' Rebecca admitted angrily, though the cost of her confession was pride. ''And then when things grew more and more difficult between Levi and me, I was sure there was something wrong with me, that I was somehow inadequate. And now you expect me to forget all that?''

''Not to forget, 'Becca. Only to forgive.''

''That's asking a lot.'' She jumped to her feet, moving toward the window where just a short while ago she had watched her son struggle to play. Now the grassy commons was awash in moonlight, silent but for the soft cadence of grasshoppers singing the world to sleep. ''I don't know if I *can* forgive you.''

''I'm willing to take that risk. People change. We both know that.'' Aaron watched her slim back grow rigid. He wished he could smooth away the tension with his hands.

''Are you saying that you won't ever go back to live with the Shawnee?''

Aaron froze. Her voice, her posture, all spoke of uncompromising determination. And yet he could not bring himself to voice the promise she desired. ''I'm not sure that I belong in this world anymore,'' he hedged. ''You've heard how resistant the men at the fort are to my presence. In many ways life there is more uncivilized than with the Shawnee. And there's still the matter of settling the charges against me.''

Her head turned, so that the moonlight outlined her delicate profile. "What will happen?"

"I can't honestly say yet," he said with a thoughtful frown. "I still don't know where I stand with the army. But that's the deal I was talking about before. If I'm convicted, I'll leave it up to you whether or not you tell Samuel the truth about us. But if I'm cleared . . ."

"Then what? You'll go back to the Shawnee?"

"I just don't know, 'Becca. I just don't know."

"Then you have no right to expect me to put Samuel's and my happiness at stake while you're making up your mind!" Sick with despair, Rebecca spoke with bleak resolution. Nothing was settled at all. The deal he offered had not moved them beyond the same impasse they had run into before.

Now it was Aaron's turn to jump from his seat. "For God's sake, 'Becca, what do you want from me?"

Rebecca stood tensed and waiting, peering out at the midnight-blue sky as if the answer lay in the firmaments, instead of inside her heart. She knew what she wanted, what she ached for with every fiber of her being. It was the one thing he had not yet mentioned—love. Until she was certain of that, she could not let him see the desperate hunger in her eyes.

"I want you to leave me alone. I won't let you hold me to public scrutiny and then just disappear into the woods again. I have *friends* here, Aaron! So does Samuel. Already people are talking."

"Damn it! I don't care what anyone else says."

"Of course not. You won't be around long enough to hear them. We will."

She knew her argument was pettish, and was not even the real reason behind her refusal to compromise, but Rebecca could not help herself. Deep inside she realized it would take little effort from him to break her resistance, and the only way to keep him at a distance was to keep her anger at high pitch.

After a lengthy silence, Aaron's voice grated over her like a rough stone, making her grimace.

"I'm not giving up, 'Becca. I'll come back here every day and every night until you reconsider."

"So be it. But that won't change anything."

"You were never this stubborn ten years ago."

"I didn't think I needed to be. But I learned my lesson, Aaron. The hard way."

Rebecca held her breath, wondering if her cutting words wounded him as much as they did her. Her heart throbbed, aching for solace, yet knowing that the pain she felt now was small compared to the agony that awaited if she let herself love him again.

And yet she could not quell the hopeful surge that leaped through her when he moved forward, stopping just behind her. She could feel the heat radiating from his body, could hear the tortured sound of his breaths. Her skin tingled with awareness, even though he was careful not to touch her.

Aaron could not decide which was stronger, the urge to throttle her or the desire to drag her into his arms to show her just how far her stubbornness would take her, but he managed to control them both.

"You can tell yourself whatever you want for the next few days, but I'll be back. This isn't over, 'Becca," he whispered hoarsely. "This is far from over."

CHAPTER 19

Aaron stowed the last of his gear into his bedroll, then looped a thin strip of hide over the entire bundle. Swinging it behind him, he dropped the pack over his shoulders so that the leather strap crossed his chest, the bulk settling comfortably on his back. He was glad that at this time of year it was not necessary to take much food into the forest. The pack was not heavy now, but he knew that after several miles it would take on weight.

And he would have many miles to travel before reaching the end of this particular road.

" 'Bout ready to go?'' Skulley asked from the door to Aaron's quarters.

"All set. Did you get it?"

"Yup." The old sergeant hitched a paper-wrapped package higher under his arm, then crossed over to Aaron. "Didn't open it up. That danged woman in town acted like I was gonna git it mussed or somethin' if'n I was to look."

Aaron suppressed a grin. As usual, Skulley's uniform looked like it had seen the worst of St. Clair's campaign a year ago and hadn't been off his back since. He couldn't blame the shopkeeper one bit. "I'll show you if you want," he offered.

"Naw, I'll wait till I can see it the way a feller outta, if'n you know what I mean."

Provided she would even accept his gift, Aaron thought while he carefully stowed the package in the satchel he would carry at his side. It was quite possible *he* would end up wearing it!

"I should be about a week," he said. "But when I get

back I'll try to bring them both to town for a good visit. At the rate the boy's going, he'll be ready to race me in by then.''

"That's good to hear. Glad he's makin' progress.''

Which was more than Aaron could say about relations between him and Rebecca. In the three weeks since he had begun his one-sided courtship, he had made the trip up the hillside a total of five times. On each occasion she had behaved as if his only purpose in calling was to inspect Samuel's leg.

To her credit, she did allow him plenty of time with his son. But not once had he been able to catch her alone.

"You gettin' any closer to softenin' 'er up?'' Skulley asked, interrupting Aaron's thoughts.

"I beg your pardon?''

"Miz 'Becca? She gonna marry you, or what?''

Turning a disparaging eye on the old soldier, Aaron grimaced. "At this point I'd settle for an occasional smile from her. I'm beginning to lose hope.''

Skulley grinned. "Not me. I only got one good eye, but some things're as plain as my mam's face.''

But even Skulley's confidence did little to buoy Aaron's spirits. "How can I prove to her that I won't hurt her again when she resists me at every turn? I realize there's a lot for us to learn about each other, but how can we?''

The sergeant scratched his grizzled chin. "Yer askin' the wrong man 'bout how women think, but I got me an opinion. Seems to me most gals likes to hear sweet talk somethin' fierce. But when that don't work, sometimes ya gotta try somethin' drastic.''

"Drastic? Like what?''

"Think on it a spell.'' Skulley hitched up his trousers and rolled his eyes. "You say she won't look at you the way you is now, but what if she ain't got no choice? Boy, you got to get 'er where she cain't help but look at you!''

Aaron chuckled, but already the sense of Skulley's words had made an impression. He laid a hand on the sergeant's stooped shoulder, raising a cloud of dust from his well-worn fatigue jacket. "I will give your suggestion some thought. You're a good friend, Skulley, to both of us. And just now I can use a good friend. Keep an ear out while I'm gone, won't you?''

"Sure 'nough. An' you keep an eye out for them kegs of whiskey I marked since we had that little talk. Just like I thought, there's a mess of 'em missin' from the store-house.''

His expression glum once more, Aaron nodded. "I hope to God we're wrong about liquor being traded to the Indians. The Shawnee leaders recognize that whiskey is lethal to their people. How can I convince them of our good intentions if it's our own men trying to poison them behind our backs?''

"We'll find out soon 'nough," Skulley remarked while scratching vigorously at his scalp. "If'n you see a keg with a *S* carved into one end, you'll know where it came from.''

"Right." Aaron moved to the shelf over his bunk, where he lifted a powder horn and oiled pouch full of shot. Both were equipped with long leather straps, which he slung over his head and across his chest. "One other thing," he added. "Remind Carter to soak that boil every night, and if he needs more salve, you know where it is in the cabinet. And keep Joe Kinkle isolated in that outbuilding until I get back.''

"Is it the chokin' disease?" Skulley asked.

"I don't know yet." Aaron pulled a leather cord tighter. "But diphtheria's too dangerous to take chances. I don't want to come back to an epidemic. If that extra sulfate and alum I ordered comes in, be sure to keep it dry. And the bandages—''

"I hear ya," Skulley said, chuckling. "Don't let the men use 'em to polish their boots. Y'know, I can see you're anxious to meet up with your friends, but it's a dang shame you have to leave just when you was startin' to get through to some o' the men. Never thought I'd be glad to see an outbreak o' dysentery, but it shore did help you win some folks over to your side.''

Surprisingly enough, Aaron felt the same way. He hadn't thought he could ever enjoy this forced stint with the army, but he had found great satisfaction in putting his skills to use again. So much so that he wondered if he really could make a place for himself here.

Not missing a clue, Skulley cocked his head and asked, "Does Miz 'Becca know 'bout how good things is goin' here?"

Aaron grinned. "Not yet, but if that's your way of saying I ought to tell her, then I suppose I will. It is ironic how something positive could come out of something so bad."

"Well, you pulled ever'one through, that you did. It's only too bad that Jessup didn't come down with it. I'da liked to see him tryin' to strut 'round like a rooster while he's slinkin' off to the latrine at the same time."

The image brought a reluctant smile to Aaron's face, something that rarely occurred while he was thinking of Captain Vance Jessup. He still recalled with anger and self-disgust the day when Major Carswell had called them both to his quarters. While Jessup had displayed a false attitude of respect and sincerity, Aaron had lost his temper. Looking back, he realized it was only by the tolerance and esteem of Henry Carswell that he was not cooling himself in the holding cell now.

Aaron still couldn't recall what had set him off. He only knew that every time he saw Vance Jessup his blood turned ice-cold and his flesh crawled. Aaron could have sworn the captain had something to do with his sketchy past, but the officer claimed not. Jessup had calmly explained to the major that even though he and Aaron were both at West Canada Creek, they had not been from the same unit, and therefore Jessup had no firsthand knowledge of the charges against Aaron.

Only rumors, he had declared. Rumors of murder and desertion, substantiated by the fact that Aaron had turned up alive, while the other men in his unit were dead.

Henry Carswell was too sharp to fall for Jessup's explanation completely, but since the captain had broken no law with his talk, the commandant could do nothing more than admonish the officer against spreading further unrest.

Once Jessup, wearing a smug grin, had been dismissed, Carswell then informed Aaron that he would withhold judgment until the official inquiry was completed in Philadelphia.

"But as for our other task," the major had stated firmly, "we will proceed as planned."

Now that the time had actually come to return to the Shawnee, Aaron wondered whether Carswell had purposely delayed the inquiry in order to allow his pet project to succeed. Aaron hoped not. He was glad for the chance to bring about a lasting peace between the two worlds he lived in, but he had a greater stake in putting to rest the demons of his past. He had Rebecca and Samuel to think of.

"What's the hurry?" Rebecca demanded as Aaron pulled her along behind him. She still couldn't believe she had agreed to come alone with him for a walk. But after three weeks of gentlemanly behavior, she had allowed Aaron this one concession.

The truth was, she was glad to be free of the watchful eyes of her neighbors for once, and glad to take a break from her routine. Early summer had finally taken hold of the land, and the warm, wafting air was rich with the scents of wildflowers and new leaves. A clump of violets beckoned to her from the side of the narrow trail, and she looked back over her shoulder at them longingly. "Can't we slow down?" she asked breathlessly. "I want some flowers for the table."

"We'll get them on the way back." Aaron did slow his pace, however, enough so that she could walk alongside him once the trail widened. He tightened his grip on her hand. "Are you too tired to go on?"

Rebecca glanced up at him suspiciously. "That depends. You haven't told me where we're going yet."

Curiosity filled her when he only shrugged and smiled enigmatically. He had arrived that morning wearing his buckskins and prepared for travel, but when she had asked him where he was going he had given her a noncommittal response. After spending some time stringing fishing line with Samuel, Aaron had then asked her to accompany him. She recalled that he had also spent a few minutes whispering to Lenore, but she had assumed they were discussing the lunch he probably had stuffed in the pack he carried.

He must be hungry, Rebecca figured. It was a large pack.

"Are we going on a picnic?" she speculated out loud. Her own stomach was beginning to feel empty, and the idea of resting for a while was not an unwelcome one.

"You might call it that," Aaron replied. He looked down at her, his blue eyes glinting like polished sapphires. "I wasn't sure if you'd let me get you alone long enough to talk. I was prepared to drag you out here, if necessary."

"Ah, so it's a kidnapping!" Rebecca raised her eyebrows. "And where are you taking me?"

"Someplace you'll like," Aaron promised.

They had headed toward the river, though not in the direction of Cincinnati. There were several spots along the ridge that she knew of, one in particular that commanded a breathtaking view of the Ohio Valley and the little town below. It was just like Aaron to try to woo her with pretty scenery and a secluded location. After all, he had done it once before.

But let him just try again, Rebecca thought with a smug inner smile. He would find that she was no longer an innocent young miss to fall under his spell, just because she had agreed to take a walk with him.

Aaron watched the corners of her mouth twitch, and he wondered if she guessed what he was up to. He was taking a chance, to be sure. But despite her protests, when he arrived at her cabin that morning her eyes had lit up like shimmering gemstones when she saw him. That had decided him. He was tired of waiting. If Rebecca had her way they would never get so much as reacquainted, let alone build a life together.

She would probably be angry with him for what he was about to do, but even that was better than the formal politeness with which she had treated him the last few weeks. Skulley was right. He had to force his way past her defenses, and the only way he knew how was to take her by surprise.

"This isn't the way to the lookout," she said a few minutes later when he led her down a deer trail toward the river. Her sparkling eyes, at first only surprised but quickly turning wary, turned up to him.

"We're not going to the lookout," Aaron replied with equanimity. He held her hand fast as he pushed his way through the brush. They came out at a spot just a few yards from the river on a grassy bank that led down to the water's edge. A tangle of trees that had been knocked over by the wind stretched out over the water a ways, breaking up the current at this spot. Aaron glanced over his shoulder at Rebecca. "We're going for a boat ride."

"A b-boat ride?" She stopped short, almost losing her balance when Aaron's greater strength nearly pulled her off her feet. She dug her heels into the ground. "Let go of me. I'm not going near the river."

"Now, 'Becca," he warned, turning to coax her. "I just want us to be alone for a while, to get to know one another again."

"We *are* alone, and we'll be alone the whole way back to the cabin. I will *not* take one step closer!"

Aaron frowned. Lenore had told him Rebecca still harbored a deep fear of the river, but this was worse than he expected. Unless she was just being plain stubborn about coming with him.

He hesitated for a moment, considering. The worse thing that could happen, of course, was that his plan wouldn't work. If in a week's time she hadn't come around, then he would have to consider the possibility that she would never care for him again.

But if he was right in his belief that she *did* still love him, then there was much to gain from doing this. Not only would they have the time together, but she would see firsthand another aspect of his life, a world that was important to him.

And once she did, she would understand.

"We're going, 'Becca. I know you're a little afraid, but once we get moving you'll be glad you faced up to your fear. It's your choice whether you walk or I carry you, but you *are* going."

"The hell I am!" she declared in a low, fierce voice. Twisting, she tried to break free of his grip, but he only grabbed her other arm and hauled her against him.

"Have it your way," he grumbled, trapping her shoulders with one arm while scooping the other beneath her legs. "God knows why you had to grow up to be a spitfire!"

When Rebecca ceased squirming in his arms, Aaron assumed she had reached a state of grudging acceptance. She gave only a startled squeak when he hefted her higher against his chest, her arms tightening around his neck. Otherwise she made no sound, with her face buried in his shirtfront.

He strode to the water's edge. As he waded in up to his thighs, the icy water of the Ohio frothed around his legs, sucking at his boots and soaking his buckskins. Damn, but he hoped she appreciated the trouble he was going to on her account. "Here, let go," he ordered as he lowered her into the half-hidden canoe. She still clung to his shoulders with a death grip. Chuckling, he pried her fingers loose and placed her in the middle of the craft, where she immediately grasped the sides as tightly as she had clutched him.

"The water's only up to your waist, 'Becca," he said teasingly. "No need to be afraid . . . yet." He tossed his pack into the center, just in front of her.

Her spine was straight and unmoving, her feet planted stiffly against the floor of the canoe. In the struggle her hair had come loose; it billowed around her face like a black cloud, hiding her expression. Aaron could see only the rigid set of her chin as she kept her mouth clamped shut, and he knew she was furious with him for manhandling her so.

Small price to pay, he thought complacently.

Turning, he untied the strip of leather which held the canoe to the windfall, tossed a few prickly branches aside, and, bracing himself with one hand against the log, swung a leg over the edge and quickly drew himself in. The canoe rocked back and forth as he settled, facing Rebecca, at the end opposite her. After scooping a flat-edged paddle from the bottom, Aaron crossed his long legs beneath him and used the paddle to shove off from the natural landing.

Rebecca remained frozen, a silent scream locked in her throat as the canoe spun into the current, first backward and then swinging crazily around to float in the other direction. If she had looked she might have seen that Aaron's face was intent but unworried as he steered the craft, but she dared not lift her eyes from where they focused on her knees, which were propped up only inches from her face.

Cold perspiration trickled down her sides beneath her gown, and her hands, locked as they were on the canoe's rough bark, were numb and heavy. Black specks drifted in front of her eyes like driftwood, and the only thing keeping her from fainting was the certainty that if she did, she would pitch headfirst into the river and drown for sure.

The only benefit in that, she thought wretchedly, was that Aaron would probably try to save her, and even if he swam too well to drown he might take a chill and die of fever. A fate which he did not deserve, she decided grimly. Fever was far too good for him.

To her surprise, Rebecca found that she felt better if she kept her thoughts concentrated on something other than the swift, buoyant motion of the canoe. Her lightheadedness receded when she closed her eyes and devised ways to get even with Aaron—extreme forms of torture seemed to work best. At one point she forced her facial muscles to relax, lest Aaron think she was caught in the throes of a fit.

Aaron presumed nothing of the sort, however. As he skillfully guided the canoe downriver, taking care to keep them close to the bank for 'Becca's sake since the current was not as strong there, he studied her smooth face. She was nervous, he could tell. Her knuckles were too white and her shoulders too tense for him to think otherwise. But her expression seemed relaxed—even serene—and he even thought he had seen a fleeting smile at one point.

"We are going to the village of my friend, Wind at His Feet. This is the fastest way to reach the Great Miami River," he said in a hushed voice. "The Great Miami. To the Shawnee it's one of the sacred three, and for countless years marked the western border of their homeland. I've traveled its length many times, through some of the most beautiful land on earth, but never will I forget how it looked that autumn when I first came here."

"Wh-when?" Rebecca asked, swallowing hard to combat the queasy sensation that came and went. Hesitantly, she allowed her eyes to open to a mere slit—just enough to see Aaron sitting a few feet away from her, his own eyes gazing at her with keen interest.

Though she despised him with every fiber of her being for putting her through this hell, she clung to the sound of his voice as a sign of hope. If he could speak to her so calmly, then surely she was not about to die anytime soon, her rational mind told her.

But the irrational part, the part that still held the upper hand, would not allow her to let go of her terror quite yet. She closed her eyes again.

"The autumn of '83, it was," he continued smoothly, oblivious to her fear. "I'd wandered the better part of a year, and had made my way north from Carolina to the outskirts of Baltimore. It was there I heard the peace treaty was finally signed in Paris, though the fighting had long since stopped. Still, it was a relief to know it was official."

Rebecca nodded sullenly. She remembered that autumn, too, and all the bittersweet emotions that had come with it. Levi had celebrated the ceasefire by beginning a three-month trek from Raleigh up into the Blue Ridge range, leaving her with her infant son and a bit of scrubby farmland to manage. Her own joy at the war's end had been eclipsed by her memories of Aaron, and the pain of not knowing the circumstances of his death.

Opening her eyes slightly, Rebecca studied him across the canoe. As angry as she was, she could not suppress the surge of happiness that still caught her unawares at odd moments. He was alive, and relatively whole . . . at least until she got him on solid ground again, at which point she planned to beat him senseless with the first chunk of wood she could lay her hands on.

Aaron glanced up, smugly satisfied to see a smile twitching at the corners of her mouth once more. Grinning back at her, he went on with his story. "By this time the army had been reduced to a tenth of its strength, with most of the troops and militias back home again trying to rebuild their lives. But a portion of my old regiment was garrisoned in Baltimore, so it was easy enough to find out where I stood.

"That's when I learned of the charges against me. One near escape from a blue-coat patrol was all it took to convince me to head west again, this time to Harrisburg."

"You were in Harrisburg?" Rebecca asked, her queasiness forgotten.

"For a time. Six months or so; I never stayed in one place for long. Why do you ask?"

Seconds passed before she answered, and then in a tone devoid of emotion. "Levi took me to Harrisburg once. In April of '84, I think. It sounds as if we just missed one another."

The bleakness in her expression caused Aaron to stop paddling. Laying the oar across his knees, he let the canoe glide slowly alongside the sandy riverbank. He studied her quietly, mesmerized by the dark, burning glow of her eyes and the sensuous fullness of her lips.

What might have happened had they found each other then? he wondered idly. She, married to Levi. He, scarred and weakened, both physically and emotionally. Insurmountable odds.

At least now they had a chance.

And he wanted that chance, Aaron thought suddenly. He wanted it with a fierce, hungry longing that rose up from the far reaches of his soul. For too many years he had denied himself the right to want—now it filled him, consumed him.

A chance—that was all he wanted for them now. A chance to put the darkness behind them, to reach into a future as bright as the dawn when morning finally comes. He would take that chance, by God. If she would let him.

"Did you travel with Levi often?" he asked softly, aware that talking seemed to ease Rebecca's fear.

"Not really. Most of the time he spent away he was just wandering, doing a little trading. He would hear of a place and decide to go. But he always came back."

Aaron decided to ignore that remark. "Why did you come to Cincinnati with him this last time?" He detected a tightening of her mouth, a telltale glistening in her eyes.

"Because we both knew it would be his last trip."

"What do you mean?"

The puzzlement in his voice reminded Rebecca that Aaron did not know the whole story of Levi's last year. She had forgotten that. "Levi came out here alone almost two years ago," she explained. "He returned to Fort Pitt full of plans. He called this valley a paradise on earth, resplendent with rich, fertile bottomlands, unending forests, and plentiful game."

"He was right about that," Aaron said, resuming the same steady, rhythmic stroke that had brought them this far. "So he decided to settle here permanently?"

"Not at first," she admitted. "It wasn't until he started getting sick that he decided to buy land and set up a store."

"Sick? In what way?"

"It started with a cough he contracted that winter. We thought he'd get better in the spring, but the coughing kept up for months. He just kept getting weaker, and so thin. . . ."

"Consumption," Aaron said with grim finality. Rebecca nodded.

"That's what the physician at Fort Pitt told us. He was against Levi coming out here at all, saying the trip might kill him." She paused, the irony of her words settling in with a kind of morbid horror. Quickly, before she began to panic, Rebecca changed the subject. "Tell me about some of the places you've been," she said.

Complying gladly, Aaron launched into a vivid description of the docks in Baltimore, the first place he could think of when she made her urgent request. He would keep talking forever if he had to. They were making good progress, and he was pleased that after that one moment of panic Rebecca had settled down reasonably well. But he would not push his luck just yet. They had hours to go before reaching the spot where he intended to make camp for the night; anything could happen.

His voice once again had a calming affect on Rebecca's nerves. She only listened with half an ear, allowing her mind to wander at will, as long as it stayed away from thoughts of the river.

How far was it to this village? she wondered. She had never asked Aaron before, but she had assumed it was a long way away. Surely it must be close now, or else they would never make it back by dark. Lenore would worry if they were gone too long, and Samuel . . .

Lost in her thoughts, Rebecca did not see the danger coming until Aaron's arms jerked upward, yanking the oar to shoulder height and spraying her with fine droplets of icy water.

"What—?" The question never left her lips as they struck something below the waterline and shuddered to a bone-jarring halt. Almost immediately the canoe began to list to Rebecca's right, away from the shoreline.

"Don't move!" Aaron warned, jamming the oar into the water. It was not uncommon for a canoe to become snagged by a tree limb hidden beneath the surface. Or, he supposed, they had run into an outcropping of rock. As long as the canoe was not damaged he could push them off and—

" 'Becca, don't!" he repeated when she tried to scramble to her feet inside the rocking craft. "Sit still."

Her skirts were tangled around her legs, and sheer panic filled her eyes when a wave of muddy water swept over the side of the canoe to soak her bodice. If she kept this up she would capsize them, he realized. Yet if he tried to hold her down, he ran the risk of losing the paddle.

Part of him was terrified—not for their safety, for they were near enough to the bank that he did not doubt he could drag her there if need be—but for the precarious progress they had made toward a new beginning. In the instant he had seen the pale specter of pure terror on her face he realized how badly he had misjudged the situation.

She might forgive him for many things, he thought desolately, but what he had done today was unforgivable.

His decision made, he tossed the oar into the water and lunged toward Rebecca, grabbing hold of her arms at the same moment she kicked her feet from the hem of her skirt and braced them on the canoe's curved bottom. With a burst of strength fueled by fear she threw herself forward, clawing at him for a hold as their combined weight shifted the tiny canoe, breaking it free from whatever watery hands had held it fast.

The unexpected movement caught Aaron off guard, and

he felt his balance disappear as swiftly as the oar had swept away on the muddy current. He had just enough time to turn so that Rebecca would not be caught under him, then he plunged backward into the river, pulling her with him.

Her scream rent the air in two, then was cut off abruptly as water filled her mouth and nose. The combined shock of frigid water and stark horror was paralyzing—but only for a few seconds. Almost before she was completely submerged she began fighting for her life.

As soon as he slammed into the water Aaron knew they were in no danger. He almost laughed out loud with relief, but since Rebecca's wriggling form held him beneath the water he wisely kept his mouth shut and his amusement squelched. With all his strength he wrapped his arms around her, struggling to subdue her as she thrashed and flailed and otherwise made no progress toward the surface.

Damn, but she's strong! he thought to himself as he tightened his hold around her slim torso. He could feel the convulsive shudders in her chest as she choked on the water she had swallowed. No time to waste.

He kicked out and, finding solid rock beneath his moccasins, flexed his knees, bunched the powerful muscles in his thighs, straightened . . . and stood upright.

Water poured off of them, rivulets and streams that joined the current churning around his waist. Still clasped in his arms, Rebecca continued to fight him, her legs kicking against his, threatening to knock him off his feet once more.

'' 'Becca, stop it!'' he said sternly, shaking her a little. Her breath sputtered and her hands tore at his restraining arms as if she wanted free of them, though he was afraid if he loosened his hold she would slide back into the river like a slippery trout. Bracing himself, he scooped her up, soaked skirts and all, and started for the bank just a few yards away.

By the time he reached the shore she had stopped struggling in his arms, but her body still quivered and her breath still came in choking gasps. Most of which reaction, Aaron realized guiltily, was due to fright and not to the small amount of water she might have swallowed.

"I'm sorry, 'Becca," he murmured as he knelt down.

He lowered her to the ground, still holding her close as she shuddered convulsively. ''I'm sorry.''

Dimly, she heard his heartfelt apology, but Rebecca was too busy trying to breathe to pay him much heed. She was aware of his solid arms wrapped around her, and of the firmness of the blessed earth beneath her. Squeezing her eyes tight, she tried to concentrate on how good it felt to be alive.

But the relief and the terror and the memories all joined against her, and the last thing she heard was the rushing flow of the river as it continued on its way.

CHAPTER 20

"How do you feel?" Aaron asked gently, for perhaps the fourth time in the hour since Rebecca had come to. She accepted a tin mug of tea from his hand without comment, sipping the steaming contents gratefully.

"Better," she answered after swallowing. She did not look up, but rather gazed into the crackling flames of the small campfire he had made.

He watched her doubtfully. She was still as waxen as the moment she had first lost consciousness. He had nearly panicked then, afraid that she had taken in more water than he had thought and was drowning. But her breathing had grown clear and even as soon as her body relaxed, and he had realized that she had only fainted.

"Is there m-more?" she asked shakily, handing him the cup.

"Plenty. And food, too, when you're ready."

Rebecca lowered her head to her knees, hugging the blanket closer around her. "I'm not hungry."

Aaron's chest tightened with remorse. Moving back to the fire, he poured her more tea, then sat down beside her while she slowly sipped the restorative brew. He was furious with himself for what he had done to her, and even more so because she had tried to tell him she was frightened, but he had ignored her because he thought he knew better than she.

It was an appallingly mistaken assumption, and now Rebecca was paying the price for his poor judgment. He wished he could take her back to her cabin this instant, and be damned with the rest of his scheme. But she was in no condition to walk now, and probably would not set foot in another boat for as long as she lived.

He reached for her, caressing the damp hair at the nape of her neck. To his surprise she did not pull away. "You can't possibly know how sorry I am, 'Becca. I should have listened to you. I had no idea how deeply afraid you were."

She did not respond at first, and he wondered if he had lost her irretrievably, but then her slim form shuddered beneath his hand and she leaned toward him. "Oh, Aaron, I feel like such a fool!"

Her quiet exclamation stunned him. He had expected anger—at least when she recovered enough to summon some emotion—and certainly mistrust. But instead she was seeking comfort in his arms.

"I'm the fool, m'dear," he whispered into her hair as he wrapped his arms around her. "I should never have forced you to come with me."

"Why did you?"

"Because I thought you would be glad to be with me, once we were on our way." He could feel the warmth of her slender body beneath the blanket, and was thankful that she had not slipped so far into shock that she could not generate her own heat. It had been hard enough to strip her of her dress and soaked underthings before bundling her quickly into the blanket. He didn't know how he would have behaved had he been forced to hold her naked form next to his in order to revive her.

Rebecca stirred in his embrace, turning to look at him. His eyes were solemn and as bright as jewels in the flickering firelight. A shudder ran through her, not from the cold but from the shaft of longing that lanced her heart. She had been foolish in more ways than one, foolish to try to deny what Aaron meant to her. Coming so near to death—or at least believing she had—had stripped away all pretense. In the moments before she had lost consciousness only one thought, one word filled her mind. Aaron.

"The funny thing is," she said in a choking whisper, "I *was* glad for a while, even though it was a sneaky thing to do. But I'm sorry I ruined everything."

Again, Aaron was surprised by her distress over her own

actions, when it was his that had fallen short. He stroked her silky cheek, cringing inwardly at the dark crescents beneath her eyes. "It's all right, 'Becca. The canoe drifted to shore just a little way downstream, so I was able to rescue our gear. And we're only a mile away from where I intended to camp anyway."

Rebecca's gaze widened. "What do you mean, where you intended to camp? Weren't we going back today? What about Samuel?" At last her color began to rise, in direct correlation to the pitch of her voice. Aaron waited out her questions with rising trepidation.

"Samuel is fine," he said when she ended on an indignant note. "Lenore is watching him and the store, too. By now she will have told him where we've gone."

She stared at him with an expression of utter disbelief, then closed her eyes and sighed. "You had no right, Aaron."

"I realize that now," he admitted shamefully. "My only excuse is that I was desperate to have you to myself, and when Lenore agreed to help, I suppose I got carried away."

"No, *I* got carried away," Rebecca sputtered. "Carried away, and thrown into a c-canoe and practically drowned—"

"You weren't drowning. The water was only three feet deep."

"How was I to know it, since you've arrogantly decided to take command of my life without *telling* me anything?"

She slumped dejectedly, and Aaron felt his heart twist. She was right, of course. He should have told her, even if that meant she would have refused him.

"I'm sorry for that, too, 'Becca. I hadn't really planned to bring you along, but when I got to your cabin and realized just how damned hard it would be to say goodbye—"

He stopped short, brushing the hair from his brow with a frustrated gesture. Her dark eyes met his, expectant, hopeful. He lifted a strand of her hair, letting the soft tendril curl around his hand. She looked like a child, an innocent, sitting there with her hair down around her shoulders and the blanket clutched just beneath her chin.

But she was a woman. A woman capable of making her own decisions.

Even those that might destroy him.

Rebecca sighed and shifted beneath the blanket. He looked so apologetic she could not stay angry for long. Her mouth twisted wryly. "I suppose this is partly my fault." With one bare toe she traced a line back and forth on the ground, her gaze focused in the distance. "I've given a lot of thought to what you said a few weeks ago, about compromising and getting to know one another. And even though I still don't want to get involved with you again, I am willing to admit that you've been wonderful with Samuel. But I was too stubborn to let you know."

Aaron released his breath slowly, his hand grown still upon her hair. Inside he felt his heart expand, but he was careful not to let his elation show. "All I ever asked was that we both try, 'Becca. I know there are still a lot of questions to be answered, but I'm more certain than ever that everything will work out." Quickly he told her about the changing situation at the fort, and his growing confidence.

Rebecca listened silently, then shook her head with a frown. "If you're so happy at the fort, why are you going back to the Shawnee village?

"Remember when I told you that Major Carswell asked me to act as a liaison between the army and the Indians? He wants me to speak to my Shawnee friends about a plan for peace we're working on," Aaron explained quietly. "I'll talk to my adopted brother, Wind At His Feet, and then return with a response." He hesitated, clearing his throat. "*If* you would like to go with me, I thought you could meet my friends and see for yourself how I've lived these past ten years. I want you to know everything about me, 'Becca. The good as well as the bad, the past and what might be in the future."

She did not answer right away; at first her lower lip quivered until she pressed her mouth in a firm line.

Aaron turned his gaze to the dying fire. "If you want," he said softly, "I'll take you home at first light."

Rebecca was still perturbed by his presumptive behavior today, but his concern for her overrode much of her anger.

"You would delay your meeting with the Shawnee to take me back? I thought the situation was urgent."

He reached for her hand, squeezing it. "Nothing is more important to me than you, 'Becca. I'm realizing that more and more each day. Carswell can wait."

Continuing to gaze at the fire, she nibbled on her lower lip thoughtfully. "Just how far is it to the Shawnee village?"

This was unexpected, and Aaron's expression registered surprise. "Five . . . six miles north. Why?"

She leaned back, unknowingly letting the blanket slip from one shoulder. Momentarily distracted by the sight of her creamy skin glowing gold in the firelight, he did not notice at first the smile tugging at her lower lip. But her next question gained his immediate attention.

"How long would we be gone?"

Incredulous, Aaron clutched her upper arms and pulled her closer. "Do you mean you'd still consider going with me?"

"I don't know. You haven't answered my question."

There was acceptance in her voice, and an uncertainty that had nothing to do with the length of their absence. Sensing that she had reached a crossroads of her own, Aaron curbed his excitement with an effort. "Two or three days would probably be sufficient time to learn what I must, and then a day and a half to return—more if we walk."

Rebecca lifted her gaze from the fire to the starry sky visible despite the canopy of leaves overhead. A slight wind moved through the branches, softly stirring the leaves to a rustling tune. Beneath it all was the steady sound of the river, moving inexorably toward its destiny.

Finally her eyes dropped to the sodden pile of clothing lying near the fire, which Aaron had not taken the time to spread out over bushes. Rebecca looked back at him, grinning sheepishly. "I think I would like to go with you, Aaron. There's only one problem. I haven't a thing to wear."

Sunlight streamed through the clearing where Rebecca donned the clothing Aaron had waiting for her, and for the first time that morning she was able to take note of her surroundings. He had made camp for them on a small rise a hundred feet from the river, and from here she could clearly see both the broken, muddied bank where he had carried her out of the water and the path that skirted the river's edge.

She sighed deeply, smoothing down her skirt. The gown Aaron had given her last night was made of the softest wool, as lightweight and finely woven as any she had ever seen; its color was the rich blue of a summer night. Tatted lace edged the squared color and long, fitted sleeves, and two bands of satin traveled down the front of the gown from bodice to hem. Such an extravagant dress was rare even for a burgeoning town like Cincinnati; it must have set Aaron back a goodly sum.

He had bought it, he told her, with the hope that she would wear it while dining some night with Major Carswell, as the commandant had once mentioned his desire to meet the mother of Aaron's first patient.

"I almost forgot I put it in the pack," Aaron had explained, "but I'm glad now that I did, if this'll help convince you to stay with me."

It was not the dress that weighed in his favor, Rebecca admitted to herself, so much as her own decision to mend the breach between them. On top of that, she was still embarrassed by her childish display of fear yesterday. If Aaron was looking forward to the Shawnee village, he might forget to question her irrational behavior.

"Does it fit?" he called from the other side of a stand of dogwoods.

Rebecca parted the branches, stepping back into the protected circle where they had spent the night. The remains of the campfire lay smoldering within a circle of stones, doused with water from the river. Aaron had already washed the few utensils he carried with him and stowed them in his pack along with her wrinkled, discarded gown.

"It's beautiful, Aaron," she said quietly. When he looked up at her from where he knelt beside his bedroll, his expression took on a distinct measure of appreciation.

Rebecca felt herself blush.

"*You're* beautiful," he said, rising to take her hand. Leading her to a large rock, he bade her sit while he took her shoes and emptied them of the leaves he had placed inside to soak up the excess water.

"I can do that," she said breathlessly.

"Allow me." With all the gallantry of a lord of the court, Aaron bent over her leg, lifting her slim ankle until her foot rested upon his thigh. His hands were warm, sending tingling sensations up her calves, and she wondered briefly if he knew that his touch made her feel lightheaded and slightly tipsy.

Just when she was about to accuse him of lingering overlong at the task, he lowered her foot and straightened, his eyes dancing as his gaze met hers. "Are you sure you're up to walking today?" he asked with blithe innocence.

Considering the way her knees trembled as she stood, Rebecca wasn't sure she was up to anything, but she smiled gamely. "Of course. The water damaged my gown, not my legs. But this is hardly a walking dress, Aaron. It's much too fine."

He went to his pack, lifting it to his shoulders with ease, though Rebecca had tested its weight when searching for the biscuits earlier and found it to be extraordinarily heavy. He perused her up and down, taking full measure of the gown as well as of her. "Will you be uncomfortable?"

"Not at all. It's just that I'd hate to ruin this dress. And it's unsuitable for everyday wear."

Aaron frowned. "I wasn't thinking of that when I picked it out. To be truthful, all I noticed was the color and the feel of the cloth. The woman in the shop knew who you were from seeing you at the market and she assured me the dress would fit, so I paid for it. Skulley delivered it yesterday morning."

"It *is* lovely, Aaron. In fact, it's the grandest gown I've ever owned." Rebecca looked down, from the tantalizing display of bodice to the pointed waist and full skirt. When she lifted her hand to brush a lock of hair from her cheek, the lacy sleeve fluttered in the morning breeze. "Will your friends think I'm overdressed and pretentious?"

"Probably, but they'll see your beauty, too," Aaron replied, laughing. He took her hand, then headed them both toward the northward trail.

For the first mile or so they talked little, while Rebecca grew accustomed to holding her skirts away from the grabbing branches lining the most narrow portions of the path. At times Aaron walked ahead of her, pulling back branches until she could pass, or helping her across small streams that crossed the trail. There were moments when Rebecca was certain they had lost their way, but always Aaron managed to guide them onward, until eventually the path would widen again, allowing them to walk side by side.

"Tell me about your friend," she said. "What was his name again?"

"*Mamaquit dasse,* which means Wind at His Feet."

"What an odd name."

"You wouldn't think so if you ever saw him run," Aaron replied. "The Shawnee pick names to fit the person, and Wind is among the swiftest of braves."

Rebecca smiled. "His mother must have had great foresight, or else she was an incredible optimist. What if he had grown up to be fat and slow?"

Chuckling, Aaron looked down at her sideways. "Wind at His Feet is not the name he was given at birth. His name was changed when he was a youth and had won his first footrace, beating opponents twice his age."

For the rest of the morning, Aaron described both his friend and his family to Rebecca, so that gradually her feelings of uneasiness turned into expectancy. His voice was so full of genuine caring as he talked, she could not help but believe that she would like these people when she met them.

They stopped once to rest and eat berries that Aaron had gathered in a scarf shoved inside his brimmed hat. Only once was Rebecca's cheerful mood broken, and that was when they reached the rocky shore of the Great Miami River. To her relief, however, Aaron veered toward a path alongside the rushing tributary.

"Is Samuel afraid of the water, too?" he asked, taking her arm as she stumbled over a minuscule pebble.

"H-he doesn't seem to be." Rebecca laughed weakly. "He wants Skulley to take him fishing out on the river."

"He mentioned that to me a few times, too," Aaron said with a dry chuckle, which told her that "a few times" was a serious understatement.

The subject did not come up again, thankfully, and before long they reached a bend in the river where Aaron stopped.

"We're almost there," he told her. "I don't want you to be frightened if they're a bit . . . overwhelming at first. Remember, the Shawnee will be at least as curious about you as you are about them."

"What will they do?" she asked, skepticism adding a cutting edge to her voice.

"Nothing to hurt you. But the women and children have no qualms about touching strangers, just to see if your pale skin feels the same as theirs. Or if your hair is different. Try not to be nervous. I'll be right by your side."

That, at least, was reassuring to hear, so Rebecca gave him a ready smile and they continued on.

Rounding the bend, the first thing she could see was a large, open field of waving green plants. Corn, not much above the height of her calves, sprouted eagerly among the shorter bean plants, and she could see that scattered amid them both were the vines that would later bear squash and gourd pumpkins.

Then a noise drew her attention to a place on the other side of the field, where several people stood pointing. Behind them, to Rebecca's amazement, were rows upon rows of bark huts. Some were small domes no taller than a man, but many others were at least as large as a good-sized cabin. Thin smoke curled above the tops of the domes, and tantalizing smells drifted toward her, along with the sound of children's laughter.

"Why . . . it's a regular town! I didn't expect anything so . . . so permanent."

Aaron chuckled. "It's been here since long before Cincinnati, or any of the other white towns along the Ohio." Then his expression became grim. "Unfortunately, I'm not sure how long the Shawnee will remain. This is one of their southernmost villages. It won't be long before the settlements push them farther west to the other side of the Whitewater."

Rebecca followed his gaze over the peaceful town, and watched as people gathered. "They see us," she said unnecessarily.

"Yes, they'll come to greet us now." Aaron took her hand in his firm, comforting grasp and stepped forward into the field. "Don't step on the corn."

"I'm *trying* not to," she replied. It seemed at first that there was no order to the garden, but Rebecca quickly caught on to the pattern, and was able to avoid the young plants.

From the other side, several people watched them, their shouts and the loud barking of a few dogs quickly drawing others. Rebecca's doubts grew when the number of villagers doubled, then tripled at their arrival. When they reached the edge of the field, they were rapidly surrounded.

"Aaron?"

"Don't worry," he said soothingly. "Here comes Wind now."

From the expression of relaxed pleasure on Aaron's face, Rebecca knew that he was not at all uneasy with this welcome, and she felt her own tension slip away. Now she looked around at the swarming Shawnee, and was able to return their curiosity.

Most of the gathering villagers, she saw, were women. Chattering brightly, they moved from side to side, alternately pointing at her and covering their own mouths shyly. All the women had dark, straight hair fastened in thick braids tied off with strips of hide. Some wore loose dresses made of doeskin, which fell to midcalf length, while some wore skirts of the same material, with brightly colored cloth draped around their shoulders and breasts.

The men, on the other hand, were scantily clad, Rebecca noted with some embarrassment. The few who deigned to greet them strutted toward Aaron proudly, barechested and oftentimes bare-legged as well. One man in particular seemed to command the respect and attention of the others, and it was on him Rebecca focused.

He was tall—almost as tall as Aaron—and his bronzed features were as proud and fierce as she had imagined an Indian warrior's to be. His dark scalplock bobbed above his right shoulder, adorned with feathers and bits of bright cloth. Below his bare chest he wore a leather breechcloth over deerskin leggings, fringed along the side just like Aaron's buckskin trousers. On his feet were moccasins decorated with quills and small beads.

As he neared them, Rebecca caught her breath. This was the same warrior she and Samuel had encountered in the woods several weeks earlier!

The warrior seemed to recognize her, too, for he stopped in front of her, looking down the length of his aquiline nose. Then his granite features softened.

"*Ayi-ayeh,*" he said. "Wel-come, Brave Mother, to Mi-a-mi town," he added in halting English.

" 'Becca, this is my Shawnee brother, Wind at His Feet." Aaron turned to Wind. "I'd like you to meet Rebecca."

"Re-beck-ah," he repeated in precise tones. "*Sede'koni*. You will eat *di-ohe'ko* with us. Food. My wife, White Star, will serve you."

"Oh, no, I couldn't expect—"

"Yes, you can," Aaron prodded gently, still smiling. "You'll hurt his feelings if you refuse."

Rebecca looked from Aaron, to the intimidating Wind at His Feet, to the pretty woman who had crept up behind him. On her back was a cradleboard, and Rebecca quickly remembered the baby, and White Star's other children as well, especially the boy who had stepped forward to shake hands with Samuel.

Suddenly she no longer felt so much a stranger.

"Yes," she answered, nodding graciously. "I would be honored to eat with you."

CHAPTER 21

"Do you want me to come with you?"

Aaron held her upper arms in a loose caress, smiling down into her eyes. "It's not that I don't want you with me, m'dear. But the council is not a place for a woman."

After an enjoyable midday meal with Wind at His Feet and his family, Rebecca felt completely safe in the Shawnee village. Wind spoke enough English that he could communicate easily, and between him and Aaron, they were able to translate for the women. Rebecca had been introduced to Wind's oldest daughter, Spring Wind, as well as Little Otter and his brother Cat Chaser. To her delight, she also learned of the part she had played in the naming of Wind and White Star's youngest child when they told her the child's name, Smiles at Strangers.

They were, she had discovered quickly, just like any other loving family she knew, with only a few cultural differences. Still, she was surprised by Aaron's announcement that he would leave her now in White Star's care.

"Why is it that women are never included in decisions that concern them? That's unfair."

"Perhaps." Aaron grinned tauntingly. "But at least out here the air is fresh and the sun shines. The council lodge is dark and gloomy and full of smoke, and we'll be speaking a language you don't understand. Wouldn't you rather stay out here and talk with the women? There's a Pickewa maiden here by the name of She Who Sighs. She speaks English."

It was blatant bribery, but it worked. Rebecca's eyes lit up. "She does? Where is she?"

Aaron spoke a few rapid words to Spring Wind, who nodded eagerly and scampered away. White Star also smiled and nodded, her dark eyes shining with delight.

"All right, then," Rebecca acquiesced. She arched a brow. "You go discuss your plans with the warriors. I'll stay here and find out what's *really* going on."

Aaron threw back his head and laughed heartily. "No doubt you will, 'Becca."

He squeezed her arms again, pointing her in the direction of an approaching group of women. Spring Wind led the way, followed immediately by a pale young girl with limpid eyes and lank brown hair.

"She Who Sighs is half white," Aaron explained in an undertone. "Her mother was taken hostage and lived with the Pickewa for several years. When she escaped, she left She Who Sighs behind in the care of the tribe. The girl still remembers some English."

"Good. This ought to be interesting," Rebecca whispered back. But Aaron was already striding toward the council lodge.

She watched him go, then smiled resolutely as she turned to her interpreter for the day. "Hello," she said encouragingly. "My name is Rebecca Osborne. I'm pleased to meet you."

The girl looked to be no more than sixteen years old from the shape of her willowy body to the unmarked clarity of her complexion, but it was hard to tell because she never lifted her gaze from her own toes. Rebecca sighed and tried again.

"You are She Who Sighs, are you not?"

At the sound of her name, the maiden peeked up through her lashes; then her gaze darted to the ground once more. She made a single up-and-down movement with her head that might have been a nod.

"Do you speak English?"

Again the rapid motion, and another swift glance. The girl's upper lip twitched indecisively and Rebecca held her breath, waiting for the child to speak. By this time several more women had gathered around, watching the proceedings with their dark, solemn eyes. Finally She Who Sighs raised one finger and pointed to the midnight curls that billowed around Rebecca's shoulders.

"Hair," she said haltingly. Then, with greater confidence, "Hair!"

"Ahh," White Star said, chuckling as she shifted her baby to her other hip and took a step forward. She too, pointed to Rebecca's unbound curls. "H-hair!" she proclaimed with a definitive nod.

"Hair!" The other women repeated, looking to each other for approval and praise. "Hair."

"Yes, this is hair," Rebecca concurred, suspicion winding its way through her. "But can you speak . . . *more*?" She held her palm flat in front of her mouth, gesturing outward.

She Who Sighs's eyes brightened and she offered a tentative smile, pointing now to Rebecca's feet. "Sh-shoes." Emboldened, she even went so far as to lightly touch Rebecca's sleeve.

"Doo-ress," she said.

"That's right. *Dress*," Rebecca confirmed with a sigh. So much for communicating. The girl was scarcely brave enough to test her vocabulary, let alone talk to Rebecca about the Shawnee's future plans.

The other women had moved in to surround her, and now their curious giggles and chatter drowned out the interpreter's shy pronouncements. Their excitement did not frighten her, but Rebecca was uncomfortable with the fact that the women did not seem inclined to wait for She Who Sighs to translate, now that they had begun to speak for themselves.

Someone tugged at her skirt; then another hand reached forward to finger the lace at her collar. Startled, Rebecca jerked backward, only to have the women laugh raucously and grab at her again. Though she tried to back away, she quickly found she was surrounded and had no choice but to put up with their bold assessment.

But she could not help searching frantically over the sea of dark heads for help. None was in sight.

White Star said something unintelligible, though it was clear she was directing Rebecca to remove her gown so that the women could see what was beneath it. Shocked,

Rebecca shook her head adamantly. Then she braced her feet, crossed her arms over her breasts, and dredged up a smile.

"Aaron Samuel Cambridge," she growled through clenched teeth, much to the delight of the Shawnee women, "you'll pay for this!"

Wisps of smoke curled upward from the ornate pipe, wreathing Snow Hair's white head. The smoke hovered, as did the watchful eyes of all within the council lodge, until Snow Hair exhaled. Every wrinkle etched into his bronze face seemed to stretch and then relax as he grunted. He passed the pipe to the young brave at his right, Tall Walker, his son.

Aaron released his own pent-up breath, pleased to see that his presence among the tribal leaders had not been questioned. He hoped Rebecca would be equally accepted by the women, and then wondered how she was faring. He could still see the wary expression on her face as he left her. The Shawnee women had maintained their distance while he was at Rebecca's side, but he knew that once he was gone their curiosity would overcome all reserve. He almost wished he could have stayed to watch.

Aaron reminded himself not to smile and returned his attention to the circling pipe. Smiling was a sign of pleasure reserved for youths and maidens and old women. But among warriors an open smile was considered to lack dignity. And in the council lodge such levity was not condoned, even if the issues to be discussed were not particularly serious.

Today the mood was already somber, for the issues were grave, indeed.

Though he had not offered any hint about his mission, Aaron was sure Wind at His Feet had guessed that this was no ordinary visit. In fact, Wind now stared at him from the opposite side of the circle, his proud features motionless and his eyes clear and appraising.

Aaron offered a curt nod, the only concession to their friendship he could give within the circle. During council, all participants were treated as uniformly as possible, with no special privileges given to even the family members of the chief. Aaron knew that Wind, as well as many of the others, would have harsh words to say about the encroaching white settlements. They would not stop to apologize to him or to excuse him from their tirades, for if he could not listen with a fair mind, then he would never be welcomed to council again.

Likewise, Aaron would not soften his condemnation of the Shawnee's fierce raids this past winter just because Wind was his good friend and had not taken part in those bloodbaths.

In council, Aaron's adopted brother overlooked his whiteness. Aaron only hoped that after today Wind would continue to call him friend.

Snow Hair stirred as the last participant laid the pipe in the center of the circle. His black eyes glittered in the bark hut's gloomy interior. Gnarled hands resting upon his knees, he leaned forward slowly. "What has brought you to the home of your Shawnee brethren, Gentle Healer?"

Normally, the council decided on minor business first before turning to matters which would require great discussion. This was unusual to leap at once to the question most on each warrior's mind. Several of the members looked up sharply.

So they understand, Aaron thought, keeping his features perfectly expressionless, as he had schooled himself. With deliberate slowness, he unfolded his long legs, rising to stand at his place. He gazed long and hard at Snow Hair, then pivoted slowly in order to see the eyes of every man present before he began. Each gaze he met was direct and unblinking, if a little cautious. So far, so good.

When he had finished his silent poll, Aaron faced Snow Hair once again. "Shaman of the warrior tribe of the Shawnee, I speak to you in the language of The People, so you will know that in my heart I, Gentle Healer, am one with you. You have also known me as Cain, the white name I told you when I first came to this place many summers ago. But Cain and Gentle Healer are not the only names I carry. To my white friends I am Aaron Cambridge, captain of the First American Regiment."

From off to his left someone drew in his breath with a hiss. Aaron did not look down.

"As you can see, I am only one man"—he lifted his arms and spread his palms—"though I would have wished for two more like me last winter at the time of the sickness."

As he had hoped, he heard several grunts of amusement. So they had not lost all sense of humor, he thought with grim satisfaction. Another good sign.

"I come to you today as a man with many identities, a man who exists in two worlds but with a single soul. No matter which of these names you call me, I have but one desire, and that is to keep both of my worlds from destroying one another."

"This is impossible!" Tall Walker jumped up, committing the nearly unpardonable act of interrupting another tribesman in his council. "Less than a moon ago they murdered two boys, and we could do nothing. The whites have stolen too much and killed too many for us to keep ourselves from destroying them."

With a cutting motion, Snow Hair ordered his son to sit down. Aaron remained silent until the commotion caused by Tall Walker's words had died.

"It is true that the whites have not always honored their word," he finally said. "But it is not to keep you from destroying them that I plead with you today. The Shawnee have a right to protect themselves. The Shawnee are justified to feel angry and cheated. The Shawnee would also be forgiven by Our Grandmother, the creator, if they attack those white men who have brought murder and starvation to The People.

"But know this," Aaron added severely. "If the Shawnee go to war with the white army, the Shawnee will lose."

He sat down, in order to give the council time to assimilate his words, but he knew already that they caused great dissension among the Indians. Several of the younger warriors, Tall Walker among them, vehemently denied the white soldiers' ability to conquer the Shawnee.

"What about last autumn?" one of them asked loudly. "We brought home many scalps in triumph then!"

"And two winters ago also, when the white chief Harmar fell to our superior warriors—what about then?"

Aaron listened quietly, allowing the indignant council

time to vent their anger. Some of the men did not speak, he noticed. Wind at His Feet sat immobile, in deep contemplation. Others, mostly warriors of many seasons who remembered not just the victories of recent years, but bitter defeats of the past, remained just as still.

These were the leaders he must win over, Aaron realized. They were the ones who understood the harsh realities of war. They had no need to prove their bravery and skill in battle; the scars on their toughened flesh was proof enough. All they had to keep them from bowing to the white ways was pride.

But pride, Aaron knew, was a powerful force. Even more so when pride was an enemy instead of a friend.

When Wind at His Feet stood, the younger men dropped off their boasting and fell hushed. They held great respect for the tall warrior. Aaron could only hope Wind would guide them in the right direction.

"I would speak," Wind stated calmly, then waited for complete silence. With a regal bow of his head, he began. "For many years I have known Cain, who became Gentle Healer to us and is now called Aa-ron, as well. He is as a brother to me, and to many of you he has proved himself friend and healer. When he speaks I listen, for he has never spoken false words to me. And even to this, this we do not wish to hear, I will listen, for it is the man who turns a deaf ear who hears not his own fate calling."

This brought many grunts of agreement from the older men, and even a few stiff nods from the younger ones. Aaron's chest swelled at Wind's declaration of confidence. The trust between them had remained largely unspoken, until now. To hear it out loud moved Aaron profoundly.

"I do not say I have made my decision," Wind continued cautiously, "but I have seen the great white army with my own eyes, and I believe it will not always be so easy to trick them as we have done before. My heart tells me that the time has come to consider other ways. Ways that will stop the killing.

"Have you come to tell us such a way exists, brother?"

Aaron was momentarily startled. He had expected to spend hours arguing with the Shawnee before being allowed to present his and Major Carswell's plan. Wind had managed to cut through much of the anticipated resistance with one short speech, and with a single pointed question had offered Aaron his chance to explain.

"There is a way," he affirmed, acknowledging Wind's assistance with a meaningful look. "I have talked many times with the present chief of the soldiers at Fort Washington in Cincinnati. It is his wish that we come to an agreement as to which lands belong to the Shawnee and which to the whites."

"But this *is* all Shawnee land," Tall Walker said, with a broad, sweeping motion. "Every inch of soil the white man touches was once ours."

"This is true," Aaron agreed. "But the treaty signed by the chiefs of the Delaware and Wyandot says this land belongs to the government of the United States. I can tell you now that no amount of argument will change this."

"Then we must drive this pestilence out by blood!" one warrior declared in a deep voice.

"But it will be your own blood spilled," Aaron insisted. "And that of your sons. Better to accept this treaty and learn to live within its rules."

A mutinous silence filled the bark hut as each man digested this advice. From the looks on their faces, Aaron mused, most were ready to spit his words back at him, along with whatever remained of their dinner.

After a few minutes of mulling this over, Snow Hair spoke in a low and compelling tone. "Many times the white leaders have made lines on paper to tell us where we may go. Most times it was the whites who crossed over those lines first, causing mistrust and hatred to turn into bloodshed, after which new lines would be drawn. Always taking more of our land away. Now will your new leader tell us to leave our homes again?"

"No," Aaron promised, hoping that Carswell had the influence to support his vow. "The idea is for you to stay here, and for the whites to keep clear of your villages. Certain areas will also be designated for hunting, not for villages, and the whites will avoid them as well. Part of the plan is for everyone to know where each of these areas lie, so there is no mistake."

"And what if there is a mistake?" Wind asked softly.

Aaron paused, then released his breath and continued. "Then the transgressor will answer to a board made up of both whites and Indians. That is the other part of the plan. We will all work together."

A rumbling sound like a distant roll of thunder rose in the room as the Shawnee turned to one another to comment on this unprecedented suggestion. Aaron waited until everyone had quieted before he spoke again. "In the past," he said, "the white men have had little respect for Shawnee ways." This brought a grumble of agreement from the others. "But I say that is because they do not *know* Shawnee customs.

"It is true also that The People scorn the ways of the white men, laughing at his clothing and hair and odd speech. I know this is so because I have heard it from you, Tall Walker, and you, Red Dog. But who among you has tried to learn from a white man why he thinks as he does, or what habits have shaped his life?"

"Who would want to?" Red Dog burst out. At this even Snow Hair chuckled.

Aaron suppressed a smile. "There are some," he offered. "Wind at His Feet is one who wished to learn of the white man's ways. I told him what I could, and you see where it has brought us. With learning has come understanding, and with understanding, respect and trust. Good things. Only good."

"But what of the bad? What of the men who would use their knowledge of our ways against us? Do you say there are none who would betray us?"

At Snow Hair's softly spoken question, Aaron hesitated. He thought immediately of Vance Jessup and his appetite for violence. He thought, too, of Fierce Stalker, who was not present at this council, but whose hot temper and cold heart made him well known among the Shawnee.

Shaking his head, Aaron said, "You know as well as I that there are men who will *always* let hatred guide them. It will take great courage to look beyond those few, and into the hearts of the many good and sincere men who would honor the dictates of their leaders, Shawnee *and* white."

Doubt showed on many of the faces before him, but at

least there was little hostility, Aaron thought. Judging that he had said enough for one day, he stood abruptly, waving aside any remaining questions.

"Think hard on what I have told you today. For three nights I will dwell with my Shawnee brothers. When I go back to Fort Washington, I hope to take with me the goodwill of all present here, so that we may begin to heal the wounds between our races.

"Please, my friends," he added once more in a low voice, "listen to your hearts."

CHAPTER 22

Amid the gay chatter of the women, Rebecca sat perched upon a tree stump, her eyes bright with interest as she watched preparations take place for that evening's revelry. At her side crouched She Who Sighs, who was not so shy that she would forgo her role as Rebecca's protector, even though her knowledge of English was limited to a few words. Fortunately, White Star had found another woman in the village, one Aaron apparently did not know, who was able to translate most of the goings-on.

Bird Woman, as she had told Rebecca, had once lived near the British fort at Detroit. That was where she had learned to speak the white language, so many years ago. Of indeterminate age, Bird Woman laughed often and talked much. She was dreadfully outspoken and her vocabulary was bawdy, to put it nicely.

Despite this, Rebecca liked her immensely.

"See how the others dress themselves up to catch a man?" Bird Woman chided the young maids who were sorting through a satchel of clothing. One would pull out a feather or string of beads, hold it to her hair or breast until the rest of the group shouted an opinion, then trade the item for another until a consensus was reached. The older, married women watched indulgently, adding occasional comments.

Only Bird Woman seemed to treat the ritual as unimportant. "They do not know yet that men look only at what is *under* doeskin, huh, Re-beck-ah?" Bird Woman repeated the comment for the sake of her Shawnee sisters.

White Star looked around and made a good-natured

comment, which Bird Woman translated for Rebecca with
a hearty chuckle. "She says I talk like this because I know
that no amount of decoration can hide my ugly face."

Uncertain how to respond to such banter, Rebecca
merely smiled and shook her head. She was still amazed
at how easily the women had accepted her into their community, once she showed them that she was as interested
in them as they were in her.

The first few minutes, naturally, had been unsettling,
until she realized there was no maliciousness among the
women—just simple curiosity. After they had satisfied
themselves as to the details of her person, the Shawnee
wives had one by one presented themselves and their children for her inspection. Once done, they treated her as
one of their own, addressing her with lighthearted comments as they showed her around the town.

Now they were getting ready for the celebration to be
held later that night, and Rebecca found their excitement
contagious. "Why is this night special?" she asked Bird
Woman.

"We celebrate because the winter is over, and spring
has given us hope and new life. The fields are planted, the
sun warms us by day, and the moon lights the cool, pleasant nights. Soon the hunters will go out, but for now all
the men are here, and so that is another reason for women
to celebrate. Even those who are not quite women yet, like
She Who Sighs."

Rebecca followed Bird Woman's teasing glance, seeing
that She Who Sighs had lowered her eyes and was blushing
furiously. "What will happen?"

"Maybe nothing," Bird Woman provoked. She spoke
again in Shawnee. The young She Who Sighs looked up
quickly, her eyes wide with dismay.

"But I have seen Swift Arrow around today," Bird
Woman added with a grin, "and he looks over this way so
much that I think he wants very much for *something* to
happen."

At this, a woman holding two small children spoke up,
and her instructive tone was met with laughter from the
other wives. "She says be sure he is quick with his bow,
and not just his arrow," Bird Woman translated for Re-

becca's benefit. "A man must provide meat for his woman's belly and wood for her fire, too."

She Who Sighs turned even redder. Bird Woman pointed
at her and laughed raucously. "She Who Sighs has no
need of a fire. She is already hot, just thinking about her
man!"

Though she was a little embarrassed by this talk, Rebecca could not suppress a smile. It was nice to be part of
a group of women like this. Here was proof that people,
even of different races, were essentially the same. Perhaps, she thought, it should be up to women to negotiate
for peace. Give each one a chance to show off her children
and start them comparing funny stories about their men,
and soon they would all be laughing like sisters.

Rebecca's secretive smile did not go unnoticed by Bird
Woman, though the woman misunderstood its source.
"Ah-hah," she said loudly, first in the Shawnee dialect
and then in English, "I can see that Re-beck-ah wishes to
dance the frolic dance with us tonight!"

Rebecca shook her head. "I don't know how. Can't I
just watch?"

Bird Woman's straight black eyebrows shot up.
"Hmmm. I would dance if I were you. Gentle Healer is
much admired by the women of this tribe."

"What do you mean by that?"

Bird Woman merely shrugged.

"What exactly is this frolic dance?" Rebecca asked
warily.

"It is part of the celebration. The best part for some."
Bird Woman spoke again to She Who Sighs, who nodded
shyly. "For many people it is only a time of high spirits.
For the married couples the dance is a chance to be together without the problems of children and *wigewa,* the
home, to interfere with their pleasure. But for the young
men and women, it is also a dance of courtship. This is
the night when some maidens will declare their desire for
a particular man. *That* is why it is a special night. For She
Who Sighs, and for others, too."

She grinned knowingly, and Rebecca suddenly understood her meaning. There would be more than flirting going on after the celebration ended, she realized.

Her thoughts darted immediately to Aaron, and she pictured him as he had looked last night, with the firelight reflecting off his smooth, muscled flesh. She had watched him from her blankets, moving around as he banked the fire and prepared for sleep, and had wondered breathlessly if he would try to make love to her. Disappointment had outweighed her relief when he whispered a gentle good night and settled onto his own bedroll.

Rebecca was too honest to deny that the attraction between them had never been stronger, and the laughter and closeness they had shared these past two days only increased her longings. Would he dance with her tonight, or with some woman of this tribe? Was there someone here who secretly yearned for him?

She was hardly aware that she frowned as she peered at the beautiful young women around her, who still laughed and preened with their dark eyes glowing and white teeth flashing brilliantly.

"Are you certain," Bird Woman asked, her eyes slanting slyly, "that you do not wish to learn the dance?"

Rebecca felt her own cheeks grow hot, and waves of alarming desire rolled through her abdomen.

But there was no harm in just dancing, she told herself. She had promised Aaron she would go along with whatever the women wanted. And if she truly wished to know and understand the Shawnee ways, then shouldn't she join them in celebrating the rebirth of spring?

With a stubborn lift of her chin, Rebecca said to Bird Woman. "I will dance. Please tell me what I need to know."

Wind at His Feet had followed Aaron from the council lodge, and the two spent much of the afternoon together. Though they were both careful to avoid discussing Aaron's quest, the problem seemed to hang over them like a threatening rain cloud. Aaron knew better than to push his friend too soon for an answer. He sensed that Wind understood the difficulties of straddling two worlds and that his friend was saddened by Aaron's dilemma.

How easy it would have been, Aaron thought, to simply

stay with the Shawnee forever. But then he would never free himself from his shameful past.

And he never would have found Rebecca.

He searched for her now, having left Wind to begin preparations for the night to come. Already the village hummed with anticipation. Children scampered and screeched and tore around the lines of bark huts; those old enough to attend the celebration were nearly quivering from the excitement, while the younger ones fretted and fussed at being excluded from the fun. Young girls chattered like magpies, preening in their new dresses sewn beside winter fires from the soft hides of last autumn's hunt. They giggled at the young men who strutted nearby, calling to each other in voices sometimes deep and manly, sometimes cracking with the strain of newness. Occasionally one of the youths would strike out at another playfully, and this would result in a tussle of arms and legs that was more a display of showmanship than strength. Still, it impressed the girls greatly—or so the young men supposed.

Aaron grinned as he strode though the village, acknowledging each cheerful greeting with a wave of his hand. Tonight's would be an extra special celebration. There was much to be thankful for.

He turned a corner and spotted Rebecca. The smile on his face widened. She lifted her head and her eyes sought his before he could call out to her. She was hurrying along with a bundle clutched to her breast in the wake of White Star and two other women. She halted long enough to speak to him.

"Aaron! I didn't expect to see you until later," she said breathlessly.

"You almost sound disappointed. I take it you managed to make friends with the help of She Who Sighs."

Narrowing her eyes, Rebecca smiled crookedly. "I managed. Actually, it was easier than I thought."

Her soft curls were completely unbound, and adorned with a beaded quill that spun and fluttered in the wind. Around her neck hung a necklace of pounded copper shaped in intricate designs. Aaron had never seen these items before. He chuckled as he lifted the necklace from her bare throat, fingering the warm metal gently.

"I was afraid you'd be lonely and frightened, and here you are wearing gifts."

Rebecca's cheeks flushed becomingly. "Not gifts, precisely. You might call them trade goods."

"You traded for them? Good for you, 'Becca. I forgot to tell you that the Shawnee love to barter, but I see you found out for yourself. You could have chosen no better way to endear yourself to the women."

"It wasn't quite by choice," she said in a choked voice. "White Star insisted that I could not attend the festivities without jewelry of my own. And I . . . well, let's just say that I'm wearing considerably fewer undergarments than before.

"Don't laugh!" she hissed, but her eyes twinkled with suppressed mirth. "At least not until you see someone capering about in my petticoat tonight."

Unable to help himself, Aaron threw back his head and roared. Rebecca only shook her head helplessly. "I have to go now. White Star is waiting for me," she finally said. "Will I see you later?"

"Undoubtedly."

"Don't be so smug," she warned lightly before turning away. "With all my new finery, you might not even know me."

"But I'll find you."

"Will you?"

"Certainly." He grinned. "You'll be the one *without* the petticoat."

Tongues of flame leaped skyward, reaching with burning hands to grasp at the moon and stars. Clusters of sparks burst open like sacks of golden, fiery grain, scattering wide and sprinkling the ground around the fire ring with glowing embers. The loud crackling and popping sounds provided a backdrop to the much louder noise of beating drums and shaking rattles, and above it all the cries of joyful voices filled the air.

The dancing was about to begin.

From her place among the women, Rebecca watched the proceedings with something akin to a fever pounding through her blood. She could see Aaron sitting cross-legged with the men on the other side of the great fire, and she wondered if he was as impatient as she.

The celebration had begun at dusk, starting with a meal the likes of which Rebecca had never seen. The savory scent of roasting meat still lingered in the clearing where they had feasted on venison, rabbit, and bear, along with corn cakes and bowls of beans and squash. Later their treat would be dried apples—the remainder of the winter stores, Bird Woman had explained—drenched in honey and baked to a mouth-watering crisp.

Rebecca had wanted to sit at Aaron's side, but it was clear from the time she left White Star's hut that women did not mingle with the men for this early part of the festivities. Though many glances were cast over to the men's side of the fire, no woman dared be so bold as to approach.

After the meal came the storytelling. The Shawnee received several lengthy tales with great zeal. A few of these Bird Woman translated into Rebecca's ear; some were so entrancing that the woman forgot her duty and sat gape-mouthed as the shaman, Snow Hair, spoke. Though she did not always understand, Rebecca found herself caught up in the dramatic gestures, gasping when the old man leaned forward to whisper, laughing out loud when he jumped back with a comical expression on his wrinkled face.

When the storytelling was done, a group of men rose, their regal bearing marking them as warriors. Wind at His Feet was obviously their leader. His deep, resonant voice filled the clearing and echoed among the huts where only children slept this night. Rebecca decided that this part of the performance was some kind of reenactment, and she leaned back against a stump to watch.

Finally the talking and boasting and praying was done. Sitting erectly once more, Rebecca looked around, watching for some signal to rise. The drums picked up a faster beat, and suddenly the night air was rent in two by a whooping shout. As one, the Shawnee people cried out with ringing voices, answering the call.

Bird Woman reached for Rebecca's hand, yanking her to her feet. "It is time," she whispered. "Quickly."

All around her, the women pushed for a place in line.

Rebecca saw that the men had already formed a circle around the fire. Aaron stood taller than many of the others, his golden head reflecting the fire's glow. Hurrying, as Bird Woman had instructed her to do, Rebecca edged her way around the crowd to move closer to him.

She was chagrined that he did not appear to be looking for her. His blue eyes scanned the scrambling women unconcernedly; a smile of amusement barely touched his mouth. It would serve him right, Rebecca thought sternly, if she did not choose him after all.

But from the corner of her eye she saw that a girl named Yellow Feather was watching her, shoving her own way in Aaron's direction. Rebecca had noticed Yellow Feather earlier, mostly because the beautiful young maiden had seemed more reserved toward her than the others. Now she could guess why.

Despite the heat of the fire and the tingling warmth that filled her, Rebecca felt as if a cold hand had clasped her heart. Determinedly, she pushed forward.

The crowd broke now as the women found places near their chosen ones, forming a line behind the men so that two rings of people now girded the flaming pyre. Rebecca only just managed to slip into the open spot behind Aaron ahead of the dusky-skinned maiden; she resisted shooting the girl a triumphant look. Aaron still did not appear to be aware of which woman stood waiting behind him. Rebecca wondered dismally if he even cared.

The music increased in tempo, sending a pulsing, throbbing beat through the earth, which was mimicked by the stomping of many pairs of feet. Rebecca did not take her eyes from Aaron. Stripped to the waist like the other warriors, his lean, muscled torso gleamed in the firelight, as radiant as a bronze statue. His broad shoulders swayed in time with the other men as they danced from side to side; his shimmering hair, tied back with a thong, curled against the strong column of his neck.

The women had begun to chant, and though Rebecca did not know the meaning of the words, she found herself caught up in the rhythmic tune. Feminine voices rose in unison, their melodic words mesmerizing and enticing. This passionate song continued on for several more minutes. Then, after a sudden violent pounding, the drums echoed into silence.

The women stopped singing. The men turned.

Aaron had spotted her across the clearing hours before, dressed in a white doeskin tunic that fell straight from her shoulders to end at her calves above a pair of knee-high moccasins. In her hands she carried a length of fabric, the scarf Aaron knew was an integral part of this dance. As with the other women, she used the cloth as if it were an extension of herself; the billowing scarf floated and rose, twisting sensuously in a teasing manner. Her unbound hair fell around her shoulders in a cloud of curls, reaching nearly to her waist in back, adorned only by the same feather he had noticed before.

Now that she stood close enough to touch, he could see how the pliant leather clung to the curve of her breasts, softly rising and falling with her rapid breathing. Her skin, flushed from the heat and excitement, held the fiery glow of a thousand pearls.

The music resumed, driving an insistent beat. Her feet moved lightly, as if she had danced this way all her life. Aaron felt his own pulse escalate in time with the drums as her eyes rose shyly, capturing his with a gaze full of wonder and promise.

Did she know how much he had hoped for her to join him in this dance? Aaron questioned silently.

Then her parted lips quivered, just barely curving upward into a knowing smile.

He thought his heart would burst with the surge of white-hot blood that poured through his veins. His feet shuffled automatically, so that his reaction could scarcely be noticed, but Aaron felt as if every cell in his body was on fire, as if every nerve was tuned to her movements. If she danced to the left, his own legs took him in that direction. When she leaned forward, swirling the scarf before her flirtatiously, he thought his knees would buckle.

Up and down the line, the Shawnee men and women danced for each other. Most smiled with open enjoyment, pleased only to be young and healthy and happy with the moment. But some stared at one another with the kind of burning intensity that only a man and a woman in love can share. Those couples were not aware of anything else but the simmering heat of their own bodies, their own feelings.

Aaron had long since forgotten about the other dancers; no other woman caught his eye, no matter how vigorously she twirled or how loudly she chanted. For him there was only Rebecca.

The women began to shift closer now, taking the hands of their partners. Most of them kept the scarf between them, but a few, like Rebecca, did not.

When she draped the scarf around her neck and reached out her hands to Aaron, the skin of his palms felt scorched by her feverish touch. In the shifting light and shadow he could not read her eyes, but her body swayed near his, just brushing the flat plane of his chest. Her breath came in short gasps that fanned his throat, and he could feel his own heat reflected back from her as his mouth grazed her hair.

" 'Becca," he whispered huskily, "do you know what you do to me?"

Her only answer was a gusting sigh against his throat. Then her lips touched his burning flesh, trailing fire from the base of his neck, up his rigid jawline and across his cheek. When she finally reached his mouth she drew back, meeting his gaze with eyes that glittered like iridescent coals in the dark night.

"No more than what you do to me," she answered, her voice trembling as much as her hands. She did not know when she had decided to take this irrevocable step, or even if this choice was absolute. But up until now it was Aaron who had made all the effort, and it was time she made a move of her own.

She was amazed by her own boldness, but somehow, having shed the rules of one society for the freedom of another, she found herself willing to forget all the barriers between them, to rejoice in the invisible bonds that tied them together. She squeezed her fingers tighter; Aaron adjusted his grip to enfold her hands in his. She whispered, "Will . . . will anyone notice if we leave now?"

He did not need to look around to know that other couples were doing just that, slipping away into the darkness to be alone while the rest of the village continued to celebrate noisily. The drumbeat continued to throb through the heated night, but the dancing had already changed.

"The proper way is for you to follow me," he said, giving her hands a gentle tug before releasing her.

He turned, and once again Rebecca glimpsed the powerful muscles in his shoulders and back. Then his lengthy strides took him beyond the circle of light, and for an instant she lost sight of him. Willing her feet to move, she hurried after him, keeping her head up and her eyes pinned on the spot where he had disappeared. Friendly voices called out, but she did not stop to wonder whether they were speaking to her. All her concentration centered on Aaron, a needle pointing to a lodestone.

Through the darkened village Rebecca raced, her heart pounding, her breath ragged. The cool night air bathed her, making her damp skin tingle with awareness and her breasts pucker beneath the soft swishing motion of her dress. Behind her the sounds of the celebration continued, but they were a distant counterpoint to the thrumming music that filled her heart and soul.

She caught sight of Aaron near the end of a row of bark huts. He was waiting for her, and with a silent cry of joy she slipped into his arms, reveling in the feel of his strong arms enfolding her, drawing her close.

"Come on," he whispered urgently, leading her to the last hut, where he ducked into the low opening.

It was nearly black inside, with only a few rays of moonlight filtering through the smoke hole at the peak of the dome. The fire was unlit, but they had no need of an outside source of heat. Every inch of Rebecca's body burned with desire.

Aaron turned to her. Slowly he traced the outline of her cheek and the graceful curve of her jaw with his fingers. " 'Becca, you're so beautiful," he murmured, hardly able to keep from pulling her to the ground immediately. But it had been so long, and he still did not know if she truly meant to stay here with him, or if she had only wanted to leave because she was tired of dancing.

Her cheek was smooth and silky as an otter's fur, and as warm. He could feel her pulse jump erratically as his hand lingered near her throat, his thumb caressing the sensitive skin under her chin. "My sweet love, I can't get enough of looking at you—touching you. Before, when I turned around and saw you behind me . . ."

Cupping the back of her head he bent toward her, his mouth descending on hers as gently as spring rain. Rebecca welcomed him eagerly, wrapping her arms around his waist, her palms spreading up and over his sides and back. With only the supple doeskin acting as a barrier, she pressed hard against him.

"God, I want you, 'Becca!" he whispered hoarsely.

The kiss that had begun with great tenderness turned fierce as he plundered her parted lips and ravaged her with his tongue. She clung to his shoulders, straining to bring him closer, arching her back to breach the infinitesimal gap between them. Myriad sensations cascaded over her; the sound of his rasping breath, the taste of his mouth, the rigid strength of his powerful body lifting her high against him. Holding her close as he dropped to his knees, Aaron gently lowered her to the thick pile of furs on the ground.

His weight pinned her to the soft pallet. With one hand he captured both of hers, holding them above her head as he stroked her from shoulder to thigh through her dress. Each pass made her breasts ache more keenly, her heart trip faster. When he slipped his hand low beneath the fringed hem she lifted her hips to give him freer access to the damp heat awaiting him.

When he found her ready, hot and slick and pulsing, Aaron nearly lost himself. He nuzzled her temple, breathing fast as he grasped the bottom of her tunic and tugged it over her head.

Pale moonlight washed over her, illuminating her shoulders and breasts, throwing the clefts and valleys of her body into deep shadow. He leaned back from her, not so far as to rob her of his warmth, but enough to gaze wondrously at the perfection before him.

"You are . . . *exquisite*," he murmured, kissing the slender column of her throat. His mouth moved lower, cresting her smooth breast, teasing at the burgeoning nipple. She moaned his name, shuddering helplessly, her hands raking his back and her head tossing. He tried to hold on, but found it impossible to resist her ardent response. " 'Becca, I can't—I need you so much!"

Swiftly, he tore at his own breechclout, freeing himself of the restrictive garment. Rising over her, he cupped her buttocks, lifting her hips to meet him. He shook with the effort required to enter her slowly, carefully, and his tremors deepened at the feeling of hot tightness that enveloped him.

Rebecca could not breathe, could not bear the sensation of fullness that spread inside her, throbbing and swelling with each thrust he made. His movements agitated and aroused her, turning her inside out. She could tell that he struggled for control, and the knowledge empowered her, released her, allowed her to give in to the spiraling madness that began at the core of her and radiated outward to the tips of her fingers and toes.

With a strangled cry she arched upward, and he answered with a potent surge that lifted and drove her beyond the edge of reason. He murmured something incoherent that ended on a groan; then, with a harsh, indrawn breath, he ceased moving except for the deep, convulsive spasm that rippled through them both.

Resting his forehead against hers, Aaron sucked in huge lungfuls of air. He settled his weight onto his elbows. When he felt her wriggle beneath him he started to pull away, but she clutched her thighs tighter and emitted a whimpering laugh.

"Don't leave."

"Whatever you wish, m'dear." He stroked a damp tendril from her cheek with clumsy fingers. "I'm not going anywhere. This is my *wigewa*."

Rebecca smiled shakily. "I wondered. I suppose we're not apt to be interrupted."

He made a rocking movement with his hips, and she responded with another involuntary whimper. "Not a chance. Even if we don't emerge tomorrow morning, or the day after. But if there's no sign of us after the third day someone will come."

She bit down on a soft moan as he eased to his side, taking her with him. He tucked her head against the fleshy pad of his shoulder and wrapped his arms around her, reaching with one hand to draw a fur over them.

"Three days—is that usual after a frolic dance?" she finally asked.

"For some." He gazed directly into her eyes, reveling in the shining warmth he found there, though he hesitated before saying, "Not everyone joined hands without the scarf, you know. You didn't have to do it."

After all they had done, Rebecca still had the ability to blush. "Bird Woman said if I wanted to follow you to your hut, I had to show you by touching you with my bare hands."

Aaron thought his heart would melt with tenderness. She *had* known what she was doing. At least in part. He drew her close, resting his chin on the top of her head. "But did Bird Woman tell you what it means?"

"It means . . ." she said quietly, her breath moist and sweet and hot against his throat, "that I love you."

Now his heart did melt, dissolving into a pool of liquid flame that warmed him to the farthest reaches of his soul. Not for years had he felt so full, so complete. So redeemed.

His breath seemed locked in his chest, but there was no need to breathe as long as he held her. "It means more than that, 'Becca." Her sigh fluttered against his skin. He felt it like the kiss of a summer wind, and the strength flowed back into his limbs with a sudden rush. He tightened his arms.

"It means, m'dear, that we are married."

CHAPTER 23

"M-married?"

"According to the Shawnee, yes." Aaron felt the unsteady beat of her pulse and wondered at how it could so closely match his own. He said cautiously, "Does that bother you? I thought Bird Woman would have explained. . . ."

Rebecca released a shaky breath. She didn't know what to think. Just now she did not want to think at all. She only wanted to feel. "Would I have been allowed to stay with you otherwise?" she asked quietly.

"Not without raising questions. A Shawnee woman has the right to invite any man she wishes to share her pallet, but since you are not Shawnee and I am, The People might have looked oddly upon any other arrangement. It is done—couples living together without benefit of marriage, I mean—but as a rule it's not considered completely respectable."

"And you need their respect," Rebecca said softly. She sighed. "I suppose as long as we're here, we have no choice but to follow the Shawnee ways, right? But you should have warned me, even if this is only a temporary arrangement."

Aaron shifted, his eyes searching out hers in the dim light. "It's not temporary to me, 'Becca, any more than our joining was ten years ago." When she stiffened involuntarily he stroked her cheek. "Don't worry, I won't hold you to vows you didn't realize you made. But I won't pretend I don't want you."

Caressing his rigid jaw, she placed a kiss on his firm

mouth. "And I could no longer pretend I didn't want you. That's why I joined in the dance."

Rebecca watched his face as he gazed down at her with an expression of great tenderness and underlying passion. She had wondered if by sharing physical love with him he would assume that her doubts had all fled. Now she was grateful that he seemed to understand.

She snuggled against him once more. Aaron continued to stroke her back, his palm sliding lightly over her smooth skin. Amazingly, he felt himself growing aroused again.

"There should never be a reason for pretending, 'Becca," he said in a strangled whisper. "Only honesty."

Then why can't you say it? his own conscience haranged. *Why can't you tell her you love her?*

Because he would not bind her to him now, Aaron argued silently. Not while his own future was so uncertain. She was right about that. She had Samuel to think of, and her own security.

But she was thinking of neither at the moment, he realized when she squirmed closer, sliding her silken belly against him. A shudder rocked through him as he gripped her bottom, pressing her nearer. "God, 'Becca!" he groaned. "I cannot bear—"

She silenced him with her lips and urged him with her hands, until the protest died within him, replaced by a need stronger than any he had felt before. He took her again—or rather, she gave herself to him, opening her arms and her heart to welcome him home. This time, though, he gave back to her measure for measure, slowly bringing her to the peak, again and again, before allowing them both to plunge over the edge of the abyss.

And when at last they lay trembling in each other's arms, Aaron held her close to his heart. The sounds of the revelry had faded and the moon had risen higher. Now the hut was like a cocoon, warm and replete and glowing. Everything he needed was here.

He kissed her hair and she shivered, sighing against his chest. "I-I didn't know it could be this way ever again."

"Neither did I," he answered. "It's been such a long time . . . ten years."

She stirred, and he felt her hold a breath before it fluttered at last across his cooling flesh. "It's been that long for me, too."

His muscles tightened. "But you said—"

"I mean like this. With Levi . . . well, it just wasn't the same," she admitted softly. "I didn't want it to be. It was as if I had something special—something only we had shared—to hold on to. Even when I thought you were lost to me forever."

Aaron groaned, rolling over her, pinning her to the soft mound of furs. He cupped her face gently, peering hard into her dark eyes. "We do have something special, 'Becca, and it will *never* die. Maybe I shouldn't be, but I'm glad you kept that much of yourself for me."

She wound her arms around his neck, hugging him close, but he caught the note of hesitation in her voice. "When you said it'd been a long time for you . . . you didn't mean—?"

The darkness hid her blushing face, though he felt the heat suffuse her cheeks as he caressed them gently. "There have been a few women, 'Becca. But no one I cared for so much."

"Then you've never lived with anyone? Surely there were women willing to do that, like Yellow Feather. You said such things are accepted by the Shawnee."

"They are"—Aaron chuckled—"and Yellow Feather takes advantage of that freedom." Then his tone grew serious once more. "But the Shawnee also teach that a man must be master of himself. It seemed unfair to live with a woman when I had no love to return."

When Rebecca lapsed into silence for a long moment, he kissed her brow. "Enough talk. You must be sleepy." Her halfhearted protest did not sway him. He eased to his side once again, scooping her closer with one arm so that her slender back lined his chest and her soft, round buttocks fit against his hips. She sighed contentedly, and he inhaled the scent of her hair, burying his face in its silkiness.

So where is your self-control now? his inner voice chided. How fair was it to make unspoken promises now, when he had no idea whether he could keep them or not? How far would good intentions take him if Rebecca and

Samuel were forced to pay for his sins, whatever they might have been?

Those thoughts swirled through his mind, but they were soon eclipsed by the warmth and tenderness he felt toward Rebecca. He was far too comfortable, too satisfied, too pleasantly tired to dwell for long on trouble.

Trouble would come to him in its own time, Aaron decided. For now he would sleep.

Rebecca picked her way among the rocks, a basket balanced on her hip and her skirts hitched up over bare feet and ankles. Ahead of her, White Star led the way confidently, leaping nimbly from foothold to foothold, though she carried a larger basket on one shoulder and the baby, Smiles at Strangers, strapped to her straight back.

"So! Re-beck-ah finally joins us once more." Bird Woman's voice carried from the opposite side of the creek, where she knelt next to a flat rock, pounding on a piece of soiled fabric as if she could physically beat the bloodstain into nonexistence. "Your man pleases you well, I see. We wondered how many nights would pass before you grew hungry."

Despite her resolve not to, Rebecca blushed at the woman's loud observation. "Hello, Bird Woman. *Ayi-ayeh,* Yellow Feather," she greeted.

The young maiden with whom she had vied for a place in the dance turned her head and coughed deeply, then looked back up with a sullen expression.

Still sulking, Rebecca thought to herself, trying not to feel smug. After making her way across the trickling water, she glanced at Bird Woman, who grinned mischievously.

"It was a good celebration, was it not?" she crowed. "We *still* have not seen She Who Sighs, though someone told me Swift Arrow was bathing in the river late last night, singing under his breath. Perhaps She Who Sighs will sigh no more, huh?"

White Star spoke up as she, too, waded across the creek to join Bird Woman, and the older woman replied in her native tongue, then burst into laughter. "I did not choose a husband for myself," she explained, sending Rebecca a sideways grin, "because there is no man of this tribe with blood hot enough to suit me. In De-troit my man was big"—she dropped her cloth into the creek and spread her arms wide—"with much flesh to keep me warm at night. These young braves are too skinny. I will wait for one to fatten up.

"But you, Re-Beck-ah," Bird Woman pointed, swiftly diverting attention away from herself, "you are happy with your man as he is. Do not try to deny it. I can see by your eyes."

"It's true, I am happy," Rebecca admitted with a rueful laugh, following White Star to kneel beside the creek bed. "But I have not been in the hut all this time. Aaron took me through the forest to visit the village of Bear Dancing yesterday."

"Ahhh." For once Bird Woman had nothing more to say, but she glanced around at some of the other women, who all watched Rebecca curiously.

Rebecca pretended not to notice, bending instead to wash the soiled garments in her borrowed basket. Though the council meetings Aaron had attended did not include the women of the tribe, it was clear they all knew about his purpose here. Yesterday's attempt to gain support from other Shawnee villages had proved inconclusive; Bear Dancing was apparently willing to wait for Wind at His Feet to arrive at a decision before committing himself.

"It's a beginning, though," Aaron had told her hopefully. "At least they are giving my suggestions consideration. I would not have been surprised if Bear Dancing had tossed me out of the council lodge with his own hands. He's known for his temper."

Rebecca doubted the towering chief would have carried the matter to such an extreme; it was obvious to her that all the Shawnee held a great deal of respect for Cain. Everywhere they went, the villagers treated him with deference, and she had been showered with kindness and friendship, as befitted the "wife" of a valued tribesman.

Wife. Rebecca dipped her head low, wringing the water from her petticoat, which White Star had returned. She turned to lay it across a large rock, glad that for the moment her face was hidden from the other women.

It had been easy in the past few days to forget that another world waited for them. Once they left here, Aaron would have to report back to his duties at Fort Washington and she would return to home and Samuel as if nothing had changed.

But much had changed, she admitted freely, and most of it in her own heart. She loved Aaron, and she loved being a "wife" to him, in more ways than just those they shared in the intimacy of his *wigewa*. He had trusted her with the details of his meetings, and had asked her opinion on several points. Theirs was becoming a true partnership—of spirit as well as of body.

If only there were not so many questions to be resolved, Rebecca thought. As lovingly as Aaron treated her, he still had not said he loved her. And as much as he tried to make up for the past, she still resented the fact that he had not returned to her after the war. His past actions were still too much of a mystery for her to completely trust the future.

Swallowing her uncertainty, Rebecca reached for another item of clothing, leaning forward over the crystal-clear water of the stream. She could see her wavering reflection in the moving water, and for an instant she was startled by the stranger staring up at her.

That was how she felt these past few days. Distanced from her real self. Like another person wearing her skin and hair, but quite unlike the steady, practical woman she had become. She felt more like the carefree girl she once was.

Aaron made her feel that way. For that she would always be grateful. No matter what happened, she vowed silently, she would not regret this adventure, nor would she blame Aaron when it ended. She *wasn't* a naive child anymore. This time, she had known the risk of loving him, and she had accepted it with her eyes wide open. If she was hurt, she could hold no one responsible but herself.

"Re-beck-ah," Bird Woman called, interrupting her thoughts, "What will you tell the white women at the fort of your Shawnee friends when you return? That we are so dull you cannot hear our words without falling asleep?" Several more women had now joined the group at the creek bed, and their giggles rippled in the morning air like the sound of the sparkling stream.

"I'm sorry," Rebecca said quickly, "I was thinking."

"About your man, no doubt." Bird Woman chuckled. "Too much thinking in that direction will make you hot, and this day will become warm enough from the sun, don't you think?" She gestured toward the clear blue sky. "Better to talk with me about the way to tan a deer hide."

White Star murmured a soft phrase, her doe eyes slanting toward Rebecca with compassion and gentleness.

"She says, are you longing for your son?"

Rebecca smiled back at the woman, recalling that the first time they had laid eyes on one another, it was the presence of their children that had created an instant understanding. "Tell her I do miss my Samuel. I am anxious to see him soon, though then I will miss my new Shawnee friends."

Bird Woman relayed the message, which was met with smiles all around. "You will come to visit us again?" she urged.

"I'll come back," Rebecca said, nodding hopefully. She let her fond gaze drift over the happy, cheerful women, and her heart ached at the knowledge that such a promise might be difficult to keep.

"I will come back," she said once more, "if I can."

Their farewells the next morning were slightly more subdued than their welcome, since Aaron had insisted they leave before dawn. In the gray half-light, they said goodbye before the *wigewa* of Wind at His Feet, who stood straight and proud with a fur draped over one shoulder. Next to him, White Star remained silent, but there was sadness in her eyes.

"You will come back?" Wind at His Feet asked Aaron.

"As soon as I can. If the white soldiers agree to all your requests, then we can start working on a permanent agreement."

Wind bowed his head regally, but Rebecca sensed that doubt weighed heavy in his heart.

"Between brothers there is no need for symbols to mark our friendship," Wind said, "but I would give you a gift to show your leaders the trust I have in you, Cain. These are the first weapons I ever owned." He handed Aaron a pair of tomahawks, decorated with bands of paint and bright feathers. "One my father made for me, the other I carved with my own hand. Now they go with you, to show that Wind at His Feet is prepared to lay down his weapons of war."

Aaron drew in a deep breath, then nodded and took the gifts, handling them reverently. "You honor me with your trust, Wind at His Feet, though you spoke truly when you said there is no need for symbols between friends. I, too, will give you such a gift, so that you may show your people that the white man can put aside his guns as well."

From his pack, Aaron withdrew the long, breech-loading rifle that was army issue for all officers. Wind accepted the gun with a dignified smile.

Rebecca was deeply moved by the exchange, for she could clearly see the bond of affection and respect between these two men. This was what Aaron had wanted her to understand, and she was glad now that he had brought her here. If two people could break through the barriers of race to find mutual trust, then so might two hundred, or two thousand.

And if only others could be made to see that such feelings were possible between the white men and the Shawnee, then the Ohio Valley could exist in peace.

It was dusk of the second day when they arrived back at Rebecca's cabin, and she surprised herself with tears that stung her eyes at the welcome sight of her snug home. Tendrils of smoke curled from the stone chimney, and though the entrance to the store was barred shut, light pooled beneath the window from the keeping room.

"I thought Lenore would have kept Samuel at her place at night," she said in a choked voice. "But it looks like they're here. I can't wait to see them."

Aaron said nothing as he followed her hurrying footsteps. He was ashamed of the sudden pang of jealousy that had stabbed him when he heard the eagerness in her tone. Of course she was glad to be home, he told himself. He only wished it was his home as well.

She raced ahead, and at the sound of her call the cabin door flung open with a hearty bang. A shadowy form appeared on the small porch, small but fast as it launched itself down the single step and into Rebecca's arms.

"Ma!" Samuel cried happily, flinging his thin arms around her neck. "Aunt Nora said you'd be home today or tomorrow, so we made some bread and a big pot of stew and even a cake."

"A cake? That sounds wonderful! Oh, Samuel, I've missed you so."

Even in the semi-darkness, Aaron could see that she struggled against real tears. His own heart thumped painfully, nearly turning over in his chest when Samuel released his mother and hopped toward him, his crutches nowhere in sight.

Aaron hunkered down and opened his arms wide. "It's good to see you, son."

"You, too!" Samuel chirped, offering a willing hug. "Did you bring me the bow and arrows you promised?"

It was so good to hold him tight, to inhale the clean scents of soap and water, to feel the boyish excitement thrumming through his sturdy young body. Aaron released him reluctantly, not wanting Samuel to notice that his arms trembled or that his words came thick. "Sure did," he answered. "And did you do what I asked?"

"Yup! Every day. And I drank all that tea you made Aunt Nora give me, too, even though I don't know how swallowin' that stuff'll help my leg," he said doubtfully.

"It will." To Rebecca's quizzical expression he replied, "I told Lenore how to brew an infusion of comfrey and cherry bark. For strengthening his bones."

She smiled encouragement. "That's good. Let's go inside. I can't wait to see Lenore."

But the peaceful reunion Rebecca anticipated was not to be. From the moment she walked through the door she sensed that something was wrong. Lenore's eyes turned to her and Aaron sadly, and though she crossed the keeping room in a few quick strides to embrace her sister-in-law, the gaunt woman's expression was anything but joyful.

"Lord, but I was worried 'bout you two," Lenore said as she squeezed Rebecca tight. She gave Aaron an equally enthusiastic hug, thumping him hard on the back. "I didn't say anythin' to Samuel when I heard the news, for fear he'd fret over it, but he found out anyway from the other boys. I sure am glad you're both back, safe and sound."

"Lenore, what news?" Rebecca asked anxiously. Her eyes met Aaron's over the other woman's shoulder. He shrugged, just as perplexed as she.

"Sit down first, and I'll dish out some supper. I don't suppose you had anything hot today?"

"Not since breakfast. But don't make us wait. What's happened?"

Lenore slipped a questioning look at Aaron as she placed a steaming bowl on the table. "Dunlap's Station was attacked night before last," she said grimly. "Those folks'd been there less than two months, struggling along in only two strong cabins and a half stockade, without a proper supply of ordnance laid by. It was a blessin' they held out as long as they did."

Rebecca's throat tightened, and her stomach did a slow roll at the frightening picture Lenore painted. As if through a heavy curtain she heard Aaron's muffled voice, low and dark.

"Casualties?"

"Five killed, two wounded bad, and a woman near dead with grief from losing a husband and a son. Bad enough."

"Who did it?"

A long silence pervaded the room; even Samuel had remained still throughout this exchange, leaning against Rebecca with his arm around her neck. Lenore glanced over at her with an odd expression on her face, then looked back at Aaron.

"Injuns, of course."

No movement showed on his strong, etched features. But Rebecca saw his hands fasten around his trencher with a white-knuckled grip. Until this moment she had not truly understood how much it must hurt him to hear derogatory remarks about his adopted tribe. She herself could barely keep from retorting in defense of her new friends.

But people had died. Not soldiers—homesteaders like herself. Families.

Somebody's husband.

Somebody's son.

"How could this have happened?" she asked in a weak voice, pulling Samuel closer.

Aaron stood slowly, towering over them all, even the rawboned Lenore. "Did anyone say which tribe?" he demanded quietly. "Was there evidence?"

After serving up the last platter, Lenore faced him with her hands on her hips. Her face held no condemnation, but it was clear she was too upset for much lenience, either. "There was evidence, all right. Four scalps taken and a tomahawk left buried in—" She stopped, gulping loudly. "Never mind that. We got a new bunch of soldiers here at the post for protection now, and they said the word is it's Shawnee."

"Impossible!" Aaron spat the word out like it was bitter poison. "The Shawnee made no attack. We were there."

But they had visited only two villages, Rebecca thought woefully. Two out of at least a dozen in the whole territory. And not all of them knew or cared about Aaron the way Wind's people did.

"Well, if it wasn't Shawnee it was some other band," Lenore replied steadily. "And most folks don't care if there's a difference or not. Word from the fort is they're planning to retaliate."

The blood drained from Aaron's face, making his scar stand out like a smear of ink on white paper. He stared hard at Lenore, then shifted his gaze to Rebecca. She was stunned by the open despair she saw in his eyes.

"I'll have to leave right away."

"Of course." Standing on wobbly knees, Rebecca helped Samuel to a chair and then hurried to wrap some of the bread in a clean cloth.

He stayed her with a gentle touch to her arm. "Don't bother, 'Becca. I have some corn cakes in my pouch."

"It's no trouble. You'll have plenty, then. I can always bake more tomorrow morn—"

"I'll be back," he murmured, stopping her frantic prattle with a light squeeze. "Don't worry."

She tried not to let him see the panic those words evoked in her, nor the ready tears that threatened to spill from her

eyes though she blinked several times to hold them back.
"I'll walk out with you," she offered.

Once outside, Aaron wrapped his arms around her, and
they clung together in silence and misery. All the bright
promise of the past few days seemed to have disappeared
like the sun behind seething clouds. It was the moment
Rebecca had dreaded, though it had come much more
swiftly and painfully than she had expected.

"I thought I'd have a chance to stay a little longer here
with you—with you and Samuel. . . ." He paused to clear
his raspy throat. "But that's not possible now."

"There'll be time for that later. But . . . oh, Aaron,
what will happen now?" she whispered, wishing they
could simply stay this way forever, standing cheek to
cheek, heart to heart.

"I don't know, 'Becca," he answered in a troubled
voice. "It depends on what I find out when I get to the
fort. Maybe nothing."

They both knew, however, that Lenore's warning was
not a light one. If there were rumors of a pending coun-
terattack, then most likely one was truly in the works.
Rebecca cringed inwardly as she thought of her new friends
and the danger they were in, perhaps unbeknownst to them.

Concern for Aaron, however, overrode all other worries. She threaded her fingers through his hair, massaging
the taut muscles at the back of his neck. "If the army
decides to retaliate, will they expect you to go with them?"

She felt him stiffen, as if the thought brought him so
much anguish he had to steel himself to bear up. He did
not answer for a moment, but his arms tightened around
her, conveying a desperation belied by the resolve in his
voice when he finally spoke.

"I intend to prevent Carswell from making that decision. If he values my opinion at all—if he *ever* did—now
will be the time to prove it. I just hope it's not too late."

CHAPTER 24

Aaron paced the width of Carswell's second-story office, stopping first to peer out the window overlooking the peaceful village of Cincinnati, then crossing to the opposite window, where below drilled two full companies of blue-coated infantrymen. The eager sounds of full-throated battle cries and the brisk, rousing tattoo from the drummer rose up to strike Aaron like a palpable wave of hot air, oppressive and threatening.

They wish for war, he thought inconsolably. *The fools.*

Too many of the soldiers below had never seen any conflict, except perhaps for that moment when they broke the news of their chosen profession to weeping mothers and staunch fathers. Those who were experienced in battle remembered too well their humiliation at the hand of the tribes six short months ago. Vengeance drove them now to put aside the horror and pain of war in favor of a chance to settle the score.

In all, Aaron had seen not one grim expression from the moment he had returned. Instead, Fort Washington teemed with hearty grins and rank excitement, like a schoolroom full of boys awaiting the tutor's dismissal.

God help them, he thought. *God help us all.*

Behind him, the wooden palisade shook with approaching footsteps. Aaron straightened and turned, bringing his heels together sharply and the fingers of his right hand to his sweating brow.

"At ease, Captain," Henry Carswell commanded.

The major's broad shoulders filled the narrow entrance as he came through the door, trailed by the ever-present

Corporal Lutz, who clutched a sheaf of papers in both
hands while struggling to keep three rolled maps from
slipping out from under his arm. Despite his efforts, one
tipped forward and dropped to the floor, the wax seal
breaking open on impact. The map unfurled amid the
sound of rustling paper and the corporal's muttered ob-
scenities.

"Leave everything here, Corporal," Carswell said be-
nevolently, indicating the map table beneath the outer
window. "And see to it that we're not disturbed."

Lutz threw a disgruntled look at Aaron, who studied
him at length through hooded eyes. How was it that Carswell seemed to trust the little weasel? He would have
guessed the major was a better judge of character.

Lutz positioned himself so that his back was to the officers as he spread the maps on the table. "Should I bring
refreshments?" he asked as he made a show of straightening the fallen map.

"Cambridge? No?" The major turned to the fumbling
Lutz. "Very well, then, that will be all, Corporal. I'll see
to those. And close the door, please."

Major Carswell waited until Lutz had waddled from the
room before turning his perceptive gaze to Aaron, who
was frowning at the clerk's back. Carswell's upper lip
curved beneath his full, graying mustache. "Is there anyone in this entire fort whom you trust?"

Aaron relaxed his stance, glancing once again to the
readying army outside. "One or two. Considering the current mood, it might be more prudent to wonder if any of
them trust me."

"Good point," the major agreed, moving to his place
behind the table. "But let me ask you this. Do you trust
me?"

His strong hands were clasped behind his back, giving
him the appearance of a scholar about to lecture a crowd.
Aaron was once again struck by the air of quiet dignity
the man exuded. Dignity, and honor.

"I trust, sir, that you are a man who will hold to your
word . . . as well as you might."

The major angled his head, his mouth quirking. "A very

astute observation. But hardly the answer I was expecting. Do you doubt my ability to command here?''

"It's not your ability that worries me." Aaron gestured abruptly toward the window. "It's a strange mood brewing out there. I've seen what can happen when the blood becomes stirred and the talk bold. I saw it when we fought the British. I've seen it here in the valley, though from the other side. The Shawnee incite and arouse such feelings with their war paint and war dances, urging their men on to greater feats of bravery and daring. Such a temper, once provoked, is difficult to control." He turned his head toward the major. "That's what worries me."

Carswell closed his eyes contemplatively, then opened them to face Aaron straight on. "Can you blame them for feeling as they do? The safety of the valley is threatened, and the army responds. It's what they've trained for, you know. The reason most of them are here."

"How well I know," Aaron answered with a grimace. "But I thought you understood why I cannot rejoice in this manner of wholesale reprisal."

"Do you wish the guilty to go unpunished, then? Would you be so forgiving if the roles were reversed, if it were your friends who were murdered? Perhaps you have made the wrong choice, Captain Cambridge."

Carswell's voice was so low, almost subdued, that Aaron was startled by the veiled recrimination there. He felt himself turning red in the face. "I have no objection to catching and charging the party responsible for the attack. If it will allay your doubts," he added bitterly, "I will find them and bring them back myself."

The air inside the room grew stifling. Aaron waited for some response from the major. Outside, the fifes and drums called a piping "to arms" and the ensuing shouts and sound of running feet whirled upward. A practice, only, he thought drearily. But to what end?

The major moved then, riffling through the stack of papers before him with long, aristocratic fingers, until he found the one he sought and pulled it from the sheaf.

"This dispatch arrived yesterday from Philadelphia. The Military adjutant is still investigating the situation at West Canada Creek." He hesitated, peering dolefully at the message in his hand. "It's only fair to tell you that charges are pending."

A cold fist closed around Aaron's heart. "Charges of desertion?"

"No, of murder." Carswell flipped the paper over as if searching the backside for more information, then sighed and let the dispatch flutter to the table. "After you disappeared, the rest of your unit was found along with the patrol sent out later to back them up. All seven men were dead."

Aaron pushed himself away from the window, where he had braced himself against the onslaught of emotions sweeping through him. Icy fear settled over him like a numbing blanket, though he fought it off with anger. His fingers curled into tight fists at his sides. "Have they forgotten that I was wounded as well? Or that those woods were crawling with British regulars and their Mohawk allies?"

"But apparently they were not. The enemy had disbursed by that time, according to the remainder of the company. And a survivor of the original band claims that you were alone with the wounded while he left to scout the area. His report stated that he heard shots fired and hurried back to find the rest of the patrol massacred."

"And they think I did it?"

Carswell placed his hands behind his back again, moving to the opposite window, where he scanned the horizon for a moment before turning back to Aaron. His voice was grim. "They did not—until you showed up alive."

Aaron turned away, cushioning his forehead on his arm as he stared across the courtyard full of drilling soldiers. All his high hopes of redemption were coming to naught, he mused. An illusive fantasy, this idea of freedom from the past, when no matter what he did the past seemed ready to rise up to strangle him.

The only good to come of his attempt to discover the truth was his reunion with Rebecca. Those memories of the past were good ones, made sweeter by the promise of a future. But if he wound up in prison or worse, she would not thank him for dredging up old feelings—emotions that might have been better off left alone.

"So what next?" he asked sourly. "Prison, or hanging?"

Behind him Carswell let out a huffy breath that might have been a laugh. "Don't be so quick to condemn yourself, man! I'm not yet convinced that there are sufficient grounds for the charges, which haven't been formally laid to begin with. I filed a report of my own after our last discussion. A favorable one. But I may as well warn you, if this comes to trial my opinion won't carry as much weight as the testimony of that single surviving member of your unit. He'll likely be the one who decides your fate."

Carswell paused again before adding, "I suppose you can guess who that witness is."

"Jessup!" Aaron's voice was barely above a whisper, swept away by the breeze and lost among the noisy shouts from below. Helpless rage surged through him. Already the man hated him, and no wonder: Jessup believed he had murdered fellow soldiers.

But he was mistaken, wasn't he? The hell of it was, until he regained his memory of that time, Aaron could not say for sure.

"When I questioned Captain Jessup myself he clearly stated that he knew nothing about this incident, and yet his report from ten years ago proves that he did. Given this discrepancy," Carswell said firmly, "the sooner I speak to Captain Jessup, the better. I intend to do so immediately after his return."

Aaron jerked his head around. "His return? Where is he?"

"I sent him to Fort Miami to deliver reinforcements there. He left three days ago—*before* the attack on Dunlap's Station. I expect him back anytime now."

"He'll enjoy this, no doubt," Aaron said humorlessly. "Not just seeing me brought down, but all this, too." He waved a hand at the scene of fomenting excitement below, then swung around, determined not to accept defeat. "You cannot let my work of these past days go to waste, Major. Not if you truly mean to bring peace to this valley. There's still a chance."

"I believe so, too," Carswell said after a brief pause.

He returned to the map table, where the chart they had worked on depicting Indian towns was already spread open for his perusal. Aaron moved closer to his side.

"Everyone is full of talk of the attack, but I've heard nothing about which tribe was responsible. Do you know?"

"That's what I want you to find out," Carswell admitted. He ran a long finger from the irregular shape that marked Fort Washington, northward along Mill Creek and then west to Dunlap's Station on the Great Miami River. "If anyone can read the clues, it's you, Cambridge. I want you to lead a unit up there to check out the situation, then report back to me with your findings. You'll have to hurry, though."

Aaron nodded, his mouth pulled into a thoughtful frown as he studied the map. Obviously this was Carswell's way of proving his confidence in him. But it was just as obvious that the major wanted him away from the fort, where he was viewed as less than trustworthy by most of the other men.

And he would not be present for Carswell's interview with Jessup, either.

"All right. I can be ready to leave in an hour. On one condition. I go alone."

Carswell's brow lifted. He was not accustomed to having his orders altered. "This mission will not be without its dangers, Cambridge. That war party may still be in the area, not to mention scattered groups of angry settlers. There is no time to delay."

"All the more reason for me to make my way through the forest trails in silence. I can move faster by myself. You'll have your report in three days."

The major seemed about to ask another question; then he nodded abruptly and smiled. "Very well. Three days, Cambridge."

Aaron scanned the map once more, though the details were already emblazoned in his mind. This was land he had traversed for years; he had no need of charts and squiggly lines to show him how to get to the beleaguered settlement of Dunlap's Station, nor to the other stops he was privately planning.

Carswell could not begin to realize the danger involved, but that was just as well. His success could well depend on utmost secrecy.

Aaron's thoughts then turned to Rebecca, and his heart beat faster with a desire that could not be suppressed even by this dark turn of events. If for no other reason, he must succeed for Rebecca's sake. Not because he was so arrogant as to think she could not live without him, but because he understood too well the pain of losing love.

He had failed her once, Aaron thought resolutely. He would die before putting her through that turmoil again.

Rebecca was hanging sheets from a line behind the cabin the morning after Aaron left when she was startled by a high-pitched whooping that made her drop her wooden clothespins as she spun around. The wind whipped the damp cloth so that it clung to her with desperate, clammy hands. She batted it away frantically, her heart pounding and her head swiveling back and forth to see the cause of the din.

Footsteps pelted the ground around her just as the sheet billowed high once again, and she felt her skirts swirl upward along with it, lifted by the breeze and by the quick, agile bodies brushing past.

Her throat locked around a scream—then choked on reluctant laughter as she heard another familiar whoop just behind her.

"Samuel Osborne!" she cried, peeling wet linen from her cheek and shaking herself free. "You frightened the life out of me!"

"Aw, Ma! We was just playing."

"*Were* playing." Clear of the impeding laundry, Rebecca glared down at the four mud-streaked faces surrounding her. Two of the figures were shirtless and had chicken feathers tied to their heads; the other two, one of them Samuel, were covered from head to toe in ashes, presumably from the roasting pit located just outside the stockade walls. "What on earth?"

"We're Injuns, Aunt 'Becca," Zeb piped up. Lenore's youngest son peered at her innocently through wide blue eyes.

"An' we're white trappers," chimed in Arnold Gates.

"Hardly," Rebecca scoffed. "Turn around and march away from these clean sheets this instant—all of you! You're far too dirty to be playing this close to my laundry."

"We had to hide, Ma, else the Injuns'd scalp us sure!" Retreating with his friends to a safe distance, Samuel grinned up at her proudly.

With only one crutch beneath his arm he scrambled around quite well—better than before she and Aaron left for the Shawnee town. Though he could not yet support his full weight on the splinted leg, he was clearly in far less pain than just a few weeks earlier. Rebecca's heart immediately softened. How could she fault him for playing the way he ought, with the carefree exuberance of youth?

But after making friends with the Shawnee, she took exception to the violent theme of the boys' play-acting.

"If you must pretend to be Indians and trappers, then why not play friends?" she suggested. "You could set up a trading post, or perhaps have a peace celebration."

The boys glanced at one another with skeptical frowns. "But that's no fun, Miz Osborne," one of them pouted. " 'Sides, that's not the way Injuns really act."

"And when was the last time you talked to an Indian, Arnold? Why, the Shawnee around here can be just as friendly as you or I. And their children, too, are polite and clean and well-behaved. . . ." Now the frowns deepened. "So I'll hear no more of this nonsense about scalping. Agreed?"

The four boys regarded her solemnly; then one by one they nodded.

"Good. Then you may go into the store with Samuel. You can each have one nugget of hard candy, and if you want you can take two blankets and some tools to play trading post, if you promise to bring them back when you're done. But please don't touch anything else," she called after them when they turned as one to sprint toward the front of the cabin.

Once the boys were gone, Rebecca finished hanging the wash with her thoughts elsewhere. She remained vaguely disturbed by the incident, convinced that the flying rumors and high emotions of the day had contributed to the boys' attitude.

She could not bear to think of what would happen if *all* the settlers felt the same. Rebecca prayed that Aaron would be successful in averting trouble for Wind at His Feet and his people.

It was later that same evening, when the settlement lay quiet, that Rebecca had a chance to think about the consequences to herself if Aaron was successful in establishing a place for himself in the valley, as he claimed to want.

Sitting alone before the dying fire with a pile of mending in her lap, it was easy to let her mind drift playfully over the time she and Aaron had spent together. And with those thoughts, too, came the fierce longing that had been sparked by mutual desire, but had been kindled and fanned to flame by friendship and growing trust.

She could no longer deny that she wanted Aaron, not just in a physical sense, but for all the reasons she had loved him before. But she was still disturbed by his occasional moodiness, and frightened by the unanswered questions that kept him from pledging himself to her.

A light thumping on the stairs behind her drew Rebecca's attention. She smiled lovingly as Samuel limped into the firelight, his nightshirt scarcely covering his knees. The bark splint peeked out from beneath the loose garment, the only reminder that her son was not perfectly healed.

"Can I . . . can I ask you somethin', Ma?" he said quietly, pausing at her side.

"Of course, darling. Come here."

He was reluctant at first to approach, then appeared relieved when she moved the small stack of clothes from her lap and patted it for him to sit down. He squirmed into place and lay his head against her shoulder.

Rebecca wrapped her arms around him, hugging his thin body tight. "What is it?" she prodded.

He sighed and wiggled closer. "Today, after we was here—"

"*Were* here," she corrected automatically, then smiled at herself. "Go on."

"After we were here, we all went to Tommy's cabin with the things you said we could take, 'cause his pa has a big shed we wanted to use for a trading post. But when his Ma found out what we was . . . *were* doing, she got real mad."

"Did you ask permission to use the shed first?"

"Uh-huh. But that's not why she was mad."

Rebecca was seized by a sense of foreboding, though she gave Samuel an encouraging squeeze. "Tell me, then," she murmured.

He hesitated, burrowing his head into her shoulder. "She said we had no business actin' like Injuns was friendly, when they killed her brother and his young'uns last year. When I tried to explain that Cain—that *Aaron* and you thought different, she got even madder. She said Aaron was no better'n a damn Injun himself. And she said . . ."

"What did she say, Samuel?"

"She said no decent woman would have truck with an Injun, and if you did, then you was no decent woman!"

This last came out in a rush, and Rebecca could hear the tears lacing his words. She closed her eyes and pressed her brow against his smooth, soft hair, fighting off her own tears with a huge gulp.

"I'm sorry, Samuel, that you had to hear such a thing. Mrs. Brownley must have been terribly sad to lose her brother in such a horrible way. Now it sounds as if she's unwilling to change her mind about the Indians. I only wish she had not taken out her anger on you."

"It's all right, Ma," Samuel said, shuddering. "I didn't mind so much, except that she made it sound like Aaron was a bad person. I like him! How could she say that when she don't even know him?"

For once Rebecca did not correct his grammar. An aching sadness welled in her heart, both for the boy struggling to come to grips with an unfair world, and for a world where bigotry existed at all.

"That's exactly the problem, darling," she said softly. "No one should ever make an assumption about other people if they don't know the truth. It's called prejudice, and it's one of the worst ways that one human being can hurt another.''

"Like sayin' someone's bad, when really they might have a good reason for doing whatever they're doin'."

"Exactly. Or by behaving in a way that you *think* others might act.''

Samuel tipped his head to meet her eyes. "You mean like today, when we was playing Injuns?''

Rebecca nodded thoughtfully, then hugged him to her chest again. "Samuel, do you know why I went with Aaron to visit the Shawnee?''

"Sure," he replied readily. "Aunt Nora said he tricked you into goin'."

"That is true," she said, amused. "Though once we were on our way I was glad. Did Aunt Lenore tell you that Aaron and I knew one another when we were much younger?''

Samuel nodded rapidly. "She said that's why my middle name is Aaron. He was your friend, and Pa's, too.''

"Yes, a very good friend. But it was many years since I'd seen Aaron, and . . . and we both had changed a great deal. We needed a chance to get to know one another again. I wanted to learn more about how he lived with the Shawnee, and Aaron wanted to visit his friends."

Puckering his brow, Samuel asked, "Is he gonna go back there someday?''

Good question! "I don't know," Rebecca said honestly. "A lot depends on what happens in these next few weeks. I think Aaron *wants* to stay near us, but he may not be able to.''

After a long silence, Samuel sat up, pulling away from her enough that she could see his expressive face as he mulled over his thoughts. His blue eyes, so much like Aaron's, rested on her unblinkingly. "Are you gonna marry him?''

Rebecca had wondered how she might broach this subject; she had not thought that Samuel would dive right to the heart of the matter. Her mind flicked back to the night of the frolic dance. Like him, in her heart she was as bound to Aaron as if they had stood before a parson and uttered more familiar vows.

And yet, even now, she could not give Samuel a definitive answer. "I don't know that, either, darling. There are many, many problems we would have to work out." She touched his soft cheek. "But now that you've brought up the subject, how *would* you feel about it if I did marry again?"

"Would Aaron be my pa then?"

She had meant to keep the discussion hypothetical, but there was no skirting the issue with Samuel. "Yes," she said after a moment.

She waited with bated breath for her son's response, surprised by how nervous she was. Even while claiming all along that Samuel's welfare was her first concern, she had never truly expected him to object to Aaron becoming a part of their lives. If he did . . .

Her worrying came to naught, however. With typical boyish glee, Samuel's eyes began to sparkle and a grin lit his face. "Did he ask you to marry him yet?"

"No . . . not exactly."

"Then why don't we ask him?"

Relief flooded her, but it could not suppress the doubts that still crowded her thoughts. She drew her son close again, hugging him tightly. "It's not quite that simple, darling. But I am glad to know that you . . . like Aaron so much."

"Next time he comes here I'm gonna tell him," Samuel proclaimed decisively. "Then he'll want to marry you for sure!"

Rebecca chuckled softly, but did not answer. Once again, comforting silence filled the room. The only sounds were an occasional snap from the burning wood and the low hiss of the dying flames. She continued to rock until Samuel's body grew heavy and lax, but her own mind would not cease worrying about what would become of Aaron.

Snuggling her cheek against her son's flaxen hair, Rebecca sighed. She envied the ease with which he slept— envied the way he could solve life's dilemmas with childlike candor.

If only it were so simple, she repeated silently. So simple.

CHAPTER 25

The first shot came unexpectedly. The sound exploded through the silent woods with a thunderous warning that gave Aaron only a split second to dive into the thick underbrush. The blast seemed to linger amid the branches like foul smoke, its reverberations still pulsing beneath the indignant cackle of a thousand birds taking wing. Their startled cries followed them high aloft, over the canopy of leaves above, to the freedom of the sky.

Lying on his back, Aaron watched them go. His heart beat as rapidly as the birds' wings, and for an instant he wished he could fly with them, away from this madness. Automatically his hand touched his scar. Was his memory playing tricks on him? Again?

But then the stinging sensation worked its way to the surface of his cheek, and he knew this was no dream. After probing the burning flesh carefully, he drew his fingers away.

His hand was wet with blood.

Another shot ripped through the night. This one missed by a wide margin; he could hear the ball ricochet from one tree before coming to rest with a splintering thump into the trunk of another. Aaron dropped his hand and rolled carefully to his side, peering through a screen of leaves into the small clearing where he had stopped to rest just a few minutes before.

Though he had not bothered with a fire, not wishing to take the time, the area was well lit. Moonlight bathed the loamy earth in silvery light; it danced off leaves like pale droplets of rain and turned stark, bare branches into shimmering wands.

And it made hiding near impossible.

Aaron scanned the clearing helplessly. Over near the largest tree lay his pack, spilled open where he had dropped it at the first shot. Strips of dried venison and a slab of Rebecca's fresh bread lay in full view—the supper he had been about to eat. And leaning against the tree, so close his fingers itched for it, was his musket.

With an effort he mastered his breathing, needing all his senses tuned and alert. His eyes flicked back and forth in their sockets, searching for the least movement in the brush surrounding the clearing. His nostrils flared as he attempted to locate the direction of his assailant from the drifting scent of powder. Now that the birds were gone, only the faint rustling of the breeze through the treetops tickled his ears.

Nothing.

Not daring to move more, Aaron licked his lips and swallowed carefully, tasting the blood as it dripped from his cheek down into the crevice of his mouth. He shuddered uncontrollably, not from cold, but from a sudden jarring recollection.

No, not really a recollection, he thought, squeezing his eyes closed to try to keep the sensation from fleeing. But it slipped away like a wisp of fog, lacking substance and form. Not quite a memory; not quite a vision. But the shock of it went through Aaron with a very definite jolt.

He knew without a doubt that his injury of ten years ago had come in just this way. At night. In the dark of the woods. From behind.

How long he lay that way, his breath shallow and his heart pounding in his throat, Aaron wasn't sure. But it seemed only minutes before the birds returned, only now instead of roosting silently, their raucous chirping welcomed the dawn.

Slowly, moving with caution as much to ease the cramped muscles of his own limbs as to keep from setting the birds off again, Aaron pushed himself to his knees. When no reaction came—beyond the impatient twitter of a robin—he raised himself above the protective covering of bushes and looked around.

There was no sign of another human soul, but he decided he must have fallen asleep at some point, because the bread had been dragged off a few feet from the pack and was now half the size that it was before. The gun and the rest of his gear lay untouched. Deliberately, he stood.

Under normal circumstances, Aaron would have trusted fully the instincts that told him he was alone now, instincts honed by many years of surviving in the forest. But that keen sense had failed him in the night, and he was still shaken by the revelation brought on by the ambush. He waited several minutes before stepping all the way into the clearing, and once there stopped only long enough to thrust his gear into the haversack and shoulder his musket. He would not wait around for another shot. The next one might do more serious damage.

Thinking of it made him touch his cheek again. Already the blood was dry, caked at the edges of a narrow gouge that neatly traced his old scar. The abrasion was still tender, but it did not hurt overmuch. Nor was it very deep, Aaron decided wryly. It would likely heal without changing his appearance at all.

It was a reminder, however, of the dangerous line he now treaded. Someone had tried to kill him, and likely as not he would try again.

Once under cover of the dense forest, Aaron stopped to remove one strip of venison from his haversack, then swung the leather pack to his shoulder. With a glance to the sky to locate east, he turned in the opposite direction and continued his trek westward.

Perhaps he should have gone straight to Dunlap's Station as Henry Carswell had ordered, instead of taking a detour to the Delaware village of Stalking Wolf. Grim-faced, Aaron chewed on the tough meat as he concentrated on putting miles between himself and the place of attack.

His appearance at the Delaware village had been met with surprise and suspicion. Aaron was becoming accustomed to dealing with the latter; it was the first reaction that he was relieved to find. If Stalking Wolf had been responsible for the raid on the white settlement at Dunlap's

Station, he would have been prepared for a reprisal. Instead, Aaron had walked into the village unchecked, with only an escort of curious boys and two youthful sentries to guard him.

But that did not mean he was made welcome. Stalking Wolf's people had heard of the legendary Cain's defection to the white fort, and they were not as tolerant as the Shawnee who admired him. And so, after a tense and watchful conversation with the proud Stalking Wolf, Aaron had left at dusk to make his own camp several miles away from the village, where he had thought himself safe.

Yet he did not believe that Stalking Wolf's men had followed him so far. Not because he trusted them, but because it was unlikely they would use a noisy gun to dispatch him. Besides, they could have killed him as he sat at their fire, with no one the wiser.

So if not the Delaware, then who?

Ducking a low branch, Aaron plodded onward, his mind ticking off the possibilities. A hunter? There were a few isolated farms, but none that he knew of in this immediate vicinity. Most of the settlers built their homes in the shadow of the stockades that dotted the valley. For one hunter to range this far alone was unusual. Unusual, but not impossible.

So, then, it could have been a stray shot that grazed him. For some reason the idea of such random carelessness was far easier to accept than an intentional assault. But Aaron did not give the thought more than a moment's consideration.

Even if he *had* been mistaken for wild game in that bright, moonlit clearing, why had no one come thrashing through the brush in search of a carcass? And there were two shots fired, not one—the second well after he was hidden.

Just like a warning.

But a warning for what? Aaron asked himself. A warning from the Indians to stay away from the white men? Or a warning from the white men telling him to break his Indian ties?

Or perhaps no warning at all.

It did not really matter which, he thought resolutely. His path—at least for the next few days—was already decided.

No hunter with poor aim or malcontented warrior would deter him from reaching his goal. He would heed no advice save his own, relying only on himself for guidance. He would put this incident from his mind and heart, and concentrate on his mission.

But if he was also extra cautious when choosing his next bed, that was only common sense. After all, he could be no good to anyone if he were dead.

A flash of lightning lit the sky to the west, illuminating the rounded, tree-covered hills in the distance and filling the yard with white light. Bellowing thunder followed; it ripped through the dusk with an unearthly rumble, seeming to push the crackling air ahead of it like a helpless boat propelled upon a current of doom.

Overhead the trees swayed and trembled beneath the sudden onslaught, and Rebecca was thankful that she had fastened tight the shutters on the upper windows. Samuel was sound asleep by now, and with luck the storm would pass without waking him.

Another streak of lightning speared the earth. Rebecca hugged her shawl tighter, but did not cower from the resounding answer. Instead she stood brazenly on the small front porch, watching the approaching tempest with excitement and awe. She loved the violent spring storms that swept this valley with regularity, as some of the older settlers had told her. They aroused something deep within her, primal emotions that were unleashed only when the heavens opened wide and the wind tore loose all her defenses.

Through the mass of dark hair swirling around her head, Rebecca watched black clouds brewing, rimmed with orange and gold from the sun descending beyond the rolling horizon. She could just make out the river as it curved to the northwest, churning as sheets of rain swept closer and closer. She could smell the rain; it's dank scent hung in the air, a cloying aroma that would always bring to mind heady thoughts and wild impulses.

She shivered lightly, but not from the cold.

Only when the rain finally came did Rebecca escape to the haven of her keeping room, only after the first huge drops had splashed upon her upturned face, soaking her dress in uneven splotches and turning her hair to tangled, limp ringlets. Leaving the south window open so that the room was filled with the essence of the storm, if not its wetness, she stoked the fire hotter, then pulled a chair to where she could enjoy the warmth of the blaze and the magnificence of the tempest.

For the next hour, both roared with equal intensity—then in the aftermath the pattering rain echoed the fire's dying crackle. Though she had not intended to stay the night there, the rhythmic sounds eventually lulled Rebecca to sleep.

It was the tickling sensation on her cheek that woke her.

At first Rebecca though it nothing but a lock of wet hair trailing over her face; she brushed it away halfheartedly, not quite waking but roused from the depths of slumber.

But her hand encountered only soft, dry curls, and with a start Rebecca opened her eyes. The room was completely dark now, save for the feeble glow of the embers on the hearth. Outside the storm had abated, though thick clouds still blocked the moon. Slightly befuddled, Rebecca touched her cheek again, expecting to find it damp even though her dress and hair were now thoroughly dry.

A deep chuckle sent her bounding to her feet. She whirled to face the intruder with a scream hovering in her throat.

" 'Becca, it's me," he whispered, stepping closer. "Don't be afraid."

He was no more than a hulking shape emerging from the blackness, but she knew the voice as well as her own. "Aaron?" she managed to choke. "What are you doing here?"

"You left your door unbarred," he said mildly, reaching for her, "and your window wide open." Clasping her arm, he led her around the chair between them, then gathered her still-shaking form into his strong arms. "You're lucky you weren't wakened by some disreputable fellow with de-bauchery on his mind."

Overwhelmed with relief and joy, Rebecca clung to him as she laughed weakly. "Anyone who would sneak in like a thief is disreputable to me. And if it's not debauchery you have in mind tonight, then I'm afraid I'll be terribly disappointed."

Aaron's mouth swooped down over hers in answer, a gentle, crushing kiss that made her tingle all the way to her toes. Instantly, vitally awake, Rebecca responded with complete abandon, pressing as close to him as her dress and his buckskins allowed. She had not known she was chilled until his warmth enveloped her; she had not realized how much she had longed for this until she felt her blood stir and her limbs buckle.

"I've missed you, 'Becca," he muttered against her mouth, then her hair. "God, how I've missed you!"

She rubbed her cheek against his shoulder, surprised, now, that it was wet with happy tears. "It's only been three days."

"Yes, I know. Three long, torturous days."

"They're behind us, Aaron. You're here now. You're here."

She lifted her face for another kiss, and Aaron obliged most willingly. Her shawl dropped to the floor as she wound her arms around his neck, drawing him nearer, raising on tiptoes to better feel the entire length of him against her.

His hands stroked her back from waist to shoulder, then down again to curve around her buttocks. Through layers of skirts his touch branded her, sending licking flames down the backs of her thighs and through the core of her being.

With one swift movement he lifted her; her feet now dangled helplessly as he held her suspended in his arms. Then he carefully lowered her to the floor once more, tearing his mouth from hers long enough to ask: "Where can we go?"

Hot blood suffused her cheeks as she lowered her eyes demurely, but not before a meaningful glance at the braided rug lying near the hearth.

He grinned in the dark, but paused nevertheless. "Samuel . . . ?"

"Sleeps like a stone," she finished breathlessly, tugging him toward the fireplace.

Aaron needed no further invitation. In the dying light, he lifted from around his neck the leather straps holding his musket and powder horn, then shrugged off his pack. Unconsciously, he raised a hand to one shoulder, massaging the stiff knots there.

"Let me do that," Rebecca commanded softly.

She urged him to sit, then knelt behind him, grabbing the fringe at the bottom edge of his shirt and pulling it up over his lean torso. With his elbows on his knees, he hunched before the fire, letting her soothe away the kinks and ease the tension from his tired muscles.

She could almost feel the tightness flowing out of him as her fingers and palms glided over his firm, supple flesh. When he sighed deeply she smiled, pleased, and pushed the heel of her hand harder against one particularly taut muscle until he groaned with contentment.

Such a simple task to bring such enjoyment. Such a wifely task.

Resting her hands on his shoulders, she leaned forward, brushing her lips to the tender skin at his nape. A few light hairs had escaped from his usually neat queue, and she nuzzled them softly. Gooseflesh prickled beneath her sensitive fingertips.

"Do you like that?" she murmured.

Aaron uttered something like a grunt. Taking it as an affirmative, Rebecca continued to massage his back, only now she added tiny, nibbling kisses to her ministrations. He remained so still she wondered if he were sleeping, then smiled to herself when she thought of the perfect way to test him.

With one hand she alternately scratched lightly across the width of his shoulders and tugged the leather thong from his hair, while with her other hand she unfastened her own bodice. Taking a shaky breath, she wrapped both arms around Aaron in a loose embrace, letting the tips of her breasts brush against his bare back.

A huge tremor swept through them both, though it was difficult to tell who had started it.

"Lord, 'Becca!" he hissed, clasping her hands tightly.

"Just when I was thinking I could let you rub my back all night . . ."

His voice trailed off in a hoarse whisper, and he pulled her around by one arm so that she ended up lying halfway across his legs. His eyes gleamed like molten lava in the dimly glowing light as they flicked up and down her exposed breasts, then came to rest on her flaming cheeks and lowered gaze.

"Don't turn shy on me now." He chuckled, lifting her chin with one finger.

She trembled anew when she met his ardent stare, and her shaking continued as he trailed his finger down her throat, past the throbbing pulse point at the base of her neck and into the valley between her aching breasts. His touch was as light as air, and yet her body responded greedily, her nipples rising to meet his palm even before he moved to caress them.

Her breath came in rapid gulps. "I was afraid you were f-falling asleep."

"It had occurred to me," he answered between the light kisses he bestowed upon each budding peak, "how nice it would be to sleep tonight with my head cradled in your arms. An hour ago I was so tired of walking . . . only the thought of holding you . . . kept me from finding my bed underneath a log, rain or not."

He shifted her in his arms so that now her hip rested in his lap. Rebecca settled against him, assuring herself that he was no longer as weary as he professed. "In that case, I'm very glad you didn't give up." She splayed her fingers through his hair, her lips tracing fiery kisses across his brow. "And you are quite welcome to use me as your pillow. Later."

Aaron gently laid her down upon the worn rug, holding himself carefully above her. With the embers lighting only the unscarred side of his face, he looked to her like some beautiful angel, like a god of fire and passion gazing down at her.

"Later," he murmured in agreement. "Much later."

For the second time that night Aaron woke her.

This time, however, it was not with a feathery kiss.

When she first came to awareness, Rebecca was not sure
what had pulled her from her deep and contented sleep.
Aaron's head lay against her breast like a heavy weight,
damp and hot with perspiration, and though she tried to
ease herself out from under him, he did not stir.

Not immediately, anyway. Soon enough, though, the
rough jerking motion began again, and now she was certain that it was this that had awakened her. This and the
low mumbling that fell from his lips, stretched taut with
remembered pain.

"Aaron?" she whispered quietly.

He did not answer, but soon afterward his body con-
vulsed again, and this time he clutched her tightly, groaning. Truly frightened now, Rebecca placed her hand on his
shoulder and shook him lightly. "Aaron, wake up.
Aaron!"

Like a shot he was away from her, so suddenly her head
fell back to the rug with a dull thump. He sprang over her,
crouched in readiness for . . . for what?

She grabbed the blanket they had pulled from a shelf
close around her neck. "What's wrong, darling? What is
it?"

For a long moment Aaron remained poised; in the darkness she could only sense, rather than see, the tension
coiled in him as he cast his gaze around, gathering his
wits. Then, as quickly as he had jumped up, it was over.
He shook his head hard, slumping back to the floor beside
her.

"God, 'Becca," he said, gathering her to him. "I'm
sorry if I woke you."

She could feel him shaking as he held her tightly, almost
frantically, and heard the unsteadiness in his voice. "It's
all right now, my love," she said. "You were dreaming,
weren't you?"

"I suppose I was."

"What about?"

He held her in silence for a few seconds more, then
released her, turning to face the window, which remained
unshuttered. Though it was only a short time before dawn
would turn the sky gray, no light fell through the open
portal yet. This was the darkest hour, Aaron knew. The

weakest hour. The hour when it seemed morning would never come.

He could not stop himself from shuddering.

"Jessup was there," he said finally. "At least, I think it was a memory and not just a nightmare. He looked different—younger, of course, and less grim. But it was definitely Vance Jessup hiding in the trees with me."

Rebecca scooted closer, lifting the edge of the blanket to enfold him in its warmth. "Aaron, I don't understand," she whispered. "When were you with Captain Jessup?"

"Not Captain," he said, shaking his head. "He was a corporal then. During the war. I remember now—the report Carswell received was right about that. Corporal Vance Jessup was a member of Willett's regiment, all right, and he was present at that last battle, I'm sure of it."

The feverish intensity in his voice disturbed Rebecca, but it was the anguish underlying his words that knifed through her. It was no secret that he and Vance Jessup did not like one another, but why would the knowledge of Jessup's presence at West Canada Creek cause Aaron so much pain?

She could not help feeling that there was more, *much* more. "What else, darling?" she urged gently.

His stomach churned with fear and his pulse raced; cold sweat made his flesh crawl and dampened his palms. Aaron paused, feeling so much like he was hovering on the brink of an abyss with only one step between him and disaster that he could scarcely choke out the words to tell her.

"There was a moon that night. I could see Jessup's face clearly. He was telling me something, handing me a gun and ordering me to use it. But I can't—" He shrugged with frustration. "Nothing! I can't remember anything else. Damn!"

"Nothing?" Rebecca squeezed his arm. "If there was a moon, what else did you see? Was there only you and Jessup? What about the others?"

Aaron bent his head in concentration, forcing deep breaths in and out of his lungs. Already the dream was blurring in his mind. Panicked that he would lose what he had worked so hard to recall, he forced himself to replay it over and over, searching for the detail that might trigger another vital memory.

Even if it was one he did not care to see.

At first his sentences seemed rambling, disjointed. Rebecca listened silently, wishing with all her heart she could help. She did not need to see his face to know the struggle there; she could feel it in the quivering tension beneath her hand, could sense it by the painful hesitation with which he described his dream.

Then he stopped.

Midsentence he broke off, his words trailing into the night like the dying fragments of a shooting star. His body heaved in one shattering sigh. "Eli was there, too," Aaron whispered, his voice so low and rasping she could scarcely hear him.

"Dr. Winthrop?"

He nodded once. "He died . . . he died in my arms. I remember now. There were others—they were all dead, too, or dying. But it was Eli whom I wanted to save. And couldn't."

Lowering his head to his arms, Aaron gave in to the racking shudders that swept over him in waves.

This sudden burst of emotion startled Rebecca, and she stared wide-eyed for a moment before hugging him close. *O God!* she prayed fervently. *What can I do?*

She felt so utterly helpless, so inadequate in the face of his grief. What good was it to wrap her arms around him and whisper meaningless banalities? She could not take his pain away, though she would do it in an instant if she only knew how.

And she could not change the past for him.

Several minutes passed in which Aaron's shaking subsided. Finally he sighed dishearteningly and wiped his face on a corner of the blanket.

"Don't try to remember any more, Aaron," Rebecca pleaded softly. "It's not worth it. I can't bear to see you hurting so badly."

"But I have to, damn it!" He lifted his tortured gaze to her, pounding a fist against his own leg. "It's worse not knowing. Not knowing what I've done, what kind of man I am!"

"*I* know you," she insisted, not the least bit frightened by his anger. She held his cheeks between her palms, keeping him from turning away again. "You *can't* have done anything wrong. Not you!"

It was a moment before he smiled grimly; she felt his lips curve beneath her thumbs. "A few weeks ago you called me heartless."

"I was mistaken."

"No, you weren't." Aaron tried to pull away, but she would not let him. "After . . . after whatever happened that night, I *had* no heart left. Not for you, not for anyone. It was easier that way."

He raised his hand, still shaking abominably, to brush a lock of hair from her damp cheek, and his heart lurched once more to know that she had wept along with him.

So that was it! Rebecca thought. His love for her had not died. It had been killed. Killed by a ruthless war, an accidental victim of a violent and troubled time. But she had once thought Aaron a victim, too, and now he was alive. Could love have survived as well? "That's not true now. Is it? The past is all behind us."

Aaron's eyes were becoming accustomed to the dark, he thought. Either that or dawn was nearer than he had first suspected. He could now see Rebecca's beseeching expression, could see the yearning in her face.

The sight of her made his chest ache with a sudden fierceness that assured him that he did indeed have a heart, or else it could not be breaking.

"It will be soon, 'Becca, m'dear. I pray to God this'll all be behind us soon."

CHAPTER 26

They were both dressed and ready when Samuel woke, and though Rebecca anticipated several awkward questions, the boy seemed to accept Aaron's presence as a matter of course. He was not so agreeable, however, when he heard that his idol could not stay the day.

"But you only just got here! Why do you both have to leave so soon?" he complained loudly—loud enough that Lenore heard him from the yard as she approached the cabin.

"Now, Samuel, you know this is the day your mother always goes down to trade at the market," she chided her nephew. Shooting a glance toward the pair that was only mildly curious, she continued. "And leastways now she won't have to walk all that way alone. Besides, you'll have plenty of chances to see him. Ain't that right, Aaron?"

"Absolutely." Kneeling in front of the boy, Aaron touched his shoulder fondly. "I wish I could stay, Samuel, but I have important work to take care of. Tell you what, though. If you keep exercising that leg, we'll see if I can't come back in a week or so to take off the splint. And maybe then we'll spend some real time together."

"Truly?" Samuel's grin nearly jumped off his face. "That'll be fun. Ma won't let me go near the river, but we can fish in the creek. I can show you where Zeb an' me caught the biggest fish last week. It was this long."

He held his hands a good twenty inches apart, though Rebecca clearly recalled cooking up a smallmouth bass that measured only half that length. She hid a smile. "If you finish those chores I mentioned yesterday, you can go fishing again this afternoon when I get back. Perhaps then you'll catch a whale.''

Samuel was still laughing as they left, she carrying a small purse full of coin tucked into her bodice and the empty basket intended to hold the fabric she planned to purchase. Aaron shouldered his own pack as well as the bundle of pelts she had accepted in trade over the past weeks.

They walked in companionable silence. Aaron did not bring up the subject of his dream, and though she was glad to see that he was not overwrought, Rebecca guessed he had not dismissed it so easily, either. Every now and again she stole a glance at him, just to reassure herself that all was well, that he was still beside her.

But she noticed almost as soon as they began the descent down the ridge toward Cincinnati that Aaron's jaw had tightened imperceptibly, and the grooves on either side of his mouth had deepened.

"What is it, Aaron?" she asked, drawing nearer as he stopped on the trail. She followed his gaze across the sun-drenched valley, past the last dissipating pockets of fog and to the bustling community below.

Except bustling hardly described the scene of commotion surrounding the nearby fort.

Even from this distance they could hear the high-pitched piping and staccato drumbeats of the regimental musicians—unusual at this time of the morning. Troops spilled from the barracks, the men, tiny in the distance, clustering around an approaching group on horseback. The breeze must have been moving toward them, Rebecca thought, for she could distinguish the sounds of shouting voices in the air, though they were yet a mile from the town.

"What's going on?" she asked again.

"I'm not sure," Aaron replied grimly, "but I have a feeling—" He stopped, his gaze narrowing as he watched the soldiers in their obvious excitement. Shifting his musket to his other arm, he took Rebecca's hand and clasped it firmly. "We'd better get down there, and fast."

She nodded, for the next several minutes saying nothing as she strove valiantly to keep up with him. It was a good thing the trail was mostly downhill, she thought, breathless and perspiring from the exertion. Once they reached the lower plain, their view of the fort was blocked by trees. But the din from the milling soldiers was louder now, and Rebecca grew more alarmed with each passing moment.

Had there been another Indian attack? What had Aaron seen that made his brow pucker with worry and his scar grow dark and angry upon his cheek?

The trail broke through the trees just a hundred yards from the western ravelin, and it was around this triangular abutment that the commotion centered. Aaron halted suddenly, pulling Rebecca off the path before they rounded the corner to the front of the fort.

"Maybe you should go on down to the village," he suggested firmly, handing over the bundle of pelts. "Cut through the trees here to the top of the next street. No one will see you."

Rebecca gazed at him, astonished. "But I want to know what's happened!"

"I'll find you and tell you later. This is no place for a woman."

"Nonsense. I always trade at the fort, and so do half the other women in Cincinnati. Skulley gives me the best bargains."

Aaron's jaw tightened. "Then come back in a few hours, after things have settled down. Look, 'Becca," he added, softer now, "won't you let me just see what's going on first? There's no need for you to get upset."

Eyes blazing, Rebecca jerked her chin upward. "Aaron Cambridge, you can't send me off to play as if . . . as if I'm a child with no sense. I understand that you're trying to protect me, but I don't need protection. You should know that by now. Whatever is wrong, I can face it. *We* can face it."

He stared at her long and hard, his eyes unfathomable. "I hope you're right," he finally said with a cryptic smile. "Come on, then. Just stay back a ways, so Jessup doesn't see you right off. He's apt to get nasty again."

Jessup? Was he part of this? As Rebecca followed Aaron around the wooden stockade she shivered lightly, glad that he could not see her sudden apprehension. She had reasons of her own to dislike Vance Jessup, but now that Aaron's returning memory appeared to involve the overbearing officer as well, she was seized with an alarming mistrust of the man. Men might make light of a woman's intuitive sense, but she could not dismiss her strong belief that Jessup meant Aaron some harm.

And she knew just as instinctively that she would do anything to prevent him from being hurt again.

When they entered the gates of Fort Washington she forgot all about these thoughts. They followed the crowd of soldiers who still surrounded a group of several horses and riders who were causing all the stir. Rising on her toes, Rebecca tried to see what was going on.

Aaron continued to push ahead, and she quickly hurried along in his wake, thankful when the muttering throng parted enough to allow them to slip through. Several of the men fell silent as Aaron passed, their stares ranging from questioning to outwardly challenging. As they neared the center, she understood why.

She knew immediately what it was; she had seen a scalp before.

In the middle of the yard, his back to them, a blue-coated soldier proudly held aloft a spear adorned with dozens of ghastly trophies. Blood matted the dark hair of each scalp, and from two still hung the feathers which marked the Shawnees' personal achievements. A few bore the scalplocks of warriors, but several more were braided, indicating that they came from women.

And as Rebecca watched in horrified fascination, the soldier sent one scalp spinning around the shaft of the spear. She saw that it was smaller than the rest. Much smaller.

"Dear God, stop it!" she cried out, but her plea was drowned by the laughter of the men around her. Swallowing bile, she looked quickly to Aaron, hoping he would intervene. But he stood rigid, fury and hatred turning his face to granite.

"Jessup!"

The captain turned, his grin frozen in place for a moment. Then he threw back his head and laughed. "Well,

316 ROBIN LEANNE WIETE

if it ain't the Injun-lover himself! I got a present for you, Cambridge.''

With that he raised the spear over his head, then thrust his beefy arm forward as if to aim the weapon straight at Aaron's chest. At the last moment a twist of his wrist sent the spear arcing through the air. It landed, quivering in the hard-packed earth, at Aaron's feet.

Rebecca gasped and tried to run to his side, but unknown hands held her back.

"There's what's left of your damned Shawnee," Jessup said in a crooning, mocking voice. "You thought you warned them all off, didn't you?"

"You son of a bitch!" Aaron grated. "You had no orders—"

"I had orders to check out the settlements. Ain't that right, Major?"

This last question was directed toward Henry Carswell, who had descended from his quarters to see what all the commotion was about. Carswell glared straight ahead at Jessup, sparing only one disgusted glance for the trophy spear before raking the triumphant captain from heel to hat. "You had no orders to attack. Explain yourself, Captain Jessup.''

Rebecca watched the captain's weathered face turn a deeper shade of russet. Even for one inexperienced with military protocol, she realized how unusual it was to reprimand an officer in public. But if Jessup felt any humiliation, it was well hidden behind his bravado.

"My orders, sir, were to learn what I could about that last raid and to make sure the settlements were safe. And that's just what I did.''

"By murdering innocent people?" Aaron spat. The amount of control required to keep from launching himself at the captain was evident by the white-knuckled fists balled at his sides. He pointed at the spear. "Women? Children?''

Jessup sneered. "Those Injun friends of yours weren't too particular about who they slaughtered. I just paid them back.''

"Paid whom back? The renegades who attacked last week?''

"If you please, Cambridge," Major Carswell snapped, "I will conduct this interview. Go on, Captain Jessup."

"As it happens, Major," Jessup said, never taking his gloating eyes from Aaron, "I did pick up the trail of a band of stirred-up Shawnee braves just south of Dunlap's Station. Tracked 'em for half a day before losing the scent. They was headed west—the same direction Cambridge here took after he warned 'em I was on their trails!"

A murmur of discontent arose among the soldiers, and many who had heretofore listened with only impartial interest now turned to Aaron with accusing looks. Even Skulley, who had positioned himself next to Rebecca just as soon as he realized she was part of the crowd of onlookers, peered at Aaron with a thoughtful frown.

Major Carswell considered Jessup's explanation for a moment, then turned to face Aaron. "Is this true? Did you speak to your Indian friends? Did you warn them of our intent to track down the renegades?"

"Of course I spoke to some people," Aaron said slowly. The muscles in his neck stretched into taut strands. "You asked me to learn what I could about the attack last week. But the tribe I visited knew nothing about the raid, except by rumor."

"How do you know they're tellin' the truth, Cambridge?" Jessup took a rolling step closer. "How do we know *you're* telling the truth?"

"Did you give warning?" Carswell pressed.

"Warning for what? They weren't the ones—" Seeing the disbelief in the major's eyes, Aaron raised his hands in supplication, then let them fall back to his sides. "I did tell Stalking Wolf to be on guard against possible repercussions," he growled. "I suggested he keep his people close to his village and out of trouble for the next few weeks. A lot of good it did them."

"See what I told you?" Jessup fairly crowed. He was no longer addressing only the major, but had raised his voice so that all the astounded audience could hear. "He cares more about the injuns than he does his own. The bastard can't be trusted, that's for sure."

"That's not true!" Rebecca cried out, shoving her way out of Skulley's grasp. She did not stop until she reached

Aaron's side, gasping and furious. Despite his ill-concealed expression of displeasure at her interference, she glared at Vance Jessup with all the withering disdain she could muster. "Aaron cares about everyone. He's trying to *stop* the fighting to save your miserable lives—all of you!"

"Is that right?" Jessup's tone shifted subtly. He stared at Rebecca, then turned back to Carswell. "You ordered Cambridge to check out Dunlap's, but instead he went to warn this Stalking Wolf. And you can bet your life them renegades was hidin' out in that village before I followed 'em. What more proof do you want?"

Pensively, Major Carswell frowned. "None of what you say is proof, Captain. Though I will admit it all seems rather more than coincidence. You have not explained, however, what prompted this." He gestured toward the scalp-covered spear.

Unthinkingly, Rebecca turned to look as well. Close enough to see the dried blood darkening the spear's shaft and the curled flesh around the edges, she now suffered the full impact of the horror those lank patches of hair represented. Suddenly queasy, she swallowed back the sour taste rising in her throat, fighting off the wave of nausea that made her sway like a drunken seaman.

A warm, steadying hand clasped her arm. "Don't look," Aaron ordered gently. "Go back to Skulley."

Shivering, Rebecca moved to obey. But before she had taken two steps Jessup's insinuating voice halted her.

"Recognize any of 'em?"

She snapped her head up to meet his taunting eyes. "W-What?"

"You heard. I asked if you recognize any of 'em, though I didn't expect you would. Truth is, they all look the same to me, too." He seemed pleased by her stricken expression, and even more so by the unleashed fury that blazed from Aaron's eyes.

With a smug grin, Jessup turned back to Major Carswell. "I told you I followed the renegades west from Dunlap's Station. Those stupid heathens led me straight into their village alongside the Miami. 'Course, when the guards caught sight of us coming, the bastards turned around to fight. They didn't leave us any choice but to stand our ground.''

Alongside the Miami River. Wind's village. Rebecca's breath caught in her throat.

"You could have backed off," Aaron said bitterly. "They were only defending themselves."

From the look on his face, Rebecca knew he had come to the same conclusion as she. Her heart twisted painfully for him; the people of Wind's village were her friends, but to Aaron they were family.

Jessup did not look around. "They were defending themselves, all right. With this." Reaching for the scabbard hanging from his saddle, he withdrew a broken rifle, regulation issue. The bayonet had been snapped in two; only the blunted end remained. The wood stock was splintered.

Despite its condition, Rebecca recognized it as part of the rifle Aaron had given to Wind as a symbol of peace. A gasp escaped her before she could help it.

"How did you get that?" Aaron asked. His voice sounded distant and hollow.

"Grabbed it off the Injun that tried to kill me. Damn fool was swinging it like a club. Maybe you should've left him some powder to go with it, eh, Cambridge?"

A shocked silence filled the courtyard, until even the faraway sounds from outside the fort's walls could not penetrate the tense anticipation of the waiting soldiers.

"Is this true, Captain Cambridge?" Henry Carswell sounded as if he wished the answer to be "no" though his voice held little hope. "Did you give this weapon to the Shawnee?"

Aaron seemed not to hear him; his stare was pinned solely upon Jessup. "What did you do to Wind at His Feet? Is he dead?"

"He oughta be," Jessup chortled. "I walloped him good, but I saw him getting up while we were riding away. Too bad, considerin' he was a particular friend of yours. And that's not all, Major." He turned to Carswell. "Before Carter joined up with me he found this in Cambridge's billet. Further proof that Cambridge is more blackhearted Shawnee than white."

Jessup withdrew from his saddle a decorative toma-hawk, one of the pair given to Aaron by Wind at His Feet as a token of trust. The bright feathers which had danced proudly from the neck of the hatchet now hung limp and dirty. The once glistening stone head was dark, stained with blood and mud. Jessup tossed it at Aaron's feet.

"There were two, but I left the other right where it belongs—there'll be one less stinkin' Injun boy growing up to kill fine, Christian people."

Without warning, Aaron lunged at Jessup fists first, catching him hard on the jaw and in the midsection at almost the same time. The captain fell back, arms pin-wheeling, landing flat on his back in a puddle left from the previous night's downpour.

The sudden activity seemed to stir the other men to life, for at once they began to yelp and cheer, their shouts sounding shrill and loathsome as they echoed through Re-becca's head like torturous thunder. Several men surged in front of her, temporarily blocking her view of Aaron and Jessup, but she could hear the muffled grunts and sharp blows of the skirmish.

It felt as if she endured hours of agony, waiting for it to end, but in fact only a few seconds passed before two soldiers dragged Aaron from Jessup's flailing form. Aaron looked none the worse for the brawl, excepting the ex-pression of pure rage and anguish that ravaged his fea-tures.

Jessup, on the other hand, bled from both mouth and nose, and took an inordinately long time sitting up. When two of his men—Carter and Fellows, if she remembered correctly—tried to assist him, the surly captain shoved them away. The look in his eyes was one of unadulterated hatred.

"I ought to kill you," he said in a low and deadly voice. He shook his head to clear it the way a mongrel dog rids itself of water. Then his split lips parted in an evil grin. "But I s'pose I can let the hangman take care of you. You might've talked your way out of prison once, but you won't be so lucky this time.

"Major!" he called out loudly. "Captain Aaron Cam-bridge is a known consorter with the enemy. Now here's the proof that he's dealing them firearms and protecting them against punishment by the law. I charge this man with treason against the United States of America and the territory of the Northwest Ordinance!''

"No! No, that's not true!'' Rebecca's frantic cries went unheeded by the grumbling crowd of soldiers, even those she elbowed as she pushed nearer to Aaron again. She broke free of the circle of onlookers just as the major stepped up to Aaron.

The commandant wore an expression of sadness, but no emotion could be heard as he spoke. "These are serious charges, Captain. Have you anything to add?''

Aaron stared stonily ahead. "You know the real truth, Henry. Not this twisted, trumped-up version.''

"I thought I did. However, this will require further investigation. Until then I'm afraid I have no choice but to place you under arrest.''

Rebecca turned, wild-eyed, to Aaron, expecting to see him resist with another violent display, or better yet, to argue with Major Carswell until the commandant fully understood how insane Jessup's rantings were.

But Aaron did neither of those things, and the sight that greeted her made Rebecca's throat swell and her eyes burn. He remained stiff and unyielding between the twin grips of the soldiers on either side of him, and his head did not hang low. Still, she could see the defeated expression in his eyes, now weary and bleak where just moments before they had flashed with fire and righteous anger.

She stepped forward cautiously, reaching to touch his arm. "Aaron? Are you all right?''

He lifted his gaze to hers, and she was struck at once by the emptiness there. For an instant she doubted if he even knew her, his blank stare reminding her that this was not the first time his mind had closed like a protective shutter.

She whirled to face Vance Jessup. "Why are you doing this?'' she demanded hysterically. "What are you hiding that makes you want to destroy him?''

"Come along, Rebecca,'' Skulley pleaded in firm, gentle tones. "I'll take you home.''

Vance Jessup only stared in her direction, his eyes unfocused and unseeing. The leering smile he generally wore now looked brittle, as if he had forgotten it was still there.

After a few moments, however, the malicious gleam returned. "Sure wish I knew what you were talking about, Mrs. Osborne. I'll just pretend you never said that. In fact, once you spend a few nights alone after the hangman finishes with *him*"—he hooked a thumb toward Aaron—"you might just wish you could take back those words."

Rebecca sucked in her breath. Before she could reply, however, Major Carswell interceded.

"That's quite enough, Captain Jessup. There's no need to involve the lady. Now, men, listen up!" he called out loudly. "The excitement is over. Everyone, go about your duties."

As a body, the crowd snapped to attention, disbursing immediately after the major pivoted on his heel to return to his quarters. The two soldiers who flanked Aaron swung him around as well, making ready to follow the commandant. One prodded him between the shoulder blades, then pushed harder when Aaron's first steps seemed too hesitant, causing him to stumble.

Rebecca started forward, but again Skulley's gruff voice restrained her.

"You can help him better by keepin' yourself safe," he advised. "Yourself and the boy."

"But how can I leave Aaron?" Tears pooled in her eyes, and at last fell burning to her cheeks. "Didn't you see the way he was? He needs me."

"I don't doubt that, but the fact is, there ain't nothin' you can do for him now, even if they was to let you see him."

Rebecca choked back a sob. The majority of the soldiers had cleared the courtyard, and she had an unobstructed view of Aaron as he was led away. His sun-streaked head towered above those of his two guards; his wide shoulders were straight and proud.

They stopped in front of a small, cubed building with no windows and only a half-sized door. One of the soldiers bent to open it, while the other shoved at Aaron, forcing him to duck his head to enter the cell.

Look at me! Rebecca cried silently. *Oh, please, Aaron,*

look up just so I can see your eyes. Just once. But her wish
went unanswered. Aaron crouched down and moved
through the small, dark entrance.

Behind him, the door slammed shut with the sound of a
death knell.

Darkness had descended over the fort, but inside the
wooden shack it was perpetually dark. Aaron sat propped
against the back wall with his legs bent, his forearms resting on his knees. He could, by watching the fading light
through the cracks in the ceiling, almost gauge the time.
And what he could not determine by that method, he knew
by the angry rumbling of his stomach.

Not that it mattered. He was no more interested in food
than he was in what was going on outside his stuffy prison.
The pain was too great for any thoughts beyond his aching
heart.

With a stifled groan, Aaron let his head fall forward
against his arms. God, what had he done? So many of The
People massacred, according to Vance Jessup and the grim
evidence he had brought back with him. And what of
Wind? At the very least his friend—his *brother*—was injured. Perhaps even dead. But worse than any wound to
the proud Shawnee chieftan would be the decimation of
his people. That, along with the sense of betrayal he must
feel.

And for what? Aaron lashed himself inwardly. For what
had these good people died? For his pride? His damnable
arrogance? This time his groan would not remain silent.
Grief and anger churned to the surface, threatening to spill
from him in an agonized scream. Instead he clenched his
teeth hard, unaware that he was biting his cheek until the
coppery taste of blood filled his mouth.

Voices sounded outside the cell, interrupting his self-
deprecating thoughts. He lifted his head in anticipation of
one of the guards bearing a dinner bucket. He was not
prepared for the jolt he received when he heard Rebecca's
softly questioning tone.

"Aaron? Are you all right?"

The small door was flung open, admitting a rectangle
of lantern light to fall across his legs.

" 'Becca?" he rasped, too stunned to do more than stare stupidly at the empty doorway.

"Come on outta there for a spell, boy," came Skulley's scratchy command. "Carswell says for me to take you 'round the perimeter to stretch your legs. I brought you some comp'ny."

Spurred to movement, Aaron crawled forward, panting heavily as he emerged into the open air. It felt good to stand, to flex his legs and straighten his back, for the confining cell was a mere square of only about five feet in all directions. He blinked at the brightness cast by the lamp Skulley held until the old soldier turned the wick down to a low gleam.

"Been a long day, eh, boy?" he said, sending a frowning glance into the gloomy prison. "Bet you're hungry."

Aaron did not answer. His gaze had locked on Rebecca's, and the concern and love shining from her dark eyes made his breath catch in his throat. A few moments passed before she spoke—before, he thought, she trusted herself to speak.

"Oh, Aaron," she said haltingly, her hands folded and pressed between her breasts. "Aaron. . . ."

Just seeing her was like balm to his wounded soul, but he forced his eyes away. "You shouldn't have come, 'Becca."

He felt, rather than saw, the stunned hurt in her expression. "I—I was so worried for you when they first took you away. You didn't . . . you didn't look like yourself. I was afraid—"

"Afraid I had lost my mind again?" he finished for her. "No, not this time. Though for a little while I almost wished I had. Even hanging is better than knowing that my friends have suffered, all because they trusted me."

"It's not your fault."

"Indirectly it is. Somehow Jessup must have located the maps I drew for Major Carswell. How else would he have known where to find Wind's village?"

"He said he followed the Shawnee there."

Aaron remained stoically silent for a moment, wishing he could wrap his arms around her soft, womanly warmth. Then he shook his head. "No, that's impossible. I've had all day to think about it. There are no trails going directly from Stalking Wolf's village to Wind's. At least none that a mounted patrol could follow in the time Jessup claims they did. He must have traveled north along the river trace. The very same way we did."

"Aaron, you mustn't blame yourself," Rebecca insisted, trying to peer into his bleak eyes. "You mustn't fault yourself for trying to bring peace. Why, if you do, then this is my fault, too. I encouraged you to agree to Major Carswell's plan just so you'd stay here to help Samuel. Does that mean I'm to blame?"

Skulley had moved away, taking the lantern with him, but it was still possible to see the glistening tears that streaked her soft cheeks. "Of course not," he whispered raggedly. "You were only doing what you thought best."

"And so, too, were you."

He wanted more than anything else to bury himself in her sweet love and forget all the suffering he had wrought. But he could not. Nor could he forget that there were others who would remember as well. Remember, and seek revenge.

"I want you and Samuel here at the fort," he finally said, looking away from her once more. "You can use my quarters. I'll have Skulley get word to Henry."

"H-here?"

"Where it's safe."

Her expression was at first puzzled. Then she smiled sadly, shaking her head. "No, Aaron. We'll be fine right where we are. There are dozens of other settlers around us."

"What if Wind retaliates, 'Becca?"

"Aaron, we're practically within sight of the fort! Do you expect all the outlying settlements to pull up and return to Cincinnati?" When he did not answer, she put her hands on her hips. "I thought not. I think, too, that you're being overprotective again. The Shawnee won't attack, and even if they did, Wind would not hurt me. He's your friend."

"And I understand him better than anyone else. If what Jessup said is true, Wind will not only renounce our friendship, he *will* seek revenge."

She stared up at him, her hair a dark halo of curls around her impassioned face. Her mouth was set in an expression he was coming to know all too well.

"I don't understand you, Aaron Cambridge. You wanted me to make friends with the Shawnee. Now you ask me to fear them. That's exactly the kind of thinking, the kind of mistrust, that's invaded the minds of too many people lately. Misunderstandings occur. Accidents happen. Someone has to stop bowing to panic and assuming the worst every time something goes wrong."

Deep down Aaron knew she was right—at least in theory—but he could not quell the sense of hopelessness, of doom, that filled him at the very thought of letting her out of his sight.

He had only one weapon to convince her, the only one that bore any chance of success. " 'Becca, please reconsider. If you won't have a care for yourself, then do it for Samuel."

As he expected, her determined expression slipped away for a moment, replaced by doubt and concern. She nibbled at her lower lip, then glanced over her shoulder toward the bobbing lantern that now approached them again. "Perhaps Samuel could spend some time here with Skulley. A few days at most. But truly, Aaron, I can't believe we're in danger."

He sincerely hoped she was right. Only one thing was certain; she would not change her mind.

"Anythin' else you need, then?" Skulley asked as he neared them. He did not comment on the fact that Rebecca stood with her fists planted and her chin thrust upward, or that Aaron's arms were folded stubbornly across his chest.

"Any word on how long I can expect to enjoy my new quarters?" Aaron asked dryly.

Skulley harrumphed and swung the lantern in a wide arc. He appeared reluctant to speak in front of Rebecca, but her determined stance was equally as obstinate. "Couple days, I hear. Truth is, Carswell ain't sure what to do with ya, an' he's afraid to let you loose on account o' Jessup an' his wild talk. But he'll deal with ya himself 'fore he let's the 'lynch law' have ya. If'n he don't wait too long." He swung his shaggy head and squinted his one good eye. "Carswell's a good man, but he sure ain't one to make up his mind quick."

"He *is* a good man. And the decisions he faces have not been easy ones to make," Aaron agreed. "I don't hold this against him."

"That's good, 'cause there ain't too many sees things your way right now, boy. Ain't too many at all."

With Skulley's ominous words in his ears, Aaron looked once more to Rebecca, gazing at her with haunted eyes.

"You were right not to tell Samuel about me," he said tonelessly. "In fact, you'll both be best off to forget me altogether."

"Aaron, please, don't talk that—"

"Good-bye, 'Becca."

Though it caused him considerable pain not to look at her one last time, Aaron returned to his prison without a backward glance.

CHAPTER 27

For three days Rebecca worried incessantly about Aaron, unable to sleep or even work as long as she had no word from him. Every time she closed her eyes, she relived again the anguished moment when the soldiers first dragged him away. Even awake, her thoughts turned at every moment to wondering whether he was being mistreated, or if his own sense of guilt was torture enough.

More painful still was the knowledge that she could offer him no comfort, that he had not allowed her to share his pain. She wanted him to know that whether they were physically in touch or not, she was with him in spirit.

In those endless days, her only salvation came from Lenore, whose stalwart strength and earthy wisdom provided Rebecca with exactly the calming effect she needed. Lenore would sit for hours on end, sometimes listening to Rebecca's nervous ramblings and sometimes only sharing the tense silence.

But it was due to her companion's forthright sense of honesty that Rebecca finally realized a harsh truth about herself. "He's not letting me help him, Lenore," she had fretted, "just like ten years ago. Doesn't he think I'll stand behind him no matter how bad it gets?"

"Why would he?" Lenore had stopped her rocking chair by planting both feet firmly on the ground. "For more than a month, now, you've been sayin' you won't have nothin' to do with him until all his troubles are settled. Seems to me Aaron's only abidin' by your wishes."

Stunned, Rebecca had sunk to the bench, her mouth slack and her eyes filling with tears. "Do you really think so?'' she had whispered shamefully. "Oh, Lord, how could I have been so selfish?''

Lenore had been quick to offer encouragement with a gentle pat on her back. "You had your reasons for bein' careful, 'Becca. And the best one is right out there carryin' a fishin' pole now instead of a crutch. No one blames a mother for protectin' her own. Just make sure you're not usin' Samuel as an excuse to keep from makin' up your own mind.''

And so, aside from anxiety over Aaron's well-being, Rebecca now had remorse to add to her list of woes.

On the fourth day after Aaron's arrest, Samuel failed to appear when she summoned him for the evening meal. She had not bothered to take him to the fort as Aaron wished, believing that Aaron's fears were unfounded. But when she called once more with no result, Rebecca felt a swift shaft of doubt pierce her composure.

"Samuel!'' she shouted repeatedly, her eyes darting around the small settlement as she leaned over the wooden porch railing. She *never* should have let him and Zeb walk over to the Brownleys' cabin alone, despite the fact that she could see the residence in question even in the waning light of late afternoon. She shouted again, a little more frantically, and from across the way Lenore poked her head from her own cabin.

"He's not home yet?'' she called out.

"No, what about Zeb?''

She ducked back inside, then reappeared scant seconds later. "He's here. Came in an hour ago.''

Rebecca's eyes widened, and she clutched the railing tighter. She thought Lenore would not notice, but in an instant her sister-in-law had sailed out her door, her long legs flying across the grassy yard until she arrived breathless at Rebecca's side.

"Darned young'uns,'' she said smoothly, though her lined face was etched with worry. "I've been telling them boys to stick together. I just assumed they were both home. But I asked Zeb just now, and he said Samuel stayed at the Brownleys' a little longer.''

Not bothering to grab a shawl, Rebecca lifted her skirts and stepped from the porch. "I'll go for him.''

"Hurry back. It'll be dark soon," Lenore said needlessly.

Breathless, Rebecca mentally scolded her son as she raced toward the distant cabin. *Samuel Aaron Osborne, just wait until I find you! How dare you frighten me like this, you little imp? Why, I ought to tan you, brace or no brace!*

She had, of course, no intention of striking Samuel, but somehow pretending anger toward the wayward boy kept her panic at bay. She would find him, chances were, deeply engrossed in a game of ninepins with Tommy, so intent on knocking down the wooden pegs that he hadn't noticed the lengthening shadows or the hungry rumblings of his own stomach.

Samuel? Ignore a call to supper? she thought uneasily. *Not likely.*

"Samuel, where are you? Answer me this instant!" she demanded, not caring that Mrs. Brownley would either think her a shrew or completely lunatic. But no response came from the cabin as she neared it—not from Mrs. Brownley or from her son. "Is anyone here?"

A sound from the woods behind the house pricked her ears. Rebecca stopped dead in her tracks, looking uncertainly from the empty windows to the dark trees towering over the cabin. Surely the children must be playing out back, she tried to reassure herself. And Mrs. Brownley? Why, she could be visiting another neighbor.

But as she glanced around apprehensively, Rebecca realized that the nearest cabins were her own and Lenore's, in opposite corners of the field, and that Mrs. Brownley would never have left Samuel or her own children unsupervised during these uneasy times.

"Samuel?" she called again, fear diminishing her voice to a croaking whisper. Rebecca looked back over her shoulder to where Lenore was but a lanky shadow against the distant porch. She was glad at that moment for her sister-in-law's watchful gaze, though she wished it did not come from so far away, or that the sun had not sunk so quickly behind the western hills.

The sky would not grow lighter by her hesitation, however. Nor did she have the time to wait for reassurance. *If*

Samuel was in trouble, Rebecca knew, she could delay no longer. Gathering her skirt in one hand, she marched up to the cabin door, fist raised as she prepared to knock.

The puncheon door, as heavy as two men, swung open easily beneath her hand. "Mrs. Brownley? Is anyone here?"

The cabin was empty, but it showed signs of recent occupancy. A stew bubbled from a kettle balanced on an iron tripod over low flames, and the sturdy plank table dominating the single room was set neatly with wooden trenchers and tin mugs. A bowl of wildflowers—violets and lady slippers, the same kind Rebecca had gathered herself that afternoon from the brambles behind her own cabin—graced the center of the table.

At one end of the cabin was a loft, beneath which a low-slung bed lay covered with a bright quilt. From pegs on the opposite wall hung the family's Sunday clothing, a well-oiled musket, and a man's battered felt hat. Mr. Brownley, then, had come in already for the evening meal. Where were they? Where was Samuel?

Urgency lent wings to her feet as Rebecca sped from the cabin, again searching back and forth across the clearing for any sign of her son, though she felt as if her limbs were weighted and her movements inordinately slow. It was like waking gradually from a nightmare, she thought distractedly as she rounded the cabin to scour the woods behind it. She prayed this *was* all a nightmare, for then she would wake soon. She would wake to find Samuel laughing up at her from the safety of his own b—

The hand that clasped her across the mouth allowed her no time to gasp, let alone scream. Hard and implacable, it clamped down on her face with the strength of a bear trap.

In the same instant, another hand twisted her arm so high behind her back she was nearly lifted from her feet. Sharp, sudden pain knifed through her shoulder, so intense it was accompanied by a wave of nausea. Beneath the suffocating palm Rebecca screamed voicelessly, arching against the rock-solid body behind her. But her struggles were for naught. The grip on her arm did not lessen; the stranglehold on her face did not ease.

"Naga e'tek," a voice hissed in her ear. Her Shawnee captor gave her arm a small jerk. Rebecca needed no translation. She ceased her struggles. He pushed her forward—a few, stumbling steps and they were well behind the cabin, hidden from view of the rest of the settlement.

Within moments two more painted figures emerged from the woods. In the dusk of night she could barely see them until they stood less than three feet from her. Both were tall and sleek and bare-chested, decked out for battle from the twirling feathers on their scalplocks to the array of knives and tomahawks tied to their waists with leather thongs. She did not recognize either warrior by name, but was certain she had seen them both during her stay at the Shawnee village.

If they recognized her, they gave no sign. No glimmer of friendliness relieved the black hatred in their eyes. No softening of their rigid mouths to give her hope. Only that same fierce pride and watchfulness she had seen first on Wind's face as he stood behind his son in the woods not so very far from here just weeks ago.

One of the warriors stepped behind her quickly, and before she could resist, Rebecca found her hands tied securely behind her. The other brave removed a length of cloth from a pouch at his waist, moving closer to replace his companion's palm with this filthy gag. He jumped back with a stifled cry when she bit down as hard as she could on the side of his hand.

For a moment the Shawnee stared at her, dumbfounded by her bravery. Or her stupidity—Rebecca would never know for sure. Before she could draw breath to scream he was upon her again, the slap he laid across her cheek leaving her head ringing and drawing tears to her eyes. The first captor had been gentle by comparison. This one knotted the gag so tightly she feared she would choke on her own tongue.

Terror and misery and pain all warred within for the right to claim her, but only one thought engulfed her mind as the vengeful Shawnee dragged her farther into the woods. Only one fear filled her heart with terror.

What had they done with Samuel?

* * *

The trees surrounded Aaron, dark sentries in an unbroken line, an impregnable enemy. He had never before seen trees like this, so many and so tall, one upon the other with huge, menacing branches and black boles wide enough to crush a man with their weight.

There'd not been trees like this in Carolina, he remembered vaguely. Those had been scrubby, ineffectual things, mere brush upon the sandy earth. These were a living, breathing entity, these trees of the northern frontier, so much a part of the land that they dominated all his waking moments.

And now, too, his dreams.

This *was* a dream, he knew in some reflective corner of his mind. A dream and a memory—unbidden, unwelcome—yet he was completely incapable of stopping it once the drama had begun. He saw himself kneeling among the trees. He *was* one of the trees. Now another of them moved, coming to kneel beside him and whatever it was that he held in his hand.

"Will he live?" asked the tree that was now a man in a voice strangely, hauntingly familiar.

"No," he heard himself reply.

Then the trees moved forward, blocking what happened next. Aaron fought to push them back. *I want to see!* he cried out in his dream. *Hide this from me no longer. I want to see!*

And so it was. The black tracery of gnarled limbs moved from his eyes, and he watched with growing horror and dim recollection as the man reached out for him, that part of him he saw kneeling among the leaves, and slashed at the shapeless form on the ground between them.

"You . . . you killed him," the young Aaron said incredulously.

"Shut up," Vance Jessup replied, "I had to kill him." *I had to kill him.*

Aaron woke with a start, shivering in his sweat-drenched clothing. The morning air was chilly, even inside his stifling little cubicle, and he sat up straight, wrapping his arms around his legs for comfort. Comfort against the dream as much as the cold.

Dear God! he thought, bowing his head shamefully. *Had it truly happened that way?*

But the reality of his dream was not in question, he admitted to himself. Nor the truth of it. Only the reason why it had remained locked inside his mind for so long. There must be more!

Aaron drew in a deep, cleansing breath, held it for a long, tremulous moment, then released it with a huge sigh. His eyes, blurred and itching despite more hours of sleep than he normally required, squinted against the early sun seeping into his cell via the cracks and crevices in the aging wood. Outside, the sounds of the morning were well advanced. Soon someone would arrive with his breakfast, and shortly after would escort him to the commandant's office, where Henry Carswell would continue the round of questions begun three days before.

Today, at last, Aaron would at last have something to tell him.

They had walked all night to reach the first river, though Rebecca could hardly call it walking, this relentless half trot which the Shawnee forced on her. Seven braves, she counted. She knew the name of only one—Swift Arrow, the husband of young She Who Sighs.

Her eyes sought out her son once again, relief and frustration mingling when she found him. Samuel had been so brave when they dragged them together from the clearing, not weeping or moaning, though his eyes had been wide with fright. They had removed his gag at the same time they retied her hands in front of her, once they were out of range of the settlement. And they had not hurt him.

It was Swift Arrow who now carried Samuel straddled across his back. Throughout the night the warriors had taken turns carrying the boy in order to keep up the pace. Rebecca was amazed at how the strong braves could trot for hours without becoming winded, burdened as they were. She was just about dead from fear and exhaustion.

By sunup they had reached the Great Miami River, where to her dismay the Shawnee uncovered three large canoes and proceeded to float them out into the swiftly flowing river. Until this moment she had managed to maintain a certain calmness, mostly for Samuel's sake, though they had been forbidden to speak to one another. But now she could only stare at the frothing water as it swirled and churned over stones near the bank. She struggled to keep the panic from overwhelming her.

"Umbe. Neg-nech!" the brave nearest her muttered as he shoved her toward the water.

Her knees buckled and she pitched forward, managing to brace her fall with her hands. Her strangled cry drew the attention of the others, including Samuel.

"Stop that!" he demanded, kicking at his captor as he tried to free himself. "Don't you hurt my mother!"

Swift Arrow easily retained his hold on the boy, wading out to the nearest canoe. He quickly deposited Samuel into the broad center, then joined another brave in pushing the craft out into the current. On scraped knees, Rebecca watched her son and his captors disappear around a bend in the river.

"Samuel!" she tried to call out through the smothering cloth binding her mouth. Helpless tears filled her eyes. She could not bear it if anything happened to him. What would the Shawnee do to them?

Once these people had been her friends. Hers and Aaron's. But now she could not stop one repulsive scene after another from slashing through her mind, visions triggered by the many stories she had heard—tales of torture and inhuman atrocities. What had happened to the Brownleys? Would she be clubbed to death, or perhaps even burned alive? Or worse, would her son face a similar fate?

Before she could dwell further upon the horrifying possibilities, her captor hauled her to her feet with a brutal twist of her arm, then thrust her forward once more.

And then it came to her, with a sickening jolt, just what she had yet to endure. The churning water before her brought a deluge of memories worse than those visions of torture.

She barely kept her balance, her head spinning with fear and confusion. Her stomach pitched violently. If it weren't for the cold alarm clawing at her chest Rebecca would have almost laughed at her own unreasonable fear. After all, she might be dead by this time tomorrow, and surely by a method far more painful than drowning!

Nevertheless, she could not contain her dread at the prospect of another river voyage. This time, she realized dismally, there would be no leisurely pace, no hugging the banks of the Great Miami as Aaron had done to ease her dismay.

And no one to comfort her when the memories grew too vivid and the anxiety too real.

Be strong! she commanded herself. *For Samuel's sake.*

But her son was moving upriver already, and as the Shawnee warriors lifted her bodily into the waiting canoe, Rebecca feared she would not be able to hold back the veil of darkness waiting to claim her.

A deep stillness settled over her as the Shawnee maneuvered the canoe away from the bank, watching her with smug expressions of triumph.

But it was not resignation that calmed her senses now. It was sheer, blinding terror.

"It's about time," Aaron growled when he heard the jangling of the key as it slid home in the lock outside the door.

Hours had passed since he had awakened—hours in which his frustration had grown with the sounds of activity outside his cell. Hours since his vivid dream jolted him from the trancelike stupor that had held him for the past few days.

He was grateful to be free of that particular state—it was too much like the nightmare he'd lived through in those months following his injury. He only wished Rebecca had not been forced to witness his weakness. He'd spared her once. He would have spared her again.

But inside the cramped cell he paced like a caged animal, snarling for release, impatient to be rid of the physical imprisonment now that the mental one seemed to have relinquished its hold. When the door rattled open, Aaron turned on the hapless orderly who delivered his long-delayed breakfast.

"You're late!" he snapped. "What's going on?"

But it was not the fresh-cheeked private bearing sustenance, nor was it Corporal Lutz, who usually escorted the prisoner to his daily interrogation. Instead, Skulley ducked into the darkened interior, twisting his head back and forth so as to scan the small cell with his good eye.

Then he scurried inside, pitching the room into near darkness as he pulled the door almost closed behind him. Surprised by this turn of events, Aaron remained silent as the old sergeant bent his creaking knees until he was hunkered above the floor. The crack in the door threw in just enough light to allow Aaron to see his hunched form. His head twisted upward.

"Sit easy, boy," he advised. "We gotta talk. Rumor is you been stingy with yer words these last days. I'm not sayin' I blame you—gets so a fella don't know who to trust. But things are turnin' downright sour out there, an' you got a right to know what's happenin'."

"Did Carswell put you up to this?" Aaron asked in a voice thick from lack of use. He slumped against the opposite wall.

Skulley's gray head drooped. "The major's too busy organizin' the march to pay no mind to you. He's caught himself 'tween a tempest and a storm, and there ain't nothin' for him to do but hope the wind dies down some before he gets blown clear back to Philly-delphia. Time was, he figgered you might be the one could weather it out with 'im. But he's losin' hope in you, boy, an' you closin' up like a danged clam ain't helpin' your folks."

"What march, Skulley? What are you talking about?" Aaron's empty stomach cramped painfully, but not from hunger.

"The march to rescue 'Becca and Samuel. The Shawnee got 'em last night."

Stunned beyond speech, Aaron merely stared at Skulley's hunched shadow, until the sergeant finally continued his explanation. "Happened 'round suppertime, accordin' to 'Becca's sister-in-law, Miz Lenore. She stumbled in here this mornin' with a broken ankle and all covered with briar patches. Seems none of the men up there was willin' to risk goin' for help in the dark, so the dang-fool woman set out on her own. Slipped and fell halfway, she says, and crawled the last mile.'' Respect tinged Skulley's voice, but Aaron had only one concern.

'' 'Becca . . . ?''

"Alive, last Miz Lenore could see. Kidnapped alive, and no sign of Samuel, so the folks up at the settlement reckoned he was took, too.''

"I was afraid this would happen,'' Aaron rasped, clenching his fists fervently. As long as they were alive there was hope. But what hope, with him locked up here? "You've got to get me out of here, Skulley. I have to go after them.''

"That's exactly what the major's plannin' to do, boy. They're goin' after the Shawnee in a big way this time. Natur'ly, Jessup's flappin' 'is mouth somethin' awful. Dang, but I wish you'da found them marked whiskey kegs so's we could shut 'im up. He rode up to the cabin a little while ago to check for clues, an' he came back with the rest of that rifle you gave to your injun friend. He says he's pretty sure he can lead the whole danged army straight to the village where they're holdin' 'Becca.''

Aaron leaped to his feet, nearly crashing his head against the low planked ceiling. His long limbs swung him about the narrow space until he towered over Skulley. "Those fools! They don't know what they're doing! That rifle was left as a sign. It's *me* the Shawnee want!''

Skulley did not budge from his position, except to shake his grizzled head. "Could be, but that don't change the facts. A white woman an' boy's been kidnapped, an' it's Carswell's duty to commence a rescue.''

"He'll cause their deaths instead,'' Aaron growled. "Wind doesn't want to hurt 'Becca and Samuel, but he won't let Carswell's army anywhere near them, either.''

"Then why'd he take 'em in the first place?''

"To get to me. He believes I betrayed him and his people. The revenge he seeks is aimed only at me, Skulley. No one else is in danger.''

"Hmmmph. Tell that to the folks who're scared outta their homes. The fort's crawlin' with 'em.''

Aaron made an impatient chopping motion in the air. "Tell me one thing: Did the Shawnee harm anyone else last night?''

"Nope. They tied up a couple people in a shed—a kid an' his folks—but they'd nary a scratch on 'em."

"That confirms it, then." Crouching in front of Skulley, Aaron grabbed his shoulders. "Help me, my friend. If the army goes crashing through those woods, Rebecca and Samuel won't live long enough to see their damned blue coats."

"Weeelll . . ." Skulley's tone was doubtful, but there was a glint in his good eye. "I s'pose with most of 'em gone we'll have a chance to slip you past them guards. An' there ain't no question you an' me can move through the woods together faster'n any army."

"Not together, Skulley. Just me. Alone."

The old soldier pressed his lips together, his brow furrowing. Aaron suspected that despite their mutual respect, Skulley wasn't sure whether Aaron could be wholly trusted. Once free, there was nothing to prevent Aaron from bolting, from disappearing into the wilderness as completely as he had ten years ago.

Nothing, that is, except love.

"It's our only hope of saving them, Skulley. Please believe me."

A long moment passed before the sergeant nodded abruptly, pushing his weary body to his feet with a grunt and a groan. "I cain't promise nothin'," he warned, "but I'll give 'er a try. You stay awake, now, y'hear? No tellin' when or how I'll do it, but when the time comes you'll have to hightail it outta here right quick."

"I'll be ready." Aaron clasped the older man's hand appreciatively. "My thanks."

"Don't thank me," Skulley replied. "Like as not you won't make it past the main gate without a ball 'tween yer shoulders. But if yer willin' to risk yer hide, I s'pose I am, too." He sent a well-aimed splatter of tobacco juice through the crack in the door, then turned back to Aaron with a bleak smile. "I just hope you know what you're doing."

Their entrance into the village caused quite a stir, though not in the same way as before, Rebecca noted. This time the figures running toward them across the field were not smiling, nor were the shouts that preceded them cries of gladness and welcome.

Instead she heard the angry demands of hatred and revenge.

She shuddered, drawing Samuel closer now that the two of them had been allowed to walk unbound. A harsh laugh from one of her captors drew her attention, and she saw at once that the first Shawnee to near them was her friend Bird Woman. A twisted smile was frozen on the translator's face as she stopped in front of Rebecca.

"You come back," she said bluntly. "Once you saw the joy of The People. Now see our sadness." She turned, indicating the village before them.

Rebecca lifted her eyes, shock rippling through her as she became aware of even more changes. Where before had been neat rows of bark *wigewas,* now only a few huts stood, surrounded by the charred remains of their neighbors. The large council lodge, where Aaron had spoken his promise of peace, was no more than a blackened skeleton of poles and heaped ashes. The wind whistled mournfully through the gaping spaces between its framework.

But it was the sound of the village that most disturbed Rebecca. Gone was the musical laughter that once permeated the air and the constant hum of a happy, productive community. In its place hung a deadly silence, punctuated occasionally by a soft keening that sent shivers down her spine.

No children scampered down the town's paths, no maidens flirted with young braves as they went about their chores. In fact, except for the hostile-looking group who had come out to meet their party, there was little sign of life in the village.

"Where is everyone?" Rebecca asked. Her question drew a spate of rapid talk between her captors and the villagers. She hugged Samuel closer at the speculative look that passed over the face of one of the women.

"Come," Bird Woman ordered without answering. She began the long trudge toward the town.

"I thought you said they were friendly," Samuel whispered anxiously as he started forward, leaning on the stick one of their Shawnee captors had found for him after they disembarked from the canoes.

"They are," Rebecca assured him. "But just now they're angry. Perhaps after I've talked to Wind at His Feet he'll let us go home."

"D'ya think so?" Samuel asked hopefully.

Squeezing his shoulder, Rebecca concentrated on helping him negotiate the muddy, churned-up earth. The group did not bother to follow the narrow path which had once divided the field of green shoots. The new corn was now trampled and broken, scarred with many hoofprints and scorched where flames had taken hold.

What would The People eat, come winter? Rebecca looked at the devastation around her, and anger rose to momentarily cover her fear. Damn Jessup and his men! This was not honorable battle, this was genocide!

Her fear returned hundredfold, however, when they halted in front of the *wigewa* of Wind at His Feet. The crowd around them had grown by now; Rebecca could hear their angry grumbling behind as she lifted her chin to face the warrior chieftain as he came through the cloth-covered door. She felt Samuel trembling beneath her hand.

As always, Wind at His Feet stood still, as straight and solid as a mighty oak. Despite the bloody bandage wrapped around his head and the scabbing wounds across his arms and chest, he seemed as invulnerable as ever. It took all her courage to speak.

"Why have you brought us here?" she demanded staunchly. "What are you going to do with us?"

No emotion showed on his granite face, though she thought she detected a flicker of light in his coal-black eyes. He stared at her unblinkingly. Then his gaze lowered, coming to rest on Samuel.

He uttered a harsh command.

Rough hands reached for them, pulling Samuel from her grasp. "No!" Rebecca shouted, fighting the unyielding grip of the man behind her. Another warrior lifted Samuel from the ground, carrying him toward a nearby *wigewa*. He yelled and struggled, to no avail.

Rebecca was dragged backward, and though her eyes were pinned on her son, she was aware of Wind at His

Feet standing immobile throughout the ordeal. Soon she was flung to the ground before another *wigewa*, and the warrior's barking order left no doubt but that she was expected to enter it.

"Samuel!" she cried once more as she kicked at the bare shin of the man who guarded her. He only laughed and kicked her in return, so hard that the breath left her lungs with a whoosh.

"Don't worry, Ma!" Samuel called back to her. "I'll be brave."

Rebecca could not answer. Her cheek pressed to the dark ground, she could only fight for her breath. And pray that his bravery would not be tested.

Rebecca passed a long night, unable to sleep with concern for Samuel and worry over what would happen to them now. She was watched over by two women who took turns resting so that one could always remain vigilant. Before nightfall she had refused a meal, but now that the morning sun was long arisen, Rebecca regretted her hastiness. It would do her no good to starve to death for the sake of pride.

She tried to indicate to the women that she was hungry, but they merely looked at her with hostile expressions. Shrugging, Rebbeca turned her attention to brushing the mud from the hem of her skirt. Before she could complete the task, however, a young man stood inside the doorway, and after spitting rapid instructions to the women, he grabbed Rebecca's arm, hauling her out into the blinding sunlight.

She blinked hard, but was given little time to revel in her relative freedom. The brave continued tugging at her arm until she followed him, and within moments she found herself once again outside the chieftain's home.

Rebecca swallowed hard as the Shawnee leader was summoned. When he stood before her, she glared up at Wind at His Feet. "How dare you treat us like this? I thought you were my friend! If anything happens to Samuel . . ." she choked on these last words.

"Come," he said tonelessly, stepping backward into his bark home. Rebecca's escort pushed her forward, then released her as she passed into the darkened interior of the *wigewa*.

She stood at the entrance, rubbing her arms and staring mutinously at the towering chieftain, whose stony visage was lit by a low-banked fire in the center of the room. Within minutes her eyes became accustomed to the dim light, and she saw that they were not alone. Some of Wind's children peered at her from a pallet of furs against the curved wall, and on the other side of the hut crouched a forlorn figure. Rebecca could scarcely tell that it was a woman; her flesh was covered with mud and ashes and scored with angry welts, while tangles of black hair hung in clumps over her face.

Then a soft moan rose from the woman's hoarse throat, and Rebecca's heart squeezed painfully. "White Star," she breathed, taking a step toward her friend. "What—?"

"She mourns for our son," Wind at His Feet said, his powerful voice warning Rebecca to stay back.

She halted abruptly, reeling slightly at the impact of the warrior's statement. His son? Quickly, her gaze returned to the huddled children, counting. Seeking.

"Little Otter?" she asked with a hoarse croak.

Wind at His Feet remained silent, stoic. Rebecca's heart lurched once more. She recalled Little Otter's cheerful countenance with an overwhelming sadness; he had been just Samuel's age.

"I'm so sorry, White Star. I had no idea." She looked back to Wind. "Was he . . . was he injured in the attack?"

"Little Otter is with Our Grandmother, the creator. His blood was spilled by treachery. The treachery of the white men."

This last word was spoken with such loathing that Rebecca's mouth went suddenly dry. And just as fast she understood what the proud Shawnee meant.

"You *can't* believe Aaron had anything to do with this," she said incredulously, shaking her head. "He tried to *stop* the army from attacking! And when he found out what happened . . . why, he's just sick about it. And worried for you, too."

"Cain should worry for himself," Wind replied with

great bitterness. "He has brought down upon us the white man's sickness, and he has betrayed The People. Now he will die."

For the first time, Rebecca was glad that Aaron was locked safely away within the unbreachable walls of Fort Washington. The coldness in Wind's heart showed clearly in his black, glittering eyes. This man, she knew, was capable of murder.

She drew a bolstering breath. "Aaron did not betray you, or your son. He is in the army prison now *because* he stood up for your people. He is truly your brother. You must believe that."

"This I believe." Wind reached beneath a pile of blankets, withdrawing the mate to the tomahawk which Vance Jessup had thrown at Aaron's feet. The same weapon that Wind had once given to his brother in friendship.

At the sight of the stone hatchet, White Star keened loudly, then covered her face with her hands. As if the villagers, too, were aware of what was happening inside the *wigewa*, outside their voices rose in stunned outcry. Rebecca's stomach pitched at the thought that this was the weapon that had killed Little Otter. She swallowed convulsively.

"No longer is Cain my brother," Wind at His Feet pronounced solemnly. "His hand is stained with the blood of my son. Soon I will have his blood, when he seeks to rescue *your* son."

"Never," Rebecca whispered, shaking her head. "He will not come."

"Then I will find him to avenge my people's honor," Wind promised, "if I must walk over every mile of the world."

At that instant the hide flap over the hut's doorway flung open, and Aaron stepped through. Rebecca gasped. Dressed in breechclout and leggings similar to Wind's, his wide chest bare and his shoulders thrown back, he looked as wild and untamed as the fiercest Shawnee brave. He met the Indian's unflinching stare without looking her way.

"You will not need to search, my friend," Aaron said calmly, his head lifted high. "I am here."

CHAPTER 28

"You shouldn't have come. He's very angry."

Rebecca watched from her place beside the small fire as Aaron remained near the entrance to his *wigewa* after Wind stalked out, the hide door flap pushed back with one clenched fist as Aaron stared out into the darkness. His bare back was rigid, each muscle as well as the cords on his neck showing clearly. He had stayed that way, stoic and unemotional, throughout the entire long council meeting to which Wind had subjected them. Rebecca wished he would tell her what the Shawnee had said. She wished he would look at her.

From the eerie blackness outside the bark hut came another nerve-shattering moan, followed by a ululating cry that sent a shiver down her spine. She had lost count of the number of times she had heard the same mournful sound since that morning. Aaron lifted his head to listen.

"What is it?" she asked.

He was silent for a long while before answering. "Someone has died. Another child, from the sound of it."

"Dear God," Rebecca whispered. "Samuel."

"Samuel's fine." Dropping the flap, Aaron turned. The firelight threw his features into sharp relief, making his angular jaw more prominent and deepening the shadows around his eyes. His scar looked like an angry slash. "They're keeping him safe, with the other children who are well."

"What's wrong here?"

"The People are dying. First the white man's guns; now his disease."

He speaks as if he's more Indian than white, Rebecca thought uncomfortably. It was bad enough he was dressed like a Shawnee, now he had taken to talking in that same terse, inexplicable manner that Wind had.

"Wind at His Feet mentioned before something about the sickness. I didn't know what he meant, but he blamed you for that, too. Did he explain it in the council meeting?"

Aaron smiled ruefully, then moved to her side, hunkering down to take her cold hands in his. His own gut churned ruthlessly, but he knew he had to stay calm for Rebecca's sake. "It looks like diphtheria. The outbreak began right after we left here. What else are they to think?"

"The truth! The Shawnee are your friends. You would never bring harm to them."

"Yet I have, 'Becca. Not the disease, and not willingly, but that makes no difference to The People. It was my poor judgment that led Jessup to them; Wind and everyone else knows that."

"Then you shouldn't have come here," she repeated stubbornly, "knowing they would hold you responsible."

"Wind might have harmed you if I hadn't. I couldn't take that chance."

Rebecca gazed up at him tearfully, her heart swelling at the knowledge of the risk he took. How could she ever have thought that he cared for no one but himself? He had come for her—and for their son. "What will they do to us now? Did the council decide? Is Samuel all right?"

The fire made a loud snapping sound, causing her to jump skittishly and swing her head toward the entrance. Aaron held her hands, his thumbs soothing her with a gentle, circular motion on her wrists.

"Relax, 'Becca. No one will bother us for the rest of the night. Come sit here." Tugging her forward, he leaned back against a pile of furs, pulling her onto his lap.

Her head lay against the smooth expanse of his chest. His strong heartbeat thudded beneath her ear, steadying her. For the first time in days she felt completely safe.

His voice was a comforting rumble. "One thing about the Shawnee: They love children. I'm sure Samuel's getting royal treatment. Tell me—how did he hold up on the way here?"

"Well enough. Better than his mother when they brought us upriver," she added in a self-deprecating tone. "I nearly swooned again at the sight of the canoes."

"But you didn't, did you," Aaron murmured. "And his leg?"

"Seems to be fine. He's—wait just a minute! You're purposely avoiding the subject! I want to know what's going to happen next." She pushed herself up to study his face. His eyes were tinged with regret, a rueful smile curving his mouth.

"There's nothing we can do tonight, m'dear. Let's get some rest and—"

"Not again, Aaron!" Angrily, she pulled away. Her hair had become tangled around his wrist and she jerked it loose, tears stinging her eyes. It was bad enough they were caught up in this nightmare. Now she felt the way she had days ago when he'd held this same remote look in his eyes. Worse than the fear was the terrible loneliness, the desolation that swept through her at his refusal to share his thoughts and feelings.

"Please don't shut me out again. I was wrong for placing all the blame and responsibility on you. I *want* us to face this together. I want your trust. Please, Aaron, *tell* me."

His granite expression softened as he gazed at her. With great tenderness he brushed a willful strand of hair from her cheek. "Never believe I don't trust you, my love. I've trusted you with my heart, which is more than I ever thought I could manage again. But the habits of a decade are not easily broken. Perhaps if I'd come to you ten years ago, your love would have proved the healing balm to my broken spirit. Or perhaps you would have grown to resent me. Who can say?"

Incredibly moved by his admission, Rebecca pressed her cheek against his warm palm. "Though I'd like to believe I'd have loved you regardless of your wounds, both external and otherwise, I'd be foolish to insist. I was very young then. My expectations about love and life were not always realistic. From what you told me, you received all the care and acceptance you needed from Wind and his people, and for that I am grateful. But we're together now, and we must find our way out of this together.''

The kiss he placed on her lips was as gently sweet as the spring rain, in contrast to the rough emotion in his voice. ''You and Samuel will be out of here tomorrow, I promise.''

''Why not tonight?'' she whispered. ''I know where they're keeping Samuel. At least I saw where Wind's men took him yesterday. We could find him and get away now.''

Aaron cupped her cheek and tipped his head sadly. ''Wind's no fool. Samuel will have been moved by now. No, darling, there'll be no getting away. At least not for me. This hut is surrounded by guards, and the village perimeter is equally protected. But you'll be on your way in the morning; Wind gave me his word.''

''And you?'' she asked querulously, already knowing the answer by the rapid cadence of her heart. ''Oh, Aaron! Wind really does mean to kill you, doesn't he?''

'' 'Becca, m'dear,'' he murmured soothingly, settling down onto the pile of furs and drawing her into his arms, ''do you think I don't know what Wind wants? His people have been slaughtered. Those who survived the attack are weakened and ill. He *owes* them their revenge. It is the only way they can recover and go on from here.''

''Then let them take revenge on the men who are truly guilty,'' Rebecca cried, ''not on you! I tried to tell Wind that you had nothing to do with the attack, but he won't listen. What kind of friend is that?''

''One who has lost his favorite son,'' Aaron replied. His voice was tinged with sadness and acceptance. ''One who knows that revenge will not erase a death. Revenge *will* bring back pride and spirit to his heartsore tribe, however. That is why Wind must take my life: to appease his people.''

''But I will make him relinquish you and Samuel first, 'Becca, darling. And you won't be forced to witness my execution. The others in council disagreed vehemently, but Wind had the final say. Believe me, if he weren't my friend he would not even consider setting you free.''

But I don't want to go without you! Rebecca wailed inside. *I don't want to live without you.*

As if reading her thoughts, Aaron tipped her head so that firelight glistened upon her damp cheeks. With his thumb he traced the soft flesh beneath her chin. His other arm tightened around her waist. "Don't even think about defying me in this, 'Becca. I don't want to leave you, either, but you must get Samuel home. I'll try to follow. You'll have to be strong, m'dear."

"But how can I, Aaron? How can I leave here knowing that you might be . . . that you might suffer unspeakably?" Huge tears rolled down her face, catching on her quivering lips before plunging from her chin to the blankets and furs she clutched around them.

"I won't suffer," Aaron insisted, though it gave her scant reassurance. "That's another reason I know Wind has not completely forsaken our friendship. He informed me earlier that I will die by the tomahawk. That, at least, is quicker than some of their other, ah, methods. And no matter what *he* believes, I don't intend to give up without a fight."

This did little to ease Rebecca's mind, however. Two days without sleep combined with an all-consuming fear, threatening to break her, but she was determined not to give in to further tears. Aaron was already skeptical about treating her as an equal; dissolving into helpless hysteria now would not convince him otherwise.

"A-Are you certain we can't escape tonight? I could create a diversion. Or maybe I can pretend sickness to delay my departure for a few days. You said Wind agreed that Samuel and I would not have to stay to see—"

"We can't wait that long, darling." His eyes were shadowed with remorse. "Even one more day could prove fatal to Wind's tribe. I came as fast as I could, but the army is only a few days behind. Jessup is hell-bent on 'rescuing' you, this time with Major Carswell's full cooperation. The only way to prevent a full-scale massacre is for you and Samuel to return quickly."

And so they were caught. Utterly and completely, like rabbits lured to the hunter's snare. Rebecca had once heard that a terrified creature would chew off its own foot in order to escape a metal trap, only to later bleed to death in the forest. That was the choice she had now. To lose Aaron would surely kill her. Perhaps not immediately, but how could she survive when a part of her, much more vital than a mere limb, had been torn away? And yet the alternative was to face certain death, or at best a lifetime of captivity.

When it came right down to it, she rationalized, there really was no choice. Rebecca could not—*would* not—expose her son to further danger. Also, the practical side of her nature told her that with release lay the best chance for them all. Aaron could concentrate on his own escape without worrying about her and Samuel.

Rebecca shivered—not from cold, for the little fire continued to blaze beside her, but from the searching intensity in Aaron's eyes as he watched her struggle for acceptance. It was the look of a starving man before he devours his last morsel of sustenance. Never had she been more frightened.

She laid her palm gently against his cheek, her eyes locked with his. "I—It seems there's nothing for me to do but take Wind's offer," she whispered earnestly. "But I will wait for you this time, Aaron. I will wait for the rest of my life."

Capturing her hand in his, he turned to her cupped palm, kissing the soft skin there. She could feel the tremors rip through him, matching her own quaking need, and she uttered a low moan of desire.

Then, surprisingly, he lowered his hands to her waist and lifted her away. "You should try to get some rest, 'Becca," he suggested tenderly. "It's a long trip back and you'll leave first thing in the morning."

Rebecca's lips parted first in shock, then curved into a bittersweet smile. "Are you merely being noble," she asked shakily, "or don't you *want* to make love to me?"

He was silent for a time; then, with a movement as slick as silk, Aaron swept her onto his lap and turned her around so that she faced him.

"God, 'Becca!" he rasped, his voice hoarse with emotion, "I've never wanted you more than at this moment. But it doesn't seem right—"

"It *is* right, Aaron. Never more so." Her words were thick with desire, her eyes burning as they searched his. "I want you to touch me, to make me forget everything but your love. Most of all I want to do the same for you."

"I've never loved you more, my 'Becca. My beautiful, brave love. The Shawnee believe that a man's spirit is most alive when he is closest to death, and now I know what they mean." His hands traced the curve of her hips and moved together to slide up her slender back. "But as much as I desire to show you now, I don't want you to go through what you did before. The shame and the hardship. If you should conceive—"

"I would be glad!" Rebecca declared fiercely. "Just as I was ten years ago when I lost you the first time. Oh, Aaron, it was knowing that I carried a part of you that helped me survive. That precious life inside me was my salvation; never my shame. I *hope* I conceive again.

"It's possible," she added solemnly, "that I already have."

When Aaron searched the depths of her eyes, he saw in them the truth, and understood, too, her need for him now. In the face of death, they both needed to join in that greatest celebration of life, to worship instead of revile, to create instead of destroy. "My love," he whispered brokenly.

Pulling her to a reclining position, he turned so that she lay beneath him, supporting him, yet protected by him as well. His hand found her belly, caressing the firm plane through her clothing.

She lay passive beneath him, drinking in the sight of him, absorbing the warmth and love and tenderness of his touch. His hair fell over his brow, shading his face, but she knew each line and shadow as if it were etched in her memory for all time. "I love you, Aaron," she whispered throatily. With her fingertips she traced the ridge upon his cheek. "I love every part of you. This scar used to be a reminder of your pain, but now when I see it I think only of your strength and endurance, your courage." She caressed his temples now with a feathery light touch. "In the same way, I no longer care about the time we spent apart. It's the time together that counts. Only this."

He lowered his head to kiss her, his mouth gentle, yet

demanding. She welcomed him with her lips and tongue, all sweetness and desperation, urgently drawing him nearer.

Rebecca's arms went around him, her hands moving over his shoulders and back. She wanted to feel his warmth and solid strength against her, to know the special closeness of true intimacy.

Sensing her desire, Aaron fumbled at the back of her dress for the buttons that fastened it, then tugged the garment free. In much less time he removed his own clothing, and soon he was lying close to her once more, making certain with his hands and lips that she did not feel abandoned.

He kissed her mouth, a deep, soulful kiss that was tender and pleading and commanding all at once. Then his lips descended, forging a burning trail beneath her chin and down her slender throat. He worshiped her full, aching breasts with his hands and mouth, teasing the dusky nipples to taut, tingling awareness before drawing on first one, then the other, with an intensity that made Rebecca moan out loud in exquisite pleasure.

His kisses wandered farther, becoming reverent as they reached the soft curve of her belly, then tormenting once more as his mouth dipped even lower. She recoiled when she realized what he intended, but his expert hands had already begun to pave the way for what his lips would continue, and so she lay quivering and helpless while he brought her near the precipice of ecstasy.

"Aaron," she cried almost soundlessly, her fingers curving, grasping only air. He understood what she wanted, rising to bury himself in her, to complete their joining together. His own quick gasps marked how close he was to explosion; with infinite care he moved his hips to increase her arousal.

Rebecca wanted to prolong his pleasure, to make this loving and this night go on forever, but all logical thought fled as Aaron moved deep, deeper inside her. With her body and her heart she enveloped him in her love, tightening, trembling, until at last she cried out with joy and desperation. She clung to his shoulders as his own body

shuddered to magnificent fulfillment, his exultant cry mingling with hers in a union of mouths and hearts and souls.

In her release Rebecca found the peace she had sought,
and temporary comfort from the heartache that was yet to
come. Only their love mattered now. Only the lives they
had created.

Aaron's breathing had slowed to a normal rate before he
could bear to loosen his fervent embrace, and even then
he relaxed only enough to roll to his side, pulling her with
him. Their bodies fitted perfectly together, and though he
had noticed it was so on other occasions together, never
had it felt more right to have her warmth and softness
pressed so close that it was difficult to tell one heartbeat
from the other.

He turned his head to look at her face, and she opened
her eyes to gaze back at him. Her dark eyes glowed in the
firelight like chestnuts; her sable lashes were tipped in gold
by the dancing light. Softly, he touched her cheek, surprised to find them wet. " 'Becca?" he asked, his voice
a low rumble in the deadly still night.

She shook her head, then buried her face against his
chest. "I love you, Aaron."

"And I love you, more than you can know."

"Please . . . hold me tight and don't let go until morning comes."

"I won't, my love," he whispered. His heart thumped
achingly at the knowledge that their loving had not erased
her fear. "I'll never let you go."

CHAPTER 29

Aaron slept for perhaps an hour, somewhere between making sweet love to Rebecca once again and the gray approach of dawn. The rest of the time he lay still, holding her as she fell into the deep slumber of emotional and physical exhaustion. He was content to watch her, to simply absorb the warmth and wonder of her, and to contemplate what might occur on what might be the last day of his life.

He heard the sounds of the awakening tribe, his mind registering the changes wrought by battle and sickness while his heart grew dismal with grief. He missed the quiet, relaxed voices and the soft hiss of steam from the cookfires of dozens of happy homes. Instead he heard anger and bitterness, weighing heavy like the predawn mist. He wondered if these people would ever know peace again. Perhaps they would, he thought with both hope and resignation. But it would not be in this valley.

Eventually the sounds grew louder, loud enough that Rebecca stirred in his arms. He smiled tenderly as she yawned and stretched, snuggling closer to him for warmth.

A grunt just outside the *wigewa* startled them both; his arms tightened around her and her eyes flew open wide. Aaron lifted his head to see the door flap fly back, admitting only the pale light of day.

"Rise, Gentle Healer. Rise quickly."

At his side, Rebecca stiffened, a low moan coming from deep in her throat. "Oh, God, no! Not yet!"

"Shhh, it's all right," Aaron murmured, hugging her

once more before throwing off the fur that covered them. "This is something else."

Dressing rapidly, he listened for more signs of what was happening, but Wind at His Feet stood motionless and silent just beyond the door. "Hurry," Aaron urged Rebecca while standing in front of the opening to give her some privacy.

Once Rebecca dressed, Wind at His Feet entered the hut. Even in the darkness, Aaron could see that his friend's eyes were troubled and his countenance strained. "What is it?"

"The choking sickness," Wind answered without hesitation. "It has come in the night to my house."

"Who?"

"It is the babe who lies ill. Smiles at Strangers."

"Aaron, the baby," Rebecca breathed, as if he had not heard it for himself. She clutched his arm and looked up at Wind at His Feet, compassion driving the fear and mistrust from her gaze. "Can you help?"

"I can try." Aaron continued to meet Wind's stare. "Is that what you wish?" Wordlessly, simply by the expression of simple entreaty in his black eyes, his friend gave him the answer.

Now Aaron turned to Rebecca. "Wait here while I go have a look."

"What if they try to take me away before you get back?"

"Then go. Take Samuel and go home as fast as you can. You must try to stop Jessup and Carswell from making a mistake."

"No, I won't leave you!" she said adamantly. "Not now."

Gripping her shoulders, Aaron resisted the urge to shake her. " 'Becca, we've been over this—"

"I can help you."

"The risk is too great."

"But I had diphtheria as a child, so I won't be—"

"That's not what I meant."

His tone was forbidding, but it was the fear in his eyes that prompted her to comprehend. If she stayed with him now to assist with Wind's daughter, she might lose the only opportunity she had for freedom, for if the child died,

Wind and his people might change their minds about letting her and Samuel go.

But on the other hand, saving the infant Smiles at
Strangers could be the salvation of them all. Aaron had
already told her that Wind was punishing him to appease
his people. This might be Aaron's chance to prove his
loyalty to the Shawnee.

"I know you're only concerned for my safety," she said
in quiet desperation. "But I'm thinking about us."

Aaron's hands tightened, then relaxed. He took a deep,
contemplative breath. " 'Becca, there's no telling how bad
off the baby is. I might not be able to save her."

"You won't know until you try," she replied with a
defiant tip of her head. Her dark eyes glittered with determination. "Wind said the illness has just begun, so there's
hope. I know you can do it, Aaron. Please let me help."

Her faith in his ability was humbling. Aaron closed his
eyes, fighting the heaviness in his chest. Then he looked
at her again, bolstered by her expression of confidence and
love.

"All right, then," he said in a rough voice. "Let's go."

The *wigewa* of White Star and her husband, Wind at His
Feet, was somber and dark. Because they had removed the
other children to the care of the tribe's women, the hut
was quiet but for the strangled breathing of the tiny Smiles
at Strangers.

White Star had risen from her mourning to care for the
baby, and now she cradled the infant gently, holding her
upright to ease the passage of air into her gasping lungs.

"When did this start?" Aaron asked in the Shawnee
tongue. When White Star uttered a soft moan, Wind at His
Feet came forward.

"The first of my people to be stricken was Yellow
Feather. I was not aware of her sickness at the beginning
because she hid herself away, not wanting the others to
know."

Rebecca was about to ask why not when Wind cast a
meaningful glance toward his wife. "The women tell me
now that Yellow Feather shared her sleeping mat with one
of the white whiskey traders. She was ashamed for The

People to know that her loose ways had caused her to be ill.''

White Star moaned again, her slight form rocking back and forth as she knelt with her baby. She whispered something which Rebecca did not understand, until Wind interpreted.

''My wife blames herself for not sharing with me the actions of Yellow Feather, even though I do not care to hear the gossip of women. I have told her it is not her fault that Yellow Feather was careless with her favors.'' He lowered a gentle hand to White Star's shoulder and said gravely, ''Yellow Feather died on the third day of her sickness. Since then, six others have died, and many are ill.''

During all this Aaron had been watching the infant, silently counting her struggling breaths and gauging her listless response to her mother's touch. Now he approached the grieving White Star, touching her gently upon the shoulder.

''May I see her?'' he asked quietly.

White Star glanced once to her husband, who nodded his approval, then handed the baby to Aaron.

He moved closer to the fire, where the more favorable light would allow him to thoroughly inspect the child. Immediately he could see the signs of distress, from her dry and feverish skin to her blue-tinged lips, a sign that she was not getting enough air into her tiny lungs.

'' 'Becca, start some water boiling,'' he ordered quietly, still bent over the infant. He laid her onto a soft fur, then used a flat piece of wood to depress her tongue while he examined her throat.

It was all he could do to keep from exclaiming out loud. Instead he tossed the stick into the fire and sat back on his heels. The tiny form lay nearly still, hardly reacting at all to his touch.

''It's bad?'' Rebecca asked fearfully.

He nodded. ''Diphtheria is rare in a child this young. She can scarcely breathe, let alone fight the fever.''

''What will you do?''

''Prepare a decoction to loosen the phlegm in her throat, and another to use as a plaster on her chest. And we'll have to get the fever down. Cold cloths will have to do, and willow bark if any of the women have some already dried.''

Hearing this, Wind went to the door. He called out to one of the villagers waiting outside, giving to the woman instructions as to what Aaron needed.

Rebecca was glad to have something to do. She filled a black kettle with water from the skins handed to her by Wind at His Feet, then threw additional wood on the fire to make it hot. Poor White Star, still bedraggled and cowering in her grief, could do nothing but hunch down in a corner to watch others take the life of her youngest child into their hands.

What must she feel? Rebecca wondered with aching sympathy. First Little Otter and now Smiles at Strangers.

Her thoughts turned then to Samuel, and she was seized with an irrational fear, not that he was unwell, for she believed Aaron when he said the Shawnee would care for him as one of their own, but that she would never see him again. If anything went wrong now . . .

She lifted her stark gaze to Wind at His Feet, who watched Aaron's ministrations to his daughter with ill-concealed impatience. Would he credit Aaron for at least trying? Or would they both suffer the result if Smiles at Strangers succumbed to the disease?

As if sensing her regard, the proud Indian turned toward her, and his eyes darkened at the sight of her defiant stance. Then he returned his gaze to Aaron and spoke softly in the Shawnee tongue.

Aaron looked at Rebecca without expression. "He said you are a strong-spirited woman, worthy of the great Cain."

She gave this a moment's contemplation, then looked Wind straight in the eye and said, "Tell him he is an honorable leader, worthy of an enduring friendship with a man who does not break his word. Go on, tell him," she prodded when Aaron did not answer.

Wind stirred from his place near the door. "I hear your words, Brave Mother, and my heart tells me it is so."

She continued to stare at him, suddenly afraid that if she broke contact they would lose this fragile understanding. Unblinking, he stared back at her, his black eyes glittering like polished onyx. Then his head moved—a small movement only, barely perceptible—but Rebecca sensed he was nodding his approval.

She sighed and let her shoulders relax.

The vigil had begun.

For a day and a night they watched over Smiles at Strangers, taking turns bathing her feverish body with cool water and spooning the medicine Aaron had made into her small, gasping mouth. Near dawn the second morning Aaron lifted her into his arms, his palm stroking the downy black hair that lay so limp upon her skull.

"We're losing her, 'Becca," he whispered urgently, rousing her from a half slumber.

Instantly she was on her knees beside him, her own hands reaching for the tiny body as if she could infuse life back into the infant with merely a touch. "Oh, Aaron," she murmured in return, softly so as not to wake White Star, who dozed at last, or to disturb Wind at His Feet, who crouched on the opposite side of the *wigewa* in silent meditation. "Is there nothing else we can do?"

"There is, but it's risky. She can't breathe through the thick phlegm blocking her throat and nose. I can try to cut a hole in her windpipe in order to ease the passage of air, but it will be difficult with so small a baby."

Rebecca suppressed a shudder at Aaron's suggestion, but she knew from his dismal voice that this was Smiles at Stranger's only hope.

"What will you need, my brother?" From behind them Wind at His Feet spoke, startling them both into turning around.

Worry had etched deep grooves into his normally smooth face, his eyes had lost their fierceness, and now held only concern. Surprised that she could feel sympathy for the man who held Aaron's life in his hand, Rebecca blinked back sudden tears.

Quickly Aaron described what he needed. Wind bowed his head, then left the *wigewa*. At the sound of their voices, White Star roused herself, creeping over toward her daughter. Aaron allowed her to cuddle the child while he prepared himself to perform the surgery.

Rebecca watched him move toward the fire, feeding the flames to produce more light. The muscles of his back strained beneath the fringed tunic he wore, stretching the supple leather taut across his shoulders. Just as inflexible were the hard lines of his face, etched deeply over his brow and along the sides of his mouth. She wished there were some way she could ease his worry, yet at the same time she realized that the same compassion and precision that caused him such inner torment were the qualities she admired most about him. Love for him surged within her, growing and pulsing like a living thing.

He lifted his gaze to her then, and the same love was reflected back in his intense blue eyes.

"I'll need your help," he said quietly, confidently.

Rebecca nodded, but did not speak. Her voice was locked somewhere deep in her throat.

"Smiles at Strangers must be held perfectly still. We can't give her anything to numb the pain because she's too weak already. Fortunately, this will go fast."

"What will you do?"

"Puncture a hole through her throat and into her windpipe. Once the incision is cleared, I'll insert a small button with a hole in the center to keep the passage open. The most important thing will be to keep blood from seeping back into her lungs."

Swallowing hard, Rebecca nodded once more. Grimly, she clung to the thought that she had managed to hold herself up during Samuel's ordeal. Surely she could do the same for the tiny Smiles at Strangers.

Within minutes Wind at His Feet returned to the hut with the necessary items, and to Rebecca's surprise, he held back the tent flap to admit the aging shaman Snow Hair.

"Greet-ings, Cain," he said in halting English, then spoke in the Shawnee tongue for several minutes.

Through this, Aaron listened with an attitude of respect, nodding occasionally. At one point Snow Hair poked his hand from beneath his robe, holding it out so that all could see the tremors that shook his gnarled fingers. Aaron said something then, and the old man grunted. He hobbled to the other side of the fire and lowered himself onto a pallet of furs, then began to chant quietly.

"Snow Hair said he has performed this particular surgery twice in his lifetime, but cannot do so again because he is too old," Aaron explained to Rebecca when she edged closer to him. "He has given me permission to proceed."

"Did he tell you if it worked . . . those other times?" she whispered.

Aaron met her gaze. "One time, yes."

But once, no. He did not have to say it. The specter of that other failure hung over them both, increasing the already considerable tension inside the bark hut.

At Aaron's quiet request, Wind at His Feet motioned for White Star to rise. With great reluctance, she handed her baby to Aaron, then followed her husband to a spot behind Snow Hair, where they both crouched. Wind at His Feet put his arm around his wife's shoulders.

Aaron peered down at the baby in his arms, then looked back at Rebecca. "Are you ready?" he asked.

Squaring her shoulders, she lifted her chin high and nodded resolutely.

It was all over in a deceptively short time. Rebecca was amazed at how Aaron's hands could remain so steady and sure when her own quaked like leaves in a windstorm. She had almost dropped the tiny button into the fire when Aaron asked her to remove it from the kettle of boiling water with a pair of crude tongs.

Fortunately, the near mishap did not prevent Aaron from deftly completing the surgery, and within minutes he knelt back from the pallet where Smiles at Strangers lay. He had already bundled the baby up in a clean blanket.

"That's it," he murmured, wiping his brow with the back of his hand. "Now we wait."

Rebecca peered at the infant skeptically. Smiles at Strangers remained as deathly still as she had during the entire procedure. The only difference was that now, instead of gasping for air, her tiny chest rose up and down in an even rhythm.

"Now that she can breathe," Aaron explained, "her body has a better chance to fight off the disease. We'll have to watch to make sure her fever doesn't rise too high, and I want to keep this room filled with steam.''

Aaron stood wearily. He approached Wind at His Feet and the silent White Star, then dropped to one knee before his friend. Holding out both hands, he waited until the chieftain grasped them.

''Now is the time to pray,'' Aaron said thickly.

Wind grunted. ''I have been doing that,'' he replied. ''I have been praying that my brother, Gentle Healer, would forget the hard words between us.''

''They are forgotten.'' Aaron bowed his head. ''Now pray for Smiles at Strangers. Her life is in the hands of the gods.''

After the high drama of the morning, Rebecca had half expected the baby's recovery to be equally as spectacular. Instead, her progress was gradual and painfully slow. The infant's color was the first noticeable improvement. Though still pale, Smiles at Strangers had lost that bluish tint underlying her skin within an hour after her breathing became regular. Aaron continued to trickle small doses of the herbal decoction down her throat, and by afternoon her fever was almost normal.

But the true mark of achievement came when White Star hugged her and Smiles at Strangers began to root for her mother's breast. Tears stung Rebecca's eyes when White Star, weeping openly, lifted her face to the heavens.

With the permission of Wind at His Feet and Snow Hair, Aaron simmered a large batch of medicine and proceeded to visit some of the other villagers who were ill, while Rebecca remained in the *wigewa* with White Star and her sleeping baby. He returned a few hours later. Rebecca was shocked at how tired he looked. She remembered that he had not slept in nearly two days.

''Did you see Samuel?'' she asked quietly after he checked Smiles at Strangers and then seated himself before the fire.

''No, but Wind tells me he is safe in the home of his sister, Laughing Woman, with his other children. They are far away from all this, thank God.''

''Is it that bad?'' Rebecca knelt beside him, handing

him a steaming bowl of cornmeal. He bowed his head over it wearily.

"A dozen or so sick," he answered. "I treated most of them, but a few were beyond help. Who knows if the others . . ."

His question trailed off, and Rebecca was struck again by the knowledge that Aaron cared as much for these people as he did for her and Samuel. Before, this would have filled her with anger and jealousy, but now her heart expanded to understand his greater love.

She placed her hand on his arm encouragingly. "You have done your best," she murmured. "You told Wind to leave his daughter's life in the hands of the gods. You must do the same, Aaron, or you'll never find peace with yourself."

He turned his aching gaze to her. "That's a difficult thing to ask, but I know you're right." He cleared his throat, then gave her a half smile. "Thank you for helping, 'Becca. Having you by my side did make this easier."

She pushed a lock of hair from his brow, smiling back at him tenderly. "Someone has to take care of you while you take care of everyone else."

"We'll take care of each other."

Aaron hugged her close then, and Rebecca gladly gave herself over to the warm, protective feeling of having his arms around her. It was all the more precious for knowing that this might be the last time they could hold one another this way.

Throughout the long night Aaron continued to check on the patients in his care, stopping back at Wind's hut whenever he could for food and rest. Rebecca asked if she could go with him, but he replied that the other villagers might feel uncomfortable in her presence, and so she assisted by keeping the kettle of medicine brewing over the fire and making sure that each time he returned she had a bowl of hot food and an encouraging smile for him.

By morning, Smiles at Strangers was greatly improved, and though two of the Shawnee had died, the others seemed to be responding well to Aaron's treatment.

Despite this, she noticed that he still appeared grave and concerned. His face was nearly haggard with exhaustion and worry. When she asked him why, he explained, "Even though no one else has become sick in the past two days, it's very possible that the outbreak isn't over yet. The problem is, with the army on its way Wind should not delay in moving his people to another site."

"Have you told him this?" Rebecca had almost forgotten about the threat of attack, but now she understood Aaron's dilemma.

"Yes, but until the disease stopped spreading they could do nothing. Now he is consulting with Snow Hair and the other tribal leaders again. I expect we'll find out what he intends to do soon enough."

What he intends to do. She had also put out of her mind the fact that Aaron's own life was still at stake. Wind's gratitude toward Aaron was obvious, but would the other Shawnee warriors view the matter in the same way?

They did not have to wait long to learn the answer, for only a short time later Wind returned to the *wigewa*. His stance was once again proud and tall, and after stooping to greet his wife and place his palm upon his napping daughter's head, he came to crouch before the fire, facing Aaron and Rebecca.

"I have spoken to the others again about leaving, my brother," he began slowly, his dark eyes staring into the fire. "I will tell you now that many of them were not prepared to believe you."

Rebecca started, opening her mouth with an indignant reply, but Aaron's steady voice calmed her. "Your warriors have reason to be cautious. But I trust you were able to convince them that I speak the truth. You must move the village immediately." He paused. "And you must also keep your promise to escort Rebecca and Samuel home."

Again Rebecca began to protest, but this time it was Wind who forestalled her with a raised hand.

"If I am to move the village, then I cannot spare my men," he said with quiet emphasis. "You will have to take Brave Mother and her son back to the white village."

It took a moment for his meaning to sink in, but finally Rebecca's eyes widened, a broad smile dawning over her face. She met Aaron's gaze and he squeezed her hand. His expression remained somber as he addressed his friend once more.

"Thank you, Wind. We will leave as soon as we can gather provisions for the journey. There is still a chance we might head off the army before they come near."

"I will pray for this," Wind acknowledged with a bitter twist of his lips, "and I will also pray that you find peace and happiness in your life. It is my selfish wish that you would return to the Shawnee someday, for I will miss my brother, Gentle Healer. The People would benefit greatly from your skill." He paused before addng, "But my heart lies heavy with the knowledge that this can never be."

Tears formed in Rebecca's eyes when she realized that Wind was bidding his last farewell. She had come to admire these people and their proud ways. It nearly broke her heart to know that no matter how hard they tried, they could not fight the changes that would come over the land.

Aaron, too, felt the loss of an entire way of life, for his voice was hoarse when he finally spoke.

"I, too, will pray for peace and happiness in the life of my brother, Wind at His Feet." He swallowed before adding, "Even if our paths never cross in this lifetime, know that my spirit will always walk by your side."

CHAPTER 30

Wind escorted them to the banks of the river, where his sister, Laughing Woman, waited for them. Rebecca could not hold back her tears when she embraced Samuel, who looked brown and healthy and extremely happy to see her and Aaron both.

"I missed you, Ma," he whispered as he hugged her neck fiercely. Then he pulled away and proclaimed, "I wish they woulda let me stay with you, but I had fun anyway. Can we come back sometime?"

Rebecca's eyes met Aaron's over the top of Samuel's head, and her heart ached for him. Already the Shawnee were preparing to leave the village that had been their home for many years. Their future in the Ohio Valley looked bleak.

Wind stepped forward, placing his hand on Samuel's shoulder. "The son of Gentle Healer is welcome in my village anytime," he said. "We will call you Hopping Boy."

Aaron stiffened suddenly at his friend's comment, and Rebecca caught the movement from the corner of her eye. She turned to him with an expression of approval, hoping he could see by her action that she did not mind. It was time, she had decided, that all truths surface.

Aaron relaxed, his eyes conveying to her both his love and understanding. It was unclear whether Samuel had even heard the oblique reference to his parenthood, or had simply accepted it as good-naturedly as he did everything else.

His face split with a grin. "Hopping Boy! That's funny. But what about when I don't have a limp anymore?"

"Then we will change your name. Perhaps you will have accomplished much by then, and a different name will be more suitable." Wind looked at Rebecca, and for the first time she saw his proud features soften with a smile. "My daughter has been given a new life. I will mark this great event. No longer will she be called Smiles at Strangers. From this day she will be known as *E'nau-bin nekah*, Smiles at Friends."

Rebecca could not speak for several moments. Aaron saved her from the necessity by moving closer and taking her hand. "You honor us both, Wind. It is good that we part with only friendship between us."

Wind at His Feet nodded regally, then gestured for two lads who waited behind him. "I have another gift for you, my brother. You told me to look for the strange markings upon the whiskey my people have traded for." Before yesterday I had not seen any, until I entered the *wigewa* of Red Dog to summon him to council. I found this."

The boys lifted between them a small keg, about two feet long and as big around as a tree stump. When they placed it in front of Aaron he could plainly see the crude *S* which Skulley had carved into the end.

Aaron stared at the marking with disbelief written on his face. He broke into a grin. "Wind, you have no idea how valuable this gift is to me," he said wryly. "No idea."

They covered the first part of their journey by canoe, after Rebecca's gentle insistence that she could bear up if it meant getting to Major Carswell sooner. Aaron was glad for her staunch effort. Deep inside he realized that every hour was precious in the race to intercept the army, and that already it might be too late.

From his place in the stern of the craft he watched her slim back bend to the task of paddling, for Rebecca had also insisted on handling an oar, claiming that the work would give her something to think about besides her fear. It had not taken her much practice to adjust to the easy rhythm of paddling downstream, and before long they were

moving swiftly down the Great Miami River toward the
Ohio.

Seated in the middle, Samuel faced Aaron, and shortly
after they embarked he was sound asleep, lulled by the
gentle rocking motion of the canoe and the peaceful surroundings.

That peace was disrupted too soon, when from off to
the left they heard the loud retort of a rifle, followed by
an accompanying volley. Rebecca jerked her paddle from
the water, twisting so that Aaron could see the questioning
fear written on her face.

"This way," he murmured quietly, pointing to the riverbank lined with overhanging branches. He used his oar
to turn the canoe while Rebecca continued with steady
strokes. Within moments they were brushing against the
shoreline.

Samuel awakened at the abrupt motion; when he started
to speak Aaron shushed him with a finger held to his
mouth.

Now that they listened, the faint sound of voices came
to them from the same direction as the gunshots, though
it was difficult to tell how many men were hidden in the
forest.

"What now?" Rebecca mouthed to Aaron.

He peered into the thick trees for a long moment, as if
trying to discern their next move from the darkness within.
"I'll try to close in to see what's up. I doubt this is the
entire army; not enough noise. It could be the advance
party."

Rebecca nodded. He had already explained the likeli-
hood that they would meet up with a scouting expedition
first. The bulk of the army would proceed slowly, requir-
ing a road to be cleared in order to move the cannons and
supply train. It was not uncommon for them to cover only
a few miles a day.

The advance party, on the other hand, was responsible
for marking a likely trail, as well as for detecting signs of
the enemy. This was a role given to experienced scouts;
Rebecca did not need Aaron to warn her that the leader of
this group could very well be Captain Vance Jessup.

"Shouldn't we go with you?" she asked softly. "If their

goal is to rescue Samuel and me, then perhaps if we show ourselves to be out of harm's way, they'll stop.''

As he studied her earnest expression, Aaron was struck again by Rebecca's courage and resilience. It seemed incongruous to him that he had ever doubted her ability to weather any storm. But the one facing them now might prove beyond their endurance. And there was Samuel to consider.

"Wait here for me, both of you," he ordered quietly. "At least until I see what we're up against.''

Almost before she could bid him Godspeed he was on his way, melting into the forest like a wild creature equipped with the ability to change its appearance to suit the terrain. Rebecca nibbled on her lower lip as she followed his movement until he disappeared. Then she settled back against a fallen log to think. Samuel limped to her side, taking her hand.

"Don't worry," he whispered manfully. "I won't let anyone hurt you. Look.'' He produced the small bow and a clutch of three arrows that he had brought with him from the Shawnee village. "I'm getting good. I can shoot through a hoop from twenty paces.''

Rebecca smiled, but inside she was praying that Samuel's newfound skill would not be put to the test. She knew that Aaron hoped to keep them both far away from whatever confrontation might occur, but she persisted in the belief that only Samuel's and her appearance would stop the troops from attacking Wind's village. Skulley and Major Carswell trusted Aaron, but the rest would be all too ready to ignore his explanations. What if they arrested him and tied him up again?''

It seemed like an hour passed, though it was probably only a few minutes, before Rebecca reached a decision. She would not wait here another moment, wondering whether Aaron had walked into a trap.

The men in her life were not the only ones with the instinct to protect their own.

Aaron crouched behind a white oak, scanning the clearing before him. It was not a large clearing, merely a break in the trees caused by nature, but it was a spot where a few men might pause and gather to rest. The canopy of leaves overhead blocked the sun, casting the landscape into shade so deep it appeared almost as black as night.

Uncannily so.

Aaron thrust away the cloud of mist that seemed to envelop his mind. His back prickled with cold sweat and his legs turned suddenly numb. Something about this whole scene felt strangely familiar, as if he had waited here before. Waited for something—some*one*—to step through the trees.

Voices drifted toward him, but whether they were voices of the past or the present he could not tell. Dread welled up inside him, surrounded him, tried to burst from his throat in a scream that would rend the air in two.

Instead, Aaron fought the panic, forcing himself to concentrate on Rebecca and Samuel waiting for him near the river. He would not succumb to this nightmare—would not let his past suck him down into the mire again. Not now that he finally had a future.

The voices grew louder, nearer, approaching the clearing without caution. He heard the crackling of underbrush and the heavy tromp of bootsteps upon dead leaves. A horse whinnied softly, followed by the jingle of harness and a wordless, soothing response.

He tensed even more, until he thought each muscle might snap like a bowstring stretched to the breaking point. Then the first of the men stepped through the trees, and Aaron felt as if his entire body had burst open upon the ground. His mind reeled, his heart pounded. His throat went dry.

Jacob? He did not realize that the soundless question rang in no man's ears but his own. He blinked rapidly, disbelieving. *Jacob?*

At that moment the man took another step forward, moving to where a slim filament of light fell on his face. Aaron felt the tension sink from his body like blood drains from a wound. He nearly wept from the disappointment and relief.

Not Jacob.

The man cocked his head as if to listen. Now Aaron could clearly see his features. He wondered how, or why, this man could have reminded him of his long-dead brother. They were not even alike. Not even—

With the thought no more than a glimmer in his mind, Aaron stiffened once more. Two more men followed the first into the clearing, two men he easily recognized: Silas Carter and his captain, Vance Jessup. Like the first scout, they appeared to listen to the wind, then relaxed when no sound came but the noisy approach of the rest of their unit.

"We'll rest here," Jessup barked. He unshouldered his rifle and ordnance bag, dropping them to the ground with a heavy thud. "Damned horses are no good in the trees. I told Carswell we should have stuck to the river."

"Too hard to float all them cannons upstream," Carter said, spitting a mouthful of tobacco juice into the bushes. "Never git 'em—"

"I *know* that!" Jessup glared at the soldier. "Just shut up while I think. And water those horses. We've got a long way to go tonight."

"Ain't we s'posed to wait for the regiment?" Carter asked. "They ain't more'n a mile behind us." The man who had entered the clearing first grunted in agreement.

"Damned if I'll wait for anyone," Jessup muttered. "We already spent too much time waiting around, trying to track down that damned traitor, Cambridge. I warned the major the stinkin' yellow coward is halfway to Canada by now. Carswell wouldn't listen, so now he can just follow our trail the whole way to that Shawnee village, can't he?"

Aaron listened to the speculative talk, his limbs motionless but his mind racing forward. It sounded as if Carswell—or at least a portion of the regiment—was not far off. But their nearness would make no difference if Jessup pushed on for Wind's village. It was Jessup who had to be stopped first.

Before Aaron could form a plan, several things happened to force him to action. A short distance from the clearing a twig snapped, causing all three men to swing their heads toward the sound. In doing so, Silas Carter's rheumy eyes locked with Aaron's, his mouth dropping open in stunned surprise, the wad of tobacco hanging from his lower lip like a blood-fattened leech. A distant shout from another direction signaled the arrival of the regiment, and an instant later Jessup leaped to his feet, snatching his gun from the ground. He braced his legs wide and took aim in the direction of the first sound—the direction of the river.

"No!" Launching himself from his hiding place, Aaron flew across the small clearing, slamming hard into Jessup's shoulder. The rifle fired, its loud retort echoing back from the trees in a thousand fragments.

"Damn!" Jessup repeated once more as he hit the ground rolling.

"Goddamn!" Carter emphasized, staring bleary-eyed.

"Well, I'll be damned!" the third member of their party followed, surprised by the one-man attack that seemed to have come from nowhere.

Aaron hauled himself up from where he had landed just a few feet away from Jessup. Between them lay the spent rifle; both lunged for it at the same instant.

"Carter, shoot him!" Jessup ordered, grunting from the impact of the rifle butt as Aaron rammed it against his chest. Jessup pushed back hard, jabbing his opponent with the barrel.

In a contest of strength neither fighter had the advantage. Jessup was more muscular, but he also carried extra weight that slowed his reflexes and sapped his stamina. Aaron was more fit, but the strain of the past few days showed as he panted for breath and pushed his body to the limit. So closely locked were the two combatants over the single rifle, Carter could not have gotten off a clean shot if he tried.

Carter had, however, wisely decided to remain in the role of spectator. He had not forgotten the doctor's concern when he was ill, nor had he completely forgiven his captain for the lashing he had received when Jessup learned of his visit with Cambridge. If Jessup ended up on top, Carter could always tell his captain he'd been afraid of shooting the wrong man.

Carter shifted on his feet, waiting out the result with the patience of a cow chewing her cud. All of a sudden he heard a sharp, twanging sound from off to his left; then Jessup yelped and fell back. Carter swung his head around.

This time when his jaw fell open, his wad of tobacco dropped to the ground with a squishy splat.

"I got 'im, Ma! I got 'im!"

"Aaron, are you all right?"

Two figures rushed into the clearing, Rebecca pausing only long enough to ascertain that neither of the men standing held a gun at the ready, and that of the two men on the ground, it was Aaron who now wielded the rifle.

Samuel, surprisingly fast despite his limp, darted forward before she could stop him, coming to a stop near Jessup. "Don't you fight with my pa!" he demanded. His small bow hung from one hand, while his remaining two arrows sprouted from his belt.

The third arrow still quivered where it had stuck in Jessup's thigh.

"You little whelp!" Jessup roared, tearing the arrow from his flesh and flinging it to the ground. He sprang to his feet. "I'll teach you—"

"No!" both Rebecca and Aaron cried out in unison. Dropping the rifle, Aaron reached for Samuel first, scooping the boy up in his arms and sidestepping Jessup, who stumbled a little.

The wound in the officer's leg was not deep, but he winced with each movement. "Cambridge, I should have known you were with them Shawnee again," Jessup sneered. After recovering his weapon, he took a few steps backward until he was flanked by his two men. "This time we won't let you get away so easy, though. We'll just string you up. That tree looks likely." He gestured toward the large white oak at the edge of the clearing. "*Then* we'll go kill us some injuns."

"You can't hang Aaron without a trial," Rebecca retorted, her voice ringing true. "And you no longer have reason to go after the Shawnee. My son and I are fine, as you can see, thanks to Captain Cambridge."

"He's not a captain anymore. Not since he busted out of jail. They'll court-martial him. *After* he's dead. All right, men, grab him."

"Not so fast." Aaron's voice rang with authority, so much so that Carter and his companion obeyed without thought. He released Samuel who returned to Rebecca's side. "Why don't you tell these men exactly *why* you're in such a hurry to hang me, Jessup? Tell them about that night at West Canada Creek."

"Why, you son of a bitch," Jessup snarled. "The only reason I need to hang you is your own injun-lovin' self. Now stop yapping."

"What's he talkin' 'bout, Cap'n?" Carter asked. He spat reflexively, though his mouth was dry.

"Tell him, Jessup. Tell him how you lied to Major Carswell about your part in that skirmish. Tell him how you slashed the throat of a wounded man to save your own skin."

Jessup appeared ready to lunge at Aaron, but another voice resounded through the air, freezing the angered officer in his tracks.

"Yes, tell us, Captain Jessup!" Henry Carswell strode into the clearing. "Why don't you tell us what you know?"

Relief flooded through her limbs as Rebecca watched Major Carswell face his inferior officer with a keen expression. Surrounding the circle were nearly a dozen more men, and she nearly laughed out loud when she saw that one of them was Skulley. He spotted her and Samuel at the same moment and sent them both a broad wink.

"Sir!" Jessup snapped to attention, but somehow the gesture of respect seemed almost comical. "We captured the escaped prisoner, sir."

"He's lyin', Ma! That man's lyin'!" Samuel yelped.

"I know, darling." It was all she could do to keep her son at her side. Rebecca could feel indignation trembling through his small form. "But let the major handle this."

Aaron had stepped forward at Samuel's outburst, and now stood beside his son. "I'm glad you showed up, Henry. We've quite a lot to talk about."

"You can begin," Carswell replied sternly, though his eyes held a secret glint of pleasure, "with an explanation for your sudden—ah—disappearance."

"That's easy, Major. I knew that the Shawnee believed—as Captain Jessup had intended them to—that I was responsible for the attack on them. Their only purpose in kidnapping Rebecca and Samuel was to draw me back to the village. A full-scale retaliation would have endangered their lives needlessly.''

"How did you get away from the Shawnee?''

"We didn't have to. I explained the situation, and my friends allowed us to leave.''

It was an understatement of huge proportions, and yet in essence it was the truth. Rebecca tightened her grip on Samuel's shoulder to keep him from elaborating.

"I still say we go after them,'' Jessup blurted. "We're getting close now. Why wait till another time?'' He fidgeted beneath Carswell's heavy stare. "You aren't going to believe him, are you? He's a liar and a traitor. You read the reports. He's accused of murdering fellow soldiers.''

"Accused, yes,'' Aaron stated with deadly clarity. "By you. Lucky for you I disappeared after the battle, wasn't it? Even when I showed up alive you were still safe as long as I couldn't remember. But you couldn't take that kind of chance, could you? You had to make sure my memory never returned. So you set it up to look like I had caused the trouble with the Indians, knowing that if I didn't hang for it, the Shawnee would eventually hunt me down.''

Jessup stared at Aaron through eyes virulent with hatred. "You think you got it all figured out, don't you?'' he hissed. He addressed the major in a loud voice so that all could hear. "Who're you going to believe, now? A yellow injun-lover, one who ran away from a battle? Or a soldier like me?''

When no one answered, Jessup looked around, furious at the lack of response.

"Major, there's another matter that may help you decide which of us to believe,'' Aaron said after a moment. "Before I left the Shawnee village the chieftain, Wind at His Feet, gave me something that proves Jessup has been stealing from the army.''

"The keg,'' Rebecca gasped. She turned to Aaron. The incriminating evidence was still lying in the bottom of the canoe, which they had left on the riverbank not far away.

Skulley stepped forward, wearing an expression of undisguised glee. "Was it a marked one?'' he asked, then slapped his thigh when Aaron nodded. "Hot damn! I knew it'd work. Major! Me an' Cambridge here figgered someone was stealin' whiskey an' sellin' to the injuns. I carved my letter in a couple o' barrels a while back, an' the only one 'at took 'em out is Jessup, here.''

"One of those kegs ended up in Wind's village," Aaron continued. "Proof that Jessup has been dealing whiskey to the Shawnee and pocketing the money for himself."

"You filthy bastard! I shoulda made sure I killed you then. I knew you couldn't keep your mouth shut."

Before Carswell could respond, Jessup hurled himself at Aaron fists first. Unable to stop the assault without knocking Samuel to the ground, Aaron stepped into it and away from his son, taking a heavy cut to the jaw. He fell to the earth with Jessup on top raining blows upon him.

"Stop them!"

Rebecca's cries went unheeded as the men surged forward, eager to witness the savage scuffle. Even Major Carswell did not move to part the two enemies locked in mortal combat, though he did gesture for a couple of his men to step nearer in case it became necessary to intercede.

The heavier Jessup straddled Aaron, using his weight to pin him while he pummeled him with brutal blows. But Aaron had the advantage of agility—plus a few tricks he had learned from the Shawnee. He managed to gain leverage over the heavier man, flipping him over his head and spinning around in a stunning reversal.

"So it *was* you who tried to kill me," Aaron managed to say despite the exertion of holding Jessup to the ground. "I wasn't sure, even after I started to regain my memory. But I should have known you had the most to hide. You killed Mercer."

Jessup grunted in denial, his torso heaving as he tried to throw Aaron off. "It was necessary. You wouldn't understand. *Nobody* understands. Killing's what I was meant to do. *You* couldn't do it, you stinkin' coward! You'da died that night if it weren't for me. Along with your own brother!"

A collective mutter rose from the gathered soldiers, followed by deadly silence as Aaron froze, wearing an expression of agonized rage. His fingers were wrapped around Jessup's throat, the tendons on the backs of his hands clearly visible as they strained and stretched.

"Go ahead," Jessup taunted in a choked voice. "Don't let up now, you bastard. Anyone that can take aim at his own brother oughta be man enough to kill me."

Never in his life had he hated so much, Aaron knew. But his gaze dropped from Jessup's mottled face to his own hands clasped around the evil man's neck, forcing him to see what he was about to do. Hands that had held a lifetime of healing within their grasp should not take life.

And yet they already had. Jessup had pronounced as much, and Aaron's own memory would not deny the claim. He could settle his past. He could destroy the man who had caused much of his pain with one quick twist of his wrists. He had the strength. He could do it.

Then Aaron felt the weight of many eyes upon him, though only two pairs demanded his attention. He searched for Rebecca. She knelt helpless and trembling, embracing Samuel as they both looked on in horror.

Over what he had done? Aaron wondered. Or what he was about to do?

Their shock released his rage like a breaking dam allows water, too long held, to flow at last. And along with his rage, the last barrier in his mind dissolved. He saw himself clearly as he was then: young, frightened, wounded in both flesh and spirit. And he saw what he had become, through Rebecca's eyes.

With a shuddering sigh, Aaron released his grip. "I won't kill you, Jessup," he said wearily. "Better you should rot in prison. Killing's too good for you."

"But not for you!" Pushing upward, Jessup threw Aaron back, at the same time unsheathing a long, lethal hunting knife from the side of his boot. "I'll finish what I started ten years ago!"

Rebecca screamed as he rose over Aaron, lifting his arm to strike. But a loud, double explosion ripped through the clearing before Jessup could plunge the blade into Aaron's waiting heart. As she watched in terror, Jessup's arm dropped, not in driving fury, but in defeat. His body fell backward, toppled by the shot which had blasted through his chest. Rebecca turned her head questioningly.

"Dang," Skulley said in a weak voice. He lowered the rifle from his shoulder and repeated, "Dang, I was aimin' for 'is arm."

From off to his right, Silas Carter also brought down the rifle he had fired. "Ya didn't hit 'im a-tall, ya one-eyed coot. I did."

"How d'ye know?" Skulley demanded. "Coulda been either—"

"Gentlemen," Henry Carswell interrupted, "it hardly matters at this juncture. We'll discuss this later . . . back at the fort." In two long strides he reached the body, peering down at it solemnly before turning to Aaron. "He was a good soldier at times. But in his mind he equated power with righteousness. In a sense, he was a victim of war as much as anyone. Are you all right, Cambridge?"

This was the question uppermost on Rebecca's mind as well. She held her breath, silently praying that the accusation Jessup had made would not send Aaron back the way he had come, through that torturous path of self-loathing and shame. But after a long moment to collect himself, Aaron took the hand Carswell offered and pulled himself upright.

"I'll be fine," he answered the major.

But it was Rebecca's eyes he sought, Rebecca's gaze he held.

Carswell cleared his throat, regaining Aaron's attention. "I'm afraid there are still a few matters to settle once we get back to Fort Washington. As imperative as your reasons were, the fact remains that you escaped from a federal jail, Cambridge."

Aaron straightened, offering a weary salute. "Sir, I am placing myself in your custody." Lowering his hand he added, "I'm through with running, Henry. Put me in chains if you must, but let's just get the damned thing over with."

Henry Carswell appeared to mull this over, leaving Aaron waiting as he ordered a few men to lift Jessup's body over his horse and to head back toward Cincinnati. Finally his gaze rested on Rebecca and Samuel, both standing behind Aaron.

"No chains," he said at last. "It's obvious you have

more compelling reasons to stay than to leave. Besides, I have need of a regimental surgeon, not another prisoner. What say you, Cambridge? Are you still game?''

Aaron swallowed hard. ''I'd like that, Major. And, Henry?'' he added as the commandant turned to leave. Carswell looked back over one squared shoulder. ''Thanks.''

Released from the paralysis of fear, Rebecca raced to Aaron's side and into his waiting arms. ''Oh, Aaron,'' she whispered joyously. ''I was so afraid for you.''

He held her in a rib-crushing hug. ''To tell you the truth, I was little afraid for myself,'' he whispered hoarsely. ''But it's behind us now. All of it.''

She tilted her head, her eyes searching his for confirmation. What she found was a wellspring of love and a lifetime of hope. Nothing could have torn her away from that promise—nothing except the brightest hope of them all.''

''Hey, you two,'' Samuel pleaded in a quivering voice. ''Don't I get a hug?''

Aaron looked down at the boyish face and felt his heart expand once more. With one arm still tight around Rebecca, he stooped to lift his son with the other. They clung together for a long time, sheltering one another while the voices and movements of the soldiers swirled around them, preparing to retreat.

When all but Skulley had left the clearing for the long march back, the old sergeant harrumphed deep in his throat. ''You folks plannin' on comin' home anytime soon?''

''You bet!'' Samuel replied, wriggling from Aaron's arms to limp over to his friend. ''Wait'll I tell you 'bout the Indian village, Skulley. It was a real adventure, an' I found out Shawnee kids go fishin', too. You woulda liked it.''

''Y'know somethin', Samuel?'' the grizzled soldier replied, taking the boy's hand. ''I bet I would.''

The two of them headed toward the trail the others had beat through the underbrush, so eager to share news that they were unaware that Rebecca and Aaron did not follow immediately.

Aaron's mouth quirked, but when he looked down at Rebecca his gaze was intense and questioning. "Are you sure you're all right?"

"Of course I am," she whispered avidly. "It's you I'm worried about. Aaron, did Jessup mean . . ." She proceeded in a halting voice, knowing how delicate a matter this was. "What did he mean about Jacob?"

Silently, Aaron drew her toward a fallen log, holding both her hands in his as they sat down. His expression was troubled, his mouth rigid. "I began to remember as soon as Jessup's men entered this clearing. That last night at West Canada Creek, Jessup and I were trapped together, surrounded by British patrols. At least we thought so. We fired at the first group that came across us, and—" He stumbled over his words then, swallowing thickly before going on. "It was one of our own units, probably sent out to search for us. Jacob was one of the men."

Tears of compassion filled her eyes, and Rebecca withdrew her hands from his grip to touch his cheek. "Oh, Aaron, how awful for you. No wonder you didn't want to remember."

He grimaced, lowering his head. Her gentle fingers traced the edge of his scar. "According to what Jessup said today and to what I'm starting to remember, there's a good chance I didn't actually hit anybody that night. But I *might* have, 'Becca. If my aim had been more sure or if I wasn't so green and scared, I might have killed my own brother. That's something I'll have to live with for the rest of my life."

"But you will live, Aaron. That's what's important now. And I'll be right beside you, wherever you decide to go."

He nodded, unable to speak just yet. After a few moments he raised her hand to his mouth, pressing his lips to her wrist before lowering it again. "It's all coming together now: the reason I used the name 'Cain,' why Jessup stirred such crazy feelings in me, even why I was afraid at first to love you again. But I was wrong about that, 'Becca. I was afraid my problems would destroy our love. Instead our love has helped heal my wounds."

"And mine," Rebecca said softly, searching the crystal depths of his eyes. "I lost a part of myself, too, when you left. All this time I blamed you for taking away that passionate, confident girl, when I should have known that only by loving you could I become that girl again. I love you with all my heart, Aaron. And I'll still love you if you choose to live as Aaron Cambridge, or Cain, or Gentle Healer.''

"How about if I choose to live as your husband?" he suggested, a smile creasing his face.

Rebecca inhaled deeply. "Where would we live?"

"I've developed a fondness for a certain little cabin, though I'm afraid it'll be much too small before long. Or if you'd rather, I'll take you back to Carolina where this all started. It makes no difference, 'Becca."

Her heart nearly overflowing, she placed her hand tenderly to his cheek, not covering his scar, but adoring it.

"We can live in Beaufort if you want," she murmured lovingly, "or anyplace else, for that matter. But we cannot go back. Only forward." She smiled. "Besides, I rather thought we'd end up in Philadelphia for a while. There's a medical college there, you know."

" 'Becca," he groaned, pulling her hard against his chest. Her warmth, her womanliness were both things that drew him to her like a moth to flame, but it was the inner strength beneath the softness that captured and held him. "I would not ask that of you. It's a hard life, and who knows what might follow? I thought you wanted security."

She shrugged, her smile growing tearful. "I've learned that your love is the only security I need. Wherever you go, we'll all go. Just tell me what you want."

He held her for a while, silent and thoughtful, before attempting to define his dream.

"Wind at His Feet plans to move his people west, to a new land. This valley had been their home for so long, it won't be easy to carve out a new life for themselves."

Leaning back in his arms, Rebecca peered up at him insightfully. "They will have many needs," she acknowledged. "Food for sustenance, friends to lend them support. A good doctor."

He smiled, amazed at her perception. "Perhaps. It would be good to at least visit once in a while. And the conflicts won't be solved by their moving, either. I think the past month is bitter proof that idealism is no match for a lifetime of prejudice. But if we don't start somewhere . . ."

"We can only try," she murmured, placing soft kisses upon his jawline.

In wordless agreement, he nuzzled his chin against her hair. For so long their emotions had hovered at such an intense level, it was difficult to sit close without recalling every instant of painful fear and aching sweetness.

They kissed now, keenly aware of every nuance of touch, taste, and scent. Rebecca's body responded to his caresses with melting compliance, and though she knew that he, too, must be as weary as she, his arousal was evident.

When they could take no more torment, Aaron pulled away, holding her at arm's length until he could breathe normally again and mutter, "Lord, 'Becca, just wait until I get you home!"

He drew her up and spun her around to march her toward the trail back to Cincinnati, but not before placing a fiery kiss on her slender neck. One hand curved over her abdomen, the other gently clutched a fistful of silky hair. Her flesh tingled with pleasure and anticipation.

Her lips burning and her eyes heavy-lidded with desire, Rebecca raised one hand to caress the rugged plane of his cheek and murmured, "We are home, my love. We are home."

HISTORICAL NOTE

The U.S. Army, led by General "Mad" Anthony Wayne, eventually redeemed itself for earlier losses against the Indians. In 1794, two years after this story takes place, the Shawnee and other tribes of the Ohio Valley suffered a resounding defeat at the Battle of Fallen Timbers, putting an end to their influence in the area. In the following years, most of the surviving tribes migrated west into Kansas and Oklahoma, where they settled in peace until western expansion again encroached upon their lands.

ACKNOWLEDGMENTS

I would like to acknowledge the members of the re-created First American Regiment, especially Mr. Steven Sininger and Mr. David Heckaman, for providing military details and data. Their enthusiasm and dedication help keep the spirit of the Ohio frontier alive.

I would also like to give a special thanks to Mr. Fred Shaw for supplying the Shawnee words and phrases included in *When Morning Comes*. In instances where exact translation proved difficult, I have taken the liberty of improvising. These and any other errors of fact or fancy are mine alone.

ROBIN LEANNE WIETE

Columbine. She welcomed him with her lips and was re-

ABOUT THE AUTHOR

Robin LeAnne Wiete was born and raised in New York State. After marrying her college sweetheart in 1976, she lived in Cincinnati, Ohio, for several years, where she worked for a national investment firm. It was largely through the enthusiasm of a co-worker there that she discovered a deep and abiding passion for romance novels, and decided to write one of her own. *When Morning Comes* is her fifth historical romance.

Ms. Wiete has recently returned to Cincinnati with her husband and two children. She spends her nonwriting time enjoying her family, reading, and working with other writers.

She welcomes comments from readers at the following address:

P.O. Box 58608
Cincinnati, Ohio 45258